ROMANCING THE RAKE

Brotherhood of the Black Tartan
Book 2

NICHOLE VAN

Fiorenza Publishing

Romancing the Rake © 2020 by Nichole Van Valkenburgh
Cover design © Nichole Van Valkenburgh
Interior design © Nichole Van Valkenburgh

Published by Fiorenza Publishing
Print Edition v1.0

ISBN: 978-1-949863-05-5

Romancing the Rake is a work of fiction. Names, characters, places and incidents are the products of the author's imagination or are used fictitiously. Any resemblance to actual events, locales or persons, living or dead, is entirely coincidental.

All rights reserved. No part of this publication may be reproduced, stored or transmitted in any form or by any means without the prior written permission of the author.

To Scotland,
And the warm, kind-hearted, generous people who live here.
I am grateful every day for the joy you bring into our lives.
Slàinte.

To Dave,
For suggesting we move to Scotland in the first place.
Best. Idea. Ever.

Before...

Four years earlier

London, England
1815

1

Lady Sophie came to a decisive conclusion six weeks into her first London Season—

Ballrooms were a microcosm of the entire animal kingdom.

And she belonged to a nearly-invisible species.

Neither fact particularly surprised her.

Sophie had long felt metaphorically invisible. Rendering herself *literally* unseen had simply required a bit of drapery.

She currently peeked out from behind a damask curtain. The small alcove with its heavy drapery provided an excellent vantage of the ballroom, allowing her to carefully study Lord Rafe Gilbert as he flirted with the young, widowed Lady Lilith Westover.

The pair were typical of the human species of the *ton*. Sophie had already spent weeks categorizing Polite Society into sub-classes and species according to the rules of Linnaean taxonomy.

For example, Lord Rafe—

Genus . . . *Rakus*.

Species . . . *Lasciviosus*.

Lady Lilith? *Venus admirata.*

Of note, those of genera *Venus* and *Rakus* generally disregarded women like Sophie. After all, she belonged to another genus altogether—*Femina studiosa,* often considered the most peculiar of all the *Femina* genera.

Or in the laymen's vernacular . . . a bluestocking.

Hence, Sophie's invisibility.

She was spending this ball like all the others she had attended this Season—fourteen so far and counting—studying the room from the security of an obliging curtain, forgotten by her mother, unnoticed by her father and siblings. Instead, Sophie had her field notebook in hand and scribbled the occasional observation of romantic behavior.

Lady Lilith's blond head gleamed in the candlelight as she leaned toward Lord Rafe. She giggled, tapped his arm with her fan, and angled her upper body in a way that displayed her bosom to particular advantage.

Never one to dissuade a beautiful woman, Lord Rafe responded with his standard romantic lure—tilting his head to an angle of 45 degrees, raising both eyebrows, and slowly smiling. It was a maneuver Sophie had noted over and over at previous balls.

Tall and strikingly handsome, Lord Rafe was a prime example of *Rakus lasciviosus*—an attractive gentleman whose endless charm and wit excused his scandalously hedonistic behavior.

Sophie had a rather lengthy journal entry dedicated to him. It read like this:

LORD RAFE GILBERT

Taxonomy: Rakus lasciviosus

Description: Twenty-four years of age. Dark brown hair. Brown eyes. Height slightly above six feet (though precise measurement has not yet been taken).

Parentage: Second son and spare heir of the Duke and Duchess of Kendall. *Pater veras* and *Mater veras* assumed. The duchess, his mother, is the former Lady Elspeth Gordon, third daughter of the Earl of Ayr in the Scottish peerage (Source: *Debrett's Peerage of Scotland and Ireland, Volume II, 1814*).

Notable Behaviors: Excessive flirtation, striking appearance, given to much laughter.

Sophie watched Lord Rafe lean in to whisper to Lady Lilith, his hair tumbling across his brow in dramatic fashion. Pursing her lips, Sophie quickly added *dashing coiffure* to his list of traits.

To be fair, Lady Lilith's record was similar: *Venus admirata*, the third daughter of a marquess, charmingly beautiful, the widow of a wealthy banker, Mr. Westover.

Sophie's own entry—endlessly edited and tweaked—was not nearly so compelling:

Lady Sophronia Catharine Sorrow

Taxonomy: Femina studiosa

Description: Twenty-two years of age. Brown hair. Green eyes. Height of precisely five feet, six and three-fourths inches.

Parentage: The fifth acknowledged child of the Earl and Countess of Mainfeld. *Filia veras*—true daughter—of Anne Sorrow, Lady Mainfeld. A member of the Sorrowful Miscellany, an epithet often used to describe the children of the Sorrow family whose *Pater veras*—true father—is not Lord Mainfeld. Identity of Lady Sophronia's *Pater veras*? Currently unknown.

Notable Behaviors: Student of the natural sciences, given to rambling on about biological topics, nearly invisible to other *genera*.

She went back to studying Lord Rafe, noting how Lady Lilith seemed nearly entranced, hanging on the man's every word.

In truth, Sophie found it most puzzling.

The scientist in her longed to speak with a *Rakus*, just a brief conversation or a passing comment. Women flung themselves at rakes with such shocking regularity. Her scientific mind was desperate to understand one simple fact—

Why?!

Why did women cast themselves into a rake's clutches?

To Sophie, interacting with a rake seemed akin to casting one's self upon a funeral pyre, burning one's reputation to ash for little gain. She had certainly watched her mother respond to their charms over and over.

As if he had heard her unasked question, Lord Rafe lifted his head and pushed back that dashing lock of hair, his gaze drifting across the room to look in Sophie's direction.

His eyes locked with hers.

Oh!

But . . . why would Lord Rafe look at *her*? She must be mistaken.

And yet, a quick glance to her left and right confirmed that Lord Rafe, was indeed, looking straight at her.

His gaze held, steadfast and intent, trapping her with its intensity.

Sophie's heart lurched in her chest, a startled *thu-thump*.

He continued to stare, as if she were anything but invisible to him.

And then . . . he winked.

Sophie jerked her head back behind the curtain, biting her lip and pressing a hand to her sternum.

That was . . . unexpected.

Moreover, her entire body bore evidence of the brief interaction. Her heart raced and bounced in her chest. Her lungs heaved, and a thin layer of moisture dotted her upper lip.

How . . . *fascinating*.

Utterly, absolutely intriguing.

Was *this* the explanation she sought? That a rake could cause such a reaction in a woman even from a distance?

If so, the allure of *Rakus* was more formidable than she had supposed. No wonder women fell so thoroughly for their charms. Perhaps she should have more compassion for her mother. There were hitherto unknown factors at work.

Sophie tapped her pencil against her lips, pondering, before scribbling notes.

She had *many* follow-up questions.

Was this reaction unique only to a member of *Rakus lasciviosus* such as Lord Rafe? Or did all members of the *Rakus* family—*Rakus ferox* (feral rake) and the mythical *Rakus reformus* (reformed rake)—possess the power to incite heart palpitations from a distance of fifty feet?

She made a few additional notes and then poked her head out of the curtain again. Unfortunately, Lord Rafe had moved out of sight. Lady Lilith was now flirting with a baronet, employing the same giggle, fan tap, lean maneuver.

"What a lovely, cozy spot you have here," a deeply masculine voice said behind her.

Sophie barely stifled a high-pitched squeal.

She whirled to find Lord Rafe a mere three feet away. The man had slipped behind the opposite edge of the curtain without her noticing.

Gracious heavens above!

She clutched her field book to her chest, as if the bound sheets of foolscap would keep her overly-excited heart in her chest.

Or, at the very least, could act as a defense against a *Rakus*, like a crucifix against a vampire.

Stand back, you flirtatious fiend, or I shall scourge you with scientific minutia and logical deductions. Begone!

Lord Rafe had been potent at fifty paces. At close quarters, he was positively overwhelming. That lush dark hair sweeping across his brow, the sharp angles of his handsome jaw casting shadows on his pristine neckcloth, his brown eyes melting puddles of rich chocolate, and—

Oh no!

How truly unnerving!

He had *dimples* . . . deep, luscious dimples punctuating the smiling corners of his mouth.

Words escaped her. Thoughts fled.

She was, in all honesty, fortunate to still be standing.

"Oh!" was all she managed, followed by a weaker, "you!"

"Yes." Those dimples deepened along with his grin. "Me."

Sophie willed herself not to stare, mouth flapping agape like a simpleton.

But . . . Lord Rafe was just so . . . *him*.

"I hope I am not intruding." His wide smile said no one ever considered his presence a nuisance. "The curtain kept twitching over here." He flicked his wrist indicating the damask fabric behind her. "I had to investigate its cause."

Sophie disliked how much she liked his instinctive curiosity. It reflected her own.

He bowed as much as possible in the small alcove.

"Lord Rafe Gilbert at your service, madam."

Such a *thrillingly* improper greeting, giving her his name without a formal introduction. Her governess would have an apoplexy.

Sophie mentally added, *Displays a blatant disregard for propriety,* to his list of *Rakus* behaviors.

She immediately curtsied, a reflexive, involuntary motion that she always found vaguely troubling. If someone bowed, she curtsied. Could she break free from the muscle memory of it, if she truly wished?

Regardless, she lifted her eyes back to his.

Seize this moment, Sophie. Research.

To that end, she breathed in deeply, inhaling an enormous whiff of air.

That . . . he did notice.

His easygoing manner stiffened slightly, shifting from flirtatious to more alert.

"Did you . . ." He paused, sending a dark eyebrow upward. "Did you just *smell* me?" A slight trace of Scotland laced his words.

"Yes." Lying was not one of Sophie's strengths. She was, after all, a scientist at heart. She might never have another chance to conduct such research. "You smell divine." She took another deep sniff. "'Tis most distressing."

He blinked, eyelashes drifting up and down. "My smell?" A small frown appeared. His spine stiffened further. "You . . . you find my smell divinely . . . distressing?" That same hint of Scotland lingered in his speech, the slight rolled 'r', the sibilant 's'.

"Well, yes," she said mournfully.

If Sophie were the type to be easily embarrassed, she was quite sure her cheeks would be flaming.

Instead, she soldiered on. "You see, I have long considered a man's scent to be inversely proportional to his moral character."

A momentary pause.

She could practically see the gears in Lord Rafe's brain recalibrating their conversation. He mouthed her words.

Inversely proportional to his moral character.

"Interesting," he said after a brief pause. "You assert that there is a correlation between scent and conduct, that the better a man smells, the worse his behavior?"

"Precisely. And based on this measurement—"

"You mean . . . my *distressing* smell?"

"Yes. To be quite clear, you smell marvelous." A brief pause. "Therefore . . . your behavior must be truly appalling."

His dark eyebrow hiked further. How did he do that? she wondered. Why would a man be given such expressive eyebrows?

"And *your* name?" he prompted.

His face relaxed again into a slow smile that said she could trust him.

Sophie was not entirely sure that would be wise.

But he didn't raise both eyebrows, as he had for Lady Lilith. Did he reserve that signature lure for the genus *Venus* then? And why did that thought invoke a sinking sensation?

"Lady Sophronia Sorrow." She cleared her throat. Again, a biological reflex.

She knew how others reacted to her name, to the weight of all that it implied. Lord Rafe, in particular, would realize that he likely should not be speaking with her.

"Lady Sophronia Sorrow?" he asked, forehead wrinkling, that same eyebrow lifting.

Did he not make the connection to Lady Mainfeld then?

"Yes." Sophie should have just left it at that, but her brain decided to babble on. "It's a terrible name, Sophronia Sorrow."

For so very many reasons, least of all that it confirmed her a member of the Sorrowful Miscellany, as the *ton* called them.

Lord Rafe's solitary eyebrow angled sideways, as if asking a question.

Her mouth took that as permission to continue. "Sophronia Sorrow

. . . it's dreadfully melodramatic. It's the name of a simpering miss from a gothic penny novel. You know, the foolish girl who doesn't survive an early encounter with the villain and then spends the rest of the book as an object lesson for the true heroine."

His head went back. "Ah."

"Sophronia Sorrow is never the heroine." She had to clarify that point. "Imagine living your life as a cautionary tale."

He paused and then said, "Now that, I do understand."

An emotion rippled behind his easy-going gaze . . . something tense and serious and entirely un-rake-like. For a brief second, he appeared a different person, one more akin to herself—a student of life rather than an active participant—

But then Lord Rafe gave a nearly imperceptible shake of his head, and the moment was gone.

"So, I presume you are a daughter of Lady Mainfeld?"

Ah. So he had made the connection. Was he not concerned about being caught speaking with her? It would certainly cause tongues to wag.

"Yes." Sophie did not miss that he had mentioned her as being her *mother's* daughter, not her father's.

His dimples faded and a puzzled 'V' appeared between his brows. Sophie could practically see the cogs turning in his brain.

It was obvious that she was not one of the *Filii veri*—true children—of the Earl of Mainfeld. Lord and Lady Mainfeld were both fair of feature, blond-haired and blue-eyed. Sophie's dark hair and green eyes loudly proclaimed her sire to be someone other than Lord Mainfeld.

Lord Rafe tapped his lips. "The Italian dancing master?"

Sophie instantly understood. "No, that is my brother, Richard."

"Lord Farris?"

"My sister, Mary."

She batted aside his comments in much the same way she attacked a ball with a cricket bat—with practiced ease and ready anticipation.

This was a game she knew how to play.

Anne Sorrow, Lady Mainfeld—Sophie's mother—was a notorious flirt and, to put it bluntly, an adulteress. A *Femina adultera*. She was easily lured by rakes of any species.

Of Sophie's eight brothers and sisters, only three were undoubtedly the children of Lord Mainfeld. The rest of them were the result of their mother's illicit liaisons. Such muddying of a bloodline only underscored, yet again, why genus *Rakus* was a problem.

Sophie's father-in-name, Lord Mainfeld, accepted his wife's children as his own.

Why, Sophie couldn't quite say.

Unlike an animal, her father (for lack of a better way to describe him) *knew* that she and her siblings were cuckoos in the nest. And yet, he acknowledged and treated them all as his own, shouldering the obligation to care for his wife's illegitimate children.

Was her father genuinely oblivious to their true parentage? That seemed incredibly unlikely; all of London knew of her mother's indiscretions. Or did Lord Mainfeld do it as a means to silence scandal? Or did he truly love her mother enough to accept the result of her flagrant infidelities?

It was most puzzling.

Regardless, despite their lofty titles, Sophie and her siblings were on the edge of respectability, tolerated and received but only barely.

For example, Lord Rafe's father, the Duke of Kendall, had been appalled to meet her. Sophie had been introduced to Kendall at a musicale evening five weeks past. But instead of a murmured greeting in reply, His Grace had stared at her, caught between astonishment and loathing. Finally, he had nodded his head, muttered something incoherent, and then turned his back on her with an outraged scowl. Not quite a cut-direct, but close enough to set tongues wagging.

And then, oddly, His Grace had spent the rest of the evening staring at Sophie, tracking her movements around the room the way a cat tracks a mouse, sending a chill up her spine and gooseflesh scattering.

Thankfully, Kendall had studiously ignored her ever since.

At the moment, however, Lord Rafe, was still trying to puzzle out who her *Pater veras* might be.

"Sir Edward Markham?" he asked.

"No, that's my brother, Anthony." She took pity on him. "I'm one of the unknowns."

A *Filia incognita*.

"Ah." His head went back. "Is this your first Season in London then? I am quite sure we have not been properly introduced."

His words were spoken simply, but the warm intensity of his gaze gave them a flirtatious flavor, implying that she was so captivating that he would absolutely remember such an introduction.

Well done, Rakus lasciviosus. *Well done.*

She chose to ignore his tone, as well as the racing of her own heart. "Yes, this is my first Season, though I am somewhat long in the tooth being nearly two and twenty. But my mother had my older sisters to marry off first. And then she was simply too busy to bother with my come-out. For my part, I did not mind the delay—"

A commotion in the ballroom outside the curtain cut through the bubble of isolation surrounding them. They turned toward the sound, both peeking around the drapes.

It wasn't hard to understand what had sent a ripple of awareness through the ballroom.

The Duke of Kendall had arrived, pausing in the doorway several steps higher than the rest of the room, his duchess on his arm. Kendall looked every inch the powerful duke that he was—meticulously groomed, head held high, eyes flinty. The duchess clung to her husband's arm. She did not go out in public much, as her health was often poorly.

But the arrival of the duke wasn't the cause of the commotion.

No, *that* was reserved for Sophie's own father and mother.

Unfortunately, Lord and Lady Mainfeld had chosen to exit the ballroom at the precise moment Kendall and his duchess had arrived.

The two men stared one another down—Kendall haughty, Lord Mainfeld narrow-eyed—neither saying a word. The moment stretched and pulled until Sophie could practically taste the violence in the air.

Finally, the stalemate was broken by their hostess, who sailed to Kendall's side, pulling the duke away, allowing Lord and Lady Mainfeld to exit.

Sophie felt rather than heard Lord Rafe's hissing exhale behind her. She turned to face him, both of them shrinking behind the soothing shield of the curtain.

"We should likely not be speaking with one another." Sophie darted a glance at the curtain, indicating the scene that had just transpired.

"Aye." Lord Rafe's dimples faded.

The man was likely mentally reviewing their fathers' ongoing feud.

It played out like a Drury Lane melodrama.

It had supposedly begun when the Duke of Kendall (age nine) had been sent down from Eton for bloodying the Earl of Mainfeld (age eight) in a fist fight.

Ten years later, Lord Mainfeld (a devoted sportsman) delivered Kendall (not quite as devoted) a resounding defeat in a carriage race to Brighton. Kendall left for Italy the next morning, so thorough was his humiliation.

Most notoriously four years after that, Kendall and Mainfeld had fought a duel over Sophie's mother, the former Miss Anne Montague. The tale went that Kendall had slighted Miss Montague. Mainfeld, naturally, had taken offense to Kendall's behavior. Kendall, of course, refused to apologize. The subsequent duel had resulted in Kendall crowing in victory, and Mainfeld sporting a bandaged left arm while marrying Miss Montague via special license three days later.

It was said neither gentleman had spoken to the other since. Kendall had withdrawn into the superiority of his title and flawless reputation. Mainfeld had retreated to the country and pretended to ignore his wife's rampant promiscuity and his own tarnished reputation, living for hunting and fishing on his estates.

So on the rare occasions that the men did encounter one another, everyone waited with bated breath to see what would transpire.

"Do you not find the animosity between our fathers somewhat medieval?" Lord Rafe finally asked.

Sophie shot him a wan smile. "I would have used the word *absurd*, but *medieval* is also adequately descriptive. Our fathers are like a pair of *Cervus elaphus scoticus*, butting antlers and pawing in the dirt to impress one another whilst the rest of the deer herd munches grass, completely uncaring."

Sophie pursed her lips, instantly wanting to take her last sentence back. Sometimes she tended to see the world only in obscure, biological metaphor.

"Did you . . ." Lord Rafe stopped, that 'V' reappearing between his brows. "Did you just compare our fathers' behavior to that of Scottish red deer in rut?"

How did he know—?

A longer pause, Sophie's eyes darted sideways. The only way out of this conversation was through it, she feared.

"Erhm . . . yes."

"And you feel that *Cervus elaphus scoticus* best resembles their behavior? Not perhaps, *Falco peregrinus*?

He spoke the words lightly, but something in his tone said the question had not been as careless as it seemed.

Was he testing her?

And if so, to what end?

More to the point, why was her heart *beatingsofast*?

Sophie did not understand the games of a *Rakus*. And so she answered him truthfully.

"Yes, comparing our fathers to a peregrine falcon is also appropriate. They defend their supposed territories with similar ferocity, chasing off intruders."

Lord Rafe stilled.

A fraught pause ensued.

He spoke first. "You have made a rather tenacious study of Linnaeus's system of species classification."

"As have you, it seems."

"Yes, well, but I have just completed three years of study at St. Andrews focused on the natural sciences and biology."

Oh.

Be still her heart.

A biology-educated rake.

The man was truly a menace to bluestockings everywhere.

"And you are a young woman in your first London Season," he continued with a deeper frown.

"Are you asserting, my lord, that being a woman excludes one from being an aspiring biologist? Are the two subspecies incompatible?"

He swallowed, eyes widening for some unfathomable reason.

"No," he said on a hush.

They exchanged another long, weighty stare.

Lady Lilith's cascading laughter sounded through the curtain. A deeper voice responded.

Lord Rafe stiffened, eyes darting to the damask that hid them from view. Abruptly, it seemed emblematic of her life . . . in the room, but never an active participant.

Perhaps Lord Rafe realized the same, as he said, "You are correct, my lady. We should not be speaking with one another. I bid you good evening, Lady Sophronia."

He bowed.

Sophie, of course, curtsied.

And then he was gone.

But the *feel* of him lingered. Sophie was singed, as if she had sat too long in the sun and the heat of it would remain in her skin for days.

Thoughts of Lord Rafe assailed her during the next two sets.

Could their shared interest in biology be the beginning of a relationship? Would they spend long hours discussing the minute differences between a feral domestic cat and a Scottish wild cat?

Most importantly, was her oddness perhaps not the cloak of invisibility she had supposed?

This state of wondering euphoria lasted for approximately an hour.

And then Sophie glimpsed Lord Rafe kissing Lady Lilith in the same alcove, a careless gap in the drapery allowing others to see in. The Duke of Kendall had certainly noted his son's behavior with a grim expression.

All in all, the experience was a brisk dowsing, a reminder of the behavior of *Rakus lasciviosus*.

She hadn't minded her invisibility until Lord Rafe had singled her out. She hadn't felt alone until he noticed her.

His rejection stung, amplifying her outside-ness, her sense of being a species apart. As if, as a biological observer, she had finally managed to see herself clearly in the wild.

In short, it was a jolt of painful self-awareness.

Despite what she had thought to be a momentary connection, Lord Rafe was still a *Rakus lasciviosus* through and through. And as the Bible states, a leopard never changes its spots.

Or, in other words—once a rake, always a rake.

Sophie vowed to remember the moment as a much-needed physic—a dose of heart-saving medicine.

Though she did add another line to her own biological entry when she returned home several hours later.

Like her mother, Lady Sophronia is highly susceptible to the mating charms of Rakus lasciviosus.

2

Rafe opened the front door of Gilbert House, his father's townhouse in Grosvenor Square, slipping inside without making a sound. All was quiet, which was to be expected given the late hour.

His mind still hummed and buzzed from the evening, thoughts of Lady Sophronia Sorrow refusing to be silenced—her frank bluntness, the clever turn of her mind, her endearingly determined scribbling in her notebook.

She was an Original, a woman utterly unique within her kind. Like finding a brightly feathered parrot among a flock of sparrows, she glowed with difference. A difference he longed to know.

Rafe smiled, remembering her lament over her melodramatic name.
Imagine living your life feeling like a cautionary tale.
He related more than Lady Sophronia could ever understand.

But knowing the animosity that existed between their fathers, could he risk spending more time with her?

Rafe closed the front door carefully, twisting the handle so the latch made no sound.

A single candle flickered on a half-moon table to the right of the entry hall, casting long shadows up the gilded, gold-and-blue wallpaper and across the marble tiles.

The hall boy was curled up in a ball on the floor beside his stool, fast asleep. Poor lad. He had to be only eight or nine years old.

The hall boy stirred, blearily opening one eye before lurching awake with a start.

Rafe pressed a finger to his own lips. *Hush.*

The boy scrambled into his chair with its sloping seat, hair rumpled, livery askew.

Rafe winked at him. The boy would be dismissed if anyone caught him sleeping.

Giving Rafe a thankful grin, the boy came forward and took Rafe's hat, overcoat, gloves, and walking stick before silently nodding toward the silver salver on a sideboard.

A letter sat atop it addressed to Rafe in a flowing script.

Ah.

A letter from Andrew Mackenzie, his closest friend, a Scot he had met while studying natural sciences at St. Andrews.

Rafe palmed the letter and winked at the hall boy again before taking to the stairs, walking on tiptoe.

Now he simply had to make it to his room without disturbing—

"A word, boy," the Duke of Kendall's voice reached Rafe as he rounded the first-floor landing. A glance down the hallway showed that the door to his father's study stood ajar, flickering firelight streaming into the hallway.

Damn and blast.

Rafe's heart lurched in his throat. He had been so careful and quiet, but to no avail. A midnight summons from his father *never* ended well.

"Sir?" Rafe said, pushing open the door and stepping into his father's lair.

His father stood before the fireplace, hands clasped behind his back. The firelight rimmed his form from behind while a candelabra on the desk to his left illuminated his face.

The Duke of Kendall was a formidable presence. Equal in height to Rafe and just as broad shouldered, he dominated any room he entered. Kendall's pale gray eyes and silver hair enhanced his sense of authority. An ice king ruling over his domain.

As a child, Rafe had thought his father's venom tongue and endless dominance stemmed from Rafe's own negligent behavior. If only Rafe were better behaved, then his father would treat him with kindness.

As an adult, Rafe recognized that Kendall simply delighted in cruelty. His father took sick pleasure in controlling and hurting others.

Rafe had hated the man for years.

Worse, his father *knew* how much Rafe disliked him and delighted in rubbing his son's face in it.

Rafe's only weapon, at the moment, was to not give his father the satisfaction of a reaction. And so he kept his face impassive.

Kendall's eyes dipped to Andrew's letter, still clenched in Rafe's fist. His father waved a hand toward the letter.

"You shall not be allowed to accompany Mr. Mackenzie on this ridiculous voyage he is planning." Kendall turned, reaching for a glass of brandy on the mantelpiece. "I will not have a son of mine roaming the South Seas with some motley crew."

The air whooshed out of Rafe's lungs, as surely as if he had taken a blow to the solar plexus.

He glanced at the letter again, noting the broken seal. Blast the man! Kendall had no shame. Rafe was twenty-four and far too old to have his father monitoring his post.

What Rafe wouldn't give to have his own bachelor accommodations, a set of private rooms somewhere, anywhere else in London. But . . . no. Kendall would not tolerate any distance between Rafe and his own iron grip.

At the moment, Kendall ensured Rafe's obedience by controlling his purse strings. If Rafe obeyed and did as his father requested, he was flush with funds.

Without his father's support, Rafe would be thrust into the street. And anyone who attempted to help him—like Mr. Andrew Mackenzie, for example—would be ruined. Kendall was powerful enough to ensure it happened. More to the point, Rafe would never put his friends in such dire straits.

Just a few more years, he promised himself.

Thank goodness, Rafe was only the second son. His elder brother, Earl Hawthorn, would never be free of their father. Though Hawthorn did not chafe against their father's control; his brother was cut after the same mold as their sire. Quite literally, as Hawthorn had their father's light eyes and premature gray hair. Rafe was eternally grateful he took after his mother's darker coloring.

And his mother's family gave him hope of freedom. His maternal grandmother had promised to leave the bulk of her Scottish estate to Rafe upon her death, gifting him a source of funds completely out of Kendall's reach. Rafe loved his Gran and wished her a long life, but she was quite elderly. And he was honest enough to acknowledge that her death would solve many problems for him.

Notably, removing him from under Kendall's controlling fist. But until then . . .

Swallowing his anger over this invasion of his privacy, Rafe opened Andrew's letter, tilting it toward the candelabra.

Words jumped out at him . . . *secured final funding for our voyage of scientific discovery to the South Pacific . . . set sail in October . . . have finally hired a physician, Dr. Alexander Whittaker, and an artist, Mr. Ewan Campbell, . . . please say you will come . . .*

Rafe refolded the letter, straightening to his full height.

Yes, Rafe wished to accompany Andrew on the trip . . . more than anything. But he gritted his teeth, refusing to show even an ounce of his disappointment.

Time, if nothing else, would strip Kendall of ways to control him. Rafe simply needed to wait, to breathe through the hatred and loathing until he was free of his father once and for all.

"Was that all you wished to say, Sir?" he asked, proud of the steady timbre of his voice.

Kendall took a slow sip of his brandy, eyes glittering in the flickering light.

"I saw you speaking with Lady Sophronia Sorrow this evening."

Ah.

And now they came to the crux of it.

Rafe decided to face the accusation head-on. It was usually the best course with his father . . . give a semblance of capitulation.

"I did indeed speak with the lady in question, Sir."

"You appeared quite taken with her." Kendall traced a finger around the rim of his glass. "She seems a lovely creature, I imagine, to those less discerning."

Alarm bells clanged in Rafe's head. Did Kendall suspect the depth of Rafe's interest in Lady Sophronia?

Giving a nonchalant shrug, Rafe replied, "Perhaps. But once I learned of her familial connections, Lady Sophronia ceased to be attractive. Lady Lilith was a much more agreeable companion."

Thank goodness he had kissed Lilith so openly. That would put Kendall off the scent. Lady Lilith was a decent sort, but not at all to Rafe's tastes.

"I am glad I need not remind you about the state of matters with Mainfeld." The duke practically spat the earl's name. "That man and his pack of mongrel children are an abomination."

Kendall paused. It was his *you-will-now-agree-with-me* pause.

"I could not agree more, Sir," Rafe obediently replied.

His father studied Rafe intently, as if looking for cracks of insincerity.

Rafe held the man's icy gaze, unflinching, ignoring the roil of emotions in his chest.

"See that you continue to avoid them all . . . Lady Sophronia, in particular," his father intoned.

Well.

Lady Sophronia's green eyes danced in Rafe's memory.

Anger rose in his chest, the eternal feeling of helplessness where his father was concerned. But Rafe knew he had to acquiesce. The past had taught him as much.

Several years ago, Rafe had taken a brief fancy to a well-educated parson's daughter, a Miss Hawthorn. Despite the lady's genteel elegance, Kendall had been nearly apoplectic—the son of a duke did not stoop to court a parson's daughter. Miss Hawthorn and her family had abruptly quit London not long after, and Rafe had found himself on a painfully short tether for the remainder of the Season.

Rafe had been infinitely more careful since then. Most of his flirtatious ways were simply a ruse. Kendall encouraged Rafe's virile reputation as a rake, as he wished for his son to be 'man about town.' Better Kendall think Rafe a man like unto himself.

Sometimes Rafe dreamed of just . . . leaving. Of selling everything of value he owned, adopting a new name, and sailing for America, disappearing into the wilderness—anything to escape the reach of Kendall's long arm.

But he never could quite make the leap. His life was *here*. His friends and interests . . . and most importantly, his mother, the Duchess of Kendall, and his sister, Lady Katrina.

His mother, in particular, needed him. Her moods swung from day-to-day, moving from normalcy to melancholy and back again. She needed the steadiness of Kate and Rafe's presence. He could not abandon his sister and mother to his father's cruelty. Nor could he take them with him, not without more than the few paltry funds available to him.

And so . . . for the moment . . . Rafe could do nothing but nod his head and comply.

"As you wish, Sir."

"I do wish," his father said, tone menacing. "Stay away from *that woman*." Kendall spoke through clenched teeth. "No son of mine will tarnish himself with such an association. Am I clear?"

"Yes, Sir."

His father continued to watch him with hooded eyes, chest heaving. The depth of Kendall's vitriol surprised even Rafe.

How could a duel over three decades past still engender such hatred? Kendall had been the victor, after all. The one whose honor had been restored.

Of course, Mainfeld had won the lady in the end. Was *that* the source of the conflict? Had Kendall wanted Anne Sorrow *neé* Montague for himself?

If Rafe remembered correctly, his father had been betrothed to his mother—Lady Elspeth Gordon, daughter of Lord Ayr—at the time of the duel. His parent's marriage had been one of convenience, arranged when Rafe's grandfather had wished an alliance with the wealthy Scottish Lord Ayr. Had Kendall chafed against his father's will, too?

But if so, why fight over Anne Sorrow? The woman was scandalous. And because of that, why would Kendall care if Mainfeld married her? Moreover, given the lady's reputation, she would not refuse a dalliance even when married. Had Kendall and Lady Mainfeld been lovers at some point? Was a lover's quarrel the true source of Kendall's vitriol?

Or perhaps it was her ladyship's *current* behavior that so repulsed Kendall?

Lady Mainfeld was grudgingly received, and her daughters bore the brunt of their mother's shame. Despite Lord Mainfeld acknowledging her as his daughter, Lady Sophronia was clearly a *nullius filia*, a child of nobody.

A bastard.

Lord Mainfeld's acceptance gave Lady Sophronia the veneer of legitimacy; legally, she was his child. But that did not matter to the high sticklers of the *ton*.

And the Duke of Kendall was the highest of sticklers. The man believed firmly in an ordered society, preferably one under his strict control. Lady Sophronia with her odd ways and murky parentage did not meet those standards.

Kendall sipped his brandy. "I have been lenient with you for the past several years, allowing you to associate with those not of your station." His eyes dipped to Andrew's letter. "Do not force me to rethink my decisions." He waved his hand. "I am for Parliament tomorrow, but I will leave a list of tasks for you with Beadle. You are dismissed."

Nearly biting his tongue to stem wayward words, Rafe bowed and left the room.

Once over the Trinity term holiday, Rafe had been forced to go fishing with Hawthorn. His brother had been his normal, boorish self, but fortunately, the salmon were plentiful. Eventually, Hawthorn abandoned his fishing pole, preferring instead to skewer the fish with his long hunting knife, pulling them onto the river bank, laughing maniacally at Rafe to join him.

As he climbed the stairs to his chambers, Rafe sympathized with those salmon, thrashing on the tip of Hawthorn's sharp blade, pinned into place.

Unable to escape.

3

The second time Lord Rafe Gilbert encountered Lady Sophronia was eerily similar to the first.

The scene was Lord Bushnell's mid-summer house party, and Lady Bushnell was the overly-anxious woman Rafe was avoiding.

Hearing her voice calling to him, Rafe ducked into the library, knowing Lady Bushnell had a frightful aversion to learning. But just to be sure, he darted behind the heavy curtains framing an oriole window. He pulled himself rigidly against the wall, the weighty fabric easily hiding him.

The door snicked open a second later, skirts rustling.

"Lord Rafe?" Lady Bushnell tentatively whispered. "Are you in here?"

More skirt rustling. The sound of timid footsteps.

"Lord Raf—"

"What are you doing in here, my dear?!" A man's voice boomed, practically rattling the windowpanes.

"Eeeek!" Lady Bushnell gave a startled screech.

Rafe's heart nearly stopped.

"Heavens above, dear husband," Lady Bushnell tittered. "You gave me such a start."

"How is it you are alone in here? You detest libraries. Are you meeting someone?" Lord Bushnell was no slow-top, Rafe would give the man that.

Rafe finally darted a glance to his right, looking across the bay window.

Lady Sophronia Sorrow met his gaze with pursed lips, her hands clasped together holding a burlap sack.

Rafe barely squelched his own jolt of surprise.

Lady Sophie, as he heard her called, was tucked behind the curtain opposite him. Clearly there had been a chain of events in the library this afternoon.

Rafe did not remove his gaze from her. As he had noted in their previous encounter two months past, Lady Sophie had breathtaking eyes, the shocking green of newly-grown grass in April.

Lady Bushnell giggled again. Papers crinkled.

"I was merely hoping to find that poem Mrs. White mentioned, the one by Lord Byron." Her ladyship's voice had taken a whining edge.

Lady Sophie rolled her beautiful eyes, communicating her opinion.

Rafe grinned. Unlike Lady Bushnell, Lady Sophie employed no artifice.

"How many times have I told you to leave off Lord Byron, my dear?" Lord Bushnell harrumphed. "'Tis a load of rubbish."

Light from the window between them skimmed Lady Sophie's face, catching reddish glints in her otherwise dark hair.

Rafe pondered her unusual beauty. Her wide-set eyes, high cheekbones, and pointed chin lent her face a nearly fey look, as if a wood sprite had suddenly come to life.

Most importantly, he appreciated Lady Sophie's quick mind and straight-forward manner.

Case in point, Lady Bushnell had now resorted to tears, accusing a beleaguered Lord Bushnell of upsetting her nerves with his loud accusations. Her noisy weeping filled the space.

Lady Sophie shook her head, eyes rolling again, carefully shifting the burlap sack to her left hand.

Rafe smiled wider.

Blast, but he liked her.

Which explained why he had been utterly avoiding her.

Rafe had heeded his father's angry ultimatum.

No associating with Lady Sophronia Sorrow. Full stop.

But . . . he was hard-challenged to care while staring into Lady Sophie's brilliant eyes.

A roll of frustration surged through him. Damn his father and his authoritarian ways. What did it hurt if Rafe spoke with Lady Sophie?

Lord Bushnell ushered his sobbing wife out of the library, the door shutting behind them with a resounding *clack*. Lady Sophie raised her eyebrows at him.

Rafe knew he should walk away—bow, take his leave, and hope to hell that Kendall never caught wind of this encounter.

But Lady Sophie's impossibly green eyes pinned him in place.

"We have a habit of meeting behind curtains, my lady," he said, waving a hand at the gap between them.

"Indeed, my lord." She bit her lip. "I am beginning to think you are quite the connoisseur of them."

She did have a point.

"These are a lovely velvet." He pushed the heavy fabric, causing it to ripple. "Italian, I should think."

"Useful for hiding from angry husbands?" Her tone held a slightly acerbic edge.

"At times."

"Is it instinctual?"

Rafe blinked.

He remembered this from their previous encounter. Lady Sophie had a way of abruptly turning a conversation.

"Pardon?"

"Is your raking instinctual?"

"My . . . raking?"

"Yes. Or do you create premeditated plans to rake women you encounter?"

His lips twitched. "I was unaware raking was a verb in this context."

"It is—" She mimed a raking motion with her right hand. "—you bring them to you."

Rafe smothered a chuckle. "I wonder if you understand what it means to be a rake." He leaned toward her. "Not to mention . . . etymology."

Her eyes narrowed. "Fortunately, we are not discussing grammar, but biology. And *biology* I do understand."

"You do?"

"Yes. I have undertaken a study of the *primus* of each social group."

As usual, Lady Sophie's thoughts were racing ahead of him.

"The *primus*? I am unaware of that term."

"It is my own word, in this context." She bit that lower lip again. "You see, I spent last autumn with my father in south Yorkshire."

Rafe pursed his lips, as he did *not*, in fact, see. He was unsure as to the precise direction of their conversation.

But Lady Sophie was so charmingly earnest and her face so lovely with the sunlight washing from left to right, that he simply did not care.

Basking in the husky timber of her voice was sufficient at the moment.

Lady Sophie thankfully continued. "My father is monstrously fond of hunting and even more passionate about hunting dogs. He keeps a large stable on an estate in Yorkshire. More importantly, the stables are home to a thriving colony of nearly feral *Felis catus*."

"Cats?"

"Yes, barn cats, to be precise."

"Of course." Rafe said the words like it had already been a foregone conclusion that their conversation would progress from greetings to grammar to barn cats.

"So while my father happily purged the estate of pheasant and grouse, I spent my time studying the clowder of barn cats in the stables."

"The . . . clowder?" Rafe paused. "I thought a group of cats was called a *clutter*?"

"I prefer the more modern *clowder*." Her side-look said, *Please keep up.*

"After several weeks of carefully observing the barn cats, I realized that there is a strict hierarchy among them. For example, a large male cat was the *primus* of the clowder."

"The *primus*? The first?" he asked, translating the word from Latin. His brow furrowed. "What precisely do you mean?"

"The *primus* is the dominant feline, like the *primus* of a Roman cohort—the one who commands everyone else. For example, the *primus* of my barn cat clowder was a large, ginger tomcat. Other cats moved out of his way and offered him their spots when he wished them. Sometimes, they brought him offerings of mice and voles. When a kitten misbehaved or another cat balked, he would hiss and intimidate them. The *primus* acted like the lord of the manor, and every other member of his fiefdom had to bow to him."

A thrill chased Rafe's spine.

A *primus* of a biological group? Rafe had never considered the concept before, but it made absolute sense. Most groups of animals did seem to have a dominant member, like a Highland red buck over his harem of does.

This woman. She was utterly brilliant.

And so he said so.

"That is utterly brilliant."

It was Lady Sophie's turn to be taken aback, drawing that bottom lip fully into her mouth.

"Th-thank you," she said, though her words were hesitant.

"And you bring up your clowder of barn cats and the idea of this *primus* because. . . ?" His voice trailed off, a question mark.

"Oh, because I cannot decide if you are a *primus* or not."

"Me?"

"Yes. You."

"You think I resemble a dominant barn tomcat?"

"There are some similarities."

"Truly? How do you figure?"

"Well, you patrol the edges of a ballroom, as if wishing to maintain your harem."

"My harem?!"

"Well, yes, the pool of women you deem available for your . . . raking." She mimed raking leaves again. "And, at times, you will chase off other males who express interest in a member of your harem, like I have seen you do with Lady Lilith, for example."

Rafe's head reared back. That was not . . . untrue.

"Based on your description, I am unsure if being labeled a *primus* is a good or bad thing," he said.

A pause.

"Me, too."

"Oh."

"And, as I said, I am unsure if the label truly fits. Because there are other times, like this one—" She motioned to indicate the space where they were hiding. "—where you act not so much dominant as evasive."

That was also true.

Lady Sophie was alarmingly perceptive.

Rafe paused, unsure how to navigate this conversation. He adored having no idea what Lady Sophie would say next. But he was also painfully aware that he should not be speaking with her. The consequences would be dire if Kendall found out.

"You have certainly been observant of my behavior," he finally said.

"I find the genus *Rakus* to be a most fascinating subject."

That startled a laugh out of him. "The genus *Rakus*?!"

Lady Sophie continued to bite her lip. "Erhm, yes."

"You assign people to genuses?"

"Don't you mean *genera*? That is the plural of genus, and you have already asserted a rather obnoxious attachment to proper word usage—"

He laughed again. "Yes, of course, but I belong to a genus?"

"Genus *Rakus*, yes. Species . . . *lasciviosus*."

"So I am *Rakus lasciviosus*, a licentious rake . . . and you are?"

"*Femina studiosa*."

A beat as Rafe parsed the label. "A studious female . . ." He thought further and then snapped his fingers. "A bluestocking!"

"Yes."

"And do you often separate men and women into genus and species categories?"

"It seems appropriate, given the vast differences between male and female behavior, despite how mutually interdependent they may seem . . ." She paused and met his gaze, a hesitant wariness there. As if she had been lost in their conversation but abruptly awoke to the reality of him.

Did she assume that he was teasing her? That he mocked her?

"I am sincere with my questions." He had to reassure her.

"I believe you."

The silence stretched between them. It should have been awkward and clumsy, but instead it felt . . .

. . . comfortable, an aching sort of security. Of belonging.

Rafe longed to spend the entire day talking to her. He wanted to know everything that she saw and observed, every brilliant thought that winged through her clever head. He feared he would never tire of it.

In short . . . it was an unmitigated disaster.

She is not for you. You must leave.

Kendall's position on Lady Sophronia was clear.

But first . . .

"Dare I ask why the sack you are holding is wriggling rather distressingly?" He pointed to the burlap bag in her left hand. It had been rolling and turning as she spoke.

"This?" She lifted it upright.

"Yes."

"'Tis an albino *Rattus norvegicus*." She paused. "The hall boy caught it in a trap and then wanted to torment it. I paid him six shillings to give it to me instead."

"You have an albino brown rat in a burlap sack?"

"Yes."

Rafe laughed. It burst free from his chest, a startled reflex.

This woman.

She would destroy him.

"May I?" He held out a hand for the sack.

She passed it to him.

He carefully peered inside.

A pair of blood red eyes stared up at him.

Why, yes, indeed it was an albino brown rat.

"Fascinating." He passed the sack back to her. "What will you do with it?"

She shrugged, those lovely green eyes slid back to his as she spoke, pinning him. "Set it free, of course. It cannot help that it is different."

Lady Sophie *would* rescue a wee beastie that stood apart. Such an action was, in the end, merely a reflection of her own uniquely astonishing self.

Rafe's heart thumped in his ribcage, each beat more painful than the last, the organ seemingly expanding larger and larger, even though he assumed such a thing to be physically impossible.

He teetered perilously on the brink of falling head-over-heels in love with Lady Sophronia Sorrow.

And *that* would be the equivalent of declaring war on his father, a war that Rafe would not win.

Rafe was desperate to be free of his father's iron grasp. Desperate to make his own decisions, to accompany Andrew on his trip to the South Pacific, to be his own man. But until he came into his inheritance, complying with his father's demands was the only way to retain a modicum of freedom.

So Rafe did not spend hours talking with Lady Sophie, as he wished.

He did not bask in the warmth of her smile, or imagine a life where he could call upon her tomorrow.

Instead, he . . . panicked.

He did what he should have immediately done. He handed the burlap sack back to her, bowed with exacting precision, and left the room.

Because falling in love with Lady Sophronia Sorrow with her vivid eyes and sparkling intellect would destroy him in truth.

4

Rafe tried to stem the tide of his admiration for Lady Sophie. Truly he did.

Over the next three months, he threw himself into helping Andrew make final preparations for his voyage to the South Pacific. He bowed to his father's every whim, hoping against hope that Kendall might relent and allow him to accompany Andrew. But that hope did not materialize. Andrew's ship, *The Minerva*, was currently docked in Leith outside Edinburgh and would depart in the next two weeks. Rafe remained in London.

He had finally given up on the dream of accompanying Andrew.

But Lady Sophie was not so easily vanquished. Though Rafe did not actively seek her out, he still found himself in her company from time to time over those months. Their all-too-brief interactions stood out in vivid relief—shining beacons of delight, each interaction adding further fuel to the fire of his regard.

Lady Sophie's laughter from an adjacent box at the theater, giggling over the gaffes of Mrs. Malaprop in a production of Sheridan's

The Rivals, while Rafe's own female companion yawned and missed the humor entirely.

Lady Sophie's fine seat on a prancing filly while riding Rotten Row in Hyde Park.

The impromptu rescue of a litter of kittens found half-drowned in the Serpentine one July morning, Lady Sophie directing his efforts from the bank as he fished each scrawny kitten from the shallow water and deposited it back with her, near ruining his favorite pair of Hessian boots.

A stolen conversation while taking shelter from the rain under an awning on Bond Street, discussing a recent paper which proffered theories on the formation of vegetable epidermis.

The list went on, each encounter stoking his admiration of her.

Then one afternoon in mid-September, Rafe spotted Lady Sophie riding in Hyde Park beside a golden-haired, red-coated officer—Captain Jack Fulstate. Lady Sophie looked resplendent in her military-style riding habit, a jaunty hat atop her head. She handled her spirited mare with the easy grace of an accomplished horsewoman. Captain Fulstate certainly was entranced. Her shy smiles and his broad laughter left little doubt as to the captain's intentions.

The scene knocked the breath from Rafe's lungs.

A few casual questions elicited the response he dreaded: "Lady Sophronia? Why, yes. Captain Fulstate has been courting her most actively these past few weeks. The man is fortunate to have survived Waterloo and likely wishes to celebrate by taking a wife. His family is not so high as to sneer at the prospect of marrying one of the Sorrowful Miscellany."

Rafe nearly flinched at the news. Had he truly thought that Lady Sophie would remain unmarried, waiting in the wings for him? That she somehow existed outside the pressures of society and family?

He was an utter fool.

Rafe watched as Captain Fulstate and Sophie cantered off, heads leaning toward one another. It felt all too much like witnessing his very future retreat from him.

He did not know how long he sat there on his horse, staring at the place where Lady Sophie had been. Long enough for his bay to prance in agitation. Long enough for the autumn chill to seep through his caped overcoat.

Long enough for a seething rage to build in his chest.

Why was Lady Sophie forbidden? Why did his father derive pleasure from cruelly denying Rafe the things he wanted most?

Rafe finally returned to Gilbert House, teeth clenched, chest burning with suppressed anger.

A letter awaited him, sitting on the silver salver in the entry hall. Its black seal—a black, *unbroken* seal—declared that he would find grim news inside.

Rafe opened the letter, his thumping heart already suspecting is contents.

His grandmother—may God bless her soul—had finally passed on. Her estate was to be settled upon him.

Rafe inhaled a breath, sharp and cleansing.

Freedom filled his lungs.

At last!

Never again would his father use money to control him. He was done with the man forever.

Rafe raced up the stairs to his rooms, hands trembling, mind hurtling forward to make plans.

He would move out of Gilbert House tomorrow and never see his father again.

But first, he *had* to see Lady Sophie. He had to stake his claim along with Captain Fulstate. Wasn't Lady Wishart's ball this evening? Surely Lady Sophie would be there.

He would woo her in earnest now. Perhaps they could elope to Scotland and join Andrew on his voyage, meeting up with him in Lisbon or Gibraltar. Rafe intuitively suspected that Lady Sophie would relish a scientific voyage to the ends of the earth.

Rafe rushed to dress for the ball.

SOPHIE FANNED HER face, listening to Captain Jack Fulstate regale her with a story from his time in Portugal.

Captain Fulstate—or Jack, as he had been insistent she call him—was entertaining. He seemed a steady, eager sort. And—she darted a glance at his broad shoulders—he was decidedly attractive in his red regimentals. Given the number of women who openly stared at him, Sophie was not alone in her opinion.

Sophie smiled at Jack and continued to fan her face. Lady Wishart's ballroom buzzed with guests, despite it being September. Most of the *ton* had already vacated London for shooting in the country—her father and brothers among them—but clearly enough remained to fill a ballroom. Lady Mainfeld had wished to finalize a dress order, and so they had lingered in London.

At least, that was her mother's excuse. Sophie thought it more likely that Lady Mainfeld wished to encourage Captain Fulstate's attentions toward Sophie herself.

Captain Fulstate—Jack!—had made his intentions toward her most clear.

For her part, Sophie could not decide how she felt. She had little prior knowledge of him, but what she had seen recommended him to her. He made her laugh with his antics and stories, and he was consistent in his affections. Her sisters insisted that she was falling in love with Jack.

Was this love then? It seemed a tepid sort of emotion, nothing akin to the sweeping force most poets described. Was love simply a sort of hyperbole then?

There were things about Jack that puzzled her. Sometimes he would tell a story that he found humorous—like hiding a fellow officer's glasses and watching the poor fellow stumble about half-blind—and then would become taciturn when Sophie did not join him in laughter. Worse, he showed little interest in her scientific studies. These things displayed a dissimilarity of thought that concerned her.

No, the only man she consistently found similar to herself was Lord Rafe Gilbert. But despite a few vivid encounters over the summer, Lord Rafe had shown no inclination to court her in earnest.

To be honest, his behavior ran hot and cold. He would ignore her at Lady Smith's musicale—looking right through her—and then two days later rush to stand beside her in Regent's Park, chatting amiably as if they were old friends. But given the animosity between their fathers, such behavior wasn't entirely unexpected, she supposed.

Her last encounter with Lord Rafe had been only last week, underneath a shop awning on Bond Street. Sophie had been waiting for her mother to finish flirting with a handsome haberdasher when Lord Rafe joined her. They had talked for a solid thirty minutes, ideas pinging between them, until Lady Mainfeld had pulled her away with a tight smile.

The carriage ride home had been tense.

"You cannot be seen speaking with Lord Rafe," her mother admonished.

"Truly?" Sophie' eyebrows flew upward, unable to contain her surprise.

Her mother currently *lived* to see Sophie married. The woman delighted in Sophie speaking with an eligible young man.

Her mother fixed Sophie with a stern, unyielding look. "Your father will never countenance a connection between yourself and Lord Rafe. The enmity between our families is too great." Concern lined Lady Mainfeld's face. "You would be wise to forget you ever knew him."

Sophie had been nonplussed, replaying the conversation over and over. How unlike her flighty mother to issue such a warning.

Clearly, Lord Rafe was not for her.

And yet, Sophie's heart thundered every time someone mentioned his name, or she caught a glimpse of him from afar. Surely that meant something, right? Or was it merely the lure of a forbidden *Rakus lasciviosus* at work?

She felt more in five minutes of Lord Rafe's company than an entire day with Captain Fulstate.

Case in point. Jack continued to speak about Portugal, leaning toward her as they stood at the edge of the ballroom.

"... the weather was delightfully warm, of course, and General West was most glad of my company..."

Sophie pasted a smile on her face and nodded when needed, encouraging Jack to continue, but her thoughts were far away. She feared that if it were Lord Rafe discussing the same things, she would be hanging on his every word.

As if to punctuate this point, Sophie felt a prickle chase her spine, a shift in the air.

She turned her head slightly to the right.

Lord Rafe stared at her from across the ballroom.

Her heart leapt into her throat, pounding like a crazed beast, as if trying to escape her chest and run to him—

Heavens.

How absurd.

Sophie swallowed and ordered herself to look away, she truly did.

Look away, now!

But her stubborn eyes refused to listen. And Lord Rafe held her with his gaze, dark and intent.

Jack and the rest of the ballroom faded.

And in that moment, Sophie simply . . . knew.

Lord Rafe Gilbert was here for her and her alone. Something had happened. Something had changed.

Later, Sophie would laugh over the melodrama of her thoughts, over her absurd perceptions of the moment.

Surely ladies and gentlemen had not obediently separated to allow Lord Rafe to pass like Moses parting the Red Sea?

Surely he hadn't held her gaze the entire time, the force of his eyes nearly mesmerizing her?

And then he was abruptly before her, his wide shoulders blocking the light flickering from candles in the chandeliers overhead.

"Lady Sophie." He bowed.

"Lord Rafe." She curtsied.

A small pause, and then . . .

"May I have the honor of this dance?" He extended his hand to her, eyes expectant.

His words snatched her breath.

Those dimples were utterly irresistible, a siren call.

She stared at his gloved palm. Would this be more of his odd push and pull?

But, no. It felt more momentous . . . like the first shot fired over the bow.

Will you join me? She sensed he was asking. *I am ready to defy my father. Are you willing to defy yours?*

Well.

She lifted her gaze from his hand, meeting his eyes.

Heavens. They were pools of warm amber, earnest and painfully . . . *solemn* . . . a direct channel to his very soul.

Oh.

Here was the true man, then. No *Rakus lasciviosus*. No flirtatious insincerity.

Her eyes darted back to that extended hand. Taking it would be a declaration of war. A glove slap to both their parents.

Sophie was not rebellious by nature, but . . . this family feud was absurd. And she and Lord Rafe were hardly going to be torn apart in some Romeo-and-Juliet melodramatic farce.

She met his gaze boldly, allowing herself a broad smile.

"Why, yes, Lord Rafe. I will dance with you." She placed her gloved hand in his, his much larger palm utterly engulfing hers, sending a wave of heat up her arm and a jolt of electricity down her spine.

His matching grin was radiant, taking his expression from merely handsome to resplendent.

He tucked her hand into his arm, leading her to the dance floor.

Dimly, Sophie thought she heard a disgruntled, "I say, Lord Rafe, badly done that," from Jack, but she could not be certain.

Lord Rafe whirled her into a waltz, the room spinning past at dizzying breath. Or perhaps it was simply the close proximity of Lord Rafe that caused her lungs to gasp for air.

His gaze never left her face, as if cataloging everything he saw there, committing it to memory.

"You look breathtakingly beautiful tonight, Lady Sophie," he finally said.

"Thank you," she murmured, surprised at the blush that threatened her cheeks.

She *never* blushed, and yet two minutes in Lord Rafe's company, and she was abruptly flushing and off-kilter.

Was it because she was seeing more than the gallant rake this evening? Because he had shed his chrysalis like a *Danaus plexippus*, a monarch butterfly taking flight and showing its brilliant colors?

"How fares your clowder of barn cats?" He asked after another moment.

"My barn cats? I believe they are doing well. I have not seen them in nearly a year, unfortunately. All the cattens will be long grown—"

"Cattens?" Lord Rafe's brow drew down, but a smile still twinkled in his eye, as if he found everything she said unbearably fascinating.

But now she had to explain . . .

"*Cattens* are how I describe an adolescent cat," she said.

"An adolescent cat?"

"Well . . . yes. Have you never thought it strange? We have a word to describe a baby cat—a *kitten*—and a word for an adult—a *cat* or a *tomcat*—but why do we have no words for animals when they are between those two extremes? We call humans *adolescents* or perhaps, more rarely, *teen-aged person*. But we do not have a similar word for animals."

Lord Rafe's grin nearly split his face. "Hence . . . *cattens*—a word somewhere between kitten and cat."

"Precisely."

"That is . . . clever." He nodded as if he approved of cleverness in a woman.

He spun her in a circle, once, twice, mouth pursed, as if thinking.

"So would it be a *duppy*? Or a *pog*?"

Sophie laughed. "I have not quite decided. Though I prefer *lamb-o-lescent* for a sheep."

He joined in her laughter.

Something in Sophie's chest fluffed and puffed outward. A sense of giddy hope, of wonder that this man was willing to defy his family for her.

When their waltz ended, Lord Rafe claimed another set, a shocking occurrence sure to set tongues wagging. Yet, Sophie sensed that he would dance the entire evening with her if he could.

They talked throughout the entire set, their conversation pinging between a recent reclassification of the common brown bat by the Linnean Society to the implications of the on-going Congress of Vienna.

As the second set finished with a trilling flourish from the small orchestra, Lord Rafe tucked her hand through his arm again.

"I cannot bear to stop our conversation, my lady. Allow me to escort you to the refreshment room," he murmured in her ear, leading her from the stuffy ballroom.

Sophie's entire body hummed like a plucked violin. How was it that the world appeared more brilliant when on Lord Rafe's arm?

He led her across the entry hall and into the dining room. Settling her into a small table on the perimeter, he soon returned with a plate piled high with biscuits and pastries. For another hour, they laughed and talked, existing in a quiet cocoon.

Sophie basked in the full force of Lord Rafe's rapt attention, the magnetism of his charm. The longer they talked, the more Scotland wove through his speech. His 'r's rolled and his vowels elongated and his 't's became more a suggestion than a reality. Everything about him radiated sincerity. Sophie sensed no practiced insouciance, no *Rakus* wiles.

Dimly, Sophie noticed that the occasional matron or lord darted them an astonished glance, but she could not bring herself to care.

They finished eating, and Lord Rafe led her back across the expansive entry hall with a large staircase winding up the middle. Casting a quick glance about and ascertaining that they were alone, he pulled Sophie into a curtained alcove beneath the stairs.

"Gracious!" Sophie gasped, staring up at him in the dim light.

The lovely herbal scent of his cologne eddied around her.

"I figured our night would not be complete without a meeting behind a curtain." He grinned down at her, grasping her hands in his. "I likely should apologize for dragging you in here, but I cannot."

"You . . . cannot?"

"Nae, because that would imply that I am sorry. And I will never be sorry for claiming more time with you, Lady Sophie." He punctuated his words by pressing a kiss to the back of her gloved hand.

And then, turning her hand, he placed a kiss on the barest strip of skin showing between the pearl buttons of her long gloves. And then, leaning down, he pressed a kiss to her cheek.

His lips were soft there. His warm breath danced across her skin, the rasp of his evening whiskers sending gooseflesh skittering.

Be still her heart.

Unthinking, Sophie wrapped her free hand around the back of his neck holding him in place. She rose on tiptoe and turned her head toward him, her lips finding his with astonishing ease.

The press of his mouth snatched her breath and increased the ache in her chest. His kiss was new, but yet, achingly familiar. As if she had already spent a hundred lifetimes kissing this man.

He clasped her cheek with his palm, a palm that *trembled*, as if this kiss were just as momentous to him as it was to her.

"May I call on you tomorrow?" he murmured against her mouth.

"Please," she whispered, pressing to give him another kiss. Now that she had a taste, she never wanted to stop. The man was shockingly addictive.

Lord Rafe did not appear deterred by her eagerness. In fact, it was quite the opposite.

Nothing was said for several more minutes.

At last with one final, lingering kiss, he pulled back.

"Prepare yourself, Lady Sophie," he said, voice husky and low. "I intend to be most devoted in my attentions to you."

Sophie nearly shivered at his words.

"I will await your visit tomorrow, my lord."

He grinned. "See that you do."

5

Rafe returned home that evening, his head spinning.

He had kissed Lady Sophie, and it had been glorious.

He had intended to pack his trunk and remove himself from Gilbert House immediately after the ball, but he had spent too much time with Lady Sophie and the hour was far too late. The staff were all asleep when he let himself in the front door. Even his father's study was dark.

And so Rafe took himself to bed, determining to rise early and remove himself forever from his father's household, from his father's life. Hopefully, his father would be off at Carlton House visiting the Prince Regent and not even realize that Rafe had gone.

He fell asleep to the vision of a life with Sophie. He would call on her the following day and begin his courtship in earnest.

But his euphoric dream of Lady Sophie was shattered by a bucket of ice-cold water.

Rafe spluttered awake, gasping for breath.

Beadle, his father's ever-loyal butler, stood beside Rafe's bed, rimmed in the faint light of dawn.

"His Grace would like a word with you," Beadle intoned.

Given that two burly grooms flanked Beadle—arms folded, eyes menacing—Rafe understood that the audience with his father was *not* a request.

Hair dripping, hands shaking in fury, Rafe wrapped himself in a banyan and followed Beadle.

"Are the rumors I am hearing true?" the Duke of Kendall demanded from behind his desk as soon as Beadle closed the door. "That you danced with Lady Sophronia Sorrow yesterday evening?" His father's dark eyebrows were drawn down into a thunderous line. The weak sunlight left the duke's face shadowy and menacing.

This was it, Rafe realized. The moment he broke with his father forever.

Good riddance!

"Yes, Father." He imbued his words with all the resolve in his breast.

Rafe met his father's dangerous gaze head on, biting back the anger bubbling in his throat. No matter how satisfying yelling at his father would be, it would only give the man ammunition. When dealing with the Duke of Kendall, it was paramount Rafe remained as cold as his sire.

Silence was always the better option with Kendall.

"I thought that I had made my stance on interactions with Mainfeld's mongrel progeny clear." Menace laced Kendall's every word.

"You had, Sir."

More weighty silence. Kendall was fond of them. Rafe, after all, had learned his silence from the master.

Rafe knew better than to squirm. He met his father's displeasure head-on.

Kendall understood the import of Rafe's silence.

"Ah." His father's head went back, dark eyes ominous. "You foolish, idiotic *cretin*. You could have any woman in London, and yet you stupidly choose the one that I have *expressly* forbidden. Why do you thwart me like this?"

Rafe refused to give an answer, though his chest heaved, and bitterness left a metallic tang in his mouth.

He has no hold on you. Do not give in. Listen and then walk away.

Rafe was his own man.

His father leaned forward in his chair, eyes narrowing. "I presume that you heard the news about your grandmother. Are your actions related to her demise? Do you consider yourself and your behavior independent of me now?"

There was no way to answer that which didn't give Kendall more power.

Rafe held his tongue.

"You are, and always will be, my son," Kendall continued. "You will obey me in all things. I dislike being placed in a position where I must be cruel to you or those you care about, boy." He seemed to ponder for a moment and then continued, laying down his words like precious cards, triumphant that he had won the table. "As you know, your mother's moods are unpredictable. I worry her melancholy grows more . . . precarious. I would hate to have to intervene."

Rafe barely stifled a gasp.

"Intervene?" He pushed the words past numb lips.

The duke threatened Rafe's mother?! His own *duchess*?

And over Lady Sophie?

Just when Rafe thought his hatred could not deepen—that the duke could not fall any lower in his estimation—the bastard revealed an entirely new country for Rafe to rage through.

Was this the man's intended way of controlling Rafe now that the threat of penury had been removed?

"Yes." The gleeful light in his father's eye confirmed it. Kendall knew he had Rafe in his clutches. The duke feigned a mournful sigh. "Your mother's mental state is so fragile. Her melancholy is most distressing to me. To be truthful, I have considered sending her to an asylum. I understand cold baths and purging are said to have a restorative effect."

Rafe's breath literally stuck in his throat, memories assailing him.

Years ago, a childhood friend had become mentally deranged, and his family, well-intentioned, had thought a lunatic asylum would help. But when Rafe visited, he found his friend in appalling conditions, chained to his bed and forced to endure brutal treatments more akin to prison torture than any true healing. Fortunately, the man's family had removed him once they saw how conditions truly were. Kendall *knew* Rafe detested such places.

Moreover, the duchess was hardly so ill. Would Kendall subject his own wife to agony and horror in order to force Rafe's obedience? Did the duke truly think to drag the family name through such a scandal?

Oh, did you hear about the Duchess of Kendall? They say she was admitted to a lunatic asylum . . .

Would Kendall really do it? Or was he bluffing?

Because if Kendall wished to admit his wife to an asylum, there was *nothing* Rafe could do. Kendall's rule over his wife was absolute. The duchess was not actually her own person under English law. Even Rafe's uncle, the Scottish Earl of Ayr, could do nothing to help his sister in a situation such as this. If Kendall decreed that his wife needed to be admitted to an asylum, no one and nothing could stop him.

Once again, Rafe had underestimated the true depth of his father's depravity, of his abhorrence of Lord Mainfeld and everything tied to the Sorrowful Miscellany.

"Of course, you can save your mother," Kendall continued. "You will cease all contact with Lady Sophronia immediately. You will *never* associate with her again."

Rafe stilled as if Time itself had taken a breath . . .

. . . and then everything rushed in on him, emotion surging in his chest.

Give up Lady Sophie?

Never speak with her again?

Like. Hell.

And Rafe *knew* in that moment—

Kendall would never stop. He would forever find ways to force Rafe's obedience.

If Rafe wanted freedom, he would have to fight for it.

This ended now.

His mind reeled, scrambling to plan, to map out options. What could he do?

First, he would call his father's bluff. Then, if needed, he would spirit his mother out of the country, out of his father's reach.

Something of his steely determination must have shown on his face.

His father sat back, fingers steepling. "If you do this—if you give up Lady Sophronia—in addition to allowing your mother her freedom, I will provide a way for you to accompany Andrew Mackenzie on this ludicrous voyage he is proposing."

Rafe's knees threatened to buckle from the surprise.

Now his father capitulated? And over Lady Sophronia?!

Andrew left in less than two weeks. There was barely time to pack and race to Scotland, catching *The Minerva* before she left harbor. Rafe would be hard pressed to call upon Lady Sophie even one last time.

He stared at Kendall.

The bastard grinned, thinking he had backed Rafe into a corner.

No!

Never. Never again.

Rafe had the money he needed. The duke had no claim on him.

He would woo Lady Sophie and claim her as his bride. They would then join Andrew on his voyage regardless of his father's decision. Rafe would finish this discussion and leave his father's house today, never to return.

Kendall was a monster, yes, but surely he was bluffing. Even the duke would not stoop to the scandal of committing his wife to an asylum unnecessarily.

"My mother is hardly so ill," Rafe said, voice measured. "And to send a healthy and whole woman to an asylum, why just imagine what the London gossips will say? It would be a black mark on your name."

Kendall met his gaze, seeing the determination there, likely reading Rafe's thoughts. His sire had always had an uncanny ability to predict Rafe's actions.

"Perhaps. But her health is tenuous, you know." Kendall nudged the inkwell on his desk. "'Twould be terrible if something were to happen which worsened her moods."

Rafe could not hold back his gasp. Was Kendall threatening to *hurt* the duchess now? To deliberately invoke her melancholic spells?

Rafe floundered. *Think, man. There has to be a way out of this!*

Kendall was not done. "And the asylums . . . I seem to remember that you disliked how that friend of yours was treated in one. Tis such a pity, as I hear a lunatic asylum can be quite restorative."

Before Rafe could reply, the duke thumped a fist on his desk, startling Rafe.

The door snicked open.

Rafe turned to see Beadle and the same two burly grooms enter the room. Menace flowed with them. The grooms moved to flank Rafe, a hulking brute on each side of him. Where had Beadle dredged up these men? They both towered over Rafe's own considerable height.

Rafe swallowed.

The meaning of this situation was not lost on him.

Rafe turned back to his father, seeing the truth in his father's determined gaze.

There would be *no* escape. Rafe could either submit or be forced to submit. The duke *would* harm his wife and condemn her to an asylum in order to ensure Rafe's compliance. His blood chilled at the thought of his mother there, listening to the screams of the truly mad. Ice baths and chains would cure nothing and, from his point of view, only make the patient worse. She would go mad in truth.

For the first time since entering the room, fear clawed at Rafe's chest. Fear for his mother and sister. Fear for himself.

A sinking sense of dread that his dream of Lady Sophie would remain just that—a dream.

He had *vastly* underestimated Kendall's need for vengeance, the depth of the duke's callousness.

A surge of virulent hatred seared through his blood, scouring his veins.

Rafe would never underestimate Kendall again.

The duke pressed his fingers together. "Allow me to be exquisitely clear, son. You will *never* again speak to nor have contact with Mainfeld's mongrel daughter. You *will* accompany Mackenzie on this ridiculous voyage. It has been your fondest wish, has it not?" Mockery laced Kendall's tone. "I understand you are already packed."

Rafe shot Beadle a glowering glance. Beadle, as befitted a butler of his station, remained impassive, but Rafe didn't miss the taunting gleam in the older man's eyes.

Beadle had always been his father's loyal lap dog.

His sire was not finished. "When I said I would *provide* a way for you to go on this voyage, I meant it. My men here—" He waved a hand at the looming henchmen on either side of Rafe. "—will accompany you to Edinburgh to ensure that you arrive safely on your ship. This is non-negotiable. You *will* go to Edinburgh. You *will* get on that ship, one way or another. Your mother and sister will be well-looked after in your absence."

The men each took a step closer to Rafe; the air in the room nearly vibrated with suppressed violence. A meaty hand wrapped around Rafe's upper arm.

Never speak with Lady Sophie again?

Leave immediately for . . . *years?!* Lady Sophie would be humiliated. The poor woman would be left to face the London gossips alone. She would think him the worst sort of cad.

Rafe pulled on the hand that held him. The second brute grabbed his opposite arm, grinning ruthlessly.

Kendall laughed, an unpleasant sound.

Rafe stilled. The brutes were too strong, and both looked ready to do damage with their meaty fists.

Kendall continued to smile, taking obvious pleasure in watching Rafe be forced to submit to his will.

Rafe struggled to breathe through his anger, hands clenched at his side, eyes locked with his sire.

Bloody bastard.

The smug glint in Kendall's eyes said that he knew he had won. Rafe had been out-maneuvered.

"You are dismissed." Kendall flicked his wrist. "Safe journey."

Like *hell.*

But Rafe had no choice but to allow himself to be half dragged from the room, impotent rage scouring his veins.

As the men led him across the first-floor landing, Rafe imagined wrenching his arms free from the brutes' grasp, dropping over the railing to the entrance hall below, fighting his way out the front door, and racing for freedom. Leaving the controlling grasp of his father forever behind.

But, if he did that, could he return for his mother and sister in time? What damage would his father inflict on them? Could he truly save them, too?

Voices on the marble floor below caught his attention.

"—we should be back in time to dress for dinner," his sister said.

His mother gave his sister a wan smile as they prepared to leave the house.

Some motherly sense had the duchess turning to look up at Rafe, their gazes tangling. A memory flooded in, of him standing in this same place years ago.

"Mama!" Rafe wrenched his arm from Nurse's hold, taking the stairs two at a time.

Mama was home. At last!

"Lord Rafe!" the woman called behind him.

But Rafe was already racing down the stairs to the smiling, beautiful woman below.

He leapt from the final step.

His mother was there to catch him.

"My darling wee Rafe!" His mother clutched him tightly, her familiar scent of heather and lavender enfolding him. She pulled back, eyes sparkling with unshed tears. "How I've missed my brave boy!"

A flood of emotion washed him, for the woman who bore him and loved him unconditionally. Who had never once wavered in her devotion to him.

Movement in the corner of his eye had Rafe swinging his head to the right. His father stood in the hallway outside his study, icy eyes glittering in the dim light. Kendall looked nearly primordial, a sinister presence from a lucid dream.

His father darted a pointed look to the entryway below. Rafe followed his eyes to see two more large grooms following his mother and sister out the door.

And in that single glance, Rafe *knew*.

His father would lock his duchess away to keep Rafe from stealing her.

And Rafe . . . he would not abandon his mother to his father's cruelty.

He *could* not.

No matter the personal cost.

A brute jerked on his arm.

Someday, Rafe vowed.

Someday he would stop being that fish, pinned in place, thrashing against the knife in his chest.

6

The day after Lady Wishart's ball was one of trial for Sophie.

Her mother scolded her for dancing with Lord Rafe—

How can you not understand that Kendall is anathema to us? Have you no care for your reputation nor respect for Captain Fulstate's clear regard? Kendall will see us pay for this!

Her mother had one of her attacks over the entire affair—chest heaving, hands shaking, gasping for breath—every line of her body trembling in panic.

Lady Mainfeld had to take to her room for the rest of the day.

Sophie, for her part, could scarcely sit still, her own chest a buzzing hive of nerves and anticipation.

Would Lord Mainfeld allow Rafe into their home? Despite her mother's hysterics, Lord Mainfeld had never forbidden Sophie from associating with Kendall's children.

And if Lord Rafe were permitted to call upon her, what would he say when he came? Would he look at her with that same intensity, that deep regard that seemed to draw her very soul from her body?

More to the point . . . was this thrumming excitement love? Or, at the least, the beginning of love?

Sophie nearly resorted to wringing her hands, helpless against the emotions battering her.

Wringing her hands!

Over a gentleman!!

And a rake at that!!!

She wanted to laugh at the sheer absurdity.

And so . . . she waited in the drawing room. Well, she embroidered in the drawing room and presided over the tea tray as a string of visitors came and went. But as she was dressed in a pretty day gown of forest green that matched her eyes and flattered her figure . . . no one was deceived as to her true intentions.

The house was inundated with friends and acquaintances, all eager to soak up the deliciousness of the situation. Lord Mainfeld's daughter and the Duke of Kendall's son . . . it had the potential to be something dramatic. A scandal? A farce? A tragedy? It scarcely mattered, as regardless it would be exciting.

Only . . .

. . . nothing happened.

Despite his ardent kisses, despite his whispered promise . . .

Lord Rafe did not appear.

In her mind, Sophie made excuses for him—

Lord Rafe had lost track of time.

Or, he had taken ill.

Maybe his mother had required his escort today.

Perhaps an emergency had arisen.

Mayhap the Duke of Kendall, in a fit of imperious pique, had forbidden Lord Rafe from ever seeing Sophie again, banishing him from the country—

Sophie rolled her eyes at the last thought. How gothically melodramatic.

They lived in 1815 not 1518, for heaven's sake.

Lord Rafe would have a good explanation when he called tomorrow.

But he did not call the next day.

Nor the next.

Captain Fulstate was there every afternoon, of course. Polite and mannerly, solicitous of her welfare.

On the fourth day after the ball, Mrs. Winters, a gossipy friend of her mother's, gleefully leaned forward and said, "I have just had the most astonishing news. I had it from my maid who has a sister in service at Gilbert House that Lord Rafe has quit the city."

"Oh." Lady Mainfeld's eyebrows lifted to her hairline. "Is that so?"

"Indeed." Mrs. Winters nearly tittered with the excitement of it all. "Apparently, Lord Rafe is off on some grand overseas adventure with a friend. They say he has had the trip planned for nearly a year now."

Lord Rafe on a trip with a friend? He had known for a *year* that he would be leaving?

Sophie's heart stuttered in her chest, her breathing abruptly labored.

Both her mother and Mrs. Winters shot a side-glance at Sophie.

Oh, that she could melt into oblivion and never again relive the pain of this moment. The shattering hurt which she strongly suspected was her own naive innocence crumbling. Invisibility had been a protective shield, and she the greater fool for stepping out from behind it.

A scorching heat climb her cheeks. This was the problem with never blushing; when one did, the sensation was horrific.

The pitying look in her mother's eyes said it all.

Sophie, for all her intelligence, was still an idiot.

Lord Rafe would never be coming for her.

Sophie had been taken for a fool.

How could she have been so featherbrained? So blinded by a handsome smile and charming wit?

Lord Rafe's behavior at Lady Wishart's ball had simply been the wiles of a *Rakus lasciviosus* in his native habitat. A flight of fancy for him that had lasted the length of two sets, a ballroom supper, and several (admittedly spectacular) kisses. A last lark before embarking on a planned journey.

After all . . . once a rake, always a rake.

Sophie was just another name in the long list of women with whom

Lord Rafe dallied. She should count herself fortunate that he had only claimed a kiss.

The pain of Lord Rafe's betrayal scoured her, causing a sleepless night and fuzzy head.

So when Captain Fulstate called the next day, Sophie was less inclined to remain aloof to his advances. He was a kind, decent man, after all. If nothing else, his attention was a balm to her bruised ego. And perhaps her more-restrained feelings toward him were a good thing. Without such heightened emotions, there was less chance of being hurt.

She had only had a taste of Lord Rafe; she had only just begun to think of him as integral to her.

Imagine if their story had continued further, and then he had abandoned her?

How cruel to learn *then* that a man could feel like home, but, in reality, be so very temporary.

No. She was fortunate, in all truth, to have had a lucky escape.

All that remained was to apply the lesson she had learned, forget about the man, and move on.

TWELVE DAYS AFTER being forced from London, Rafe was "escorted" onto the deck of *The Minerva* moored in Leith harbor to begin the first leg of his voyage to the South Pacific.

One week later, *The Minerva* docked in Plymouth. Rafe rushed from his berth aboard ship, a letter to Lady Sophie in hand. Andrew met him on the gangplank, a grim expression on his face. Wordlessly his friend handed him a copy of yesterday's *London Times* which announced the marriage of Lady Sophronia Sorrow to Captain Jack Fulstate.

After...

Four years later

Angus, Scotland
1819

7

The notice in the *Edinburgh Advertiser* was short and succinct:

> *To those who survived the wreck of* The Minerva: *Remember the debt that is owed. You shall not be permitted to forget the one who trusted you. Act with honor before it is too late.*

Lord Rafe, as one of the survivors of said wreck, found the notice disturbing for several reasons.

First, only five men had survived the sinking of *The Minerva*.

Second, those same five men were the only ones who knew the secrets *The Minerva* had taken to her grave.

Third, the men were close friends, brothers in every way but blood.

And fourth, all five of those men were currently present in the room.

"None of us posted this." Rafe tapped the paper where it lay on the table beside him. "And we have no suspicions as to who *did* post it, nor the nature of this so-called debt."

"Not to mention, what honor is owed." Andrew Mackenzie Langston, Earl of Hadley, replied, sinking back in his chair before the fire, resting his feet on a nearby footstool. He took a slow sip of whisky.

"'Tis a puzzle." Dr. Alexander Whitaker propped an elbow on the fireplace mantel, drumming his fingers along the wood.

A fire popped in the hearth providing cheery ambiance and needed warmth. Even in August, Scotland required a lit fire indoors. Rafe was quite sure the Scottish climate existed on a sliding scale of superlatives—cold, colder, coldest—rather than the more traditional summertime heat and winter chill of England.

"A bit disturbing, if ye ask me." Ewan Campbell reached for another buttery from the tea tray, spreading preserves on the golden bread, the buttery dwarfed by his enormous hand. Ewan dispatched it in two bites before reaching for another.

"Och, I likely just need to knock a few heads together down at the wharf," Master Kieran MacTavish snorted, downing a healthy swallow of whisky. "See if I cannae shake some answers loose."

Rafe smiled. The answer was so . . . Kieran.

"I'm no' sure violence is the answer here," Ewan said to Kieran, licking his fingers and reaching for a shortbread round. "The tone of the notice isnae specifically threatening."

"Aye, but it isnae friendly, either," Alex said.

They were assembled together, the Brotherhood of the Black Tartan. Rafe and his four best friends, Scotsmen whose lives had become intertwined during their voyage of scientific discovery to the South Pacific. Four years ago, they had left Leith, mostly strangers to one another. Three years ago, their bond as brothers had been sealed in blood on that fateful night in the South Pacific. Two years ago, they had finally returned to Scotland and resumed their respective lives.

The voyage had certainly altered Rafe's life for both good and ill.

The *ill*, of course, was the manner in which the journey had begun for him—dragged from London, forced to abandon his courtship of Lady Sophie.

The *good*, naturally, was this group of loyal, steadfast friends.

Andrew Mackenzie Langston, Lord Hadley, had been Rafe's closest friend for nearly a decade, since their days studying together at St. Andrews. They had planned and discussed the trip for years, until Andrew had taken steps to make it a reality. To Rafe's delight, Andrew had inherited an English earldom about a year earlier, putting them firmly into the same social circle in London. Not even Kendall could find fault with Rafe's friend now.

As for the other men in the room . . .

Dr. Alexander Whitaker had come aboard ship as a physician for the gentlemen, as well as a botany consultant.

Ewan Campbell, a talented artist, had been hired to document their finds through his drawings.

Master Kieran MacTavish had been *The Minerva*'s sailing master and their trusted liaison with the ship's commander—Captain Martin Cuthie—and her crew.

All four men were like brothers to him.

They were seated in Andrew's impressive library in Muirford House, his friend's sprawling estate near the coast north of Dundee, Scotland. The Brotherhood always gathered at least once a year in March, to commemorate the dark day that had changed them all forever.

But this was a sunnier occasion. Andrew was to marry Lady Jane Everard in the morning, and they had naturally come together to celebrate. The evening promised to be a merry one.

The notice in the *Edinburgh Advertiser* had been an unexpected jolt.

Rafe swirled his own tumbler of whisky, pondering the ramifications of the notice. "The problem, of course, is that we five are the only survivors of the wreckage. We were at the ends of the earth at the time. It wasn't as if we had regular postal service to send information home." He downed a healthy swallow of liquor, wincing at the burn in his throat. The motion pulled at the scar on his cheek, a souvenir of the events in the South Pacific.

"True," Alex agreed. "How would anyone else have learned about a debt? Moreover, beyond our immediate family and friends, who even knows we were on *The Minerva*?"

"There was the crew of the Portuguese whaler that rescued us," Ewan said, reaching for the pile of warm bannocks in the center of the tray.

Rafe nudged a pot of honey toward him. Ewan smiled in return.

Ewan was a giant of a man—well over six feet tall, broad-shouldered and barrel-chested—and had an out-sized appetite to match. Fate had a sense of humor, Rafe supposed, to have housed such a gentle, soft-spoken, artistic soul in a prize fighter's body. Watching Ewan's large hand draw a delicate flower was always a fascinating study in contrasts.

"The whaler?" Kieran said. "They didnae speak English."

"Aye," Rafe agreed. "My French was the only language we had in common. More to the point, I don't see why any of them would post such a notice." He waved a hand over the paper beside him.

"Agreed." Andrew downed the last of his whisky in one gulp, face pulling into a grimace.

"The newspapers mentioned the wreck a time or two, did they not?" Alex said.

"Aye, but it passed quickly, and I ensured that our names were never mentioned specifically in print." Andrew ran a hand over his face.

Silence hung for a moment. Kieran let out a long gust of air.

"Why are none of ye eejits saying the obvious? Ye dinnae need to spare my feelings." He drilled them with his pale eyes. "The bloody advert talks about us forgetting the one who trusted us. There is only one person who fits that description."

Rafe met Kieran's gaze, the name unspoken between them all.

Jamie Fyffe.

The sixth member of their band. The one who, despite the notice's accusation, would *never* be forgotten.

Jamie had been hired as the carpenter's mate aboard *The Minerva* as a favor to Kieran's former mentor, Charles Fyffe. Clever and good-natured, Jamie had helped them over and again, quickly earning all their loyalty. Tragically, when events turned deadly about a year into their voyage—when Captain Cuthie had betrayed their trust—Jamie had paid the ultimate price.

Tellingly, tonight they all sported the same dark tartan in some fashion or another.

Jamie's Tartan, they called it—bands of cross-hatch color against a black ground. Red for blood spilt. Yellow for hope. Green for growth. And white for the purity of their hearts.

Rafe, Andrew, Alex, and Ewan had wrapped lengths of the tartan around their chests as a sash. Kieran wore his as a great kilt, the plaid draping his body. Tomorrow, Jamie would be there in spirit, a silent witness to Andrew's marriage. Always with them, always remembered.

"Jamie's sacrifice will never be forgotten," Rafe said, voice low. "Ye know that, Kieran. Jamie set us all free—"

"Aye," Andrew agreed. "And we've sussed out those ultimately responsible for the situation in the South Pacific, for all the events that led to Jamie's death."

"Damn Captain Cuthie and his machinations," Kieran spat. "I know it's no' Christian of me tae say, but I'm right glad that bastard is at the bottom of the ocean somewhere. Drowning was too quick a death."

Kieran shook his head, a familiar bleakness in his eyes. Rafe knew his friend blamed himself for Jamie's death. Even several years on, Kieran's grief was ever-present.

Rafe had hoped that bringing those responsible to justice would ease his friend's suffering. This past spring, they had finally done just that, but Kieran was still lost in his pain. Justice for Jamie had been Kieran's lodestar for three years, his overarching goal. But now that it had been achieved, Kieran had been cut adrift. The man was awash in a sea of anguish and guilt, no shore in sight.

"Cuthie is gone, thank goodness," Andrew agreed, "but someone outside of ourselves clearly has some knowledge of what happened that night. I cannae think what debt is still owed."

"And what, if anything, we are tae do about it," Rafe said, his accent slipping from the crisp, aristocratic tones of his father to the soothing Scottish vowels of his mother.

Their voyage to the South Pacific had been uneventful until leaving Sydney, Australia and sailing for the New Hebrides. Once there, they set anchor near a village in the islands. Captain Cuthie had called a meeting and informed them that he had orders to take a group of villagers captive, to be sold into slavery on the voyage back to England. The Treaty of Paris, signed just two years before, had begun the process of abolishing the slave trade in the Atlantic, but the Pacific islands were outside the reach of any European government, as Cuthie well knew.

Naturally, the Brotherhood had categorically refused to allow Cuthie to enslave the villagers. Rafe and Andrew had borne the brunt of Cuthie's anger, leaving Rafe with a scar stretching from his right temple across his cheek. Kieran and Jamie had saved them, but at the cost of Jamie's freedom. Cuthie had taken Jamie captive and marooned the Brotherhood in the New Hebrides, sailing away. *The Minerva*—with Cuthie, Jamie, and her crew aboard—had wrecked on a reef shortly thereafter.

No one had survived.

"Like I was saying to yous,"—Kieran clenched his jaw—"let me knock some heads together down at the docks and see if I can shake anything useful loose. Sailors like the sound of their own voices. My ship is for New York next week. I'll let yous know if I find anything afore then."

"Perhaps we should also contact the newspaper and see if they will share who posted the notice," Rafe suggested.

"That's not a bad idea," Alex nodded. "Their offices are not too far from my surgery. I can call on them when I return tae Edinburgh."

"Regardless, we need to get tae the bottom of this." Andrew waved a hand. "It troubles me."

"Aye." Kieran rose and poured himself another finger of whisky. His third, if Rafe remembered correctly. The man was well on his way to becoming roaring *fou*—drunk as a wheelbarrow, as his English friends would say. Worse, given his current mood, Kieran would not be a cheerful drunk. And seeing as this evening was supposed to be a happy occasion . . .

"How goes the work with your patients?" Rafe asked Alex, attempting to change the subject.

"I have no complaints. Though I did make inquiries for ye, as ye asked."

"Inquiries?" Andrew asked.

"Aye." Rafe nodded. "For my mother."

"Ah."

No more needed to be said. The Brotherhood were well-aware of Rafe's difficult history with both his parents. Though Rafe wondered— would Kendall have forced him to go on the voyage if he understood the support Rafe would draw from his friends?

"How is your mother?" Andrew asked, voice quiet.

"The same."

"The draught I recommended didnae help?" Alex asked.

"Not significantly, I'm afraid tae say."

"A pity, as I had researched it thoroughly. There is so little written on the subject of chronic melancholy and even less that is practical."

"Aye. Though ye were correct—ceasing the repetitive bleeding has improved her color and physical energy."

Alex shrugged. "I have long thought that the black bile of melancholy cannae be balanced by bleeding the body."

"Aye. My mother is not quite as listless, at the very least. Visits from my sister, Kate, and her wee bairns help, as well."

Silence hung in the room for a moment. Rafe swallowed the rest of his whisky in a giant gulp, the liquor burning his throat.

His mother had not always suffered from such a depression of spirits. Though Kendall had forever been a menacing figure, the mother of Rafe's childhood had been a loving, doting presence. And as Rafe was the second son, not the heir, his father had more readily ignored him back then. Little had the man known how loved Rafe had been in his mother's gentle care.

"Come here, my wee love." His mother set aside her sewing and opened her arms to him. "Did ye have another nightmare?"

"Aye, Mamma." He scrambled onto her lap and snuggled into her arms, reveling in the warm familiarity of her. Mamma always smelled like Scotland, heather and pine and something else uniquely her.

"There, there, my wee boy," she murmured, rocking and stroking his hair. "I'll keep all the scary beasties away. Sleep now."

He rubbed his eyes and yawned. If Nanny found him out, he'd be in trouble. But he always slept better when Mamma snuggled him first.

Of course, all that had changed when Rafe was a teenager.

After years of believing herself past child-bearing years, his mother had fallen pregnant. Despite Kendall's caustic words and controlling behavior, Rafe's mother had been jubilant. She viewed the life growing within her as a glorious gift.

Unfortunately, the infant girl had only lived a week after birth.

Kendall had been unaffected. The baby was "merely a girl, after all, and hardly worth mentioning" as Rafe had overheard his sire say to the vicar.

But no words could capture his mother's desolation. Her distraught weeping still haunted Rafe's dreams on occasion. The baby's death had, understandably, sent the duchess into a deep depression of spirits. The Duchess of Kendall had always been prone to the occasional melancholic spell, but this one had simply never lifted.

Rafe would never know if it was the death of her baby or Kendall's endless cruelty that finally broke his mother's spirit. Likely both had played a part. Regardless, the cheery, loving mother of Rafe's childhood vanished overnight.

Though before Rafe's voyage, she had still participated in Society, making morning calls and accepting invitations. But the duchess had been markedly worse since his return from the South Pacific, Rafe's absence and Kendall's cruelty taking their toll.

Vividly, he saw his mother in his mind's eye, the scene ten days earlier as he left London for Scotland.

"I will return soon, Mother."

"Of course." She nearly whispered the words, her voice quiet in the hush.

She sat before a roaring fire, a shawl around her shoulders despite the summer heat beating on the window panes. She stared sightlessly into the flames, head slightly bowed. Even though she was well into her fiftieth year, his mother still retained a delicate beauty, a decidedly feminine version of his own face—dark eyes under a pile of dark hair only starting to gray at the temples. But her gaze was distressingly blank.

"Please keep hope," he begged her. "I will find a solution, something to ease your melancholy."

"Of course," she repeated in a monotone, eyes still fixed on the fire.

He waited another moment, but she said nothing more.

He kissed her cheek.
No response.
She did not turn her head to watch as he left the room.

The duchess would often go days without eating or speaking to anyone, staring listlessly into the fire or out the window. Worse, she would sometimes become agitated, muttering to herself and pacing her bedchamber over and over.

It was as if something had broken within her and, thus far, nothing had been able to mend it.

Rafe hated this feeling of helplessness, of being unable to relieve her suffering.

"On a positive note," Alex said, "my research efforts have not been entirely without benefit. A former university professor recommended I speak with Dr. John Ross. He is a practicing physician who specializes in disorders of melancholic madness."

Rafe's head snapped to attention. "That is good news."

"Aye. Dr. Ross himself is Scottish, actually, but he has lived and worked in London for several years. Apparently, the man prefers to focus on his patients and so doesnae take the time tae write letters for professional publications, which is why we hadnae heard of him until this point. But Ross supposedly has a wealth of practical knowledge. My professor felt if anyone could help your mother, it would be him."

Rafe nodded. "I'll write Dr. Ross immediately."

He silently prayed that this new doctor had some answers.

Something *had* to change.

Kendall was as brutish as ever, keeping Rafe on a short tether, using the duchess's health and the threat of a lunatic asylum as a bludgeon to guarantee Rafe's obedience.

Rafe acknowledged that he *could* leave. He could walk away and ignore his father, leave his mother to Kendall's cruelty.

But just the thought sent bile rising in his throat . . . the memory rose from two years earlier on his return from the South Pacific, of finding his mother chained to a bed in that asylum, lying in her own filth, gaze so empty and vacant—

No! Don't go there. Not tonight.

More than ever, Rafe understood that Kendall's threats were *not* idle words. The duke had committed his duchess to a lunatic asylum once in order to ensure Rafe's obedience. He would do it again unless Rafe remained at the man's beck and call.

However, Kendall was clever in his cruelty, tying Rafe with a silken cord. He allowed Rafe just enough freedom—to visit friends in Scotland, for example—that Rafe refrained from revolting in truth.

But after nearly three decades of bowing to his father's iron will, Rafe was so tired of swallowing his pride and doing *that* man's bidding. Just two weeks past, Rafe had been forced to evict a widow and her nine children, overseeing the duke's men as they carted the entire family to the work house. He *hated* this powerlessness, this endless game of having to choose which evil he would tolerate. Anger left a sour taste in his mouth and rage humming in his blood.

Worse, Hawthorn, Rafe's elder brother, had yet to produce an heir, and Kendall was growing impatient with Rafe's unwed state.

Unbidden, a pair of forest-green eyes flashed through his mind's eye. Even four years on, the pain of losing Lady Sophie had never really eased. The memory of her quirky mind and perceptive comments would not leave him be.

She was widowed, he had heard, over eight months ago. She would be through her mourning period by now. In his more delusional moments, he imagined defying his father and courting her again, assuming Lady Sophie didn't think him the worst sort of cad.

But Kendall had forced Rafe to the ends of the earth last time he attempted such a courtship. Rafe couldn't risk angering his father with his mother's health so precarious. He needed to find *something* somewhere that would ease her melancholy. If the duchess regained her health enough to be seen in Society happy and whole, Kendall would find it harder to commit her without sparking public outrage. It would, at the very least, perhaps give Rafe enough leverage to find a wife of his own choosing with only his father's lukewarm approval.

But in the meanwhile, Rafe seethed, simmering at the end of Kendall's binding chain.

"So what festivities do we have planned for the evening?" Ewan sat back, licking honey off his fingers. He nudged a chin toward Andrew, a grin on his face. "This bawbag is getting hisself married in the morning. Surely we have much merry tae make afore the night is over."

Trust Ewan to read the downhearted emotions in the room and attempt to change the topic.

Alex raised an eyebrow.

Kieran perked up, a cheeky light in his eyes.

Andrew, the groom-to-be, looked apprehensive, because he was a wise man and knew his friends well.

"If you're going tae give me a soot foot or some such, Jane asked that ye ensure I be presentable by tomorrow," Andrew cautioned, referring to the pre-wedding custom of rubbing soot over the groom for good luck.

Rafe chuckled, smacking his hands together. "We'll just have to be careful tae keep it off your face, then."

Nodding toward Alex, Rafe pulled Andrew out of his chair by one arm. Alex took the other.

"Come along, yer lofty lordship. There's a fair amount of fun yet tae be had tonight."

8

Sophie's family did nothing by halves, not even breakfast.

"Father, you must not permit Henry to give sausages to the dogs," her older sister, Mary, pleaded from down the table.

Mary's four-year-old son, Henry, stood beside his grandfather, holding a plump Cumberland sausage in his chubby fist, dangling it high above his head and teasing the Earl of Mainfeld's hunting dogs into a salivating frenzy. For their part, the dogs barked and whined but were too well trained to jump on the little boy and retrieve the treat.

Two footmen maneuvered around the dogs with practiced skill, pouring fresh coffee for Lady Mainfeld and replenishing the depleted sausage and bacon in the warming dishes on the nearby sideboard.

Lord Mainfeld presided over the head of the table as he always had, a benign smile firmly in place underneath his shock of salt-and-pepper hair.

"They both seem happy enough, Mary," he said, patting Henry's head. "Let it be. It's nothing worth hurt feelings."

Sophie bit back a sigh. The words summed up Lord Mainfeld's motto in life.

Let it be. It's nothing worth hurt feelings.

Whether it was hunting dogs and sausage or his wife's incessant indiscretions, Lord Mainfeld accepted it all with unflappable calm.

The dogs continued to whimper and whine, their wagging tails thumping against Sophie's chair. Little Henry giggled and turned in a circle.

"I don't understand why we must have the hunting dogs in the breakfast room at all." That was Sophie's youngest sister, Harriet, pretty as a jewel in a new blue frock with expensive Venetian lace.

Four years Sophie's junior, Harriet was in her third Season and in no hurry to find a husband. That was hardly surprising, given their parents' own unconventional marriage and Sophie's disastrous one. It was enough to render any sane person skittish.

In Sophie's case, Jack had revealed himself to be typical of gentlemen on the fringes of the *ton*. He had been chronically unfaithful and often gambled deep, racking up debts. Jack had broken her into pieces, one biting word, one thoughtless act at a time.

She had spent the months since his death fighting to reclaim her very soul, to recover the bits and bobs of herself from the wreckage Jack had left—

Sophie stopped right there. She would not allow her thoughts to spiral into bitterness and anger. Not today.

She slowed her breathing.

Jack was gone.

Remaining angry at him only hurt herself.

Do not give him any more of yourself.

Live your life free of him.

Or taking a page from her father's book—*Let it be.*

Sophie straightened her spine and took a bite of her own eggs.

"Nonsense, Harriet." Lady Mainfeld was saying. "You know your father prefers to keep his hunting dogs in the house, not the mews."

"Yes, but why not leave them in the country—"

"Bah! Don't be ridiculous, Harriet!" That was Sophie's eldest brother, Thomas, Lord Richan. Like Jane, he was blond and blue-eyed and strongly resembled Lord Mainfeld. One of the *Filius veras*. "Town would be dreadful dull without the dogs about."

Thomas emphasized his point by offering the nearest hound a sliver of his own sausage, thereby stealing the dogs' attention from little Henry.

"Hear, hear," Robert agreed, snapping the paper he was reading. Robert was dark of feature, a *Filius falsus*, but he and Thomas were thick as thieves, always dragging each other into one scrape or another. They were focused on the dogs at the moment. However, give it five minutes, and they would be discussing a horse race, or the planned hunting trip west next week, or who would win this year's cricket match between Harrow and Eton.

Her family, in a word, was sporting mad.

Case in point: "Are we off to Tattersall's this morning, my boys?" Lord Mainfeld asked his sons. "I want your opinion on a bay hunter I have been admiring."

The men debated the matter back and forth, ignoring the dogs and their clamoring as only practiced gentlemen could.

Mary, Harriet, and Lady Mainfeld reverted to minutely dissecting the gentlemen's behavior at a ball the previous evening. Though Sophie's mourning for Jack had officially ended two month's past, she had yet to resume attending balls, thank goodness.

"Did you see Mr. Watson dancing with Lady Lilith?" Harriet mused. "She flirted most shamelessly. I wonder if she intends to finally marry again?"

"Lady Lilith has not ceased flirting in the five years since her husband's death," their mother replied. "With her, I cannot imagine that flirting alone indicates an intention to marry. The lady is quite immune to any reproach over her scandalous behavior."

Mary and Harriet nodded, neither of them seeming to note the hypocrisy of their mother's words.

Sophie found herself observing the scene, once again invisible. Sometimes she wondered if she *literally* was invisible to her family—unseen, unnoticed.

Unwanted.

She had thought that marriage—that having a person, *her* person—would alleviate those old feelings of invisibility. But, if anything, marriage to Jack had made everything worse—

It was one thing to be invisible to strangers or family members with whom one had little in common.

It was something else entirely to be invisible to one's own husband.

Sophie had married Jack, thinking to avoid the wiles of a rake, assuming that he was not one of them.

How wrong she had been.

There had been plenty of skeletons in Jack's closet. They had simply taken longer than his courtship of her to reach London . . . reports of gambling debts, tales of seducing officer's wives, stories of raucous drinking—

She placed a mental hand on that train of thought.

Enough.

Let it be.

Act. Do not wait to be acted upon.

Swallowing, Sophie calmed her breathing, pressing a palm to her sternum.

She turned her head to find little Henry stock still, watching her, his eyes too big in his face.

Oh.

At least someone noticed, she supposed. But like her, poor Henry was alone in a room of people who appeared heedless of his existence.

No one should ever feel unloved or unwanted.

Sophie smiled and beckoned him forward, shooing away the dogs. She lifted him onto her lap, snuggling him close and pressing a kiss to his forehead.

Henry, of course, did not want kisses and instead reached for her watch, dangling from its chatelaine. Sophie handed it to him. The watch and chatelaine were a favorite possession, given to her by Lady Mainfeld. The chatelaine featured a series of painted glass beads showing the eruption of Mt. Vesuvius in 1779. Her mother had purchased it as a memento while in Naples just after the eruption.

Henry passed over the exploding volcano in favor of examining the watch mechanism, listening as Sophie quietly demonstrated how it functioned, opening the back case to carefully show him the gears ticking away inside.

"... Lord Rafe was there, as usual." Harriet's words snapped Sophie to attention. "But I did not see him flirting with Lady Lilith."

Sophie stilled, her heart thumping as it always did when Lord Rafe's name was mentioned.

Stupid, useless organ.

But the thought did not stop her from leaning sideways to better hear her mother and sisters.

"Lord Rafe has shown more restraint this past year, I think," Mary said.

"Do you believe he is finally considering marrying, once and for all?" Harriet asked.

"Perhaps," Lady Mainfeld replied. "He is of an age, and his elder brother has yet to sire an heir."

"But who would be perfect enough for the son of the Duke of Kendall?" Harriet rolled her eyes.

"A *second* son," Mary clarified.

"Lord Rafe will surely marry a Diamond of the First Water. Kendall will tolerate nothing less," their mother replied, tone acerbic.

Something aching and hard lodged in Sophie's throat.

Occasionally, she would take out the memory of that night, turn it over in her hand like a souvenir, brush off the dust, and marvel at her naivety. How being with Lord Rafe had felt like a homecoming, but he was, in fact, so very transitory.

Heavens but she was the veriest fool.

Yes, on an autumn evening four years ago (four years!), Lord Rafe had danced attendance on her for two hours (two hours!), behaving in every way like a smitten swain before sweeping her underneath a staircase for an epically-searing kiss. And then he had left London the next morning and set sail for the opposite corner of the globe, leaving Sophie to deal with the wreckage of his behavior.

The London gossips had been ruthless. *Lady Sophronia Sorrow openly accepted Lord Rafe Gilbert's attentions! Lord Mainfeld's daughter is being courted by Kendall's son?! How shocking!* His abrupt abandonment had only added fuel to the fire.

Some said Lord Rafe's actions were simply the typical behavior of a rake; Sophie should have known better. Others said it was Kendall's doing . . . ordering his son to humiliate one of Mainfeld's daughters.

No one put forth the idea that Lord Rafe had actually been sincere, smitten with Sophie for herself.

That was your own delusional fantasy.

Regardless of Lord Rafe's reasons, Sophie had experienced whispered glances and cutting remarks in the aftermath of his departure.

Throughout it all, Jack had been loyal, staying by her side. Unlike Lord Rafe, Jack had appeared to want her. He had been constant in his affections during their courtship—he told her he loved her, he promised to worship her. And so, thinking him a *Virum nobilis*—a noble gentleman utterly unlike Lord Rafe's *Rakus lasciviosus* ways—she had agreed to marry him a mere week after Lord Rafe had left London.

Hah! How wrong she had been.

A fortnight into their marriage, Sophie learned another brutal truth—neither professions of love nor marriage vows were to be trusted.

"—all I am asking is that you do not brazenly flirt with other women—"

"You are my wife," Jack hurled back at her. *"Am I married to those other women?"*

"Of course not." She nearly sighed. How could she help Jack understand? *"When I was studying my barn cats, the* primus *led with gentle—"*

"Enough of your damn barn cats! I'm sick to death of your bluestocking ways." Jack glared at her, his handsome face twisting in anger. *"A good wife would concern herself more with her husband's needs than prattling on about farmyard animals—"*

Sophie sucked in a steadying breath, allowing the memory to wash over her and then forcing it out.

Ironically, in the end, her scholarly pursuits were the only piece of herself she managed to cling to throughout her marriage. She could lose herself in Linnean research and forget, at least for a while, that her marriage was an utter sham.

And it *had* been a sham. Jack's attentive behavior during their courtship had simply been a ruse. He had only wanted her for her dowry and her family's connections. He had a taste for fine living and gambling debts nipping at his heels, debts Lord Mainfeld had settled at their marriage.

And once Jack had secured her as his wife—once she was utterly bound to him and unable to free herself short of death—his true colors came through. After those first months, he had declined to share their marital bed, preferring to slake his lusts elsewhere.

To be fair, Jack was never physically cruel to her. He professed to love her, but his actions and words were often cutting. If that was considered love in a marriage, then Sophie wanted no part of it.

Jack's death had been such a *relief.* Relief that she no longer had to endure his presence, his biting words . . . that her life was her own again.

But Sophie found that she was not the trusting, naive creature she had been before her marriage. Jack had broken her soul, one small bit at a time, until she scarcely recognized herself. Ironically, it took his death for her to fully realize how battered and broken she truly was.

In the months after his death, she spent hours staring out the window, unequal to the task of eating or being in the company of others. If she did leave her room, it was to wander the countryside like some ghostly wraith. But eventually, she had sorted through her chaotic emotions and began the process of repairing her fractured heart. She had moved on from the pain of Jack's behavior. She had stemmed the tide of caustic thoughts.

And she had arrived at some important truths:

Yes, she was odd and would likely never quite fit in.

Yes, her mind thought differently than others did.

Jack's low opinion of her personality defects said more about *him* as a person than herself.

And yet . . . a part of her still mourned that she had never truly been wanted. What was it an older matron had once said?

Men need to be needed, but women want to be wanted.

Sophie had long pondered the wisdom in those words.

Jack had *needed* Sophie to need him. Life had flowed more smoothly when Jack felt her dependence on him, when she had appeared helpless and feeble-witted—a featherbrained woman of the *ton*.

But Sophie struggled to be needy enough; it was not her way, after all. Lord Mainfeld had raised her like his boys, to be strong and forthright. She simply could not mold herself into the form that Jack needed. And so every angry argument, every debt notice, every dalliance he hid eventually reduced her spirit to splintered shards.

And as for Sophie herself . . .

In her more honest moments, she still dreamed of finding a true husband, a man whom she loved and who loved her in return.

In short, Sophie wanted to be wanted.

Not just wanted as a dowry or a housekeeper or a mirror to parrot back what others (*i.e.* Jack) wished to hear.

No . . . Sophie longed to be wanted for herself, for her quirky comments and scientific observations. Wanted *for* her unique oddities, rather than in spite of them.

But she was clear-headed enough to recognize the bare truth—Lady Sophronia Fulstate had never been wanted.

She was the child of her mother's illicit affair with an unknown man. Yes, Lord Mainfeld—bless him—had taken her on, but he hadn't *wanted* her. Neither of her parents had rejoiced at her birth. She was an unfortunate side effect that had to be borne.

Lord Rafe had only wanted her as a momentary distraction. Jack, for her dowry.

Yet, the scientist in her was not ready to give up. Not yet.

To her, it seemed the problem lay with her understanding of men. Given the muddle of her parentage, such confusion was to be expected, she supposed. Her problematic relationships with men likely started with her murky origins.

So Sophie needed to go back to the beginning, as it were, and rebuild them anew. She wished to uncover the identity of her true father, the man who had sired her.

She knew from her biological studies that offspring shared

characteristics with both their parents. She clearly was not Lord Mainfeld's natural daughter. *That* had been decided long ago. Two fair-haired people did not have dark-haired offspring.

Nothing of Sophie resembled Lord Mainfeld. Physical differences aside, her father was a canon boom of a man, given to hearty laughter, bracing slaps on the back, and loud hunting stories. He was far too easy-going and good-natured, brushing off his wife's infidelities with shocking ease.

As for Lady Mainfeld, Sophie resembled her enough to not doubt that the lady was indeed her mother—the shape of Sophie's eyes, the similarity of height and body structure all testified of her maternal inheritance.

But beyond that, Sophie and her mother had little in common.

Based on this, Sophie assumed she had to bear a strong resemblance to her natural father. Her dark hair and green eyes, not to mention her studious bent, had to come from somewhere outside her mother.

And if she could find her true father, uncover all the original pieces of herself, perhaps she could mend her shattered heart in truth and begin anew to find love—

The door cracked open, and the family butler entered, the morning's correspondence piled high on a silver platter. Lord Mainfeld plucked a few letters from the salver and then waved the rest on to be given to Lady Mainfeld directly. The post was quickly sorted, three letters ending up beside Sophie's plate.

Only one caused her heart to thump.

It was addressed in her Aunt Margaret's swooping hand.

At last!

Henry scampered from her lap, and Sophie took the opportunity to open her letter, scanning the lines. Aunt Margaret was a verbose writer, but the gist jumped out.

Sophie pressed a shaking hand against her chest as she read . . . which meant it took her too long to notice how quiet the room had become.

"I say, poppet, are you quite all right?" Lord Mainfeld asked.

She raised her head and met her father's concerned gaze.

"It's all good news, I hope?" Her father motioned toward her letter.

"Yes, Father." She managed a small smile while tucking Aunt Margaret's letter with the others beside her plate. "Just more of Aunt Margaret's antics."

"Ah." Her father chuckled knowingly. Aunt Margaret, Lady Mainfeld's older sister, was a bit of an eccentric.

"If you will excuse me, Father." Sophie smiled wider and rose to give Lord Mainfeld a dutiful kiss on the cheek before exiting the room for the privacy of her bed chamber.

Aunt Margaret's letter burned in her hand the entire way.

Sophie had tried for years to gently pry information about her natural father from her mother. She simply wished to know the man's identity.

But Lady Mainfeld became agitated and angry whenever Sophie brought it up, occasionally devolving into one of her panicked fits. The last time Sophie had mentioned her natural father, her mother had experienced a severe attack—chest heaving, breaths panicked, hands shaking—and had taken to her room for a solid day.

Sophie refused to ask her again.

Obviously, Sophie couldn't ask Lord Mainfeld to disclose the identity of her natural father, assuming he knew. Even her father's good nature would balk at that. The London gossip mill had proved unhelpful.

And so Sophie had finally stooped to brazenly asking her Aunt Margaret.

She unfolded the letter again upon reaching her bedroom.

Her aunt's words were not a definitive answer, but the letter offered hope:

> *Unfortunately, child, I do not know the identity of your natural father. Your mother has been astonishingly mum on that score. However, I can tell you what I do know. Your mother fell pregnant with you while taking the waters in Bath for a nervous ailment. She remained in Bath for the duration of her confinement. She once let slip that your natural father was present for your birth. That is all I know.*
>
> *I must say, given your mother's almost vehement reluctance to disclose your natural father's identity, it might be wise to let sleeping dogs lie, dear child. Sometimes, it is better to not know the truth.*

Sophie heaved a breath, swallowing.

How could knowing be worse than *not* knowing? Her mind conjured up too many possibilities.

Perhaps her father was a footman or groom? Was his lowly birth the reason her mother kept silent?

Or was her father a man of some importance in the government? The type of gentleman who could not weather such a scandal and might seek retribution?

Or was her father a criminal element? The silver-tongued leader of a band of thieves who would harm anyone who disclosed his identity?

It all sounded unnecessarily melodramatic.

Sophie did not care about her father's social status. If he was someone who clearly did not wish to know her, she would not confront him.

The hunt for her father, in the end, was a living metaphor of the search for herself. That in finding him, Sophie would start anew—rebuilding her soul from the beginning into the woman she longed to be.

She could not lay claim to a great many personal characteristics.

But *tenacity* was one of them.

She *would* discover the man's identity.

And then, once she knew, she would finish putting herself back together, piece-by-piece.

9

Rafe received a letter of his own three days after he arrived back in London.

> *I know what you did aboard* The Minerva *that night. Do not suppose that your crimes will go unpunished. You will end your days dangling from a hangman's noose.*

The words scattered his thoughts, setting his heart to pounding. A dreadful sinking sensation settled in his stomach.

His mind stuttered, trying to bring the implications of the letter into focus. Arriving so soon after the notice in *The Advertiser*, the letter felt ominous.

Who had sent this?

That awful day in the South Pacific rose in his mind.

Cuthie drew a gleaming blade from a sheath at his waist, eyes studying Rafe closely. The knife glinted in the tropical sunlight.

"How many cuts will it take before you yield?" Cuthie smiled maniacally. "Shall we see?"

Rafe struggled against the arms that held him. Sailors cackled and called encouragement to Cuthie, some rattling the rigging overhead.

"I don't think that face of yours will be quite so pretty when I'm done."

The knife slashed—

Rafe shook off the memory, resisting the urge to rub the scar on his cheek. He had escaped with only minor injuries in the end. Cuthie had been a disgrace of a human being, a man cut out of the same cloth as Kendall. Thankfully, three and a half years had lessened the horrors of what had occurred in the New Hebrides.

He turned the note over, looking for a signature, but nothing more was forthcoming. Only a partial postal stamp—Leith, perhaps?—and nothing more.

Had someone survived the wreck of *The Minerva* after all? The letter certainly wished him to think so.

Or was this simply a case of someone attempting a lucky guess? And, more importantly, *why?*

The letter contained no demand for money. Was this simply the opening salvo, and blackmail demands would follow? And if not, then what did the mysterious sender hope to accomplish? Send him running from London, hiding in fear?

And if the sender was not actually involved with the events aboard *The Minerva*, then who might he be?

Rafe rolled his shoulders, his mind cataloging all the men in London who might have issue with his existence.

Blast. It was a long list.

He received angry notes from slighted husbands and would-be paramours from time to time. But they were always signed and usually more along the lines of "apologize or name your second" rather than directly bloodthirsty. As he abhorred duels, Rafe excelled at giving heartfelt apologies.

He closed his eyes, muttering curses under his breath.

RAFE WAS STILL pondering the note hours later as he sat across from his mother in the front drawing room of Gilbert House in Mayfair.

His mother shifted in her seat, eyes staring into the fire before lifting them to meet his gaze.

The duchess had been more animated earlier in the day. Rafe's sister, Kate, and her two children had come for a morning visit. His mother had sat on the floor bouncing the baby in her arms while talking and playing with three-year-old George. The duchess had seemed nearly normal, open and fully present. She had chatted amiably with Kate about the latest fashions and even hinted that she might take a walk with George later on. Being around her daughter and grandchildren always lifted his mother's spirits.

"Did wee George show you his new tin soldiers?" Rafe asked.

"Aye, he did. Lovely wee thing." A rare smile touched her lips, her elegant Scottish accent sliding through her words. "Sometimes I feel I can breathe only when Kate and her children come to visit."

For the hundredth time, Rafe wondered how much of his mother's melancholy was static and unchanging, and how much was the result of her current situation. Her melancholy may have begun with the loss of her infant, but it was certainly perpetuated by his father's vicious behavior. Such a marriage would be hell for any woman.

As if to emphasize Rafe's mental point, the Duke of Kendall's voice sounded in the entrance hall, calling to the butler. His mother recoiled, her smile instantly fading and face turning pale, eyes going blank as she returned to studying the fire. Her flinch caused something hot to seethe in Rafe's chest. What had Kendall done to elicit such a reaction?

Damn his father.

The man had them all bound in chains of some sort or another.

Kendall had manacled Rafe to his iron will, the duke's threat always the same—*Behave or your mother will be consigned to a lunatic asylum.*

And Rafe complied.

Because she was his mother, and he loved her.

Because he remembered the light-filled lady she had once been.

Because he could not purchase his freedom at the price of her imprisonment and torture—

Rafe took in a long, steady breath, jaw clenched.

Hate seemed too tame a word for the fury that roiled in his chest every time he thought of his father.

Loathe. Detest. Despise. Abhor.

Synonyms were not much better.

Perhaps if taken as a whole, then?

More than anything, Rafe wished to see his mother freed from the Duke of Kendall's grasp.

But under British law, his mother had ceased to be her own person when she married his father. Kendall for all practical purposes, *owned* his wife, just as if she were a horse or any other chattel.

Rafe was grateful there were at least *some* laws to protect a woman from the extremes of physical harm. A husband could only beat his wife with a switch no thicker than his thumb, for example. But that was pathetic comfort to most women. There were hundreds of ways to do harm that left few marks on the body, as Kendall well knew.

And there was little Rafe could do to free his mother.

Divorce was impossibly difficult—it literally would require a new law to be written and ratified by his father's friends in Lords—and his father would never sanction a legal separation.

Though in the past Rafe had considered escaping with the duchess to another country, that was no longer possible. The duchess loved Kate and her grandchildren too much. The only time Rafe had suggested leaving, his mother had gone into hysterics. Such an action would be no less cruel than confining her to a lunatic asylum.

Only his father's death would free his mother permanently.

But if the duchess could emerge from her melancholy—be seen laughing and going about London—Kendall would lose his justification for locking her away. Rafe could then muster friends and public opinion to aid his cause. And past experience had proven that Kendall did care about his public image.

But as the duchess's health continued poorly . . .

There *had* to be better treatments out there. Rafe had sent two letters now to Dr. Ross, the man Alex had recommended, but he had yet to receive a reply. He planned to call upon the man tomorrow. His mother needed assistance, and Rafe would do whatever he could to see that she received it, despite his father's intransigence.

As if reading his thoughts, the door snicked open, and Kendall himself walked in.

As wealthy men tended to do, the duke had aged gracefully. His silver hair and broad shoulders merely added to his aura of power. But it was the icy steel of his pale eyes that had Rafe rising to his feet.

His mother shrank in her chair.

Kendall's gaze flitted over her, much as one might dismiss an annoying gnat, before returning to Rafe.

"A word, boy," was all he said before turning around, confident that Rafe would follow.

Rafe watched his father's retreating back, briefly wondering if sinking a knife into it would be as satisfying as he imagined.

He rather thought it would.

Sometimes he feared for his very soul.

He turned back to find his mother watching him. Did she know? Did she understand that he sacrificed his freedom to protect her?

He hoped not.

Such knowledge would only add to the burden of her melancholy.

Rafe shot his mother a too-bright smile—hoping it came off as comforting and not maniacal—before pecking her cheek and following his sire from the room and into the duke's private study.

"I trust all went well with your visit in Edinburgh?" His father sorted through correspondence on his desk, not even bothering to look at Rafe.

"Yes, Sir. Your steward there has the situation well in hand," Rafe replied, referring to a problem on one of his father's estates.

His father clearly hadn't seen the notice in the *Edinburgh Advertiser*, thank goodness. Rafe did not bring it up. The Duke of Kendall knew the barest outline of what had transpired in the South Pacific. Rafe intended to keep things that way.

His father nodded before finally lifting his head. "I have spoken with Lord Sykes about his eldest daughter."

A chill raced along Rafe's spine, that same anger rising in his throat.

He choked it back, clasping his hands together tightly behind his back to stop himself from doing something . . . unwise. Like wrapping his fingers around his father's neck and choking him lifeless.

Sometimes, the sheer depth of Rafe's rage terrified him. It felt boundless, a bottomless, black pool, churning and roiling.

Outwardly, however, years of practice allowed him to keep his expression benign.

Rafe knew exactly where this conversation was headed. He and his father had been on a collision course over Rafe's marriage—or lack thereof—for several years. Thus far, he had managed to dodge his father's attempts at matchmaking, but that could not go on indefinitely.

Kendall continued, sitting back in his chair, steepling his fingers. "Miss Sykes is an excellent choice for a bride. Impeccable pedigree. Pretty without being overly so. Polite, well-mannered, and biddable."

And also absolutely featherbrained and prone to giggling. But as her father was Henry Sykes, Lord Sykes, she did have a large dowry and excellent family connections, things Kendall valued above all else.

Regardless of the fury pulsing in his chest, Rafe knew he must tread carefully.

Keeping his tone bored, he began, "I appreciate the thought, Father, but I have not yet determined to marry—"

"Enough." Kendall rarely raised his voice. The quiet chill of his tone was sufficient. "I have been patient for too long over this matter, boy. You must marry. Your brother's wife has proven distressingly unable to produce an heir. The task has now fallen to you. You will not disappoint me in this. Your imbecilic Cousin Frank will never be allowed to hold the title of Kendall."

Rafe's older brother—Lord Hawthorn—was heir to the dukedom. But after nearly five years, his marriage had not been fruitful. Naturally, his father blamed Lady Hawthorn.

Rafe was of the opinion that if Hawthorn perhaps spent less time carousing in London and more time with his wife, he might yet produce the much-needed heir. But Rafe knew better than to voice that thought.

As for Cousin Frank, the heir after Hawthorn and Rafe . . . the man truly was a ninnyhammer. Frank would make a spectacularly-awful duke. Part of Rafe wished that Frank could inherit, just to watch his father's head explode from the horror of it.

But as satisfying as that would be, Rafe needed to focus all his mental strength on escaping his own matrimonial noose.

Rafe knew he must marry at some point, and he *did* believe that when paired with the right person, marriage could be a blissful, happy thing. Just remembering the look in Andrew's eyes as he wed his Jane the week previous was sufficient proof. He refused to allow the carnage of his parent's marriage to sour him on the institution entirely.

Unbidden, he thought of Lady Sophie's darling nose as she waxed on about her beloved barn cats, her opinions darting right and left, always keeping Rafe in suspense as to where she would land next.

She is a widow at the moment. Now might be your only chance.

He batted the thought back with a practiced mental swipe, dismissing the burn in his chest.

Lady Sophie was not for him. End of story.

Rafe lifted his chin. "Naturally, I share your concern, Father, but I cannot think a hasty marriage, particularly to someone I scarcely know—"

"I said *enough*, boy. I do not like having to repeat myself." The menace in his father's tone brooked no argument. "Lord Sykes will be hosting a house party the first week of November. We are, of course, invited to attend. You will make yourself amiable to Miss Sykes and begin an earnest courtship of her. I expect that you will request her hand in marriage before Christmas."

Rafe's stomach knotted. The first week of November? That was barely six weeks away. Though he had known his father would increase pressure on him to marry, Rafe had not anticipated Kendall commanding the bride and timeline.

Though knowing his sire's love of control, Rafe should have anticipated this.

Was there any way out of this mess? Fury and bile rose in his throat. He clenched his teeth, holding it back.

His father's gaze took in Rafe's reaction. The bastard missed nothing.

"The freedoms you enjoy come with a cost, boy," the man continued, voice silky. "Do not force me to be cruel. You know how I dislike cruelty, but you often leave me with no other choice."

Rafe swallowed back the angry words that bubbled in his throat. Someday, somehow . . . he would be free of this man.

"I am, as ever, deeply concerned for your mother's health," Kendall said.

And there it was. So predictable.

His father's endless threat.

He never referred to his duchess as 'my wife' or 'my duchess.'

No, she was only ever Rafe's mother, as if Kendall needed to ram that point down his son's throat.

"You know that your mother's health is my greatest worry. Why, just today, I fear Kate's visit overset her. My grandchildren can be loud and boisterous. Perhaps such visits should be curtailed?" Kendall spoke the words with measured calm, his eyes never leaving Rafe.

The man was a chillingly good liar.

"I was speaking with Dr. White again about her condition," the duke continued. "He is still of the firm opinion that his asylum is the best place for her."

No, Dr. White wished for the exorbitant fees his father would pay.

And Kendall knew that Rafe would see his mother in a lunatic asylum only over his own cold, dead body. Moreover, Rafe would bow and scrape to Kendall's whims to ensure Kate and her children were still welcome to visit the duchess.

"You will attend Lord Syke's house party. You will make yourself agreeable and do as I bid you." His father turned away, confident in Rafe's compliance.

In years past, Rafe had fought against his father's ironclad hold. But he had learned from sad experience that outright revolt only strengthened his father's grip.

In other words, thrashing against the knife that pinned him only hurt himself.

Subtle rebellion and the appearance of acquiescence were much more effective weapons.

And so Rafe bit back his angry words, swallowing the fury and hatred clogging his throat, and replied with practiced insouciance, "I shall think upon it, Father."

"See that you do, boy."

10

Sophie stared at the front stoop before her, the brass knocker gleaming in the afternoon sun.

Out of habit, she glanced at the address in her hand, but the plaque beside the door clearly confirmed her location in scrolling letters:

Dr. John Ross, Esquire
Dr. Stuart Hartley, Esquire

Swallowing, she squared her shoulders, lifted her pelisse and skirts with a gloved hand, and climbed the three stairs to the row house door.

Aunt Margaret's tantalizing hint—*your natural father was present for your birth*—had led Sophie on a bit of a hunt that landed her here. Questioning the older members of the household staff had yielded nothing. The few who were with her mother in Bath did not recall the presence of an outside gentleman. Or, perhaps, were fearful of reprisals if they disclosed what they did know.

An elderly groom *did* remember fetching Dr. John Ross to attend her mother the night Sophie was born. If her natural father had been in the next room at the time, waiting for news of her birth, Dr. Ross certainly would have seen the man. More to the point, Dr. Ross would be unlikely to have any lingering loyalty to her mother and would think nothing of disclosing what he remembered, if anything.

Sophie knew it was a slim clue—relying on a man's memory of a night over twenty-six years past—but it was the only thing she had to go on.

She *would* track down the man who had sired her. She *would* understand her own biological history and begin anew to reconstruct herself.

Tucking the address back into her reticule, Sophie rapped the knocker, the sound echoing down the hallway beyond the door.

She waited, mouth dry, hands clenched around her reticule.

Coach wheels crunched along the road, drivers calling greetings to one another, horse hooves clopping.

If the doctor remembered . . . she could be only moments away from learning the identity of her *Pater veras*. If her natural father resided in London, perhaps she could even finagle a way to meet him, unofficially of course.

And if she did meet him . . . would the man be like her? Would she feel a sense of kinship?

Now if Dr. Ross would only answer his door.

She rapped again.

A carriage rattled to a stop behind her. Sophie turned around just in time to see a tall, broad figure step out of a hackney coach. The brim of his hat hid his face as he turned to hand coins up to the driver.

Was this Dr. Ross then?

If so, he was younger and decidedly more dashing than she would have supposed. His greatcoat fell in elegant folds to his gleaming Hessian boots.

The man turned around, locked eyes with her, and froze.

All functional thoughts fled Sophie's head.

Oh.

The gentleman was decidedly *not* Dr. Ross.

Instead, Lord Rafe Gilbert's astonished expression greeted her.

Her heart lurched to attention, blood galloping in her veins.

Of all the gentlemen in London—!

Sophie tightened the grip on her reticule, knuckles surely white within her kid gloves.

At least she had the satisfaction of watching Lord Rafe attempt to control his own surprise.

His head reared back and his nostrils flared, eyes wide.

A small fraught silence ensued. As if he, too, were struggling to realign himself. As if seeing her was just as momentous for him as for herself.

And then, gravity reasserted itself, and Sophie remembered that this was Lord Rafe's area of specialty—making a woman feel as if she were treasured and important one day, and then utterly forgotten the next.

Lord Rafe regained his equilibrium as well. A small smile tugged at his lips, dimples popping, as he tipped his hat in her direction.

She, absurdly, dipped a small curtsy, as if they were in a ballroom and not a dusty London side-street.

Really? After so many years? After everything that had transpired during their last encounter and its aftermath?

This was what she did? *Curtsied?!*

Sophie wanted to hate him for the chain of events his thoughtless actions had caused. She truly did.

But . . . perhaps her heart was too battered for hate, the pieces still too scattered. Because standing here, facing him . . .

. . . she only felt a great welling of anger-tinged hurt.

Anger over Lord Rafe's push-and-pull all those years ago, flirting and kissing her behind a curtain one night, and then abandoning her the following day, leaving the London gossips in a feeding frenzy.

Hurt because for a few blissful hours, she had dreamed of something different, of a life where she was valued and *wanted*.

Worse, it appeared her physical reaction to Lord Rafe had not changed. Her blood leaped and galloped in her veins, her palms perspired, and her tongue stuck to the roof of her mouth. How could the man's mere presence elevate the surrounding ambient temperature by at least ten degrees?

She found the entire experience incredibly annoying.

Though Sophie's naive, younger self had attributed her involuntary reaction to the mystique of the *Rakus* genus, she now recognized it for what it was—

Basic human attraction.

In other words, Lady Sophronia Fulstate found she had one thing in common with at least half the female population of London—

Her treacherous body fancied Lord Rafe Gilbert.

The *thinking* part of her found the entire situation nauseatingly ridiculous.

Once a rake, always a rake, after all.

Her involuntary physical attraction to Lord Rafe left her wanting to scream.

It was just—

He was so—

Ugh!!

Did the man *have* to be so very . . . *virile?* The very definition of a *primus?*

And *why* must she, like many females of a species, be attracted to flagrant displays of masculinity?

Why, body? WHY?!

So even though she bitterly ordered her traitorous eyes to *lookaway-thisinstant!*, they refused to listen, and instead, eagerly drank in the sight of him.

The passing years had been excessively kind—more's the pity— adding bulk to his broad shoulders and filling in the hollows of his cheeks. A white scar now traced his face, stretching from his right temple to the top of his cheekbone. How had that happened? Regardless, the scar did nothing to mar his overall dashing appearance. It was less a blemish and more an exclamation mark, as if to say, *Attention, ladies! This man is irresistible!*

If Lord Rafe suspected the direction of her thoughts—staring dumbfounded at him as she was—he said nothing.

Instead, she watched him glance down at a piece of paper he held in his hand and then look right and left, before settling his eyes on the plaque beside the door. She followed his gaze.

Was he here to visit the good doctor, too?

He did another visual sweep of the street.

Trying to ascertain if there were other members of the *ton* about, was he? She could see the gears in his head practically calculating his odds of being able to speak with her unnoticed.

Heaven forfend he be seen associating with her!

She mentally rolled her eyes.

Clearing his throat, Lord Rafe took to the stairs and lifted his head.

Their eyes met once more.

Another tense silence ensued.

He had recognized her. She had recognized him. She had already curtsied, for goodness' sake. Courtesy demanded he greet her first.

The Sophie of four years ago would have waited patiently for him to greet her, and then if he did not, she would have swallowed her devastation.

The Sophie of now was not interested in waiting for his begrudging notice.

She shifted her feet, intent on pivoting away.

Unfortunately, he chose that moment to smile, those devastating dimples popping again and effectively pinning her in place.

Gracious heavens. His dimples still had the ability to send her heart lurching into her throat. She quite detested them.

She would *not* be a slave to the pull of his demon dimples. Her will was stronger than mere biology.

"We always meet in the most unconventional ways, Lady Sophie." His rich voice wrapped around her.

Ah. So she was to have charming Lord Rafe today. The Lord Rafe who chatted amiably and made her . . . *feel* things.

But she was no longer that naive girl who had pined for him, who had built fairy castles out of the crumbs of attention he flicked her way.

Marriage to Captain Jack Fulstate had cured her of romantic notions, even if she were still helpless to stem her body's instinctual reactions.

She smiled stiffly in return. "Yes, my lord—"

Her words were abruptly silenced by the door opening behind her.

Sophie turned to find a maid boldly surveying them. "How may I help you?"

Lord Rafe shot Sophie an apologetic look.

"I wish to speak with the good doctor, if he is in," Rafe said, climbing the final stair to stand beside Sophie.

Sophie said nothing, as she wished to see Dr. Ross, as well.

"O'course. Please come in." The maid motioned them inside.

Lord Rafe stood aside, allowing Sophie to pass into the small entrance hall. The smell of herbs and vinegar greeted her senses. The maid directed them into a tidy parlor to the left of the door. A small fire burned in the grate, and a bench and several chairs dotted the edges of the room.

Again, Lord Rafe stood politely back, waiting for Sophie to enter first. Her skirts brushed his great coat as she passed, sending a waft of sandalwood to her nose.

Naturally, the man still smelled divine. Blast him.

The maid spoke behind them. "You and your lady can have a seat while I inform the doctor you're here."

That caused Sophie to whirl around.

"Oh no, you misunderstand. I am not with this gentleman." She motioned toward Lord Rafe. "We merely happened to arrive at the same time. I have come to see the doctor on another matter."

The maid raised both eyebrows, her expression clearly stating this wasn't the first time she had heard such a claim from prospective clients.

"We're souls of discretion here, we are. You needn't fear that the doctor or any of his staff will gossip about you."

The maid left the room before Sophie could stammer out a reply.

She turned to face Lord Rafe, horrified to find reflexive words of apology on her lips.

Heavens, what did she have to apologize for?! She had arrived first. The situation was hardly of her own creation.

She pinched her mouth shut.

He shot her a brief smile and turned, removing his top hat and brushing a hand around its brim. He stood for a moment, gazing out the front window, rimmed in light. His caped greatcoat fell in elegant folds; his polished Hessian boots reflected the room in elongated shapes. She caught a glimpse of a silver-embroidered violet waistcoat under a more sedate dark-gray tailcoat. Lord Rafe had always had an unerring fashion sense.

How could anyone assume that Sophie and Lord Rafe were a couple of any sort? Lord Rafe was a glittering aristocrat from the highest echelons of society. Sophie belonged to the same set, she supposed, but she was not so much glittery as faintly burnished.

Lord Rafe wore his status with flair and verve, whereas she wore hers with last-year's bonnet fashions and eccentric conversation.

In short, they were not quite a matched set.

And yet . . . a hesitance lingered in the stillness of his shoulders. As if he, too, struggled to calibrate to her presence.

Finally, Lord Rafe turned back to her.

"I trust you are well, Lady Sophronia?" he asked, an intense earnestness on his face.

His eyes sought hers, open and questioning, as if he genuinely cared about her answer.

She refused to allow her stupid heart to dance and pitter-patter in her chest. This man *specialized* in making women feel noticed and important. She sternly pushed back the memory of what it had felt like to be held in his arms, the consuming wonder of that kiss—

Do you hear that, Heart? You are forbidden *to like the inconstant rake. Forbidden!*

She steeled her spine and kept her tone frosty. "Yes, my lord, quite well, thank you." She paused and then forced herself to be polite, "And yourself?"

"Quite well."

Silence hung. The brief banalities having exhausted the reservoir of her conversation with this man.

Unbidden, her eyes drifted to that scar on his face. What *had* happened to him? Was the scar a memento from some angry lover? Or a duel with a ruling sultan during his travels abroad?

Or perhaps the result of a poetry accident, slashed by his own quill in a fit of artistic distress?

Heavens, but her thoughts were maudlin today.

Why was that? Why was her entire body—heart, lungs, and mind—fixated on Lord Rafe, vividly remembering their time together? Her scientific brain analyzed the puzzle.

With Jack, she had forgotten her affection for him well before his death. Her mind remembered caring for him once, but the actual feeling was long gone, burned to ash in the flame of his betrayal and indifference.

So why, then, did her heart ache and her lungs constrict when in Lord Rafe's presence? Why did her body instantly remember his kiss—the press of his much-larger body, the hunger in his lips—as if it had happened last week and not four years past?

Why did Jack fade and disappear? And yet, Lord Rafe burned brighter?

The door creaked open, startling her.

A middle-aged man entered.

"I am Doctor Hartley," he said, extending a hand to Lord Rafe before shooting Sophie a smile. "How may I assist you and your lady today?"

Oh, dear.

"We are not here together," Sophie corrected him. "We simply arrived at the same time."

The doctor blinked.

"Of course," he said, though his tone, like that of his maid, implied he thought her a liar.

Ugh.

Worse, Lord Rafe did not correct the man, but instead jumped right in to his own affairs.

"I thank you for your time, Doctor Hartley," he said, "but I wished to speak with Doctor Ross about a personal matter. Is he available?"

"Doctor Ross is not here." The man shifted on his feet. "But I am sure I could be of assistance—"

"No, it must be Doctor Ross, I am afraid," Lord Rafe insisted.

As that was Sophie's aim as well, she nodded in agreement.

Dr. Hartley grimaced. "Doctor Ross is no longer with us."

Lord Rafe frowned. "Pardon?"

"He has retired from practicing medicine." The doctor waved a hand toward the entry hall. "I know his name still resides on the plaque out front, but Dr. Ross hasn't practiced here for over three years."

"Three years?!"

"Yes." Dr. Hartley at least had the decency to look ashamed. "I haven't had a new plaque created, as of yet."

Sophie's heart sank. Was this yet another dead end?

"Are you quite confident there is nothing I can do to help you?" the doctor continued.

"I am unsure," Lord Rafe replied, a frown on his brow.

For her part, Sophie shook her head. "My question was rather specific for Dr. Ross himself. Do you happen to know where I might find him?"

Dr. Hartley looked between herself and Lord Rafe.

The man shrugged. "I would suppose Dr. Ross to be at his home in Edinburgh."

11

Ten minutes later, Rafe stood outside Dr. Hartley's surgery, hat in hand.

Lady Sophie had left after Rafe requested a word in private with Dr. Hartley. But a brief discussion had ascertained that the man did not share Dr. Ross's knowledge of melancholy and its treatment.

Dr. Ross was still Rafe's best hope of helping his mother overcome her depression of spirits. Given the deadline looming over Rafe's head—Lord Syke's house party next month and Rafe's imminent betrothal thereafter—that help could not come soon enough.

He would need to travel to Scotland and speak with Ross directly. His previous letters had proved fruitless, so writing again seemed a waste. Time was of the essence. Fortunately, Dr. Hartley had been able to provide Dr. Ross' direction in Edinburgh.

Rafe clenched his jaw. He had *literally* just come from Scotland. To think, he had been so close to Dr. Ross.

But, upon reflection, returning to Edinburgh might be best. The threatening letter he had received the previous day weighed on him.

Do not suppose that your crimes will go unpunished.

Further study had convinced him that it was indeed postmarked from Leith, just outside Edinburgh. Someone in Scotland wanted to toy with him and knew enough about the events surrounding *The Minerva* to make a credible claim. Rafe had intended to write the Brotherhood about it today, but rather than send a letter, he might as well deliver his message in person.

The problem, of course, was how to accomplish a trip to Edinburgh without his father learning of it. Kendall left Rafe to his devices for weeks at a time, so Rafe dashing off to the countryside wasn't a problem, particularly during the autumn hunting season. But a trip back to Edinburgh would raise questions, and Rafe instinctively knew his father would resist any attempts to truly heal the duchess.

Rafe would have to sort a way to travel unnoticed.

He tapped his hat into place on his head and turned from Dr. Hartley's stoop, only to realize that Lady Sophie still stood on the pavement below, her brow furrowed beneath her bonnet.

His stupid, wayward heart had lunged at its tether when he saw her before Dr. Hartley's surgery. Would he ever rid himself of this absurd infatuation?

But one look into her forest eyes, and the intervening years had melted away. He found himself, once again, that eager young man desperate to court her, to spend hours listening to her thoughts and dreams.

This would not do.

Briefly, he considered apologizing for his behavior four years ago, letting her know that his actions after that ill-fated ball had not been his own.

But . . . to what end? Lady Sophie gave no indication that she even remembered the incident. It was entirely likely the events had meant little to her. After all, she had married Captain Fulstate a short time later.

More to the point, Rafe was not in a position to court her. There could be no resumption of their relationship. Kendall had made his position on Lady Sophie brutally clear.

Which reminded him . . .

Rafe took in a steadying breath.

He could not be seen with Lady Sophie outside a doctor's surgery, no chaperone in sight. His father would be apoplectic if he learned of it.

Damn the man for controlling Rafe's life like this. How could Rafe be twenty-eight years of age and terrified of speaking with a woman, lest his *father* find out? It was an absurdity of such outrage—

Rafe took another shuddering breath, swallowing back his habitual rage.

Instead, he chose to focus on a lesser concern:

Why was Lady Sophie seeking Dr. Ross? Rafe had overhead her request the man's address in Edinburgh as well.

Moreover, why had Lady Sophie undertaken to visit Dr. Ross without a proper chaperone? Yes, she was a widow now and free from many of the constraints of an unmarried lady, but she was still that—an aristocratic lady. Had the woman no care for her own personal safety?

Worse, she glanced up at him—still standing on the stoop like a halfwit—nodded in parting, and then began to walk down the street, likely bent on the hackney stand a full block away on the main thoroughfare.

Before consciously telling his feet to move, Rafe found himself closing the gap between them, taking a place at her left side, standing as a defense between her and the street.

Like he belonged there, as if he and Lady Sophie were a couple.

Rafe tipped his hat at a passing gentleman, causing Lady Sophie to finally register his presence.

"Oh!" Her eyes flew wide as she lurched to a stop. "I say, Lord Rafe, this is quite unexpected." Her tone left Rafe wondering if she was annoyed or exasperated.

Perhaps a bit of both?

Which was the only explanation for Rafe's abrupt accusation. "You should not be gallivanting around London without an escort, Lady Sophie."

Silence.

An open-topped barouche creaked as it rattled past along the cobblestone streets, its occupants gazing with interest. Rafe shot the woman and her two daughters a quick look. Thankfully, he did not recognize them.

Lady Sophie noticed his noticing, an indecipherable emotion flitting across her face.

"My lord, I fail to see how my gallivanting, as you described it, is any concern of yours." Her jaw set. "Did you join me to prove your point? That anyone who wanted could impose upon my person?" Her head tilted to a forty-five-degree angle.

"Perhaps."

"And did it occur to you that a captain's widow of six and twenty has little reputation to ruin in the first place? Perhaps it is *you* who should be concerned with sullying your own by being seen with me." She darted a telling glance at the carriage now well down the street.

"Your *safety*,"—he leaned on the word—"my lady, is my greater concern. You are the daughter of an earl, esteemed and prized—"

Lady Sophie cut him short with a laugh. A bitter, mirthless laugh.

Rafe paused. That harsh sound reverberated in his chest. Regardless of her actual parentage, Mainfeld acknowledged her as his own. Why should she have this reaction?

He held her focused gaze for another second, mind racing. He had been so surprised to see her, so caught up in the sheer *relief* of being near her once more, that he had failed to notice—

Lady Sophie had changed.

She was not the same bright-eyed debutante he remembered.

Had there always been that hint of sadness in her mossy eyes? A wariness?

He thought not.

"I cannot imagine that your father would be content to witness you traipsing around like this, Lady Sophie," he continued. "You should, at the very least, have a maid with you."

She returned his gaze, her green eyes holding an odd flatness. Why had her spark vanished? Where was the quirky woman of his memory?

The more Rafe studied her, the more distressing it became.

Where had she gone, his Sophie?

"My father's approval or disapproval is none of your affair. I do not need to explain my actions to you, Lord Rafe," she said.

He opened his mouth to speak.

She held up a hand, palm out. *Allow me to finish speaking.*

"I will tell you, however, that my maid, Martha," she continued, "has a somewhat nervous constitution and finds outings like this quite distressing. Therefore, I did not think to subject her to it. Given this information, I am curious as to how you think she would protect me, my lord?"

A deafening silence.

Rafe's head went back slightly. "Perhaps she swoons with deadly accuracy?"

"Hmmm. I cannot speak to her accuracy, but she is most efficient at swooning, I will grant you."

Rafe stifled a grin. Her words gave him a flash of the Lady Sophie he had once known—a fleeting glimpse.

He couldn't stop himself from asking, "What is the point of a maid who is incapable of . . ."

"Maiding?" she offered, a barest of smile on her lips.

"Precisely. If that is the case, perhaps this Martha should be replaced."

"While I thank you for the unsolicited advice concerning my household management, I find the idea of casting Martha into the streets—for no other reason than being herself—distasteful. She is a human being, not a threadbare glove two years out of fashion. Despite your opinions, my lord, everyone deserves to have a place where they are needed and wanted."

Rafe almost huffed a startled laugh. Lady Sophie was taking the mick out of him and none-too-subtly at that.

But, more importantly, her tone animated her eyes, removing that terrible flatness. Something of that spark he loved showed through—a feisty originality that was so characteristically . . . her.

He adored that spark; he always had.

How I still want her. I am nothing but want when I am near her.

The thought rattled through his brain before he could stem it, the jolt sending words tumbling from his mouth—

"I seem to remember you had a habit of rescuing things."

It was his first reference to any meaningful prior acquaintance.

Her chin lifted, as if his words had struck a blow.

"She had nowhere else to go." The words cut him with their bare honesty. "I cannot save every destitute girl. But I could save Martha."

Her reply rendered him mute, a swift kick to the stomach, knocking the air out of him.

How had he forgotten this, too? Her shocking candor, humbling in its directness.

Hawkers called down the street. Large wagons rumbled along the busy main road ahead.

Lady Sophie turned and continued walking toward the hackney stand. He fell into step beside her.

"Will you be traveling to Edinburgh then?" she asked.

Rafe blinked and then grinned. Ah yes, he remembered the struggle to follow Lady Sophie's conversational leaps.

"To speak with Dr. Ross?" he asked.

"Yes. Will you be going as well?"

Going as well?

Wait. What was she implying—

"Are *you* planning to travel to Edinburgh to speak with Dr. Ross?"

"Of course," she said with prosaic finality. "I like the thought of making a journey of it. Besides, my matter with Dr. Ross is one I prefer to discuss in person."

First gallivanting around London without an escort and now considering a trip north—

Irrationally, anger flitted through him. Had Lady Sophie been so protected and pampered that she took no thought for her safety? Had the men in her life arranged affairs for her so frequently that she had no thought for the dangers that could befall a woman traveling?

This irritation made his tone sharper than it should have been. "If you must go to Edinburgh, please tell me you will be traveling with a brother or a male relative of some kind?"

"Heavens. The last thing I need is a man along."

"I beg your pardon?" He stopped in the middle of the pavement.

She paused as well, turning back to him with pursed lips, pinning him with her mossy eyes.

"Lord Rafe," she said, "you seem to be under the impression that a gentleman of any sort would be a help rather than a hindrance."

"Pardon?!" he repeated.

"I learned long ago that when faced with a difficult task, I am better off sorting it myself rather than waiting for a man to assist me. In my experience, a man will show up days too late, half-sprung, and then complain about having to help, all while watching *me* do what needs doing. Though I do not have a habit of disparaging your gender—" she shrugged, "—you did ask."

Well.

She was taking the mick out of him in earnest now.

And why did he feel that she wasn't referring to her brothers or father with her reply, but instead her late husband? What sort of a fellow had Captain Fulstate been?

"Of course. I suppose I will have to take Martha . . ." Her voice trailed off in thought.

"The one who swoons with inaccurate efficiency?"

A beat.

"Yes." She turned on her heel and started walking again toward the hackney stand.

Rafe's heart thundered in his chest. Who had taught this woman to hold her own safety so cheaply? And why did he suspect it was Captain Fulstate?

He ran a few steps to catch up to her.

"You should perhaps have a greater care for your personal well-being, my lady," he said. "I strongly recommend taking a traveling coach with several footmen and grooms—"

"A traveling coach? Footmen and grooms? Heavens." She shot him a side-eye. "We are not all the offspring of a wealthy duke, my lord. I was thinking to take the mail coach. I have read that it is quite speedy."

Speedy? Yes.

Comfortable and safe for the acknowledged daughter of an earl? No.

"What can possibly be so important that you must speak with Dr. Ross in person?" he asked.

Her lips drew into a straight line. "It is a private, personal matter, my lord." She clutched her reticule in two hands, her head staring straight ahead.

Rafe drummed his fingers against his leg, darting glances at the brim of her bonnet as she walked, all the while having a wee argument with himself.

Lady Sophie was none of his concern.

She was neither a relative nor a lady he was courting.

His father would have Rafe's head if he learned of this conversation.

What Lady Sophie did or did not do affected him in no way.

And yet . . .

His chest ached and burned at the thought of her journeying north to Scotland.

Alone.

Unguarded and unchaperoned.

In a public *mail* coach.

If something were to happen to her . . .

'Tis none of your concern.

But . . .

But—

He *liked* her.

As in . . .

. . . definitely, decidedly, emphatically adored her.

How could she take such risks with something he so adored?!

The very cheek!

"You cannot be serious about this endeavor, Lady Sophie," he finally said. "Surely, this is a jest."

She stopped again and fixed him with those lovely eyes. A man would do a great many ill-advised things for a mere glimpse of her glorious eyes.

"Why would I jest about this?" she asked. "I am in deadly earnest, my lord."

"But . . . why?" His tone was utterly baffled.

"Why do *you* seek Dr. Ross?"

Rafe paused, surprised at having his own question thrown back at him,

Words stuck in his throat. Most knew that his mother suffered from ill health, but disclosing the depth of her melancholy felt . . . deeply private.

"*Precisely*, my lord," she continued. "You cannot speak to me of it, as I am sure your concerns are of a personal nature. I do not wish to speak to you of it, as *my* questions are also of a personal nature. And so we are at an impasse."

Grrrr.

"You cannot journey to Scotland alone, my lady."

"My lord, I understand that you have strong *primus* tendencies—"

What?

This woman and her leaps of thought. "*Primus?*"

"A *primus.*" She rolled her hand. Her voice endearingly earnest and so impossibly stubborn. "Barn cats, dominant tomcat, my theory of a *primus* . . ."

"Yes, yes, I remember." Heaven help him. He remembered everything she had said, no matter the passage of years.

She clutched her reticule tighter. "I recognize that you, as a *primus*, may feel the need to order and protect those around you. However, I am not part of your clowder of barn cats. Your *primus* urges are unnecessary and unwelcome." She flicked her wrist. "Please go practice your *primus*-ing elsewhere."

Despite her acerbic tone, his lips twitched. "*Primus*-ing? I fear you are taking more liberties with the English language—"

"Enough!" She threw her hands in the air. "My lord, I am a fully-grown woman. I do not require your approval. If I wish to *verb* a word, then I will do so. If I want to travel to Edinburgh, I will choose my form of conveyance, whether by gilded carriage, hot-air balloon, fairy dust, or heaven forfend, a public mail coach!"

"Lady Sophie—"

"Why must you insist in arguing this point?"

"Why?!" Rafe's frustration rapidly got the better of him. "A public mail coach is a quick mode of conveyance, but it renders you vulnerable. You will be seated for *days* at a time beside heaven knows who! It could be a pleasant vicar's wife, but it could also be a randy man-of-business with wandering hands or, worse, a traveling salesman with a trunk of unsold merchandise. And when you finally stop for an evening, who will procure you a room? How will you ensure that no one cheats or robs you? Even more concerning, there have been reports of possible brigands south of Grantham. What will you do if accosted by highwaymen? Discuss barn cats and *verb* them into submission?!"

Rafe's voice rose as he spoke, Lady Sophie's brow drawing further and further down, her chest heaving.

"Oh! Is that all you think a bluestocking capable of? *Verbing?!*" She bit out. "As I learned only moments ago that I must away to Edinburgh, I haven't had a chance to research the journey. I am sure there is a solution that even a *bluestocking* can manage."

This woman.

Instead of crumbling into a weeping heap, she swallowed, pinched her lips together, and rallied.

And damn if he didn't admire her all the more for it.

"Perhaps instead of berating my decision, you could offer a few helpful suggestions. Or, at the very least, words of encouragement," she finished with a toss of her head and spun around, stomping off.

Rafe had rarely felt like such an ass. Yet again, he chased after her.

"I apologize, Lady Sophie," he said as he drew abreast of her once more. "My words were thoughtless. They were borne from the fact that I travel to and from Edinburgh with some regularity and am well-acquainted with the dangers. My genuine concern for your safety got the better of me. I did not mean to disparage your sex or intellect. I am quite certain you are fully capable of doing anything you put your mind to."

They were approaching the main thoroughfare. He glimpsed several carriages rumbling down the wide street ahead, crests he knew on their doors.

He couldn't be seen walking with Lady Sophie.

Damn and blast.

He paused.

Lady Sophie stopped and again noticed his noticing. Rafe suspected little escaped her too-knowing green eyes.

"Apology accepted," she said briskly. "And though I understand the pull of your *primus* urges, I fail to see how the security of my person is any concern of yours." She paused, looking him up and down. "I am no one to you, Lord Rafe."

"Lady Sophie—"

"Good day, my lord." She coolly turned on her heel and continued toward the hackney stand.

Rafe gritted his teeth and . . .

. . . did *nothing*.

Because despite how his heart panged and thumped in his chest—emphatically insisting that Lady Sophie was *everything* to him—she was, in fact as she said . . . truly no one.

He had no claim on her, no right, and, worst of all, no freedom to change the situation.

And that was the greatest tragedy of all.

12

Sophie took a hesitant sip of her tea, eyeing the door to the inn with mild trepidation.

Her maid, Martha, looked around, expression apprehensive. "There are so many people coming and going."

Sophie hummed in agreement and took another sip of tea, grimacing at its weak taste.

She and Martha were availing themselves of a brief luncheon before continuing their journey. They had left London the previous morning, intent on Edinburgh, but the crowded roads made it seem as if the entire metropolis had followed them.

Case in point, they currently sat in the Black Bull in Stilton, one of the largest coaching inns in this corner of England. Scores of travelers came and went every hour.

The inn had been far too busy for Sophie to claim a private dining room. Consequently, she and Martha were tucked into a far corner of the public dining room, giving them a clear view of the main entrance. That is to say, she could see the door only in brief glimpses, as men-of-business and families with crying children blocked the way, over and over. Every few minutes, a beleaguered man would announce the departure of a coach and another press of passengers would exit the room, while new arrivals surged in. The bells of the cathedral down the road sounded the hour, their deep *bong-bong* causing the thin window panes to rattle.

Sophie had been disappointed to find that Dr. Ross had retired and moved home to Edinburgh. But something in her welcomed the challenge. The quest to find her natural father—to begin at the beginning when piecing herself back together—had become a journey in truth.

Initially, she had not known how to best accomplish the journey north. Her finances were not robust—Jack had seen to that—but neither was she destitute. Lord Mainfeld had ensured that some of her dowry was protected from Jack's wastrel ways, and living with her parents these past months had allowed her to bolster her reserves. That said, she did not have the blunt for a hired coach to Scotland.

But in that as well, Lord Mainfeld had come to her assistance. Sophie had voiced her wish to visit a 'friend' in Edinburgh and before she knew it, her father had lent her a light travel chaise with a groom to ride postillion and footman to sit behind. She would need to pay for the post horses along the way, as well as lodging and all other incidentals, but Lord Mainfeld's generosity helped considerably to defray the cost of the trip.

Sophie pushed back the guilt of using a false father's kindness to find a true father who had, up to this point, shown no desire to know her.

If the man had been present for her birth, then he clearly knew of her existence. And yet, he remained in the shadows. But why?

Perhaps he felt that by ignoring her, he was allowing her the fiction that she was indeed Lord Mainfeld's daughter?

Or . . . perhaps the man simply did not wish to know her? Would she forever be this unwanted, invisible burden—

"Do you think we will be kidnapped and sold into a maharajah's harem?" Martha's odd question jerked Sophie out of her reverie. "I've heard of those things happening," she continued, eyes slightly panicked, voice deadly earnest.

Sophie looked at her maid, trying to keep her face impassive.

Martha was a nervous sort, forever anticipating a catastrophe around every corner. Her family had been tenant farmers for generations on the Mainfeld estate. Sophie had hired Martha after the young woman's mother died, leaving her orphaned. None of Martha's distant family members would take on her care.

What else was Sophie to do? She could not bear to see the younger woman tossed out into the world, like an unwanted basin of water. More to the point, she had been helpless to resist Martha's earnest eyes and cheerful demeanor. The girl truly thought nearly everything would hurt or kill her, and yet she faced it all with a sort of desperate, plucky verve.

Sophie was quite sure there was a profound life's lesson to be had in that.

"No, Martha. We will not be sold into a harem," Sophie replied. "I think we would have to be in India for that to happen."

"Oh." A moment's hesitation. "But why?"

Sophie mentally sighed. It was going to be a long trip with Martha as a 'chaperone.'

"Because maharajahs only live in India. Harems are quite illegal in England."

"Yes, but aren't we going to Scotland? Scotland is not England." A pause. "They probably have harems in Scotland."

"There are no harems in Scotland, either." *Aside from the women that men like Lord Rafe collected around themselves, that is.*

Sophie did not add that last bit.

Lord Rafe was likely traveling to Scotland with an entourage befitting the son of a powerful duke—coachman and postillion, footmen, valet, and perhaps a secretary. His own personal clowder to order about.

She took another hesitant sip of her tea. It truly was vile, more lukewarm, tea-flavored water than anything. The boiled pork and mash they had been offered for lunch had not been much better.

She knew she needed to move past this absurd fascination with Lord Rafe. She had traveled this path with him once before and been badly singed; she refused to act so stupidly a second time.

It was just . . .

. . . arguing with him outside the doctor's surgery . . .

The years had simply . . . slipped away.

She had been vividly reminded of *why* she had liked him all those years ago. The quick turn of his mind, the concerned caring in his voice.

And she *had* liked him.

So.

Very.

Much.

With every word out of his mouth, she had felt that younger self rising within her—the girl she had been before Jack.

That girl had been naive in so many ways . . . so trusting, so easily deceived.

But that younger Sophie had also been full of life and fire, hope and optimism.

Her goal was to piece back together the shards of self that Jack had shattered, but into what form? The girl she had been?

No, she had no desire to go back. This journey had to be a rebirth in truth. That by uncovering the events on the night of her birth, she might begin anew—a phoenix rising from the ashes of her old self.

A coachman entered, calling for his passengers over the din. Through the dirty windows, Sophie could see a stagecoach in the yard. Like all stagecoaches, it was piled high with luggage and people, some seemingly held on with only a bit of rope and a prayer. A noisy table of school boys and their tutor rose, following the coachman out, reducing the overall chaos of the room considerably.

A tall man at the door stood aside to allow the boys to pass before entering the inn himself.

Though his back was to her, the man's height and Highland dress instantly drew her attention.

An enormous red-and-blue kilt swathed his body, starting at his knees and ending wrapped around his torso, a darker short frock coat underneath. A jaunty Highland bonnet sat at an angle atop his dark hair, and the hilt of a knife protruded from the top of his gartered stockings.

Surveying him, Sophie's heart lurched to a running thump in her chest and a pleasant tingle chased her spine.

Well, now. That was unexpected.

Or . . . perhaps not. The man was, after all, absolutely delectable.

Apparently in addition to rakes, her biological self found Scottish displays of overt masculinity unbearably attractive.

Interesting choice.

She had never encountered a clansman in traditional dress, so how was she to have known she liked such a thing?

But then, she had always found Jack dashing in his red-coated regimentals. Her late husband might have been a philandering rakehell, but he did cut a fine figure.

Unfortunately, her biological self had a preferred type of male, and this unknown Scot fit her notion of a spectacular masculine specimen. Now the man simply needed to turn around so she could evaluate him from the front.

Mmmm, perhaps she should add Scottish men as a separate genus and species. *Scottus virilis* or some such thing.

The frazzled innkeep stepped over to the unknown Scotsman.

"A Scot, are you?" the innkeep asked, surveying the man up and down.

"Och, nae," the Scot laughed, his voice a rolling boom of sound. "I'm actually a dandified rakehell sent down from London for being an utter letch. I've stowed ma starched cravat and violet waistcoat in my valise." The Scot hefted the bag in his hand.

The innkeep rolled his eyes. "Yer a Scot, all right. Can never answer a question without making a joke."

"Aye, it's our national pastime, I ken," the Scot chuckled, good-naturedly. "Nothing else tae do during a dark Scottish winter except drink a wee dram and laugh at ourselves."

The rumble of the man's deep brogue washed over Sophie, a wave of fizzing sensation, firing her senses.

Heavens.

And to think—there was an entire *country* of men who looked and sounded just like this. If the man smelled divine too, she was utterly done for.

Stop.

No more rakes. No more manly men of any sort. They are bad, bad, bad for your health.

Sophie found it endlessly frustrating. Why did her biology crave something that was ultimately so harmful?

"Right. How may I help you?" the innkeep asked the Scot.

"I'm for the stagecoach to Edinburgh at half four. Looking for a mite to eat afore then."

"Ah. Well, we're terrible busy at the moment . . ." The innkeep placed his hands on his hips, surveying the room. "There appears to be a seat near the ladies in the corner over there." The man waved a hand in Sophie's direction. "I'll send my Mary over with a pint and a plate in a moment."

"I'd be much obliged."

The Scot turned to survey the room.

And that's when recognition *finally* set in.

What the—?!

Lord Rafe's eyes fell on her from beneath his cap, his well-formed jawline and the scar on his upper cheek clearly identifying him.

He froze, his expression just as surprised to see her as she was to see him.

How—?

Here—?!!

They were in a coaching inn.

In bloody *Stilton*, of all places!

Of course, wretch that he was, Lord Rafe recovered quickly.

Worse—

He *winked*, sending another wave of corresponding heat chasing Sophie's spine.

Lord Rafe turned back to the innkeep. "Thank ye." He saluted the man.

And then *all* his attention was on Sophie.

Lord Rafe didn't walk so much as stalk toward her, his eyes lit with mischief, those dimples deep holes in his cheeks, the scar near his eye stretching.

Twice now, she had simply not recognized him. Her skills of observation required some honing.

She was blaming the kilt for distracting her. A man's bare knees had a way of upending even the soundest woman's good sense.

Though judging by Martha's stunned expression and the heads turning his way, Lord Rafe would never pass through life inconspicuously. London rake or lowly Highlander, it made no difference.

His mere presence had raised the temperature in the taproom by a solid five degrees.

"Ladies." Lord Rafe nodded at her. "May I be so bold as to join ye?" He motioned toward the empty chairs opposite Sophie.

And then, before hearing her answer, he sat down, setting his dusty leather valise at his feet. As if he had every right. As if he knew he would be welcome.

The sheer nerve!

Bloody *primus*.

Grrr.

"Please have a seat, sir." Her tone could have peeled paint with its acidity. She aimed a pointed glance at the battered case at his feet, the initials LRG for Lord Rafe Gilbert embossed on its side.

Of course, that simply made Lord Rafe smile wider, nodding his head in greeting. He stretched his legs out, flashing those bare knees below his kilt and jostling the small table.

The man had no shame.

Sophie pasted on a strained smile.

What was Lord Rafe about? Did the man habitually travel to Scotland in Highland dress?

Moreover, he said he was waiting for the public *stagecoach,* not the more prestigious Royal Mail coach, or a more aristocratic private coach.

It all seemed . . . odd.

What was Lord Rafe about? And why did Sophie abruptly feel off-kilter, as if everything she knew about this man had been upended?

"Lennon Gordon, at yer service," he said, answering some of her questions.

Ah.

A disguise.

Lord Rafe was traveling to Edinburgh *incognito*.

The mystery deepened.

Sophie surveyed him, lounging in his chair, his large body relaxed and at ease in his surroundings.

She had gravely miscalculated.

A pampered London rake did not appear in Highland dress at a coaching inn in Stilton—traveling on a public stagecoach, no less!—because he found it an enjoyable way to journey the length of Great Britain.

Why the need for such a disguise? What secrets was he hiding? Why did she care?

And why, why, *why* must he smell so delicious?!

"And ye are, madam?" he asked, his dimples flashing again.

"A lady," Sophie replied, repressively.

If he was going to pretend not to know her, then she certainly wasn't going to play anything other than the reserved societal widow that she was. Normally, Sophie would rebuff the advances of a man such as Lennon Gordon, no matter how attractive she found him.

Something flashed in Lord Rafe's eyes as he absorbed her words.

He braced his forearms on the table and leaned toward her.

"Are ye lovely lassies for the stagecoach north, too?" His brogue clung to Sophie like warm honey, deliciously sweet. "I should count myself a verra lucky man if ye were."

Sophie nearly snorted. "I do not see such luck in your future."

If she thought to quell him, she was mistaken.

Lord Rafe laughed, loud and boisterous. It was a glorious sound, pinging around the crowded dining room like a rung bell, reverberating across Sophie's sternum.

Heavens.

He seemed a different person entirely.

Lord Rafe was the consummate man about town—impeccably well-dressed, meticulously groomed, and dripping with wealth and privilege.

But seeing him at this moment . . . not a trace of the London rake remained. That man had disappeared entirely. In fact, had it not been for the scar on his cheek, she might have doubted the Scot before her was Lord Rafe at all.

The entire scenario tilted her world on its axis, forcing her to realign truths and realities, underscoring how little she knew Lord Rafe in the end.

And given how effortlessly he settled into this Highlander act, Sophie had to wonder who was the true Lord Rafe:

The Scottish Highlander? Or the London rake?

Or was the real man someone else entirely?

"You play the Scotsman quite well," she murmured, canting toward him, dropping the pretense between them.

"Thank ye." He leaned similarly forward. "I ken ye like me like this, lass."

She did.

Far too much.

It would likely prove a problem to her peace of mind.

Given the smirk on Lord Rafe's face, he had as usual noticed her noticing, the wretch.

"Lord Rafe—"

"Lennon, lass. The name is Lennon. Lennon Robert Gordon." He glanced down at the valise at his feet, nudging the LRG initials there.

Sigh.

"Lennon Gordon. Of course—"

"Is this your maid?" He interrupted, shooting a glance at Martha, who sat watching the entire exchange with bulging eyes.

"Yes."

"The one that—"

"Yes." She changed the topic. "Why the disguise?"

Was it her imagination, or did his expression freeze?

A small pause.

"Sometimes I like to keep my movements . . . secret . . ." was his reply.

Which was less of an explanation and more of an obvious statement. Clearly, he wished to travel north undetected. The son of a duke didn't take a public stagecoach because he *enjoyed* rubbing elbows with the masses.

"Secret? But why? There is no inherent shame in traveling to Edinburgh," she said.

"No, there is not."

The maddening man said nothing more, though something hard and unyielding flashed in his eyes.

Foolish Lord Rafe. Did he not know that tenacity was her one and only power? If she had been born a sorceress, *tenacity* would be her signature enchantment.

She would uncover his reasons.

"Hmmmm. Allow me to guess." She tapped her lips. "You are set to meet with a paramour and don't wish to upset her husband?"

It was a standard *Rakus lasciviosus* maneuver.

Jack had been particularly fond of it.

"Ah, no." He shook his head. "Permit me to say that I do not, as a general rule, consort with married women."

Sophie sat up straighter. That was . . . surprising.

Again, how little she actually knew him.

She glanced at the battered case emblazoned with his initials. The bottom of his kilt rested on it.

"Any other guesses?" he asked.

"Hmmm. You have an unnatural love of the works of Sir Walter Scott and decided to re-enact *Rob Roy*?"

"Nae, though I'm no' opposed to the thought."

"You wished to test my *primus* theories as they pertain to a Scottish Highlander?"

He grinned, that confusingly intense warmth in his eyes. "Nae, lass."

"Well, you have confounded me." She rested her hands on the table. "Aside from an irrational attachment to wearing a kilt and riding in public stagecoaches, I cannot think of another reason."

"Ye cannot?"

"No. Why not travel in your own carriage? Or via horseback, at the very least? I am sure your father's stables are impressive. The servants of the Duke of Kendall would never tell tale of your destination. I warrant your father hires men of discretion."

"Aye, of a surety." Was that bitterness in his tone? "But those same men will always report my goings and comings *to* my father."

Venom laced his words, that same steely glint flashing in his eyes.

Now *that* was interesting.

Fascinating, really.

She was unaware there was a rift between Kendall and Lord Rafe. She had never heard mention of such a thing and, given the tension between Kendall and Mainfeld, she would *definitely* have heard if anything were amiss in the Duke of Kendall's household. Lord Mainfeld would chuckle with glee over it.

Against her better judgment, she felt Lord Rafe drawing her in.

She leaned farther forward. "And so when you wish to avoid notice, you pretend to be Scottish?"

"I *am* Scottish, lass."

Oh. "From your mother?" Belatedly, Sophie remembered her taxonomic entry about him. His mother hailed from Ayr, south of Glasgow.

"Aye. I wear my heritage proudly."

"*That* is fairly obvious."

She struggled to see the gentlemanly Lord Rafe in his current attire, to find the English duke's son underneath it all.

But the opposite effect kept occurring. The more she looked, the more she felt like she was finally seeing the true Lord Rafe Gilbert. As if the London rake was nothing more than a polished veneer, but the Highland kit revealed Lord Rafe in his true form.

Why was that? And why did she care?!

"Do you often wear a kilt and all the . . ." She motioned a hand to indicate his attire. ". . . rest?"

He *had* to wear it often. What else could account for his ease in inhabiting it?

"Only when I want the lasses to notice me." He shot her a wink and a grin.

Her brows drew down. How instinctual was this man's need to flirt?

"Lord Rafe—"

"*Lennon*, lass."

Grrrr.

"Lennon—is that truly the case? You don Highland dress as a form of mating plumage? Display your colors like a *Pavo cristatus*?"

To his credit, Lord Rafe scarcely blinked at her comment. Instead, he lounged back in his chair, eyes laughing.

"Are ye calling me a peacock, lass?"

"Your plumage is quite colorfully loud." She permitted herself a small smile.

"Careful, lass, or I might take tae calling ye my bird." He winked again.

Oh!

His words crossed a line from charming flirting to something . . . weightier. He did not actually wish a future with her, as his words implied.

And yet, his eyes were warm, deep pools of soothing chocolate. He tilted his head, giving her that signature slow-burn smile which caused his dimples to pop, everything about him saying quite clearly, *I am overwhelmingly attractive. How can you not adore me?*

Much to Sophie's eternal annoyance, she *did* find him overwhelmingly attractive.

Fortunately, his overly-flirtatious behavior was a brisk dowsing of much-needed Reality.

He did not mean his words. He never had.

She broke away from his gaze, clearing her throat.

Just because his plumage had changed colors, she couldn't allow herself to forget that his *behavior* likely had not.

He still saw her as a plaything.

When would she ever learn?

Once a rake, always a rake.

Like the *primus* tomcats she had studied, a *Rakus lasciviosus* liked to play with his food. Lord Rafe endlessly toyed with her, pulling her near in one moment, and then pushing her away the next.

Just as Jack had done . . . ignoring her for long stretches of time, to only come begging when he needed something.

"I need you to speak to your father," Jack said, opening a conversation without any preamble, despite the fact that Sophie hadn't seen him in days.

"My father?" She looked up from her seat before the parlor fire.

Her husband swayed in the doorway, his blond hair rumpled and askew. His bleary eyes scanned her up and down.

"I need some blunt." He walked a crooked line into the room.

She stilled, the words a lead weight in her stomach. Had he been racking up debts again? After he promised he would stop?

"If you need blunt, then I suggest you speak with Lord Mainfeld yourself—"

"If you possessed an ounce of wifely feeling, you would assist me in this!" he snapped, slumping onto the sofa before the fire, head lolling back, eyes shut.

The scent of brandy and cheap perfume eddied into the room behind him, leaving little doubt as to his activities.

Sophie bit back angry words—

If you were any sort of husband, we wouldn't be in this mess.

Nausea clawed up her throat. Was this what her life had become? Tolerating a husband who spent his nights carousing around London? Begging her father for funds on his behalf?

Perhaps a legal separation between them would be for the best. Her father had suggested it last time they spoke.

Jack cracked a bleary eye, not misunderstanding her stony expression.

"Perhaps I should do more than simply speak with my father, then," she countered. "Perhaps it's time I returned to his household—"

"Ah, love. You are my wife. My dearest heart." He smiled, strained, as if professing his affection were physically painful. "You don't mean that—"

"I most certainly do—"

Sophie shook off the memory.

Never again.

Her heart and affections were not toys to be used and discarded at will.

"My lady? Are you content to leave? I have settled our bill." Sophie's footman, James, stood before the table, eyes darting between Lord Rafe and herself, clearly trying to determine if he needed to do something about the imposing Scot.

Lord Rafe raised an eyebrow at James in his livery before turning his gaze back to Sophie.

Yes, her eyes said. *I did* listen to your advice.

"Thank you, James," she replied, standing up. "I am quite ready to depart."

Lord Rafe lurched to his feet, his manners as a gentleman too ingrained to change as easily as his clothing.

"Good day, Mr. Gordon." She nodded her head, sweeping past Lord Rafe.

She felt his gaze follow her as she crossed the public dining room.

She did not look back.

She had already traversed this path with Lord Rafe, purchased a season subscription to the *Heartache and Stupidity Revue.*

If nothing else, Sophie learned from her past mistakes.

One painful lesson at a time.

13

The following afternoon, Rafe was trying to remember why he had chosen to take a public stagecoach instead of simply riding a horse north.

Ah, that's right. He *enjoyed* having every bone in his body jarred loose.

He grunted as a particularly deep rut jolted the carriage.

At least he rested atop the coach at the moment, escaping the stuffy confines of the interior for the crisp autumn weather outside. A mother and her two children sat on the bench in front of him, the woman crooning a lullaby.

Rafe leaned his back against an obliging traveling chest strapped to the roof, watching the landscape bounce past.

He tried, yet again, to tamp down thoughts of Lady Sophie—her expressive eyes, the keen sharpness of her intellect. His heart had nearly stopped beating when he spotted her sitting alone with only a maid in the crowded public dining room in Stilton.

Thankfully Lady Sophie had listened to his advice and had at least a footman and likely a coach and coachman with her, too. His concern had dropped dramatically as he had watched her leave the dining room, her footman glaring at people to keep their distance.

If only his own troubles were so easily sorted. He had no idea how he was to escape marrying Lord Syke's daughter before Christmastide. Unless Dr. Ross could offer solutions for the duchess, Kendall's stranglehold on Rafe's future felt absolute.

Furthermore, the letter about *The Minerva* and his supposed crimes weighed on him. It was the sort of thing that gave a bit of a jolt when first received, but as all the implications of it sank in, the entire situation became more of an earthquake than a simple tremor, threatening to upend his life entirely.

The largest question? Who knew about the events of that day three and a half years ago?

They had long assumed everyone involved—except for the Brotherhood—had perished. It had seemed impossible to think otherwise. Surely if some of the crew had survived, they would have heard tale by now.

So either the letter and notice in the *Edinburgh Advertiser* came from a friend or family member who knew of the events—and there were a few of those, though why they would threaten the Brotherhood was a mystery? Or . . . someone, against all odds, had survived.

Could Jamie have survived?

The thought would not be silenced.

And yet . . . if the youth had survived, Jamie would have found a way to contact them. It was impossible to think otherwise. The carpenter's mate was too loyal, too stubborn.

"*Try again,*" *Rafe called, lifting his rapier into a standard* en garde *position. Jamie matched his movements.* "*Ye're not keeping your weight properly balanced.*"

"*Balance isnae the problem, I ken,*" *Jamie replied with a helpless grin, trying to swipe the blade and failing miserably. The blade tip sank downward.* "*I'm too small, and my arms are just a wee bitty too weak.*"

"*Nonsense. Ye have plenty of strength, Jamie. Ye simply need to practice. Try again.*"

With a toss of the head, Jamie lifted the rapier, despite sporting an arm nearly shaking with fatigue. Jaw clenched in determination, steel in the eyes—

Rafe shrugged off the memory.

Jamie had been fencing like a master by the time they reached Sydney. The youth was resourceful, tenacious, and infinitely clever. If Jamie had survived the wreckage of *The Minerva*, the Brotherhood would know. There was no other explanation.

The stagecoach jolted again, causing Rafe to grunt. The children sitting in front of him laughed, climbing on their mother.

Rafe settled further into his seat, pulling his kilt tighter around his shoulders to block the chill autumn breeze.

Thoughts of Jamie and the rocking of the stagecoach called to mind the rocking of a ship. Memory took Rafe back to the South Pacific. Images floated through his mind—the village children racing Jamie and Kieran down the beach in Vanuatu, Ewan hunched over his sketchbook sketching Jamie laughing as the villagers looked on in wonder. Somewhere in his musing, Rafe drifted off to the children's chatter.

A bullet whizzing beside his head shattered his sleep.

He lurched upright as a second bullet flew past.

What the hell?!

In his disoriented state, for a brief moment, he thought he was still aboard *The Minerva*.

A pounding on his cabin door. Gunshots above deck.

Jamie screaming, "Hurry, my lord! Ye must get out tae save yerself!"

Fully awake an instant later, Rafe had his pistol in his hand and had ducked down behind the bench when the third and fourth bullets struck the side of the coach.

A single thought pounded through his brain:

They've come for me.

Whoever was behind the threatening letter and post in the *Advertiser* had decided to take matters into their own hands.

But as quickly as the idea floated through his head, Rafe kicked it away.

Focus, man.

He was no longer in the South Pacific.

He was on a stagecoach somewhere between Newark and Doncaster, being fired upon by brigands, most likely.

Rafe turned and peered through the bench slats, assessing the situation.

Yes, there hadn't been a stagecoach robbery along the Great Northern Road in quite some time, particularly in broad daylight. The age of highwaymen had passed nearly half a century ago. But it would be absurd in the extreme to think these bandits had anything to do with Rafe specifically, much less the recent threats he had received. He was in disguise, after all.

Besides, hadn't there been rumors of highwaymen in this area? He had said as much to Lady Sophie, hadn't he?

The mother atop the coach with her two children had ducked down—the bairns screaming hysterically—giving Rafe a clear view of the road in front. The coach lurched and bounced. The driver whipped the horses, sending the coach careening down the road, trying to outrun the brigands. A passenger seated beside the driver bent down to retrieve a rifle.

Trees whizzed past, the stretch of road ideal for lurking highwaymen. Shots rang out from the trees. The passenger beside the driver took aim and fired.

Spinning in his crouched position, Rafe scanned the forest, finally seeing the shadows of horsemen there. He counted four of them.

Damn and blast.

As irrational as it seemed, his first thought wasn't for his own safety, but that of Lady Sophie. There was no telling which route she was taking, not to mention where she was at the moment—she could be behind or in front of him for all he knew—but he immediately wished her far away from this chaos.

Glancing ahead, Rafe could see a narrow bridge over a river. The driver was clearly racing for it. Smart man. If they could make the bridge, the brigands wouldn't be able to surround the coach, allowing them to make a proper stand.

Another shot rang out.

Rafe whipped around.

A rifle cracked from below, another passenger inside the coach also returning fire. One of the brigands fell off his horse. The bouncing of the coach along the rutted road made aiming difficult, but Rafe took aim with his own pistol and squeezed off a shot, winging another rider.

The rifleman atop the coach reloaded, firing again. Another would-be highwayman toppled.

More shots rang out, this time coming from behind the brigands. Another coach appeared on the road, two gentlemen in a curricle, one brandishing a pistol. The remaining highwayman scattered into the trees, melting away.

Rafe should have felt elation, but instead unease threaded through him.

Had that been too easy? Had the would-be robbers given up too quickly?

Are you sure this isn't related to that letter?

He grimaced.

No. No, he wasn't sure at all.

Rafe turned around, yelling at the driver that the threat had been neutralized, but the man couldn't hear over the rattle of the coach.

Ahead, the bridge drew closer, arching over a rushing river. The carriage turned slightly to careen over it.

But the stagecoach was traveling too quickly and the edge of a wheel caught on a groove in the uneven stonework. The coach tipped precariously to the left. The vehicle was so top heavy with luggage and people that it didn't stand a chance of remaining upright. With a creaking crash, the stagecoach sloped sideways onto the bridge railing.

People screamed. Horses whinnied.

The mother and her children tumbled to the side, jarring the younger child from her grasp. Without thinking, Rafe caught the wee girl before she could tumble off the coach and pushed her back into her mother's arms.

But in doing so, he lost purchase on the bench, upsetting his balance. He scrambled for a hold, but his hands came up empty.

He barely had time to snatch a breath before crashing into the chilly water below.

SOPHIE WAS RESTING comfortably in her coach, tucked beneath a warm wool blanket, reading a treatise about the habitat of the American turkey, when she heard gunshots.

Raising her head, she and Martha exchanged glances. The gunshots were in the distance and no cause for immediate alarm. Likely just some hunters flushing game or a farmer chasing a fox off his property.

She surveyed the road ahead, seeing nothing.

Her father's light chaise was of a modern design. It featured a single bench and large panels of glass across the sides and front. There was no coachman, per se. Instead, a groom rode postillion on the front left horse, while a footman sat in a high seat behind the carriage box. All in all, the arrangement gave travelers an excellent view of the road ahead.

And at the moment, there was nothing to see. Just trees.

With a shrug, Sophie went back to her treatise, trying (again) not to let her mind wander to Lord Rafe and that odd encounter at the coaching inn.

It was just . . .

Her brain was so *tenacious*. It desperately wanted to sort the puzzle that was Lord Rafe . . . or rather, Lennon Gordon.

The man was not who she had thought him to be. She desperately wanted to put him into a box, label him a *Rakus lasciviosus,* and tuck him away on a high shelf like some exotic specimen.

But that was proving more and more difficult.

There were layers to Lord Rafe. Or, perhaps, *masks* would be a better word. The man was more chameleon than anything.

Why was he traveling in disguise? The implications of it led her mind down a rather specific logical path.

Fact: Lord Rafe was in disguise because he very much did not want his ducal father to learn of his trip to Edinburgh.

Fact: The purpose of the trip to Edinburgh was to consult with Dr. Ross on some matter.

Ergo . . . Lord Rafe assumed that his consult with Dr. Ross would anger his father.

But what could that be? What information did Lord Rafe seek that Kendall deemed upsetting?

The Duke of Kendall was a stern, foreboding figure. More than once during her marriage to Jack, she had caught him staring at her across a ballroom or a street or the opera. In her more fanciful moments, she considered his stare something of a death glance, as if he wished to will her entirely out of existence.

Which, of course, was absurd. Kendall did not wish her dead; he simply did not like her parents.

But what if Kendall were similarly chilly with his own son?

And, if so, what was so important that Lord Rafe would go to such lengths to avoid his father's notice?

And why, why, why did Sophie long to know?

It was *entirely* none of her affair.

She drummed her fingers, glaring at the scenery, frustrated with herself for caring when she knew better.

Lord Rafe is no one to you.

Let it be.

She was nearly ready to halt the carriage so she could stretch her legs (and clear her head) when they rounded a bend.

Pandemonium had erupted ahead.

A stagecoach leaned precariously against the railing of a narrow stone bridge. Another curricle was stopped to the side of the road, its horses tethered to a tree. Travelers were everywhere. One woman cared for several crying children, while another appeared to be bandaging a passenger. Half the men were unloading the luggage from the stagecoach, while others attempted to re-harness the horses in such a way as to right the coach.

All in all, Sophie wasn't traveling any further until the mess cleared— the stagecoach thoroughly blocked the bridge—but at first glance, it appeared that no one was seriously hurt.

Her chaise rolled to a stop and her groom dismounted. He asked the nearest man what had happened. The words *highwaymen* and *gunshots* chilled Sophie's blood.

Heavens.

Lord Rafe had been right, in the end.

Martha, of course, instantly devolved into a blubbering mess, threatening to swoon entirely. Sophie held her for a moment, offering comfort.

"I would like to help where I can," Sophie asked, nodding to the chaos outside the chaise. "Will you be able to manage here, Martha?"

Bravely wiping her cheeks, Martha nodded her head.

Sighing, Sophie patted her cheek and exited the carriage. She asked her groom and the footman, James, to help the men unload the rest of the luggage from the stagecoach. Sophie turned to help a mother with her two children when one of the pieces of luggage caught her eye—

A battered leather valise with the initials LRG branded into the side.

Heavens!

Lord Rafe was here?

This was *his* stagecoach?!

Sophie whirled around, looking for the telltale flash of a red-and-blue kilt. A few steps to the side and she could see all the men swarming the coach. There was no kilted Scotsmen in the group.

Biting her lip, Sophie turned back, bending down before the mother who rocked a small girl in her arms, another child nestled against her side.

"Was there a Scotsman aboard the stagecoach?" Sophie asked. "A tall, dark-haired fellow in a red-and-blue kilt?"

The woman lifted her head, eyes bewildered. She looked around, craning her neck.

"Why, yes, there was. He was most brave, firing on the brigands and scaring them off. And then when we hit the bridge, he saved my wee girl from tumbling right off. But I have been so scattered since, I haven't thought to look for him." The woman continued to search, brows drawing down. "Where *is* he?"

"He fell in the water," the child at her side offered. "He plunked right in." The child mimed something falling and plopping in the water.

Terror pounded through Sophie.

Lord Rafe had fallen into the river? Had he been shot? Worse, as she didn't see him about, had he emerged from the river? Where was he?

Surely the man could swim. But if he wasn't with the coach, something had to have gone wrong. Had he hit his head?

Whirling around, Sophie dashed to the edge of the bridge, looking downriver. The water swirled swift and fast. A minute was all it took for her to spot the red-and-blue soaked figure clinging to a rock in the middle of the river a hundred yards downstream. His head moved back and forth, assessing his situation.

Relief flooded her. Lord Rafe appeared to be among the living at the moment.

He was too far away for a shout to be heard. If she hadn't been deliberately seeking him, she would not have spotted him. No wonder no one had done anything yet to help.

Fortunately for him, she made a habit of rescuing helpless things.

Even half-drowned rakes.

She fetched James and had him retrieve a length of rope from the chaise, along with a heavy lap blanket. Lord Rafe would surely be frozen clear through after such a dunking on a chilly autumn day.

With James at her side, Sophie skirted trees and traipsed down the riverbank, drawing alongside where Lord Rafe clung to the rock.

He had one arm wrapped tightly around the jagged end of the boulder, the other braced to hold himself onto the rock. She couldn't see any blood from her vantage point, thank goodness. But she had seen half-drowned rats that appeared less disheveled and shaken. The poor man was quaking with cold, shivering violently. It was a wonder he could cling to the rock at all.

She surveyed the situation while she waited for him to notice her.

It didn't take long. As if somehow feeling her gaze, he turned his head her way.

She waved her fingers at him, plastering what she hoped was a delightedly obnoxious grin on her face.

Ah, if only she had some way to record the astonishment on his face—wide-eyed, stunned.

With a final wave, she plotted how to retrieve him.

She immediately understood his predicament. The river flowed too swiftly for him to swim to the riverbank. A series of cascades began only twenty yards downstream. A man would be dashed to death if he tried to float through there. Not to mention the chill of the cold water hampering his strength.

No wonder Lord Rafe had a death grip on the rock.

James read the situation as well.

"He's too far away for me to throw the rope to him," the footman said.

"True." Sophie surveyed the riverbank, noting a tree branch which extended over the river. "But if we secured the rope around the trunk there, I could inch along that branch"—she pointed to the tree—"and I could toss the rope to him."

James frowned. "Best let me do it, my lady."

Sophie dragged her eyes up and down the footman's tall, stocky body. "You weigh far too much, James. You'll break the branch. Best let *me* do it. Besides, you will be needed here to pull him in once he secures the rope to his person."

James continued to protest, but Sophie was adamant.

She had spent her childhood up trees, scouring for insects and checking bird nests. *Half-feral*, her brothers had called her. They were, perhaps, not entirely wrong.

Needless to say, a sturdy tree limb posed little challenge.

Rafe studied them from his rock, eyes wide.

"Hold on!" she yelled to him, tucking up her skirts. James tied the rope to the tree trunk. She made a wide slipknot at the other end of the rope.

Of course, Rafe's eyes only became wider once he realized their plan.

She saluted him, clenched the rope in her teeth, and reached upward, scrambling up the trunk with ease. Once she reached the branch, she then held onto the limb above, inching her way carefully down the tree branch, feeling with her feet. The branch dipped with her weight, lowering that much closer to Rafe. Her teeth clamped on the rope in her mouth.

"Are y-ye d-d-daft, lass?!" Rafe roared as she neared him, teeth chattering violently, his scar a slash in the pallor of his cheeks. "You're g-going to g-get yourself k-killed!"

Even in such dire circumstances, the man continued to play the Scot. Was the behavior so truly ingrained then?

Sophie shook the thought free and inched a little farther. She wasn't quite close enough to toss the rope yet. Water raced below her. One wrong step would send her tumbling in.

Rafe, of course, continued to berate her. "D-did ye not hear m-me, ye wee d-daftie?! Go back! Have the b-braw groom there do this. I w-willnae have yer b-blood on my hands!"

Almost there. She took another careful step before pulling the rope from her mouth and holding it in her hand with the tree limb above.

"Hush, you!" She called to him. "I know full well what I am about. Before leaving London, a dominant, *primus* rakehell gave me some excellent advice about the dangers of traveling by stagecoach. He mentioned something about brigands," she replied, tone becoming more and more sardonic. "I, with my bluestocking ways, initially planned to discuss barn cats and *verb* the highwaymen into submission—"

He winced. "Lady Sophie—"

"But in the end, I chose to bring rope and other aids." She waved the rope in her hand. "In other words . . . I came prepared."

A small silence.

"I s-suppose ye think you're c-clever."

"I am *excessively* clever."

Sophie inched forward another foot.

The branch cracked. She paused for a moment, assessing the stability of the limb. The tree was healthy and green, so the branch should continue to bend with her weight.

After a moment's hesitation, she continued forward.

"Sophie, I m-mean it," he said, sincerity in his voice, shoulders shaking from cold. "Ye m-must stop right there. You're g-going to hurt yourself."

"I understand perfectly what I am doing, my lord."

"Do ye? Because from my vantage p-point, it looks like you're about to j-join me in taking a c-cold swim in this river. Only you're l-liable to have your b-brains dashed on the rushing c-cascade there." He nodded toward the water racing downstream.

"Well, fortunately, I am also a strong swimmer and, last I checked, quite waterproof. If I get wet, I shan't melt." She slid forward the final foot, her head nearly above his.

"Sophie—" His voice a warning as he looked up to her.

She met his dark gaze, a wry smile on her lips. "I think what you meant to say was, 'Why thank you Lady Sophie for having the presence of mind to affect my rescue. You are so very brave.'"

She finished by dangling the rope in front of his face. Rafe snagged it with one shaking hand, fishing the loop over his head and free shoulder, securing himself.

"You are most welcome," she smirked. "I'm always ready and willing to help a laddie in distress."

And with that, she turned and nodded at James to begin pulling Lord Rafe to shore.

As her footman grunted and hauled on the rope, Sophie scooted back down the branch.

Predictably, Lord Rafe beat her back to the riverbank, water sluicing off his kilt and dripping from his arms as he freed his shoulders from the rope, body still shaking from the cold.

Ignoring his outstretched hand, Sophie jumped from the tree limb onto the riverbank, shaking her skirts free.

"Are you quite unharmed, Mr. Gordon?" she asked Lord Rafe, using his alias as they now had an audience in the curious James. "Aside from the cold, that is?"

Lord Rafe nodded and scraped a quivering hand through his hair. He unclasped the top of his kilt from a pin which held it at his shoulder, sending the long upper end of it tumbling behind him, the length nearly reaching his ankles. He began wringing the water from the dripping fabric, the tendons on the back of his hands popping in stark relief.

He finished wringing water out of his kilt and had begun shrugging out of his soaking coat before Sophie realized she was staring.

It was just . . . he was so wet. And his shirt was nearly transparent, plastering to the muscles of his arms and chest like a second skin, muscles that definitely merited a second and third glance. Throw in that scar on his cheek and the handsome cut of his jawline . . .

Sophie needed a moment to recover. Perhaps two.

She was woman enough to appreciate the view of a virile man.

It was merely biology, after all.

James cleared his throat at her side, holding out the heavy woolen lap blanket he had brought from the chaise.

Right.

No more awkward staring at the drenched Scottish rake.

More's the pity.

Sophie took the blanket from James and passed it to Rafe.

Then, to discourage her wandering eyes, she turned around and walked back toward the bridge, James at her heels.

The passengers had managed to wheel the stagecoach off the bridge, allowing traffic to flow once more along the road. However, it was obvious that the stagecoach would be going no further. The accident appeared to have cracked the front axle.

"See that Mr. Gordon's valise is loaded onto my carriage," she ordered James. "We'll drop him in the next town."

James darted a glance back at Lord Rafe, his upper body wrapped in the blanket now, coming toward them.

"Are you quite sure, my lady?" he asked, voice low.

"Yes," she replied. "I will say no more on the matter, James. I trust I can rely on your discretion."

James nodded and strode off to collect Rafe's valise, though his pursed mouth communicated his dislike of the idea.

Sophie struggled to care.

She was a widow. Who she traveled with and where she journeyed was no one's business. And she was excessively curious as to why he needed to consult with Dr. Ross. She wanted to see if her theories were true.

She was simply conducting field research. It was science, nothing more.

Besides, given what she knew of a *Rakus lasciviosus* with strong *primus* tendencies, Lord Rafe's opinion on the events of the past thirty minutes would be forthcoming in three, two, one—

"Ye are a wee bit daft to be climbing that tree in such a manner," Lord Rafe hissed, coming to stop beside her, the blanket pulled tight around his upper body. Though wet hair stuck to his forehead, the worst of his shivering appeared to have stopped. "Ye could have been seriously injured attempting a trick like that."

Sophie looked down at her pelisse which was only slightly rumpled from the escapade.

"And yet, I appear to be entirely whole, my lord."

"*Lennon*," he countered. "The name is Lennon Gordon."

"Very well, Mr. Gordon."

A beat.

"I think I would prefer it if ye called me Lennon, lass." He squinted, the motion tugging on his scar.

"That's not going to happen."

"Are ye sure?"

"Very. Speaking of very, you were *very* lucky I recognized your valise and realized what had occurred." She raised an eyebrow, resting a hand on her hip. "And you still have not thanked me. I would have thought a Scot, even a pretend one, would have better manners."

A reluctant smile tugged at his lips.

"Thank ye, Lady Sophie, for rescuing me," he said most gallantly, punctuating the whole with an exquisitely lordly bow, even while holding that blanket around himself. "But ye didnae need to rescue me. Particularly not risking yer wee neck like that. I'm no damsel in distress."

"Are you quite sure you're not a damsel in distress? Because it seems to me that you were *distressingly* marooned on that rock." Sophie shot a pointed look at his bare knees poking out the bottom of his kilt. "And you *are* wearing a skirt."

A long pause.

"Did ye . . ." His gaze narrowed dramatically. He threw his shoulders back, chest out. "Did ye just call my kilt a *skirt?*"

She raised her brow higher and added a smirk. "Why, yes, I do believe I did."

Everything in her tone added, *And what are you going to do about it?*

Lord Rafe took a step closer, forcing her to lift her chin to look him in the eye.

"Scots have started wars over an insult such as that," he said.

"Why does that not surprise me?" She cocked an eyebrow and resisted the urge to pat his cheek. "A kilt is not a skirt, then?"

"Nae." He all but growled at her. "It's called a kilt because we Scots *kilt* the last man who called it a skirt."

Another beat.

"You cannot be serious." She rolled her eyes. "That is honestly the worst pun—"

"Ye dinnae want to fash with a Scot and his kilt, lass." Lord Rafe raised a dark eyebrow and closed the remaining distance between them. She could practically feel the warmth of his breath on her cheek. And how had he recovered his body heat so quickly? The fire of him singed her. "Unless it's a more frolicsome sport ye have in mind . . ."

Ah.

And there he was.

Rakus lasciviosus, always true to form. Quick to flirt. Never sincere.

His words were as brisk as a dowsing in the river flowing at his back. Once a rake, always a rake.

And if part of her had perked up at the thought of 'frolicsome sport,' well, that was simply her wayward biology showing its colors.

Fortunately, she was stronger than mere biology.

So she did not stoop to respond to his innuendo. Instead, she took a step back, forcing herself to meet his eyes.

She wasn't sure what she expected to see. Continued amusement? Mocking irritation?

Instead, she found his eyes . . . thoughtful. Did he regret his words then?

Did *she* regret ordering James to place his valise beside her trunk?

Unbidden, her eyes drifted to that scar running down his cheek.

How had that happened? Was it the result of 'frolicsome sport'? Or something more sinister?

How little she truly knew this surprisingly complicated man.

She glanced beyond him at the incapacitated stagecoach. A local farmer had stopped and several passengers were loading their trunks into his wagon.

He followed her gaze, that same eyebrow going up, likely at the thought of hours jolting beside turnips.

Fortunately for him, *spite* was not one of her personal shortcomings.

Blunt frankness, however, was.

And so she said, "Someone recently commented on my over-eagerness to rescue pathetic things. Even those that resemble half-drowned felines."

She dragged her eyes up and down his wet, dripping body, mostly to be annoying, but also because . . . *wet, dripping body*.

She walked around him, shooting a glance his way. "Your trunk is already on my chaise, Mr. Gordon. We'll deposit you at the next coaching inn."

She walked away, making no attempt to mask the smug look on her face.

14

Fifteen minutes and a change of kilt later, Rafe found himself heading north again in the *one* place he truly should not be—

Traveling with Lady Sophie.

They sat side-by-side in the chaise, the solitary seat only accommodating two. Martha, her ladyship's maid, had been all too eager to sit outside with the handsome James.

Mainfeld had certainly lent Lady Sophie a carriage fit for an earl. The wheels were so well-sprung, the seat barely jostled along the rutted road, the cushions so stuffed, Rafe seemed to be floating upon pillows.

He could have said, *No*, and declined her offer, piled himself atop the turnips, and carried onward alone.

But Rafe had several years of his life shaved off between being shot at, half-drowning in the frigid river, and then watching Sophie inch down that branch as it dipped closer and closer. If the branch had broken and sent her tumbling into the churning water . . .

And so the thought of her journeying northward while there were highwaymen about had set him climbing out of his skin—

"How concerned should I be over those highwaymen?" Lady Sophie asked. "Are they likely to attack again today?"

Was the lady now reading minds, as well?

"The fact that highwaymen attacked us at all is . . . unnerving," he said. "Not to mention, puzzling."

"Unnerving, I can understand. By why puzzling?" she asked. "You yourself said that it was a possibility when I began this journey."

True.

And yet . . .

"The fact of highwaymen, yes. However, highwaymen rarely attack a full stagecoach in broad daylight along a rather busy stretch of road."

"Ah." She tapped her lips. "That is . . . puzzling."

"Precisely."

A moment of silence. The harness jangled. The chaise rocked to and fro over the bumpy road.

Rafe considered the highwaymen, mentally reviewing the attack. No one had been seriously injured, none of the brigands' shots finding a target. Which meant the highwaymen had either been desperate, unskilled, and green to the business. Or the 'attack' had been for a different purpose entirely.

But what?

Could it be tied to the letter he received? Someone clearly did not appreciate that he currently breathed. But surely there were easier ways to dispatch him than accosting a public stagecoach along a busy stretch of highway.

Besides, aside from Lady Sophie, who knew that he was traveling as Lennon Gordon? He employed the Scottish disguise from time to time, but it was not well-known. Tracking him in this situation would be unlikely (which was precisely why he used it).

But his scar *did* make him more recognizable, so Rafe struggled to dismiss the idea out of hand.

Sophie darted a glance at him. "My intuition tells me that you have an idea as to why the highwaymen attacked the stagecoach."

What the he—?!

How did she sense his thoughts so clearly?

"Are ye sure ye are not part fey?" The words tumbled out before he could stop them.

"Fey? As in a sorceress?" She did not miss a beat. "What is the precise genus and species for that?"

He grinned.

Oh, but he had missed this woman.

"*Femina maga?*" he offered.

"Clever." She nodded. "But . . . you haven't yet answered my question."

Mmmmm. She was tenacious, he supposed.

Rafe frowned before giving the only answer he could: "I honestly dinnae know, lass. As a scientist, I dinnae have enough evidence to estimate the likelihood of another attack."

She gave a soft half-snort, half-sigh in reply.

They rode in silence for a while, both watching the postillion as he slowed the horses to skirt a rather large series of ruts in the road.

A town came into view up ahead.

"What will you do once I deposit you at the coaching inn?" Lady Sophie asked.

"Wait for the next stagecoach, I ken." He scrubbed a hand over his chin.

"Mmmm."

Yes, Rafe would bid her adieu and wait for another stagecoach north. That was the sensible choice. Wise. Safe.

Well, safer for him.

But what about Lady Sophie? a part of him whispered. *How would she be safest?*

He kicked back the words, but just the thought of letting her out of his sight had sent his blood racing and caused panic to settle in his gut.

There are highwaymen about. She could be hurt, that same voice whispered. *Perhaps you should offer to accompany her to Edinburgh?*

He suppressed a grunt and looked out the window.

Traveling with her would be . . .

A sort of glossy haze descended over his mind, and he saw their excursion in brilliant color. Spending hours . . . *days* . . . in her company, listening to the quirky ramblings of her scientific mind, basking in the lilt of her laughter, watching her nibble that bottom lip over and over—

Whoa.

Yes, traveling with Lady Sophie would be a very bad idea.

And yet his mind had seized on it with an almost maniacal frenzy, lunging at the opportunity like a slavering dog.

No. I cannot seriously be contemplating this—

But his mind, so eager to spend time with her, conjured up reason after reason to justify the decision.

Why not travel with her, ensure she arrives safely? You are far enough from London now—the risk of recognition low—so word is unlikely to reach Kendall.

Moreover, she is a widow. The rules of propriety are not as stringent for her. You can simply tell everyone that you are cousins.

Besides, your father will see you married off to someone else soon enough. You should enjoy her company one final time.

And who knows? Maybe spending more time with her will cure you of this ridiculous obsession once and for all.

Mmmm.

Those were all excellent points.

Without consciously making the decision, his mouth decided to act of its own will.

"Lady Sophie," he began.

She turned, those clear green eyes drilling into him. Her eyebrows raised, and she surveyed him from head-to-toe.

"I believe I know that look," she said.

"Pardon? What look?" He shook his head.

"The look that says you're going to ask to accompany me to Edinburgh."

Huh.

She truly *was* reading minds now.

Rafe shrugged, not denying it. "Well, it isnae an entirely dreadful idea, ye must admit."

"It is a fairly dreadful idea."

"No. Not really. Ye are going to Edinburgh. I am going to Edinburgh. As the events of this afternoon prove, I am clearly not safe on my own."

She rolled her eyes.

He grinned. "Ye just told me not an hour hence that ye have a habit of rescuing pathetic things." He pointed to his bedraggled, still-wet hair. "Am I not pathetic enough for ye?"

She continued to stare at him, brows drawn down.

"I will be your humble Scottish cousin,"—he pressed a hand over his heart—"accompanying ye to visit relatives in Edinburgh."

"Lord Rafe—"

"Lennon, lass. Cousin Lennon."

She sent her gaze skyward, as if pleading for patience.

He grinned wider. He knew when he was getting to a lady. "I promise I'll be no bother. I'll keep to myself, not pester ye."

"Don't make promises you cannot keep."

"I'll keep this promise." He crossed his heart. "I'll leave ye in peace."

Lady Sophie pursed her lips and then sighed. A deep, long-suffering sigh.

"I suppose it does make some sense. I have space in my carriage." She looked around the plush interior. "There are known highwaymen about. And it is unlikely that we will encounter anyone from London. And even if we did, your disguise is most effective." She said the words almost grudgingly. "No one would recognize you if they weren't specifically looking for you."

"Do ye truly think so?"

"Oh aye, laddie."

Wait . . .

Had she just *mocked* his accent?

The cheeky minx.

She continued on, nearly making his case for him. "And unlike your father, *my* servants are excessively discreet."

"They are?"

"You forget who my mother is," she replied. "My father only retains servants who are utterly loyal."

"Very well, Lady Sophie, ye've convinced me." He let out a gusty sigh, as if this had been her idea from the beginning. "I will accompany ye to Edinburgh."

She laughed and rolled her eyes. Was it his imagination, or did Lady Sophie relax at the thought?

"Very well." He could hear the smile in her voice. "I think we should push on today and into the evening hours. If we manage to cover another forty miles before tucking into an inn for the night, we should be able to reach York by tomorrow afternoon."

SIX HOURS LATER, Rafe had begun to have some regrets.

The sun had just set, wrapping a cocoon of inky blackness around them, a hushed sort of privacy, as if they were vastly alone. Carriage blankets kept the autumn chill at bay.

Worse, he should have thought through how sitting next to Lady Sophie for hours on end in a rocking carriage would stoke, not diminish, his attraction to her. Every jolt and bump rocked the soft curves of her body against him and sent another waft of her rose scent his way.

He was an utter *eejit*.

How had he thought this situation would assuage his ardor?

Lady Sophie herself was no help in that regard. She had spent the passing hours asking questions about his natural science studies. They talked easily, jumping from topic to topic, ideas flowing effortlessly. She spoke of her clowder of feral barn cats and her theories on their behavior. Rafe described his finds in the New Hebrides and his research ideas.

This was the Lady Sophie of his memory, the woman who delighted him with her unexpected comments, with her ability to always be three thoughts ahead of him.

He couldn't remember a time when he had enjoyed someone's company more.

What had he said to her at the inn the other day?

I might take tae calling ye my bird.

It was an absurd thought. *Bird* was Scottish cant for sweetheart. A lass became your *bird* when courting and then your *hen* once married—

He took a slow breath.

He needed to cease these runaway thoughts. Lady Sophie could never be his bird. Too much was at stake.

As the carriage rocked through yet another sleepy village, he almost thought Lady Sophie asleep, but then she stirred, a soft sigh escaping.

"Are you awake?" she asked.

"Aye." His frayed nerves were far too agitated for sleep.

The carriage swayed over a bump, harnesses jangling. They had changed horses nearly two hours ago, the carriage pulling into an inn coach yard and grooms swapping out the team.

They rode in silence for a moment.

"Lord Rafe—"

"Lennon, lass."

Was it his imagination, or did she heave a sigh?

"Do you like playing the Scot?" She waved a hand in the dim light. "It is only us two in the carriage, and yet you still maintain this Highlander act with the accent and . . . everything. You inhabit the role so thoroughly, it seems innate."

Huh.

That was . . . discerning.

"I *do* think of myself as Scottish," he murmured, his accent sliding from a broad brogue to a more aristocratic burr. His mother's Ayrshire accent, he supposed. "I ken more tae my mother's folk."

The ever-present loathing of his father reared up. Rafe detested that he heard his father's voice in his own clipped aristocratic English accent.

Though he knew his affinity for Scotland was more than simply a rejection of his father's English heritage.

Rafe *felt* Scottish. As if all the thick Gaelic blood that ran in his mother's veins had transferred itself straight to him. He loved the smell of haggis, hot and steaming from the oven. The sound of the bagpipes stirred his soul. And, oddly, the bite of a brisk ocean wind would always say *home* to his heart.

It was no surprise that he had chosen to attend university at St. Andrews in Fife. Or that all those he counted as close friends were Scottish.

"Do you think it inevitable that you would become a rake?" Her random question broke through his musings.

As usual, her mind made leaps and connections that left him grasping.

"Pardon?"

"You being a rake. Was it inevitable from the beginning? You are named Rafe, after all."

"Lennon, lass. It's Lennon, remember?"

He could practically hear her eyes rolling.

"Rafe is only one letter off of *rake*," she continued, undeterred. "Have you ever considered that your mind may have unconsciously substituted the second consonant at some point?"

"That isn't how raking starts, I'm afraid."

"Are you sure?"

"Quite."

Silence.

"Raking isn't a matter of vocabulary," he clarified.

"Mmmm. I am not entirely convinced."

Rafe snorted. "Actions are not tied tae a label. Taxonomy alone doesn't determine behavior. A wolf is a wolf no matter what word we use tae describe the animal. The name alone doesn't call up its form. How did Shakespeare phrase it? *What's in a name? That which we call a rose by any other name would smell as sweet*," he quoted.

"Perhaps, but we aren't discussing tangibles like those of genus *Rosa*. We are contemplating malleables, like behavior. You grew up listening to a Scottish mother, and so you think of yourself as Scottish. You hear your name, Rafe, and think of raking—"

"We label the behavior when it arises, not the other way around," he countered.

"Yes, at times. But that is not always the case. If a friend or parent repeatedly calls you a dunce, at what point do you begin to believe it, despite the label's lack of veracity?"

This woman. *Why* did she have to be so clever?

He was supposed to be discovering her faults here, not falling deeper in love.

"So if enough people called me a rake," he said, following the trail of her logic, "eventually I would adopt the behaviors of one, regardless of my own inclinations?"

"The idea has merit, I think."

It did, indeed. She was closer to the truth than she could ever know.

"Or," she continued, "if you label yourself as Scottish in your head, you will eventually come to believe it. Taxonomy can call forth behavior in the end."

The low husk of her voice wrapped around him in the silken darkness. He valiantly pushed away the thought that compared it to a lover's caress.

"You have a distinct fondness for taxonomy," he said.

A moment's pause. And then—

"I like certainty. I appreciate logic and rational thought."

"Why is that, lass?"

A longer pause.

"It creates order out of chaos. It gives things a place, a space where they are wanted."

"Ah. And that is important tae ye?"

More silence.

Rafe almost thought she had fallen asleep, but then she shifted again, her skirts rubbing against his bare knee and sending heat through his body. Bloody kilts, leaving skin exposed.

"*What's in a name?*" she repeated his quote from earlier. "Scottish isn't necessarily a negative label—"

"It is tae some," he snorted.

"Oh, perhaps. But with the popularity of Walter Scott's works and his recovery of the Scottish Honors last year, public opinion about what it means to be Scottish is rapidly changing. I doubt anyone has ever disparaged you because of your mother's heritage."

"Lady Sophie—"

"People have many names for *my* mother, none of which are as complimentary. Shall I list the ones some have said to my face?"

Rafe's breath snagged in his chest.

"*Adulteress*," she said, ever so matter-of-factly, as if reciting a shopping list. "*Wanton, light skirt*, even *whore* on occasion."

"Lass—"

"No, I don't need or want the pity tinging your tone. I know who and what I am. Rakish behavior isn't only limited to men, obviously. Woman can be philanderers, too. We just use harsher words to describe them. I know I will spend my life paying for my mother's sins."

That ache in his chest grew, engulfing his heart.

This woman and her candor.

He wanted to say—

I do not judge you.

You will always have a safe-haven in me.

But the chaise rolled into a sleepy hamlet, and all further discussion was left off in favor of a warm meal and bed chambers at a local inn.

15

Sophie awoke with a horrific crick in her neck from leaning against the side of the carriage. She hadn't slept well the night before, thoughts of Lord Rafe and the emotions he stirred had kept her awake. So it was no surprise when the carriage rocked her to sleep by mid-morning.

The coach was rolling through another bustling town, shopkeepers hawking their wares.

"We'll stop here to change horses and eat a quick luncheon." Lord Rafe consulted the watch he had stowed in his coat pocket. He wore a different plaid today—this one a red ground shot with yellow—but it still wrapped around his hips and crossed his upper body. "We'll make York by late afternoon."

His voice was low and warm, enveloping her weakened senses. Their conversations the afternoon and evening before had left her . . . confused. Lord Rafe's genuine interest and perceptive questions had begun chipping away at her 'No Rakes Permitted!' resolve.

Traveling together was surely a mistake. She liked the man too much for her own peace of mind.

The coach rumbled through a red brick arch and into the coaching yard of a large inn. Passengers bustled about.

Sophie nearly stumbled when Lord Rafe handed her down from the chaise. Her legs and back ached. Odd that one's muscles could ache just as much from complete disuse as from being thoroughly abused.

Regardless, after a quick visit to the necessary, she joined Lord Rafe and Martha in the crowded dining room, as there was no private parlor to be had.

A maid came by and took their order for bacon rolls, ale, and tea. But people continued to pour into the dining room. Eventually, a Mr. and Miss Johnson, brother and sister on their way north, asked if they could share the table.

Lord Rafe, of course, smiled affably and readily agreed.

Mr. Johnson's daring violet-and-yellow waistcoat and Miss Johnson's overly-beribboned bonnet fought for Sophie's attention. The Johnsons clearly had *aspirations*.

Miss Johnson was young and pretty with china-blue eyes and golden hair and was likely as irresistible as catnip to a *Rakus lasciviosus* like Lord Rafe—or Lennon Gordon, as he introduced himself.

Lord Rafe's eyes certainly appeared to linger on Miss Johnson. Was it the lady herself or her rather garish bonnet that snagged his attention?

That question was soon put to rest.

While they all waited for their luncheon, Lord Rafe flirted outrageously with Miss Johnson. Naturally, Miss Johnson—like most woman who were young and pretty and knew it—flirted in return.

Sophie watched it all in stony silence. She could only presume that, upon finding himself thrown into his natural habitat—attractive woman, public setting—Lord Rafe behaved on instinct.

In other words, Lord Rafe was simply being himself.

She would never dream of feeling anger over an animal acting on its biological proclivities. It was a natural phenomenon—perhaps an even uncontrollable reflex—like a sheepdog chasing anything that runs, or a cat purring when petted.

Why should a *Rakus lasciviosus* be any different?

But her heart remembered that ball so many years ago. His fawning attention and then . . . nothing.

She had foolishly assumed that his request to travel with her and their like-minded conversation had somehow altered the nature of their relationship. That maybe, like herself, Lord Rafe had changed.

But as she watched him grin at Miss Johnson, giving his standard raised-eyebrows-and-tilted-head lure, Sophie feared she had been mistaken.

Once a rake, always a rake.

"The Scottish attire is most daring," Miss Johnson breathed to Lord Rafe, shooting him a demure look through her lashes.

"Thank ye." He winked at her. "We Scots are a daring lot."

"I say," Mr. Johnson frowned, the man's opinion on Scots and Scotland fairly obvious.

"The articles of clothing you wear, do they have unique, Scottish names?" Miss Johnson asked, her voice ridiculously breathy.

Sophie longed to roll her eyes. How could Lord Rafe be lured in by such obvious behavior?

"Of a surety, lass. Great kilt," he said, plucking at the tartan swaddling his hips and chest. "*Sgian dubh*." He pulled the knife from its sheath in his garters. "*Ghillies*." He lifted a foot, indicating his shoes. "Bonnet." He pointed to his hat.

Miss Johnson watched him with rapt attention.

"Charm," he continued, pointing to his cheeks. "Handsome." He fluttered his eyelashes. "Manly." He flexed an arm.

Miss Johnson giggled, a grating titter of sound.

Sophie longed to elbow *Lennon* into silence.

Instead, she bit her lip.

Not *once* had Lord Rafe flirted so blatantly with her. Not in the previous twenty-four hours. Not even on that magical evening so long ago.

How many years had she endured similar behavior from Jack? When courting her, he had been attentive and sedate, a perfect gentleman.

But it had been nothing more than an act. As soon as they were married, he ceased his attentions.

Jack had never respected his wedding vows. Her husband had lost interest in her as a woman shortly after their marriage. He claimed to be disappointed that Sophie, the daughter of a profligate adulteress, was not a skilled courtesan. Why Jack had assumed she would be, Sophie could not fathom. She had been as sheltered as any other virginal daughter of an earl.

So naturally Jack had found her shy and inexperienced in their marriage bed. And after that first month, he had declined to exercise his marital rights at all, preferring instead the company of more 'seasoned' women.

Sophie had been hurt and confused.

On the one hand, she was relieved to not be burdened with Jack's physical demands. She was just as disillusioned with his behavior as he was with hers.

But, on the other hand, Sophie was painfully aware that not even her own *husband* found her desirable. That the one person who had pledged to love and honor her above all else . . . considered her little more than an onerous acquaintance.

Instead, he would flirt outrageously with other women—usually right in front of Sophie—and then turn back to her, expression bland, as if nothing had happened. Worse, he would become aggravated with *her* if Sophie took umbrage at his behavior.

Sophie swallowed back the bitterness that threatened to swamp her.

Enough.

Enough of Jack.

Do not give that man any more of yourself.

Yes . . . she wanted to be wanted.

But that had nothing, really, to do with Lord Rafe. She and he were naught more than traveling companions. He could flirt with whomever he pleased.

Even if his current behavior did make her want to hiss at him like an angry barn cat.

As if reading Sophie's mind, *Mr.* Johnson reacted to Rafe's overly-flirtatious manner with a low growl. The man shot Rafe a deadly look before taking Miss Johnson's hand possessively in his own.

That was the point at which Sophie realized that Mr. and Miss Johnson were not, in fact, brother and sister but were more likely a couple eloping to Scotland.

Given the way that Lord Rafe looked at their clasped hands, he likely realized the same. To his credit, *Lennon* tamped down his flirtation once their luncheon arrived.

But for Sophie, the entire experience had been a much-needed physic—a timely reminder of the ways of a *Rakus* and why she never intended to become involved with one again.

Once had been enough for a lifetime.

SEVERAL HOURS LATER, Sophie was mentally and physically exhausted. The chaise rolled through the streets of York, passing under archways and through medieval gates before coming to a stop in the galleried stable yard of The George Inn in St. Helen's Square.

All she wanted was warm food, a warmer fire, a clean bed, and a complete lack of handsome, charming Scots.

After his luncheon flirtation, Lord Rafe had reverted back to his affable self with her. Charming but not overtly flirtatious. Solicitous but hardly amorous. Essentially, treating her more as a colleague than a woman he found desirable.

The man was merely adhering to the set of instinctual behaviors—when faced with a beautiful woman, a *Rakus lasciviosus* will flirt. Biological fact.

But the poultice of logic refused to take the sting out of his behavior.

As the carriage rolled to a stop, she considered telling Rafe that she would carry on without him. Perhaps it would best for them to go their separate ways in the morning?

This was intended to be a journey of healing and rebirth Not one of confused emotions and unfulfilled expectations.

To that end, Sophie left the men to deal with the chaise and horses, collected Martha, and entered the inn, ordering rooms for herself and her servants.

Lord Rafe could see to himself, could he not?

The George was a traditional galleried inn, with rooms running around the upper floors surrounding the coaching yard, the doors reached by a cantilevered wooden gallery. It appeared that other galleries branched off the main one, leading to a seeming rabbit-warren of chambers.

A chatty maid led Sophie and Martha up the gallery staircase, along the main balcony with the din of the coach yard below, through a side arch, and up another flight of wooden stairs to a second, smaller gallery that surrounded an ancient courtyard before stopping before their door.

The maid curtsied and left to have the ostler deliver Sophie's trunk. Sophie opened the door, finding a small but tidy sitting room, a fire already lit in the grate. On one side of the room, two chairs rested before the fire; a small round dining table and chairs sat on the other. A door to the bedchamber proper beckoned to the left, the room holding a double bed and smaller cot for Martha.

All of it blessedly *Rakus* free.

Sophie untied her bonnet and stripped off her gloves, stretching her sore muscles. The aches and twinges in her back were merely the last indignity of the day.

"I think I would give just about anything for a warm bath," Sophie smiled wanly.

"Let me ask for you, miss," Martha said, turning for the door. "I reckon they are used to such requests around here."

Martha was true to her word.

After eating a leisurely dinner in the sitting room, maids brought in a large hip bath, placing it before the fire in the bedroom proper, and then filled it with bucket after bucket of hot water. Sophie quickly disrobed, eager to wash away the grime of coach travel.

She moaned when the warm water hit her skin, sinking low in the luxurious heat. She could practically see the tension seeping from her body into the bathwater. Who cared about the biological impulses of a *Rakus* when there was a hot bath to be had?

She leisurely scrubbed her skin with a rough cloth and soap, the popping fire helping the water retain its heat.

The entire experience felt so glorious, Sophie insisted Martha use the water after her, as it was still warm. The maid bathed and collapsed onto her cot in exhaustion, her soft snores filling the small bedchamber.

Despite the long day, a restless sort of agitation gripped Sophie. She donned a dressing gown and left Martha to the bedroom. Lord Rafe's behavior kept racing through her brain, his flirtatious smiles and charming voice, all for women other than her.

Sitting before the fire in the sitting room, Sophie brushed her hair, section by section, meticulously working through the mass of it.

Part of her hated that she found Lord Rafe so attractive. How could she still want that which had been so harmful in the past? Hadn't Jack inoculated her against that very thing?

Why did she have such a sweet tooth for rakes? Was it a biological inevitability, given her mother's own susceptibility? Was Sophie like a drunkard, incapable of resisting the siren call of the bottle even as it destroyed her?

That was *not* a pleasant thought.

Should she part ways with Lord Rafe tomorrow? It would likely be for the best, would it not?

She had thought herself emotionally strong, but Rafe's hot-and-cold behavior had reopened old wounds.

Vividly, she remembered the aftermath of Jack's death. How the pain and anger of all she had endured as his wife ate at her very soul. A deep melancholic rage had stolen over her. She found herself, day after day, simply staring out the window, often unequal to the task of dressing or even feeding herself. And when she did leave her room, it was to roam the family estate in Surrey, walking aimlessly for hours on end, replaying scenes from her marriage over and over in her head.

In retrospect, she realized she had lost a rather alarming amount of weight. Her mother had the cook send up Sophie's favorite foods to tempt her. And Sophie did try, she *did*. It was just . . . everything felt so empty and bleak. She was simply so furious at Jack, at everything that had transpired, at life in general.

And then, one day, about three months after Jack's death, Sophie had returned to her room after a long ramble to find a closed basket on her bed. The basket hissed and rocked as she approached, a low *roawr* cutting through the room.

Was there a . . . *cat* in the basket? And . . . *why?*

A note was attached, the foolscap flicking back and forth with each shake of the basket.

Dearest Poppet,

The primus tomcat stole a ride from Yorkshire in my carriage, the rascal. I fear he has abandoned his clowder at the estate. Can you suggest a solution for him? You are always full of excellent scientific ideas.

Your father, Lord M.

Sophie looked between the note and the basket. The *primus* was here? From Yorkshire?

And somehow, *this* was the event that pushed her over the edge, the point at which she had fully acknowledged all that she had lost.

All that Jack had taken from her.

She had collapsed onto her bed, weeping so hysterically she feared her sobs would suffocate her. How could she have forgotten about her studies? How could she have so thoroughly lost herself? The poor tomcat, still in his basket, meowed and *roawred* right along with her.

Once her crying fit subsided (and it had taken *hours*), she felt as if some enormous weight had finally—finally, at last!—been lifted.

The beginnings of her rebirth, in truth.

She might have lost herself while married to Jack, but she did not need to *remain* lost. She could, and *would*, reclaim her sense of self.

Jack would get no more of her. Never again.

Of course, the primus tomcat had been far too feral to keep as a house pet. But after setting it free to find the clowder in the stables, she had rung for her maid, dressed, and joined her family for dinner. Lord Mainfeld had smiled enormously when she entered the drawing room.

The memory of it still made her weepy.

But none of this helped her to know what to do with Lord Rafe now.

She recognized that his push-and-pull behavior rattled the equanimity she had won after Jack's death, picking open old wounds that she had thought healed.

She shook her head, taking in deep, fortifying breaths, centering her mind, reaching for that peaceful state she had fought to achieve.

Reason through it, Sophie. Be logical.

Setting aside her brush, she began plaiting the heavy mass of her hair into a long braid.

Logically, Sophie knew she should not punish Lord Rafe for another man's sins. He was not Jack. He had not made vows to her before God and man; he had no obligation to uphold where she was concerned.

But did she wish to continue onward with him? To fight the emotions that Lord Rafe brought to the surface—

Thum-thum-thump!

Footsteps abruptly sounded outside the door.

She turned toward the noise. The door handle rattled, jostling the latch.

Surely Martha had locked the door? Right?

Sophie dropped her hair, mid-plait, and surged to her feet, noticing that Martha had *not* locked the door—

A large figure burst into the room, shutting the door quickly behind him.

Sophie lunged for the fireplace poker, a scream in her throat.

Finally . . . her brain caught up, pointing out the man's swirling kilt, familiar shoulders, and dark hair.

Her scream died as she, yet again, recognized Lord Rafe.

He stood with his back to the door, eyes wide, palms pressed flat on the wood behind him.

Sophie considered herself a level-headed person.

But—

"Why are you in here?" she hissed, setting the fire poker down and pulling her dressing gown tighter across her chest.

Though he still sported his kilt and ghillies, his cravat was decidedly looser, and he had removed his bonnet altogether. Unwillingly, Sophie noted his hair was deliciously rumpled and the heady scent of sandalwood had whirled into the room with him.

Sophie gritted her teeth.

You will not find him attractive.

You will cease this stupidity at once.

She huffed, "You cannot simply burst into my room. This is ridiculous."

"Yes," was all he replied. He leaned back against the door, his head turned as if listening to something in the hallway.

Honestly.

He rotated to look at her, his eyes *finally* bringing her into clear focus.

And look at her he did, gaze running over her figure before finally turning away, as if he were . . . *shy?*

Sophie blinkingly took in that thought.

Shy?

Truly?

Lord Rafe?

That seemed almost . . . impossible.

He was likely a connoisseur of situations like this—a woman in half-dress, warm firelight, a dark night.

And yet . . .

Was the man now *blushing?!*

It was difficult to tell for sure, what with the warm firelight, dark night, and her current state of half-dress.

And still he said nothing.

"Truthfully, *Lennon.*" She leaned on his false name. "Why are you here?"

"I know I promised yesterday tae not be a bother . . ." He paused, bringing his gaze back to her before taking a step into the room.

Just having him here in her private chambers sent her senses tumbling into forbidden paths. How many years had she ached for this man?

But then he spoke again—*thank goodness!*—breaking the spell.

"I require the opinion of a beautiful woman," he said.

Sophie's mind, quite literally, blanked.

What—

Beautiful woman?!

But . . .

Had he truly just said that—

Was he finally *flirting* with her?

After everything else today?!!

Blind rage flooded her mental vacuum.

"Opinion? Beautiful woman?!" She enunciated each word with exacting precision.

His eye shot wide. He was no stranger to that female tone of voice. No surprise there.

"Aye, there's something ye need to kno—"

"How dare you!?" she nearly shouted, advancing on him, jabbing a finger. "How dare you treat me like this!"

"Sophie—" he began, taking a step toward her, glancing anxiously at the door.

"I have *not* given you leave to use my proper name, sirrah!" She took a step closer and jabbed her finger into his shoulder. A seemingly muscular, hard shoulder. She maybe jabbed it again, just to be sure. She steadfastly refused to be impressed.

"Hush!"

"I will not be silent!" *Jab, jab.* "Time and again, you ignore me when others are about, but the second you have no witnesses, I am suddenly a beautiful woman who you long to be *mmmph, mmmph*."

Sophie's voice drifted into muffled mumbles as Lord Rafe wrapped one hand around her waist and the other over her mouth.

Hand. Waist. Mouth.

Him!

Shock froze her in his arms.

The sheer astonishment of being drawn flush against his larger frame, the heat of his hands pressing against her, his intoxicating male smell at such close range.

The *outrage* that he would dare touch her person—

Rakus lasciviosus, indeed.

"Please, ye must be quiet," he hissed in her ear.

"Let me go, you arse-headed rakehell!" Sophie snapped in return.

But as Lord Rafe still had his hand firmly over her mouth, the words were less emphatic and more, "*Mmmph mmmph ma grrmph.*"

Finally, Sophie's thinking brain informed the rest of her body that, as delicious as it felt being held in Lord Rafe's arms, she was not *that* sort of woman.

She wriggled, digging an elbow into his ribs, causing him to release her with an annoyed *oomph*.

"This is ridiculous!" she whisper-hissed.

"Of course, it's ridiculous!" he whispered back. "I haven't been ignoring ye."

"*Pardon?!*" Sophie all but screeched.

"Shhhh." He stepped forward, as if to wrap a hand around her mouth again.

Sophie danced out of his reach.

"You most certainly have been ignoring me!" she continued in a quieter voice. "You flirt and charm and work your *Rakus* wiles on anything in a skirt—like earlier today with Miss Johnson over lunch—and then, when you are alone with me, it's like a tap. Shut off."

He paused, as if something in her words confused him.

"Are ye saying you *want* me tae flirt with ye?"

Sophie suppressed a scream. "*That* is what you gleaned from my words just now?"

"Well, it is a logical conclusion—"

"Consistency, my lord. I am asking for *consistency* in your behavior toward me. I have spent my entire life feeling like a nuisance. An unwanted obligation. Daughter of a whore, remember?" She lifted her hand, wiggling her fingers.

His shoulders sagged. "Oh, Sophie—"

"I don't require your pity, my lord. But I would love for a man to decide that I am worth his full attention, regardless of who else might be in the room."

That stopped him short. "Oh."

"Yes. *Oh*."

"I— Well—" He stopped, frowned, and then ran an agitated hand through his hair, still glancing at the door, before speaking lowly. "I am sorry if my actions confused ye or caused ye pain in any way. I was simply trying tae remain in character as Lennon Gordon, as the man does have a reputation tae uphold. I clearly behaved without thinking—"

"I am hardly that naive, my lord." She rolled her eyes. "Spare me your protestations—"

"'Tis the truth! And it's a good thing I have been behaving like this as I just saw Lady Lilith walking along the gallery."

"Pardon?! Lady *Lilith*?!"

"Yes. Hush." He stepped closer, holding a hand out as if to silence her again. "Ye must be quiet. You'll give us away."

"Are you sure it was her?"

"Yes. Most sure."

"Why is she here?"

"How should I know? That's why I needed your opinion."

"*My* opinion? You're a rake. Rakes know things like this."

His look was one-part aggravation and three-parts long suffering.

"Perhaps she has relatives in York? Honestly, it doesn't matter why she's here. The larger concern is if she finds *us* together . . ."

Oh, for the love of—

Sophie wanted to pound her head against the wall.

Could some divine being please save her from idiotic men?

"Lady Lilith finding us together only became a problem once you *entered my private chambers*!"

He paused, blinking.

"Exactly." Sophie continued in a low whisper, agreeing with his stunned expression. "Did you believe my chamber door to be a substitute for a convenient curtain, allowing you to hide from an unwanted paramour?"

He made a strangled sound.

"Honestly," she continued, tone biting and unrelenting, "for someone who is supposedly so knowledgeable about women and raking, you make a muck of it with alarming frequency."

16

Rafe stood still as Sophie continued to rage.

Did she mean what she had just said? The words continued to pound through him:

I have spent my entire life feeling like a nuisance. An unwanted obligation.

I would love for a man to decide that I am worth his full attention, regardless of who else might be in the room.

His heart sank. He *had* contributed to her feeling like this. Earlier with Miss Johnson, certainly at that ball four years ago, and then just now . . .

He had glimpsed Lady Lilith walking along the outer gallery and, to put it bluntly, he had panicked.

No one could know he was traveling with Sophie. If word got back to his father . . .

He swallowed his anger, breathing slowly through the habitual rage that flared whenever he thought about his sire.

Though she was correct:

He should *not* be in her private chambers, facing an irate Sophie in a dressing gown with her hair unraveling from a thick plait, every gentlemanly sense he possessed ordering him to leave *righthisinstant*.

But he was struggling to do so. The soft firelight bathed Sophie in luminous light, glinting gold in her dark hair.

Holding her against him had been ill-advised, as now he could think of nothing else.

Don't imagine holding her.
Don't ponder how right she feels in your arms.

Oblivious, she continued to berate him, her voice a hissing whisper of sound. "All you had to do is turn the other direction and walk away. From behind, Lady Lilith would have suspected nothing. Instead, you come in here, risking everything!"

Rafe figured now was not the time to mention how fetching Sophie looked when in a high dudgeon. He knew he needed to answer her. But his eyes were bewitched by a solitary curl that had escaped her braid and drifted down the side of her throat.

Heavens above, she was beautiful.

A long silence ensued. Rafe struggled for an answer, but that curl seemed to have stolen his thoughts.

"Honestly, it's as if you don't know how to manage a clandestine arrangement," she went on. "For someone with your rakish reputation, you are really quite terrible at this."

That got his attention. "I didn't have time to think it all through. I just reacted."

"You just reacted?" she parroted, crossing her arms, brows drawing down. "*This* is your definition of reaction? Doing the one thing you should not? I had assumed that your raking behavior would be more instinctual."

Rafe looked up at her, dragging fingers through his hair. "Instinctual? How can raking—" *Not a verb! Grrr.* "—*being* a rake be considered instinctual?"

"What we are inhabits our very beings. You forget I have observed feral tomcats at length—"

"The barn cats again?"

"Yes, barn cats! As wild animals, they react entirely on instinct. When the *primus* tomcat encountered a problem, he behaved without hesitation—"

"Lady Sophie—"

"—but you hesitate endlessly. In fact, the more I ponder this, I see that you pursue a woman and then pull back at the last moment. Or, like this evening, you dodge a conflict in the worst way possible." A long pause. "Your heart isn't in the raking business, my lord. You lack a passion for it."

"A passion for raking? Do ye even hear yourself?"

"It is as if you want others to perceive you as being a rake, when you are, in fact, nothing of the sort."

Rafe flinched, head rearing back, his tongue sticking in his throat.

Her words had struck unerringly true.

A condemning silence filled the room.

And of course, Sophie being Sophie, she did not miss his reaction.

"Ooooohhhhh!" Her eyes went wide, mouth a perfect 'O' of surprise. "Ooooooh!!!" she repeated, her voice raising.

Rafe took a quick step forward, hand out. "Hush. Please."

His actions did nothing to dampen her enthusiasm.

"Is this actually true, what I'm thinking?" she breathed.

"I don't know what ye are thinking."

"Yes, you do."

"No, I don't."

He did know. He simply wished it left unsaid.

Don't say it. Don't say it.

"You are not actually a rake."

She said it.

That same condemning silence returned.

He could not deny it.

Her mouth formed another perfect 'O.' He refused to contemplate exactly how kissable her lips appeared at the moment.

"It's true. You are a gentleman in rake disguise. A *Rakus falsus*." She nearly bounced on her tiptoes.

Why this news was so exciting, Rafe could scarcely understand.

All her anger and frustration seemed forgotten. Abruptly, she was the Sophie of his memory—the wide-eyed innocent in her first Season, full of optimism and cheery glee.

She clasped her hands together, holding them at her chest. It was the expression his sister adopted when viewing a particularly cute puppy or an adorable child toddling about.

Not a pretend rake-shame.

"You are like a *Colubridae dipsadinae*, a hognose snake," she continued. "You raise your head and flair your cheeks like a venomous cobra, but in actuality, you are utterly harmless."

Sophie smiled. Rafe found himself lost in it for a moment.

Now she'd done it. In less than thirty seconds, she had become that amusing, quirky woman he had loved.

That he *still* loved, if he were honest.

Damn and blast.

This was *not* how things were supposed to go.

"I am hardly harmless, madam." He stalked toward her, gaze intent.

If he thought his behavior would startle her, he was sorely mistaken. Instead, her eyes merely gleamed brighter, fascination dancing within.

"Oh, that's very good. With the lean, the slow smolder, the heated look . . . incredibly effective." She pressed a hand to her chest. "I feel breathless and terrified and yet so utterly thrilled. Absolutely fascinating. I must write this down."

She darted past him, reaching for a notebook and pencil on the table, making notes.

This was . . . ridiculous.

Rafe stood, feet shuffling, glancing toward the door, feeling thirty-ways a fool—

"You must sit." Sophie sat down and then nodded toward the other chair at the table. "I have many questions."

"Questions?"

"Yes. Scientific questions."

"About . . . raking?" *Ugh. Still not a verb.*

"Yes."

She stared him down until he sat in the opposite chair, the wood creaking under his weight.

"To begin," she said, tapping the pencil against her lips, "why does one decide to become a *Rakus falsus*?"

"Sophie—"

"There you go using my first name again."

"Surely, we've reached that point in our friendship."

Silence.

"I suppose we have . . . Rafe."

"Lennon," he corrected her.

Sophie may have sighed. She definitely rolled her eyes.

"Very well, *Lennon*, why did you decide to become a fake rakeshame?"

More silence.

"Please?" she added, eyes beseeching.

Rafe swallowed. No one knew this story.

And he meant . . . no one.

Not his mother or sister. Certainly not his father.

Not even Andrew and the other members of the Brotherhood of the Black Tartan. They knew that his rakish ways were not as prevalent as he made them out to be, but they didn't know the entire story. It had felt too . . . humiliating to tell them.

As for anyone else . . . no one had been perceptive enough to see the truth behind his behavior. But analyzing behavior was Sophie's specialty. Of course she saw through him. In hindsight, it seemed almost inevitable.

And he cared enough to want her to understand all of him. It felt Fated in a way, that he would give every part of his soul to this woman.

He released a sigh of his own, sinking back into his chair and stretching his legs.

"It's a simple story, really," he began. "More of an accident than anything. My father ran with a fast set as a younger man, and so it was no surprise when my elder brother followed in his footsteps, gaining a reputation as a rakehell. My father assumed I would do the same. But, much to Kendall's dismay, I did not. My father has never understood my love of the natural sciences. He condemns it as an unmanly, priggish sort of pursuit."

He breathed through the blast of rage that accompanied the memory, the tension churning a knot in his stomach.

Kendall glared at him, eyes icy and merciless. "No son of mine will be a lowly scholar. The Dukes of Kendall are men of action. You will follow in their footsteps, boy."

Sophie gave a dismissive sniff. "Such a Philistine."

That startled a laugh from Rafe. "Truly. Regardless, my final year at Eton, I wanted nothing more than tae continue my studies at university, preferably at St. Andrews in Scotland. My father and I had a terrible row over it during the Christmas holidays. No son of his would be a weak scholar. Kendall insisted he would purchase me a commission and send me tae Portugal before seeing me studying natural sciences at St. Andrews. So I returned for my final term at Eton, angry and restless. Needless to say, I made a few poor decisions and my anger bled into my studies. I got into an altercation with another student, bloodying him."

Rafe did not disclose that the fight had begun when the other boy had slandered Rafe's mother.

"Naturally, I was sent down because of it, expelled from Eton. The headmaster told my father that the fight was over a woman." Rafe snorted. "My father had never been so delighted with me. Somehow, my being known as a philanderer and a rake filled my sire with pride. Such behaviors are symbols of power in his world, and by participating in worldly and immoral deeds, Kendall perceived I was following in his footsteps."

"Good heavens. That is . . ."

"Appalling?" Rafe supplied. "Aye, it is. But there ye have it. Philistine, remember?"

The irony, of course, was that had his father known the fight had been over the duchess, Kendall would have beaten him for being a weakling. The duke had no care for his wife. But some unknown lightskirt? That was acceptable.

Rafe clenched his jaw, fighting back the red tide of rage that swept his vision—

He shook his head, swallowing firmly. "My father granted that if I continued to behave as a man ought—his words, not mine—then I was free to attend St. Andrews."

"Ah." She tilted her head. "So you simply had to maintain the charade of your wretched behavior . . ."

"Precisely." Rafe shifted in his chair, drumming his fingers. "Of course, once I finished at St. Andrews, my father expected me tae continue being a proper 'man about town.' And so I could not relinquish my raking, as ye call it."

Coals settled in the grate, sending up a rush of sparks.

"No one else knows." He paused. "About my *Rakus falsus* ways."

A moment while she digested that fact.

"You feel . . . vulnerable . . . about it?"

A pause.

"I suppose so. I simply ask ye to keep this a secret."

"I won't tell a soul," she said, eyes pensive, pencil tapping, teeth worrying her bottom lip.

Rafe looked away before doing something ill-advised, like covering that bottom lip with his own.

"I appreciate your discretion." He swallowed, as there was one more thing. "One last item . . . over time, I fear that playing the charming rake has become habitual, as you most correctly observed. I will not pretend that my behavior has not been problematic from time to time. It is a mask that I don without thinking, as I did this afternoon when faced with Miss Johnson." He took a steadying breath. "So, I must sincerely apologize if my actions caused ye any discomfort."

SOPHIE SET DOWN her pencil, drawing in a steady breath.

I apologize if my actions caused ye any discomfort.

The revelations of the past hour. She felt oddly scrubbed raw. Like she had been tossed about in a boat and then set back on land, head spinning, skin pricking. Nothing quite in place.

Rafe was not a rake. He had *never* been a rake. A sheep in wolf's clothing, to twist the popular idiom.

How had she missed this important component of his behavior? And why did this knowledge leave a lump in her throat and a fire in her chest, both of which oddly felt like *affection* for this man?

She did not want to be *fond* of Lord Rafe.

Yes, she was attracted to him physically, but that was merely biology. An involuntary reaction she could not control.

And, yes, she found conversing with him mentally stimulating . . .

But fondness?

Fondness implied that she had given a small part of her heart to him. That she liked him for himself.

Fondness led to *expectations* . . . expectations on her part as to his behavior. And she knew from painful past experience, that this man was not to be trusted with any part of her heart.

Do you hear that, foolish heart?

Not. To. Be. Trusted!

But . . . was that truly the case now?

Sophie was unsure. Regardless of his true intentions, his *Rakus falsus* ways had given rise to hopes that he had then dashed.

She didn't know how to manage the thrum of emotions roiling in her.

But there was one thing she *knew* she needed to do.

"Apology accepted." Her voice hung in the dark quiet. "I believe I owe you an apology, as well."

"An apology?" He huffed a laugh. "Whatever for?"

"I have assumed the worst of you. My late husband . . ." Her voice trailed off. She swallowed.

Rafe had been brave. He had shared a secret part of himself with her. She could do the same in return.

"Captain Jack Fulstate was . . ." She took a deep breath, allowing the habitual loathing she felt when thinking about her late husband to roll over her and then through her, washing away. She refused to be that hate-filled person. " . . . well, Jack was a *Rakus veras*, a rake in every true sense of the word."

Rafe stilled, his head coming upright. He clearly understood everything that she left unsaid.

She shot him a sad, wan smile.

"Yes," she nodded, "every behavior you are imagining and more. I spent my entire childhood living in the shadow of infidelity and adultery. I wanted nothing more than to escape it. And yet, whom do I marry?" She gave a soft, self-deprecating laugh. "I've often wondered if it is in my biology, in my very blood. I cannot seem to escape wanton behavior."

"Your late husband's actions have nothing tae do with ye, Sophie. They reflect on him and his own demons and insecurities."

More silence. The fire popped again.

"I know that now. But at the time . . ."

Memories rushed in.

Jack shouting at her when she asked him when he would return home.

Jack meeting her gaze across a crowded ballroom, and then turning away, offering his arm to another woman, escorting her out onto a dark veranda . . .

Sophie took a shuddering breath, raising her head. She met Rafe's too-seeing gaze. She expected to see pity there. But received compassion instead.

Her throat tightened, the ache growing.

"No, I will not allow ye to apologize tae me," he said, laying his words with soft gentleness. "Your words earlier were . . . accurate."

"My words?"

"Yes . . . how did ye put it?" He paused, head tilted. " '*I have spent my entire life feeling like a nuisance. An unwanted obligation. I would love for a man to decide that I am worth his full attention, regardless of who else might be in the room,*' ye said. Or something very like that."

She had said that. She meant every word.

"I am sorry that I ever made ye feel like that." His words dripped with sincerity; his eyes plead for forgiveness. "As I said earlier, playing the rake . . . it's been a mask for so long, I sometimes forget tae take it off. Any censure or irritation ye felt was justified. All I can do is promise to try tae do better while we are traveling together. To shed my *Rakus* skin, as it were."

Sophie regarded him, his eyes dark and imploring, his evening whiskers stubbling his cheeks.

How did he apologize so effortlessly? Had she ever known a man to be like this?

She gave a shake of her head, swallowing back the emotion that clogged her throat. The kindness that welled from him.

What did it say about her life that *kindness* from a man such as Lord Rafe should bring her to tears?

"I believe you," she said and meant it.

She stared off, blinking, attempting to reconcile the man before her with the inconstant rake she had assumed him to be.

Did this explain his behavior all those years ago? He had kissed her out of force of habit?

Did he even remember her from that evening? She had been so naive and trusting then, so inexperienced and unknowing in the ways of the world.

"What is wrong, lass?" he asked, that same concern in his voice. "What did I say?"

She bit her bottom lip again, this time to stop its trembling.

Would Lord Rafe ever stop being this man to her? The one who undid her, unraveled her heart and made her yearn for things she had given up years ago. Even now, he was unearthing bits of her soul—hope and desire and longing that she had thought broken beyond recovery—and offering them to her, encouraging her to rebuild.

But . . . she had trusted him once, and he had shattered her.

"I believe you," she repeated. "I believe everything you have told me is the truth—"

"Thank you."

"Don't thank me quite yet. I believe you . . . but I do not *trust* you."

His head snapped back.

"Why would your belief not lead tae trust? Are they not the same, in the end?" His brows came down.

"Because even if the intent of your behavior is not truly rakish, it is still a deception of a sort. Such blatant flirtation gives rise to expectations, and I cannot trust those expectations."

"Pardon?"

"See?! This is precisely what I mean. You are not even aware enough to remember."

Sophie took a deep breath, blinking away the sting in her eyes. Would she actually do this? Confront him about that night four years ago? Remind him that he had *kissed* her?

Events he likely did not remember.

She would look like a fool.

She would feel like a humiliated idiot.

But . . .

The sting of it would not let her be. She needed him to understand why she withheld her trust. And perhaps in doing so, like Jack, she could release this odd hold he had over her.

"Sophie?" The concern in his dark eyes convinced her to open her mouth. "What don't I remember?"

She laughed, such a bitter, sad sound.

"Kissing me," she all but whispered. "You don't remember kissing me."

17

Rafe sucked in a stunned breath.

Bloody hell.

Of all the places for this conversation to land—

You don't remember kissing me.

He damn well remembered kissing her. The lush curve of her in his arms, the hitch in her breath as he dipped his head to hers, the gentle give of her lips as he lifted her closer—

The memory nearly undid him.

He had spent the last several years fighting to *not* remember their kiss.

But it seemed every last second with this woman ended up imprinted on his very bones. Sophie had become part of his actual biology.

You don't remember kissing me.

She looked at him, those expressive green eyes meeting his, catapulting him back four years to that night. To that glorious stolen kiss and all his hopes and dreams for the future. For *their* future.

How was he to answer?

Our kiss is all I can remember.
You are blazoned on my very soul.

He took in a lungful of air, thoughts scrambling, trying to decide what to say.

"I am not wrong." She shook her head, looking away. "You do not remember."

"Sophie—"

"No. Let me finish my thoughts." She held out a hand. "You mentioned yesterday that you feel a kinship with your mother's Scottish heritage." She motioned toward his kilt, a wistful note in her tone. "I've never really . . . belonged." Her voice the barest trace of sound. She lifted her eyes to his. "Is that so wrong? To want a place to belong? To be *wanted*."

Oh, Sophie.

My heart.

"Everyone deserves tae belong." He willed her to believe him. "Everyone should be wanted, just as I—"

"Exactly!" she interrupted him. "It is *not* wrong. I spend my days categorizing and assigning living things to their places. In a sense, I find the homes where they belong. The genus that puts them near others like them. I give them familiarity." She glanced down at his tartan. "A clan, as it were."

He nodded. This he understood. The sense of kinship he felt when visiting his estate west of Perth. The reason why he counted the Brotherhood of the Black Tartan as his brothers.

The places he belonged.

What this had to do with their kiss, however . . .

"I have no clan," she continued, gaze drifting to the fire. That same lock of hair looser now, grazing the line of her throat, a slash of darkness against her pale skin. "I have no sense of kinship, no place where I am intrinsically wanted. I am the daughter of an unknown man. Poor, cuckolded Lord Mainfeld took on my care—bless him—but that cannot have been a welcome task. Worse, I am a scientist . . . a female scholar in a man's world." A lengthier pause. "The widow of a man who never took the time to know me beyond my dowry."

Something raw and aching settled in Rafe's throat.

This woman.

You don't remember kissing me.

He understood. He closed his eyes, letting the pain of it wash him.

Ah, Sophie.

She thought he had kissed her and then forgot, left her unwanted.

He *hated* that he had contributed to her pain.

She deserved a clan.

No . . . more than that.

Acolytes. Pilgrims. A host of people dedicated to her. Like a goddess of old, worshipers to sing hymns of praise, to leave her offerings.

And yet . . . he knew her well enough to understand that she didn't want to be worshiped.

She simply wanted to be . . . wanted.

He opened his mouth—to apologize? to confess?—but she continued speaking.

"I am more than just a dowry!" She met his gaze, eyes glassy. "I may not have known that when I married Jack, but I understand it now. I have a plan for my life." A pause, and then, "The first step is finding my father, my true father."

He froze, thoughts scattering.

Her *father*?

That was . . . unexpected.

"Pardon?"

"I wish to find my natural father," she repeated. "My mother will not tell me who he is. She becomes excessively agitated anytime I mention it. No one else seems to know." A hesitant silence. "It's why I am seeking out Dr. Ross, actually."

As usual, the jump in topic had him scrambling. "Ye think he might be your father?"

"No, hardly that." She laughed, a soft, breathy sound. "I've heard tale that my true father was present for my birth. Dr. Ross was the physician attending my mother that night."

"Ah. Ye hope he remembers who else was there?"

"Exactly."

Her unexpected confidence had him off-kilter.

She was traveling to Edinburgh, risking life and limb, simply on the hope that an elderly doctor might remember who else had been in the house that night nearly a quarter century ago.

It was . . . absurd and rash and poignant and . . .

. . . the actions of a woman on a mission.

Of a woman of courage and spirit.

A pilgrimage of her own, in a way.

Was it any wonder he had been so helpless against her charm that night four years ago? How could he have done anything *but* kiss her?

His Sophie was—

Ah, bloody hell.

His Sophie.

He had gone and done it.

He was thinking of her in possessive pronouns. Words like *his* and *mine* and *us*.

A man was done for when a woman started to alter his very grammar.

He truly was a peacock, as she had said. Because Sophie had become his bird, and he felt helpless to stop this flood of emotion.

Every Scot knew that being a man's bird was one step closer to becoming his hen and marrying Lady Sophronia Fulstate simply wasn't a possibility.

His father would banish his mother to the cruelest asylum possible in retribution. Rafe would never forgive himself for it.

But one thing he could give her.

"Ye are wrong on one account, Sophie." He waited until her eyes met his. "I absolutely *do* remember kissing ye. I remember every moment of it."

He willed her to believe him, to trust that she was wanted then.

Hell, she was wanted *now*.

Desperately. Achingly. Thoroughly.

How he wanted her. Some days he could scarcely breathe for sheer wanting.

"Why?" she whispered, voice agonized.

She said the word so softly. As if it wasn't cannon fire. As if it didn't shred him bare.

Why did you kiss me?

Why did you never call on me afterwards as you promised?

Her pain was his own.

The habitual anger toward Kendall scoured him . . . fury firing through his blood, setting his heart to racing.

Why had he been forced to give up this woman?

Why could he not be free of his father's heavy hand?!

But now . . . what was he to say to her?

I love you and my father took you away.

You are more wanted than you can ever know.

I would give anything to make you mine.

Rafe took in a shuddering breath, the roar in his ears blocking all sound.

He answered her plaintive, *why?* the only way he could:

"You want to belong, tae be part of a greater whole." He laughed again, an angry, mirthless sound. "I simply want tae be free."

"FREE?" SOPHIE REPEATED, shock freezing her in place.

Rafe had morphed before her very eyes.

With his words, the carefree rake had abruptly melted away, leaving an angry, wounded animal in his place—a creature who raged at the world, furious and impotent.

The sight sent air whooshing from her lungs.

What happened to you?

Who did this to you?

And how was this the answer to her question?

Her: Why did you kiss me?

Him: Because I wish for freedom.

His face was drawn into a tense grimace, that scar a slashing punctuation mark across his cheek.

"What do you mean . . . *free*?" She laid the words hesitantly, as she knew something about being a wounded creature herself. "You are the second son of a duke—wealthy, feted, excessively handsome, and with none of the looming responsibilities of the heir. How is that not freedom?"

Rafe stilled, his eyes studying her.

She replayed her words. *Wealthy, feted, excessively handsome.*

"*Excessively handsome?*" he repeated, a faint grin causing those dimples to appear—a trace of his rakish persona resurfacing. "Dinnae stop now, lass."

Sophie rolled her eyes. "Don't confuse the obvious. You know you are absurdly handsome—"

"*Absurdly*, even?"

"And now you're avoiding my question. Freedom from what?"

His face instantly sobered, that wounded creature re-emerging.

He swallowed convulsively and clenched his jaw.

Finally, he replied: "Freedom from my father."

Father?!

Gracious. That was not what she expected.

Though it perhaps explained why he felt the need to travel *incognito*.

Sophie sat back, her mouth drawing into a frown. Her mind raced to understand.

"He holds your purse strings?" she asked. Many a peer danced attendance on an overbearing parent in order to keep an allowance.

"No. At the moment, I would be a penniless beggar before allowing *that man*"—he spat the words like an epithet—"to control me for money."

She absorbed that statement. The vehemence in Rafe's words, the way his mouth twisted when he said *that man*, the wondering absurdity in his tone, as if the prison that held him could be exited for such a paltry reason as wealth.

But if not money, then what?

Or perhaps the better question—

"Who?" Sophie murmured. If he didn't obey his father for money, if wealth and gain weren't Rafe's goals, then it had to be for a person.

Rafe was protecting someone, someone he cared about enough to subject himself to his father's whims.

And why did that thought cause her eyes to sting?

"*Whom* do you protect?" she asked.

He leaned forward, scrubbing his hands over his face. He stared sightlessly down, eyes focusing on a spot about three inches in front of her feet.

The fire popped in the grate. Silence hung in the gloom. He sat so unmoving that Sophie began to doubt that he would reply.

Finally, he shifted, bringing his gaze back up to hers, his eyes pools of helpless suffering.

Ah. Here was the wounded animal in truth.

"My mother," he whispered.

Oh!

"Your mother?"

"Aye."

Sophie's mind scrambled to keep up. She had met the Duchess of Kendall only once or twice. The woman was something of an invalid, rarely going about in public. But Sophie had lived long enough to know that being labeled an 'invalid' could encompass a great many things, only some of which were genuine illness.

"Is your father . . . cruel to her?" she asked, trying to communicate all her fears with the one word . . . *cruel*.

"Does he beat her, do ye mean?" he huffed, sitting back abruptly. "Not often, though he has struck her on occasion. Her wounds are . . . less visible."

He paused, a war playing out across his face.

Sophie remained quiet . . . waiting. Her heart ached for him . . . for his mother. That poor woman.

Sophie knew only too well the pain of a callous husband. The endless shame. The silent horror.

Oh, Rafe.

He sat up straighter. "No one knows. It's a closely guarded secret, but . . ." He released a breath. ". . . my mother suffers from melancholy."

Ah. Many things clicked into place for Sophie. But that still didn't explain how his father held Rafe hostage.

"And your father . . ."

"My father threatens tae place her into a lunatic asylum." He met her gaze, as if willing her to understand.

"No! I've heard tell that those places are horrific."

"They *are* horrific." He shifted, coming to his feet, fingers raking through his hair, sending it askew. He paced to the window, looking out over the empty courtyard, hands on his hips.

"My mother wasn't always so poorly." His words floated back to her. "There was a time when she laughed and enjoyed life. But about ten years ago . . . she lost her last child right after childbirth. She has never been the same since. The melancholy that some women experience after childbirth simply never left her."

"How dreadful."

"My father was an unkind husband before, but with her illness, he has become . . . brutish. He has little patience with her depressive moods. He wishes tae lock her away and be done with it." Rafe turned around to face her, his eyes clashing with hers.

How had she ever missed the pain there?

"Surely your father is only bluffing?"

Rafe gave a barking laugh. "Oh, I assure ye, Kendall is quite in earnest. He has already locked her away once. He will not hesitate tae do so again."

"*Pardon?!* He locked her away? I heard nothing of this. How was such a thing kept from the gossips?"

"My father can be excessively discreet when he wishes to be. Power and money will always buy silence." He braced his hands on the back of the chair opposite her. "I returned from my voyage to the South Pacific tae find that my father had sent my mother to a private lunatic asylum. He gave me his word before I left that he wouldn't commit her tae such a place, but he broke his promise. I think he wanted to ensure my immediate obedience, and harming my mother was the most effective way tae achieve it. I raced to reach her. That place . . ." He swallowed. "There was no kindness there. Can you imagine how I found her?"

"No." She truly couldn't.

"They had her chained tae her bed, like a feral animal. She lay in her own filth, bruises and cuts on her body from their 'treatments.' She didn't even meet my gaze when I first found her." He paused, his jaw tight, grinding against his teeth as he fought back emotion. "That was no cure. It was torture, pure and simple."

"Agreed." Tears stung Sophie's eyelids.

And to think, she had spent the better part of the day fuming over his *Rakus lasciviosus* ways and thinking him a bit of a cad.

She had been so utterly wrong.

How am I to protect my heart now?!

Rafe waved a hand continuing, "I instantly demanded my mother's release and was belligerent enough that the asylum complied. I couldn't bear the thought of her being there even one more day. I assumed that despite being an utter blackguard, my father wouldn't want the scandal of his duchess being treated in such a way." He gave another bitter bark of laughter. "I could not have been more wrong. I returned home with my mother, placing her feverish and listless in her bedchamber. Kendall merely called me a fool and said he was ordering her returned tae the asylum, immediately."

"Oh!"

"I wouldn't hear of it, of course. I demanded he allow her tae be treated at home with kindness and love." A moment of silence. Rafe stared ahead, lost in the memory of that moment. "Kendall refused, and that's when I truly learned the depth of his depravity. He informed me that he had sent her to the asylum *because* I had returned home. He wanted tae ensure that I fully appreciated the sincerity of his threat.

"He then gave me a single option—her freedom for mine. Kendall would not send her back tae the asylum as long as I obeyed him. What could I do?"

He looked at her then, eyes so anguished.

"Nothing," Sophie whispered.

She knew only too well how complete a husband's control was over his wife. Only Jack's death had freed her.

But for Rafe's mother . . .

"There is *nothing* you could do," she said. "No one would doubt your father's right to control his wife."

"Precisely. I had no options. There was no way tae free her from my father. He knew it. And so I agreed."

"Oh, Rafe."

"The man has owned me ever since. He is exceptionally clever in his cruelty. He lets me go days and even weeks without summoning me for a task, allowing me the sense of freedom. But then he will tug on the leash and snap my chains, reminding me that I am nothing more than his dog. And I *allow* it."

He bit out those final words as if they scoured his soul.

"I have to, you see," he continued. "If I do not acquiesce, Kendall will send my mother back tae the asylum. I cannot leave and consign her tae such a terrible fate. She is much improved, but I feel most of that is due tae the comfort of my sister and her grandchildren. Therefore, stealing her out of the country isn't an option."

"So . . . what do you do?"

"I search for a cure for her melancholy. If my mother improves, if she is seen healthy and hearty about Town, my sire has less reason tae confine her. I would perhaps be able tae rally public opinion to her side. But until she is well . . ."

Abruptly everything made more sense. "Dr. Ross?"

"Yes. His area of specialty is illnesses of the mind and emotions. If anyone can help, it would be him."

Sophie's heart ached in her chest. That poor woman, trapped in a callous marriage. No wonder she suffered from melancholy.

And then Rafe, chained to his father's cruelty . . . grasping at such a thin thread of hope, not unlike herself.

Both of them, off to find Dr. Ross, as if he were some wizard in a tower who could grant both their wishes simply for asking.

Though Sophie felt some embarrassment over the superficiality of her own request. No one's life or future hung in the balance. Hers was merely a fanciful wish.

Rafe fought to protect one he loved. Because he had someone *to* protect, someone *to* love.

She swallowed. All the unbidden attraction she had felt toward him rose to the surface, flooding her, nearly overwhelming in its force.

She had one last question, however.

"Kendall hates Lord Mainfeld. He hates the entire Sorrowful Miscellany," she said. "Was Kendall angry that you had . . . danced with me that night?"

A long silence and then one word—

"Yes."

Ah.

"Would you have called on me, as you promised, had Kendall not been angry?"

"Yes." No hesitation.

He did not look at her, however. He remained standing, eyes trained on the window and the dark world outside.

But his next words reached her nonetheless: "*Never* doubt the sincerity of my intentions that night, Sophie."

Something hot and painful lodged in her throat. She heard his unspoken words clearly.

Never doubt that you were wanted.

Rafe had not been untrue.

Sophie had not been naive or delusional in her understanding of the events of that evening.

He had *wanted* to spend more time with her, to get to know her.

But Kendall had come between them.

Sophie pressed a hand to her chest, anything to stem the tide of so much . . . *feeling.*

She didn't need this.

She didn't wish to like him.

She didn't *want* these feelings of tenderness and care. She did not need her heart to be reconstructed and resurrected from the dead.

But then Rafe turned back to her, pinning her with his dark eyes.

Their gazes held and lingered. The darkness of the night wrapped around them, promising comfort and anonymity. Coals in the grate settled, sending a shower of sparks up the chimney.

Sophie rose slowly to her feet, thinking to tend to the fire, but his eyes held her in place.

Attraction fizzed through her blood, pounding in her ears.

He took a step toward her. And then another.

She had to raise her chin to continue to meet his gaze, his wide shoulders blocking the firelight altogether. Her heart pulsed in her throat, threatening to escape her body entirely.

Another step.

She could *feel* the heat of him, the warmth of his sandalwood scent surrounding her. How she longed for the comfort of his touch . . .

It would be so easy to fall. To tumble all the way into love with this man.

But . . . even if Rafe decided to pursue her in earnest now . . . his decisions were not his own.

Kendall hated Lord Mainfeld, and therefore, by extension, Sophie herself.

She and Rafe would never become . . . *us*.

But that didn't stop her from leaning toward Rafe, rising slowly on tiptoe, canting her lips upward.

She felt his breath on her mouth—

Ughmmm!

Martha snorted from the adjoining room.

Sophie jolted back to reality with a gasp, nearly jerking away from Rafe.

She turned to the fire, snatching up the poker and stirring the coals to life.

Heavens! Had that truly almost happened? Had she nearly kissed Lord Rafe again?

She stabbed at the fire, desperately shaking the lingering effects of his spell from her head.

She was a mature woman. She would to be stronger than her biology.

"What time do we leave in the morning?" she asked, deliberately changing the topic.

A moment's hesitation. "Sunrise."

She nodded.

Swallowing, she set down the poker and dared to turn back to face him.

His expression appeared just as muddled as hers.

Finally, he shot her a wan smile and turned for the door, listening before opening it.

"Lock this behind me." He jiggled the handle. "A ruffian might burst in unannounced, ye know."

He bowed, oddly formal and very English—at utter odds with his rumpled kilt and semi-dressed attire—and then was gone.

SOPHIE CONSIDERED TRAVELING with Lord Rafe—or rather, Lennon, as he continually corrected her—to be a tortuous delight.

This was amply proved over the next two days.

They did not return to the quiet confessions of the inn in York, to the stretched tension of their almost-kiss.

But something had shifted in their relationship.

All her previous feelings of hurt had fled. The ball, so many years past, was not a scene of humiliation and naivete, as she had previously supposed.

For his part, Rafe remained the man she had seen that evening in York—a thoughtful scholar, intent and earnest. There was no more outrageous flirting with every barmaid and pretty woman. His attention was solely on her.

The quiet scholar, Sophie realized, was the true man.

As was the man who, twenty miles outside York, immediately hopped out of the chaise to help push a mired coach out of the mud, uncaring as to his status or the cleanliness of his ghillies. He saw a need and helped where he could.

Not that she was above using his charming prowess to her advantage.

They rolled into a busy inn yard outside Newcastle on a brisk afternoon. The autumnal weather had decided to hint at winter and a chill wind blew from the east. Every time they stopped, Sophie would insist on heated bricks for their feet inside the chaise, as well as for James and Martha outside.

But of course, as Sophie sat contemplating a hot cup of tea and perhaps another pair of warm bricks, Rafe turned his charming smile on her. It was his rake smile. His eyelids dropped, gaze hooded and flirtatious.

Sophie lifted an eyebrow in return.

"Yes?"

"I just realized something." He leaned toward her. "Your name is Lady Sophronia Sorrow Fulstate."

He grinned, pleased as Punch, dimples popping in his cheeks.

Sophie stared him down.

"My name, as ever, is a cautionary tale," she sighed. "'Tis almost mind-boggling in its mawkishness."

"It's hilarious, is what it is."

"Are you quite through?"

He smiled wider. "I could be. What did ye have in mind?"

Sophie leaned away from him. "Are you . . . are you flirting with me?"

"Possibly," he shrugged. "I have tae keep my skills sharp, ye know."

A pause. "Well, they are a weapon of sorts, I'll give you that."

"Thank ye."

The carriage rolled to a stop in the inn yard.

"Don't thank me just yet." She smiled and patted his shoulder. "How about you take some of that Scottish charisma into the inn there and charm the innkeep into selling us another hot brick or two?"

True to his abilities, there were *three* hot bricks waiting for her when she returned to the carriage a half hour later.

The man truly was a menace to her heart.

18

"Here we are." Rafe stretched his arms as the chaise rolled to a stop outside Alex's surgery in New Town in Edinburgh.

"At last," Sophie replied beside him.

He darted a glance at her. She returned a soft smile.

Finally, they had reached their destination —the townhouse of Dr. Alex Whitaker, one of the Brotherhood.

They had spent the last hour of the drive maneuvering through the labyrinthine medieval streets of Old Town before skirting Calton Hill and arriving on King Street in New Town.

As they wove through the tedious traffic, Rafe gave Sophie a brief history of Edinburgh. As the name implied, Old Town represented Edinburgh in its medieval incarnation—overcrowded, ancient tenements stretching nine stories or more into the sky, all clinging to a rocky mount capped by the crenelated Edinburgh Castle. A loch bounded Old Town on the north, cliffs on the east, and Arthur's Seat (another large mount) on the west. The city could only spread south, which it had.

Unfortunately, a landscape that had effectively protected a medieval population from English invasion, did not fare so well in a more modern age. The ancient city was desperately over-built and over-crowded.

About fifty years prior, the town council had decided that enough was enough with the medieval city. Instead of tearing it down, they simply drained the swampy land to the north, built a bridge over the marshy North Loch, and constructed New Town on the flat stretch between the castle mount and the Firth of Forth.

New Town with its honey stone, wide boulevards, and pedimented architecture looked more like Mayfair or Bath in England. Naturally, any gentleman who could put forth enough guineas moved from the crowded city center to New Town.

Which also explained why Alex had placed his physician's surgery there, positioning himself as a doctor to the elite of Edinburgh. Though Alex greeted patients and such on the ground floor, the remaining three floors of his town house were dedicated to living space.

For obvious reasons, Rafe knew staying in the Duke of Kendall's townhouse in Charlotte Square—a mile to the south and west—was utterly out of the question.

And why stay in a hotel when Alex had perfectly comfortable bedchambers just waiting for guests?

"Rafe, ye scoundrel!" Alex burst into the drawing room mere minutes after a maid showed Rafe and Sophie in.

Alex enveloped Rafe in a back-slapping hug before pushing back to survey him from head-to-toe.

"Playing at the Scot, are ye?" Alex winked.

Rafe tugged his great kilt into place. "I wear it better than most, I suppose."

Alex laughed and turned to Sophie, his grin stretching wider, eyes lit with interest.

Rafe did not like that interest, not one little bit.

Educated, charming, and handsome, Alex was exactly the kind of man Sophie should marry. Not that the daughter of an English earl aspired to be a Scottish physician's wife, but Sophie was not your typical,

English aristocrat. Moreover, she appeared to be regarding Alex with similarly keen interest.

Rafe barely stopped himself from frowning. "Lady Sophronia Fulstate, may I present Dr. Alex Whitaker?"

Sophie curtsied. Alex bowed extravagantly over her hand as he murmured a greeting. Sophie did nothing to discourage his friend's attentions, blast it. Instead, she smiled that warm, open smile that Rafe adored.

Voices sounded in the hallway and Ewan burst in, his large frame dwarfing the elegant furniture in the room.

"Rafe! Ye scoundrel!" Apparently, his friends had a theme when greeting him.

As usual, Rafe felt nearly small exchanging a warm embrace with Ewan, his friend having several inches on him in all directions.

The entire scene repeated itself. Introductions. Pleasantries.

Alex's sister, Catriona, arrived and they repeated everything once more.

Sophie begged leave to a hotel.

Catriona would hear nothing of it and went off with Martha to ensure the housekeeper prepared the necessary rooms.

They all sat in the drawing room, chatting about their journey and the changeable October weather. Another maid brought in a tea tray piled high with shortbread and bannocks. Sophie situated herself behind the tray, pouring tea. She fit easily into the room, appearing more comfortable here than in London. Ewan helped himself to several biscuits. The man was perpetually hungry; feeding his large body was an endless task.

"I must say, Rafe," Alex said, accepting a cup from Sophie with a too-friendly nod, "we hardly expected ye to arrive so quickly, and with such lovely company, too."

He shot Sophie a flirtatious smile. She ducked her head at his compliment. Was she blushing? It was hard to tell in the light, and yet—

"Expected me?" Rafe's addled wits *finally* caught up to the question. He froze, his own cup halfway to his lips.

"Aye," Ewan agreed, taking a cup. "Have ye even slept on the road from London?"

"Pardon?"

"We sent ye an express immediately after receiving the threatening letters, but that was scarcely five days ago," Ewan said between bits of crumbly shortbread.

"An express? Letters? Ye have me muddled."

Alex and Ewan both stilled, eyes swinging to his.

"Is that not why ye're here?" Alex asked.

"Nae. I'm still trying to track down Dr. Ross. Turns out, he retired and now lives in Edinburgh. But I received a threatening letter of my own before leaving London. You lot did as well?"

Alex sat back, setting down his saucer. "It's best to show ye, I think." He left the room.

Sophie watched him leave the room, her eyes coming back to meet Rafe's, a question mark there.

Rafe kept his expression tight. He had told her a wee bit about their trip to the South Pacific during their days in the coach. But not how the voyage ended. Not the pivotal events of that night.

Alex returned a moment later with two folded pieces of foolscap, one in each hand.

"They each say the same thing." He handed the letters to Rafe.

Unfolding one, Rafe let out a low whistle.

> *I know what you did aboard* The Minerva *that night. Do not suppose that your crimes will go unpunished. You will end your days dangling from a hangman's noose.*

He shook his head, snapping the paper in his hand.

"I received an identical letter right before leaving London," he said, setting the slips of foolscap down.

"And ye didnae write us about it?" Ewan frowned.

Rafe shrugged. "I figured I would discuss it with ye in person, as I was headed north. I assume this is related tae the notice in the *Edinburgh Advertiser* in August."

"Aye," Ewan said, "'tis the only explanation that makes any sense."

Rafe resisted the urge to drag his fingers through his hair. "But who else knows the details of that night? Have we made any headway with who placed the notice?"

"None." Alex set down his teacup. "The editor claims that no one remembers who requested the notice—"

"A likely story."

"Eh, I cannae say, tae be honest," Alex said. "It could very well be the truth. Hard tae remember one person out of the hundreds who post notices every month."

Ewan reached for a bannock. "Kieran made no progress with his questions down at the wharf before leaving for New York. Just some vague mention of a man in Aberdeen possibly having information. But Kieran wasnae able to chase it down afore he left."

"So we still assume that no one actually survived the wreck of *The Minerva*?"

"Aye," Alex nodded. "It's been over three and a half years. If someone had survived, they surely would have surfaced before now." He nodded toward the letters. "Besides, the writer claims tae only *know* what happened. That's not the same thing as being there. Our mystery writer could be someone from that Portuguese whaler."

Sophie's head bounced between them before looking at the discarded letters, clearly interested in their exchange.

"May I know what this is all about?" she asked, voice curious but ever-so-polite.

Rafe exchanged a glance with Ewan and Alex. He could see the question in their eyes.

"I'd like her tae know," he replied. And he truly did. "But obviously the story is not entirely mine to tell. Though it appears others know somehow." He waved a hand toward the threatening letters sitting beside the tea tray.

"We have nothing tae hide," Ewan said, reaching for another biscuit.

"Aye." Alex lifted one of the letters and handed it to Sophie. He then retrieved a copy of the *Edinburgh Advertiser* from a chest of drawers against the wall, allowing her to read the notice, as well.

She scanned both items, eyes going wide.

"Heavens! *Supposed crimes*? You've been discussing your trip to the South Pacific, but *The Minerva* wrecked?" She turned to Rafe, eyes so very wide. "Your ship *wrecked*?! How did I not know this?!"

Rafe could understand her surprise. But *The Minerva* had been simply one of the hundreds of merchant vessels lost every year, only mentioned in a small paragraph in the newspapers, quickly forgotten.

As for why Rafe hadn't mentioned it himself . . .

The events of that night were painful. He leaned back in his chair, knowing that reliving everything about that night would be uncomfortable, but wanting Sophie to know.

"Aye," he said, raking a hand through his hair. "*The Minerva* did indeed sink. I know I've told ye much about the trip, but only the scientific parts of it. Not the human drama bits."

"I see." She frowned. "You mean the parts where someone might accuse you of a crime?"

"Aye." Rafe turned to look at his friends.

Alex got a steely glint in his eyes. Ewan clenched his jaw and then nodded. *Go on*.

Rafe looked back at Sophie. "As ye know, Lord Hadley—Andrew Langston, tae us—funded the trip. But such voyages are expensive, and so he had a business partner who helped finance the trip, in exchange for the ship carrying some cargo. Part of our original agreement was tae take on sandalwood in the New Hebrides, as the wood had been discovered to grow there. The timber would help defray costs. So we set anchor in a lovely harbor of a native village in the New Hebrides and began to explore the island, categorizing our finds and so on. All the while assuming that the captain, Martin Cuthie, was negotiating the purchase of lumber."

He told her about their weeks on the island, befriending the villagers, exploring new species. He recounted Jamie's infectious enthusiasm, and how the youth had rallied everyone to participate.

"We thought we had found paradise. However, unbeknownst to us, Captain Cuthie had struck a more sinister bargain with Andrew's business partner. Instead of sandalwood, Cuthie would kidnap and enslave villagers from the islands."

"Pardon? Slavery?! How atrocious!" Sophie choked on her tea, instantly devolving into an explosive coughing fit.

Her reaction seemed fitting for the horror of the situation.

Sophie took a moment to gather herself, eyes tearing before she managed to take a sip of tea to calm her throat.

"I did not expect this conversation to land on slavery," she croaked. "Please continue."

Rafe carried on, "Naturally, we categorically refused to participate in such an atrocity."

"That imbecilic man—" Alex bit off. "Tae even contemplate treating other human beings in such a fashion."

"I experience nightmares yet over it," Ewan agreed. "I dinnae ken that it will ever cease tae haunt me."

"Of course, Cuthie was adamant that his orders be followed." Rafe described the scene. The memories still so vivid, images flowing through him.

Gunshots above. Fists on his cabin door, startling him awake. Jamie's voice urgent.

"Ye must away, my lord. Cuthie has his men coming for ye. Hurry!"

But Rafe had not been quick enough. His friends and the villagers had escaped, but Rafe and Andrew had not. They had been apprehended and beaten, tied to the mast and lashed. And then cut down and dragged before the captain. Andrew had received the worst of it, his large body sagging in the sailor's hold, more bloody sausage than man. Rafe feared him dead.

Then Cuthie had approached with that wicked-looking blade.

"Ye have far too pretty of a face," Cuthie cackled, running the flat of the knife across Rafe's cheek. *"How many cuts will it take before ye yield? Shall we see?"*

Rafe struggled against the arms that held him. Sailors called encouragement to Cuthie, all their attention on Rafe. Behind Cuthie, he could see Alex, Ewan, Jamie, and Kieran slipping over the railing and onto the deck. A score of villagers followed them. Jamie held a rapier with confidence. The youth excelled at hand-to-hand fighting now. But they were vastly outnumbered, the fools. They were going to get themselves killed.

"I don't think that face of yours will be quite so pretty when I'm done," Cuthie said.

The knife slashed. Rafe turned his head at the last second, causing the blade to strike his cheekbone, barely missing his eye.

Screams followed, as Kieran and Jamie attacked the sailors, determined to free Rafe and Andrew . . .

"I don't remember much of the rescue, to be honest," Rafe continued. "I was struggling tae see with my cheek on fire—"

"I pulled ye into one of the villager's canoes, rowed ye to shore," Ewan chimed in. "I was the only one strong enough tae carry yer huge carcass down the side of the ship."

"And though ye have a bit of a scar, I'll be forever proud of my stitching that night. The cut was deep. It healed as well as could be expected." Alex nodded toward Rafe's cheek.

"Aye, and for that I'm grateful. I mostly remember the aftermath of it all. The dark night air, Andrew delirious, the village on fire, and *The Minerva* sailing out of the harbor, sails catching the moonlight off the water. Cuthie marooned the five of us on the island."

"Gracious!" Sophie said. "What happened to *The Minerva* to cause her to wreck? Where is Jamie now? How did you escape from the island?"

Rafe exchanged a weighted look with Ewan and Alex. Sophie, intelligent creature that she was, did not misunderstand the gravity of that look.

"Did Jamie not . . . survive?"

Rafe silently thanked her for the small catch in her voice as she said the word, *survive*—the reverent hush, as if desperate for any other answer, but fearing the worst.

"Jamie dinnae survive," Ewan said softly. "While Kieran and Jamie led us lot tae rescue Andrew and Rafe, they were both captured in the process."

"Aye," Rafe continued. "From what Kieran has told us, Captain Cuthie had him and Jamie chained in the hold of the ship. I believe Cuthie's intention was tae force Kieran to navigate the ship out of the treacherous waters of the South Pacific, using Jamie's safety as motivation—"

"Kieran was the ship's master, and as such, the only one who had enough knowledge of the area tae navigate it safely," Alex explained to Sophie. "Sometimes the ship's captain is master *and* commander—meaning the captain is a skilled navigator, as well as a leader of the crew. But that isn't always the case. Cuthie was only the commander; he didn't know enough himself tae steer the ship through all the hazards."

"Aye, but before Cuthie could set sail out of the harbor that night, Jamie picked the lock on Kieran's chains and freed them both," Rafe said. "They fought their way to the top deck. Jamie was truly lethal with a rapier. I ken their plan was tae jump overboard and swim for shore. But at the last second, Kieran was apprehended by the first mate while protecting Jamie. Jamie ran the first mate through and pushed Kieran overboard, out of harm's way."

Silence for moment. The distant sound of the street below intruded. Carriage wheels on cobblestone.

"And then what happened?" Sophie asked into the quiet.

Rafe took in a long breath. "We don't know." He swallowed back the painful lump lodged in his throat, causing his eyes to sting.

"Aye," Ewan whispered. "Poor Jamie was left aboard the ship. Kieran swam tae shore, wounded and screaming at us tae help rescue Jamie, but there was nothing any of us could do. The ship was already under sail, headed out of the harbor."

"Jamie remained on the ship," Alex added. "Without us. Without our protection—"

"And guilty of stabbing a crew member and disobeying the captain, both hangable offenses."

"Oh, that poor lad," Sophie breathed, swiping at her cheeks, jaw firmly clenched. "So much injustice! Did Cuthie execute him then?"

"We don't know," Rafe repeated. "We were on the island for about six weeks when a Portuguese whaler stopped tae re-provision. They claimed to have sailed through the remains of a merchant ship only a week previously. The ship appeared tae have been dashed to pieces on a hidden reef in the open ocean, bodies floating in the wreckage. The launch skiffs were bobbing and empty. They found no survivors, but they did recover a piece of wood with the letters 'ERVA' carved into it."

"*The Minerva?*"

"We have always assumed no one else lived," Rafe nodded. "But then these missives arrived." He held up the letters.

Sophie darted her gaze back to the letters and notice resting on the table.

"Oh," she blinked, as if remembering the letters. "They were certainly troubling beforehand, but now they appear downright sinister."

"Precisely. We had assumed everyone had been killed. But someone knows something—"

"But who?" Sophie voice was bewildered. "Surely the only people who know are your closest friends and family. Why would they threaten you?"

"There are a few others who know," Alex answered her question. "The men on the Portuguese whaler heard some of the story, though none of them spoke English. And there was a brief paragraph about the wreck in the *London Times* at one point."

"Aye," Rafe agreed, "and Andrew had tae give a deposition to Lloyd's of London who had insured the trip, explaining the circumstances. So there is a written record buried in a solicitor's office somewhere. Someone could have acquired it and thought tae blackmail us."

Sophie snorted and pointed at the letters. "If it's blackmail, they left out the important bits about payment and such."

"Exactly." Alex sighed. "And we cannae be sure that no one else survived the wreck, obviously, without having counted all the bodies. But survival does seem unlikely."

"But no' impossible," Ewan muttered.

"Aye," Rafe agreed. "Someone could have survived. Though I struggle tae understand how."

"Even Jamie?" The hope in Sophie's eyes nearly unmanned him.

The three men exchanged a look, weighted with all the history between Jamie and Cuthie, between Jamie and themselves.

Alex spoke first. "I cannae think that Jamie survived. Even if Cuthie hadnae had the youth executed for insubordination, Jamie would have had tae survive the ship wreck somehow."

"And if Jamie survived, we would have heard by now," Ewan said.

"Aye," Rafe agreed. "Jamie would have found a way tae contact us, or Kieran at the very least. Only death would have stopped—"

He paused, needing to clear his throat, his eyes surely too bright.

"Aye," Alex whispered, agreeing with what was left unsaid.

Those same feelings rose in Rafe's chest . . .

Fury at Cuthie for forcing them into the situation.

Rage at the injustice of Jamie's senseless death.

Pain that they hadn't been able to save their friend.

Ewan met his gaze, his own eyes reflecting similar emotions. It was a burden they all carried. Even though the past summer had seen Andrew's wayward business partner brought to justice—the man who had initiated the entire failed plan—the resolution hadn't brought a sense of peace. At least, not for Rafe. He still felt Jamie's loss keenly every time he saw his scar in a mirror.

"We'll get tae the bottom of this," Alex motioned toward the letters on the table. "Someone knows something and eventually they will become careless. For now, they're simply making noise. Let them, I say."

"Aye," Ewan agreed. "We've survived too much tae be laid low by this. I'm planning on following up on the vague information Kieran received before he left. I'm for Aberdeen, as I have a portrait commission to fulfill in Aberdeenshire. I'll look into it and let yous all know if I find anything worth reporting."

Rafe shot a glance at Sophie. "You've rendered us maudlin, lass."

"And there was no' even a drop of whisky involved." Ewan's tone was mournful. "Alex doesnae believe in alcohol," he clarified to Sophie.

"Despite what anyone says, it isnae good for the body, Ewan," Alex grumbled. "Ye'd be wise to imbibe less frequently."

Ewan grunted and reached for the last biscuit. "I'm Scottish. We drink whisky, wear kilts, and curse the weather and English in equal amounts—" He shot a wide-eyed look at Sophie. "—present company excluded, o' course, my lady."

Sophie laughed, taking Rafe's friends in stride.

Yet another reason to like her. As if he needed more.

"So if ye're not here because of our missives, then why are ye intent on visiting Dr. Ross in company of a fine lady?" Alex asked, taking the opportunity to change the topic. "And a most delightful lassie, I must say," he added, raising his teacup to Sophie.

Her grin grew wider, warmth sparkling in her mossy eyes.

Rafe tamped down the burst of annoyance at Alex's friendly comment. Pity he was going to have to bloody the good doctor if Alex continued to cosy up to his bird.

"And why are ye dressed as a Scot, no less?" Ewan added, looking to Rafe. "Tae prevent your father from knowing your whereabouts?"

Rafe nodded.

"Indeed. Lord Rafe has been quite insistent on the Scottish disguise." Sophie shot Rafe a teasing look. "Is that not so . . . *Lennon*?"

"Lennon?!" Ewan choked on biscuit crumbs.

Alex chuckled.

"'Tis the name I chose tae adopt for the trip . . . Lennon Robert Gordon," Rafe said.

He shot his friends a look that he hoped sufficiently communicated a strong threat of bodily harm should they say anything further.

"Mmmm," Ewan mumbled around his biscuit.

Alex was less circumspect.

"Allow me to guess?" he asked, turning to Sophie and fixing her with another of those friendly looks that set Rafe's teeth on edge. "Rafe here has insisted ye call him Lennon at every turn?"

Sophie laughed. Again. "Why yes, he has. How very astute of you."

"Thank you. I *am* very astute." Alex gave a decidedly flirtatious grin. "In fact, ye should probably throw off this lummox here." He jutted his chin toward Rafe. "Find yerself a cleverer man—"

"Alex." Rafe pitched his voice low in warning.

"Yes, Lennon?" Alex returned, face entirely too innocent, blithely ignoring the thunderous *Beware!* in Rafe's eyes. The wretch.

Ewan nodded, as if thinking. "And why are ye in the company of the bonnie Lady Sophronia?" He shot her a far-too-appraising look before darting his gaze back to Rafe.

Ah.

It finally sank in. The pair of bawbags he called friends were teasing him, deliberately cozying up to Lady Sophie in order to wind him up.

He glared at them; he was onto their games.

"I seek Dr. Ross, as well," Sophie answered Ewan's question herself.

Sophie openly explained to his friends the purpose of her quest, Lord Mainfeld and his brood, her own wishes.

Alex was tapping his fingers as she finished. "You present lofty goals, Lady Sophronia. Though I dislike being the harbinger of bad news, ye must know it is extremely unlikely that Dr. Ross would remember who else had been in the house while delivering a baby over twenty-five years ago."

"I know." She smiled. "Or perhaps you would say it's a wee bitty daft."

Rafe chuckled.

Silence for a moment.

"I do have one question, however," Alex said. "Why would a physician who specializes in diseases of the mind have been the one tae deliver a countess's child?"

19

Sophie studied the row house as Rafe extended a hand to assist her from the chaise.

So this was the current residence of Dr. Ross?

It was an older building outside Old Town proper, tucked into Drummond Street between the University of Edinburgh and the infirmary. A generally respectable address, Rafe had told her. Not a fancy townhouse in New Town but not nearly as ramshackle as the tenements beside the castle either.

Sophie blinked her weary eyes. She had experienced one of those nights where one arises just as tired as one went to bed. So many thoughts churned through her mind, it rendered sleep elusive—Rafe's concerns about those mysterious missives and the horrors of their trip to the South Pacific; her own anticipation for today and calling upon Dr. Ross; the reality that she would likely part ways with Rafe after their visit to the doctor. After all, their journey complete, there would be no reason to remain together.

And what did it say about the state of her feelings that the thought upset her more than she would have supposed?

Somewhere during the long night, she had come to the rather startling realization—

Foolish woman that she was . . . she had begun to forfeit her heart to Lord Rafe Gilbert.

Had she learned nothing over the past four years?!

This trip had begun as a journey to find herself—to go back to her beginning and piece herself back together, bit by bit—but she had never anticipated that *this* would be the result.

All of it had kept her tossing and turning for hours.

Though given the dark circles under Rafe's eyes, he had likely experienced a similar night.

Morning light washed the street as carts clacked over the cobblestones. A faint mist rose from the damp pavement where the sunlight hit, giving the city a hazy, otherworldly appearance.

Rafe offered her his arm before taking the stairs to the front door of the townhouse.

They both had such high expectations for the visit today. Sophie still longed to know the identity of her natural father. But her small wishes paled in comparison to Rafe's quest, and so the bulk of her prayers now rested with him. She desperately hoped that Dr. Ross could recommend a true cure for the duchess, anything to help the lady escape the cage of her marriage.

If anyone deserved a miracle today, it was Rafe and his mother.

As if sensing her mental pleading, Rafe shot her a strained grin before rapping the knocker.

He had opted to wear his kilt again today, choosing to blend in more as a Scotsman than to stand out as a wealthy, London gentleman. A dark length of plaid wrapped around his hips and chest. *Jamie's Tartan*, Rafe had called it, a fabric woven in memory of the lad who had sacrificed his life for theirs. It spoke to the heart of the Brotherhood that they would cherish Jamie's memory so.

A shuffling sound came from beyond the front door, followed by the *snick* of the lock being thrown.

An elderly woman in a mobcap and apron opened the door, strands of gray hair escaping here and there.

"May I help ye?" she asked, brows drawn down, gaze taking in Rafe's great kilt and Sophie's elegant London finery.

"Aye," Rafe replied, deploying his most charming smile, dimples popping. "We seek Dr. John Ross. Is he at liberty tae receive us?"

The woman blinked, as if momentarily stunned. Sophie could hardly blame her. Lord Rafe's smile at full force felt a bit like a blast of summer sunlight—deliciously warm and dazzling.

"Dr. Ross, ye say?" she finally said. "I dinnae ken that will be possible as Dr. Ross hasnae lived here for at least a year."

Sophie's heart hiccupped at the news.

Truly? *Again*?

Where had the man gone this time?

But Rafe held his smile.

The woman blinked again and then shook her head, as if to clear her scrambled wits.

She moved to shut the door. "I bid ye good day."

"Wait, please." Rafe held up a staying hand, somehow deepening those dimples.

Heavens, he was potent when he wished to be.

The woman wavered, the dimples doing their work.

"It is urgent that we speak with the doctor." Rafe's tone took on a cajoling edge. "Do ye know where we might find him?"

The woman licked her lips. "I cannae rightly say."

She shot Rafe another look before beginning to shut the door, though more hesitantly this time.

Rafe held out his other hand, a gold sovereign in his fingers. "Would this assist in loosening your tongue?" He punctuated the question with another blast of dimpled charm.

The woman stared at him and then the coin. She darted a cautious glance behind her, as if ensuring the hall was empty. Then, she took a half-step out the door, joining Rafe and Sophie on the stoop. She snatched the sovereign from Rafe's fingers.

"Dr. Ross is like to be living with his sister in the Highlands, west of Aberdeen," she murmured, slipping the sovereign into her apron pocket. "Drathes Castle, just outside Aboyne—"

"Margaret!" A crotchety man's voice rang down the hall. "Are you yammering away with that wee Alice again?"

Unlike Margaret, the man's voice held a gentrified, English edge.

The woman startled and practically jumped back inside the house.

"Never ye mind, Robert!" she called back, hand on the door. "'Tis none of yer affair—"

"Of course, 'tis my affair, woman!"

A tall man with a ragged mop of white hair strode out of a doorway to the left of the entrance hall.

"Now see here, Robert, I was just helping these fine people with some directions." Margaret turned to the older man, shooing him away with flicking wrists. "No harm done, as ye can see."

Rafe hissed in a breath at Sophie's side.

The elderly man similarly froze, eyes drilling into Rafe.

And then he shifted to look at Sophie. He rocked back a step, as if in surprise. But he recovered quickly and took two strong strides forward, eyebrows rapidly drawing to a 'V.'

He stopped beside Margaret, nostrils flaring, eyes dragging up and down Rafe's kilt.

Rafe had gone still as a statue beside Sophie, all smiles gone, his arm steel under her hand.

"Lord Rafe," the man said, tone chilly.

Shock chased Sophie's spine.

Lord Rafe?!

"Beadle," Rafe replied, the name spat like a curse.

Who was this man?

"How may I be of assistance, my lord?" the elderly man—Beadle, Sophie supposed—asked.

Rafe shifted the weight on his feet. "I believe that we have all that we need—"

"Pardon," a new voice said behind them. A deep, menacing sort of voice that made the hairs on the back of Sophie's neck lurch upright in alarm. "Do yous lot need anything in truth? Or should I assist ye in taking yerselves off?"

Sophie turned to find another man behind them, standing on the walk between them and their carriage. Unlike Beadle, this fellow was younger and stocky, built like a pugilist. He wasn't dressed in a kilt, but the red wool bonnet on his head proclaimed his nationality before he opened his mouth. The man's eyes, however, were anything but welcoming.

Rafe froze further at Sophie's side, every muscle tensed for action.

What was going on? Who were these people? How did they know Rafe?

"Your father is well, I trust?" Beadle asked, bringing their attention back to him. The unknown thug remained at their backs, a threatening presence.

"Kendall is well," Rafe replied, though his clipped tone clearly added the word *unfortunately* to the end.

Kendall? Beadle knew Kendall? How was the duke involved in this? Sophie swallowed, hand tightening on Rafe's arm.

"Give him my regards when next you see him." Beadle's sharp gaze darted to her, something hard and unyielding there that set Sophie's skin to crawling. This Beadle fellow looked at her the same way Kendall did.

Who was this man to the duke? Who was he to Rafe?

And why the looming bruiser behind?

"I will. Thank you for your time," Rafe finally replied. "Good day."

He nodded at Margaret, before turning around. He stared down the pugilist behind them, before leading Sophie back to the waiting chaise.

Sophie allowed Rafe to hand her into the carriage, noting that Beadle and Margaret remained on the stoop, watching them, the unknown man saying something, his distinctive red hat bobbing even at a distance.

"Walk on," Rafe ordered the postillion before climbing in beside her.

Rafe waited until the chaise turned a corner before sinking his head back with a low groan, letting loose a stream of profanity that went on for a solid minute.

What just happened?

Rafe's expletives and the tense reactions of everyone involved were a rather clear indication that he considered the situation a catastrophe.

"Damnation! Of all the blasted, rotten luck!" Rafe shook his head, over and over. "This is an utter disaster. How is this even possible! *Beadle?!* Bloody hell!"

He rattled away for another moment.

"Rafe?" She placed a hand on his arm. "Who is Beadle?"

"Mr. Robert Beadle"—he spat the man's name—"was the butler for our Mayfair townhouse for over twenty years. He began as a valet to my father when my sire was abroad on his Grand Tour. Eventually, Kendall made him butler over his entire London household. Beadle retired three years ago. I had no idea my father had pensioned him off in Edinburgh." He shook his head one more time. "Beadle will surely report seeing me to my father, the bastard."

Oh! "That is truly awful. After everything you've done to hide this trip—"

"Precisely! There is no doubt that Beadle is currently penning a letter to Kendall. Beadle has always been my father's man. He's impossibly loyal. If I had shown up kitted out as Lord Rafe, perhaps inquiring after Beadle's health and seeming solicitous as a family friend, maybe Beadle would have been slower to mention it. But arriving dressed as a Highlander, asking after Dr. Ross, clearly not expecting to see Beadle . . . it's far too suspicious for him *not* to report it immediately."

Rafe's voice drifted into cursing again. He leaned his head back against the seat, pounding his skull against the soft cushions, eyes staring sightlessly at the carriage roof overhead.

"Everything we've done to hide this trip from my father . . . demolished." He made an exploding gesture with his hands. "My sire is too intelligent not to immediately understand that I am attempting to thwart him. He'll ask questions, threaten my mother . . ."

Rafe pressed his palms into his eye sockets, suppressing a frustrated growl.

Seeing his obvious distress did something to Sophie's chest. How was this the same rake she had disdained not even two weeks before? No longer a *Rakus lasciviosus*, but a *Virum nobilis*—a noble gentleman who simply wanted his mother's happiness and the freedom to govern his own life.

"Who was the other man? The one who came up behind us on the front stoop?"

"The brawny looking fellow? I have no idea. I have never seen him before, but that means little. My father likes to hire former pugilists as grooms to enforce his demands."

"Well, the man certainly felt threatening. His red bonnet seemed emblematic of his temper. Bruiser of a man, that one."

"Bruiser? Fitting." Rafe flashed her a fleeting smile. "Bruiser isn't even the worst of it, though. Beadle saw ye—"

"Me? Why should that matter?"

"I think he recognized ye."

Sophie frowned. "How would your London butler of years past know a younger daughter of the Earl of Mainfeld upon sight? I look nothing like either of my supposed parents, and our fathers give one another a wide berth."

Rafe remained silent, his hands still over his eyes.

"Rafe?" she prompted. "Why would Beadle recognizing me upset you? What aren't you telling me?"

NAUSEA CLIMBED RAFE'S throat. Of all the damned abominable luck.

Robert *bloody* Beadle.

"I feel that I am missing a critical piece of this puzzle, Rafe. Please tell me," Sophie said again, shifting on the seat beside him. The carriage bumped over cobblestones returning to New Town and Alex's house.

Rafe huffed a soft laugh.

What a tangled web.

He couldn't very well tell her the full truth: *Well, you see Sophie darling, I have loved you quite madly for at least four years now. My father, ever astute, realized this eons ago. Last time he caught us together, I was banished to the far side of the planet. What will he do this time?*

Somehow, someway, Beadle had recognized her. Beadle had made it his business to know Rafe's life. The old butler had probably followed Rafe one day, seen him with Sophie. After all, his father had always had an almost uncanny knowledge of Rafe's comings and goings. Hence the need for such an elaborate disguise on this trip north.

All for naught.

That nausea churned in his stomach, a toxic mix of frustration and impotence and blinding, *seething* rage.

What was he to do?

The chaise rocked onward. The press of Sophie's body beside him, the comfort of her presence . . . a haunting glimpse of a future he would *never* have, never experience.

Bitterness and anger washed over him, acidic in its fury.

How dare his sire commandeer his future like this? How much longer could he tolerate this? How could a man live such a life, forever bound to one he so hated?

He pressed his shaking hands over his face, sucking in deep breaths, trying to force down his more savage thoughts.

The ones that whispered terrible things like . . . a convenient accident, his father's death, and *no one would ever know.*

Pity he wasn't prepared quite yet to enact a Greek tragedy. Rafe was too much his mother's son. She had raised him to be a better man than this. No matter how convenient Kendall's untimely demise would be.

"Rafe?" Sophie's voice, soft and low.

As ever, just the *sound* of her voice was a lit fuse down his spine, sparking the nerves in his body.

"There's no help for it, Sophie." He let his hands fall. "The damage has been done. My father will find out about this particular escapade, and the consequences will be spectacular."

"Will he hurt your mother?"

He laughed, a bitter sound. "Perhaps. Just enough to hurt me, the bastard. And then he'll demand even more, put me on a shorter leash. Force me to marry—"

"Marry?!"

"Aye. He has it in his head that I will marry Miss Sykes—"

"Lord Sykes's daughter?"

"The very same. I do not wish to disparage Miss Sykes, but marriage should be based on more than a handshake between our fathers."

"I had thought arranged marriages a thing of the past."

"So had I," Rafe snorted. "And even if I can escape the matrimonial noose, I will remain at Kendall's beck and call. He relishes giving me distasteful tasks . . . evicting tenants, enacting punishments, anything to sully my soul." A knot settled in his stomach.

"That is truly terrible, Rafe." Sophie frowned, fingers tapping. "Moreover, I cannot seem to reconcile with this level of a coincidence."

"Pardon?"

"It seems nearly impossible that your father's devoted servant resides at the same address where Dr. John Ross once lived. There is no connection between the two men, is there? Between Kendall and Dr. Ross?"

Intelligent lass.

Rafe pursed his lips, his own frown deepening, mind churning.

"I'm an eejit," he said, nodding slowly. "I had never heard of this Dr. Ross until Alex mentioned him, but the puzzle is even deeper than that."

"How so?"

He drummed his fingers, forcing himself to think through the frustration seething in his brain. What *was* going on here?

"Robert Beadle, as a long-time loyal lap-dog, would have received a pension," he said. "The key piece of my father's pension promise is almost always a house of the servant's own. The dukedom owns thousands of properties throughout the country."

"So why wasn't Beadle sent to one of those?" Sophie asked. "Why a townhouse in Edinburgh instead?"

"Those are the questions, aren't they? Or, possibly more damning, does my father *own* Beadle's townhouse on Drummond Street here in Edinburgh?"

Sophie sat back, eyes wide. "When did Beadle retire?"

"About three years ago."

"Didn't Dr. Hartley say Dr. Ross left London to move to Edinburgh about three years ago?"

"That could just be a coincidence."

"Possibly, but it's an interesting coincidence. The woman at the door said that the good professor had left Beadle's house to live with his sister a year past."

"Meaning there were two years when Dr. Ross presumably lived in that same house in Edinburgh."

"Exactly." Sophie nodded. "Of course, as you said, it could simply all be happenstance and unrelated in any way. Dr. Ross and Beadle, both elderly men, simply retired at about the same time. Beadle lived elsewhere, and Dr. Ross came here to this house in Edinburgh. Then Dr. Ross left Edinburgh a year ago to live with his sister, and Beadle took over the lease and moved into the Drummond Street townhouse. But . . ." Her voice drifted off, brows drawn down in thought.

"But?" he prompted.

"The woman at the door, Margaret, spoke like she knew Dr. Ross. More than that, she was hesitant to disclose that he had lived there. Why would she care, if he had simply been a previous tenant? Instead, she acted as if it were secret somehow."

"Or she merely saw two well-dressed people on her doorstep as an opportunity to earn a quick coin?"

"That is possible, but as I review the conversation in my mind, my impression was one of hesitant secrecy, not greed. Not to mention that Bruiser fellow, showing up behind us and looming threateningly. Those were all the actions of people with secrets to hide."

Rafe pondered that, remembering how Margaret had looked behind her as if watching for Beadle, not wanting him to hear her speak of Dr. Ross.

Which, truthfully, made no sense at all. What business did Dr. Ross have with Rafe's father? What could possibly require such secrecy?

"So ye are proposing, lass, an alternative story." He sat more upright. "One where Beadle left London at about the same time as Dr. Ross and, for some unknown reason, lived with him here in Edinburgh. Perhaps even butlered for him." A longer pause. "In a house owned and provided by my father."

A pause and then Sophie's reply: "Yes."

"Why?" Rafe could hear the confusion in his voice, the bewildering thought of it. "Why would my father bring Ross to Edinburgh and place him in a household with a trusted, pensioned servant?"

"There are only two reasons I can conceive." Sophie offered. "Perhaps your father has something to hide, and Dr. Ross knows the secret. Beadle was set as a sort of guard over Dr. Ross, with people like Margaret and Bruiser to help. Or your father valued Ross in some way—perhaps Ross performed some noble deed?—and Kendall wished to reward him."

Rafe snorted. "My sire is not in the habit of rewarding people for anything other than astonishing acts of service. What must Ross have done to deserve such a reward?"

"Or, given what you have told me about your father . . . what did Ross do to merit such a punishment? Being placed into a household and watched over every moment by another man . . . a sort of house arrest?"

Rafe nodded. How he adored her clever mind.

"But if Ross was a prisoner," he said, "why send him off to the Highlands? Drathes Castle near Aboyne?"

"That . . . I cannot say."

He nearly groaned in frustration. "Blast it all! We don't have time to spend asking questions and getting to the bottom of my father's involvement with Ross. In the end, such answers will not help my mother."

"Yes. Dr. Ross seems to be the key to all this."

"Aye. All that is left is to regroup and formulate a plan." Rafe clenched his jaw, rapidly thinking through ramifications and timelines. "We've come this far, and Dr. Ross is still my best source of any help for my mother. And, as you said, the good doctor seems to be central to all this."

"I agree."

Rafe thought further. "Even if Beadle sends the letter today, it will likely be at least a week before it reaches my father. He will wait to punish my mother until I return. He needs witnesses. Brutality is useless when performed in a vacuum."

"So you will continue northward then? To Drathes Castle?"

"Yes. I've come this far. I want to see it all through. "Will you accompany me?"

She hesitated, those enormous green eyes meeting his. "I would like to, but time seems to be of the essence at this point, at least for you. I would never forgive myself if I hampered the speed of your travel."

"Nonsense. We began this journey together that day in the doctor's surgery in London. I say we finish it together."

"Are you sure?"

"Aye. We can travel faster on horseback. The road into Aboyne in the Cairngorms will likely not be passable for a carriage, which means we will have to leave your carriage and your servants with Alex." He paused. "Even Martha."

Sophie managed a wry smile. "I do not think Martha will mind being left with James."

"So ye feel ye could manage a long trip on horseback?"

She shot him a decidedly *are-ye-daft* look. "Regardless of my true paternity, I was raised by the Earl of Mainfeld. My father is a fanatical sportsman. I think I was in a saddle before I could walk. You should hope to keep up with *me*, not the other way around."

Rafe barely suppressed a smile at her outrage. Vividly he remembered seeing her riding along Rotten Row in Hyde Park. The woman had a magnificent seat.

"That's settled then. Would ye be willing to leave at first light tomorrow morning?"

"Of course." She met his gaze, clear-eyed and confident. Utterly committed to his cause.

Rafe was quite sure he would never love another woman as much as he loved Lady Sophronia in that moment.

How was he ever going to part with her once their journey was over?

20

Any doubts Rafe may have had as to the exact ownership of the townhouse on Drummond Street were laid to rest the following morning.

After an anxious night's sleep, he was up at first light to visit his father's Edinburgh residence in Charlotte Square. Rafe had several horses stabled in the mews behind the house, animals that he and Sophie would need for their trip to Aboyne.

The butler of the residence was entirely unsurprised to find Rafe upon the doorstep. Someone had told the man Rafe was in Edinburgh, and it didn't take any guess work to know who that was. Rafe did not, thankfully, encounter that Bruiser fellow as he saw to his own horses.

Kendall would know everything in fewer than five or six days. Rafe hoped to visit Dr. Ross near Aboyne and then catch a boat from Aberdeen back to London, as he was acquainted with one of the captains of the London packet boat. With any luck, Rafe would arrive only a day or two behind whatever letters Beadle sent and, from there, brazen his way through his father's censure.

But Rafe was no fool. Any hope he had of avoiding a marriage to Lord Sykes' daughter had utterly vanished. His father now owned Rafe's future. At best, Rafe might leverage the marriage as a means of keeping his mother out of an asylum for the time being. If Dr. Ross had helpful information, that space of time might be enough to turn around her melancholy, to at least give them all hope for a better future.

But Rafe had to find the man first.

And as for Sophie and himself . . . Rafe would just have to learn to breathe through the painful ache currently banding his chest.

SOPHIE PULLED HER earasaid tighter around her shoulders while clutching the horse reins in her fist. She buried further into the heavy, warm wool, hunching in her saddle. Her poor gelding had his head bowed, both of them doing all they could to shut out the bitter wind blowing down the mountain valley.

The Scottish weather had been true to its reputation over the past two and half days since leaving Edinburgh. Rain and wind had forced them to stop in Perth for a night. The second day, they had only made it to Brechin before being forced indoors.

Today, they set out on the final leg—and the most treacherous stretch—of the journey to Aboyne. The village was buried in the Cairngorms, a mountain range that stretched west from Aberdeen nearly to Inverness. Rafe had said they had just over thirty miles of ground to cover today, but it felt like more, as the terrain was mountainous and inhospitable.

The roads had been worse and worse the farther north they traveled, and now the way had degenerated into more of a track than an actual road. The innkeep in Brechin had promised that there would be a small drovers inn in Aboyne that could put them up for the night . . . provided they reached Aboyne before the weather turned.

Or rather, became *worse*, Sophie mused.

The rain at the moment fell sideways more than down, the wind whipping and pelting her face. The track zig-zagged up the barren moor, a slash of civilization in the stark landscape. Before leaving London, Sophie had not thought that such a forlorn place could exist on the isle of Great Britain.

They weren't the only people on the road, thank goodness. There was a rider or two behind them—Sophie caught glimpses of them on the path below from time to time—probably eager, like them, to clear the mountains before nightfall.

Rafe rode ahead, leading the way with two other horses between them.

He turned in his saddle to look back at her. "Are ye holding up, lass?"

His brogue had become more consistent the longer he remained in Scotland. Though he had lost the thick accent of Lennon Gordon, his tone retained a Scottish lilt.

In short, it melted her knees every time he spoke.

"Cold but otherwise in decent spirits," she replied.

He grunted his approval before turning back around.

Her words were truth. Despite everything—their continued journey, the atrocious weather, the threat of Kendall looming—she was desperately grateful to be in his company. To still have Lord Rafe Gilbert close.

The wind whipped around them, the biting air and ominous clouds hinting at more violent weather to come.

On the morning of their departure from Edinburgh, he had arrived at Dr. Whitaker's townhouse with four horses, two for riding and two as pack animals and spare mounts. The few inns they did encounter were humble affairs and hardly the sort to have horses for hire, so they had to spare their own animals as best they could.

If Sophie had found Rafe attractive as a London rake and a roguish Highlander, nothing prepared her for the spine-weakening sight of Lord Rafe in his most true element—competent, virile man.

Two days of staring at him riding before her had solidified this opinion. He had swapped out his Highland kilt for more traditional buckskin breeches and riding boots. But that hadn't stopped him from wrapping a length of Jamie's black-and-red tartan across his body underneath an enormous caped greatcoat.

After watching her shiver on the ferry crossing at Queensferry, Rafe had pulled out a second length of plaid—also in Jamie's tartan—showing Sophie how to fold and wrap it to create a sort of cloak, a second warm layer of wool between her dress and her traditional English cloak. An earasaid, he called it—the female version of a kilt.

Right now, Sophie was simply grateful for its warmth. The heavy wool kept out the wind and damp, helping her body retain its heat.

The road snaked through hills, each one taller than the last, climbing higher and higher. A battered sign at the crossroads in the village of Fettercairn far below had called this route Cairn O'Mount. The barren moor provided no shelter from the rain and did nothing to break the wind whistling through the heather and gorse. The land was desolate with only the occasional abandoned steading, likely some of the many casualties of the Highland Clearances.

Rafe's large bay trudged up the road, head down. The wind blew Rafe's greatcoat, revealing a pair of pistols tucked into his belt. A rifle gleamed across his saddle. Sophie had a pistol of her own tucked into the belt of her earasaid. There had been no reports of bandits in this area, but neither of them wanted to take any chances, not after their brush with the highwaymen in England.

Sophie's horse stumbled, causing her to list in the saddle. She easily righted herself, but not before Rafe turned around, eyebrows drawn down, a hand reaching back, instinctively moving to help her, even though he was too far away to do anything.

The path widened for a moment, and he used the extra space to pull up on his horse, motioning her to come alongside him, positioning his body between her and the wind.

Sophie clenched her teeth to stop their chattering.

Why did the dratted man have to be so caring? She kept telling her wayward heart that nothing would come of their friendship.

Nothing! You hear that, Heart!

Even if Rafe wished for more between them, she knew that their fathers' bitter hatred stood as a barrier. And if they ignored Kendall's wishes, Rafe's mother would pay the price. The woman's safety was infinitely more important than Sophie's sentimental wishes.

But *oh* how she wished—

"Is Scotland always this dratted cold?" she asked through clacking teeth.

He chuckled. "Truthfully? Aye. But it is a wee bit cooler than a typical autumn day at the moment. The rain is already turning to sleet. I fear there may be snow before long."

"Snow?!"

"Aye. It's not unheard of in the Cairngorms in late October. But provided the weather doesn't become worse, we should be able to reach Aboyne before supper."

Sophie grimaced. The rain was indeed turning to a sleety snow-and-rain mix.

Rafe glanced past her shoulder, eyes drawn to something behind them. Sophie swiveled to follow his gaze.

She had to squint to see the two men on horseback on the path far below them.

"They've been gaining on us," she indicated the men with her chin, not wanting to release her cloak.

"Aye."

Sophie stared at the men.

"Does one of them have a red hat?" she asked.

Rafe stilled, following her gaze, eyes squinting, both of them focusing on a large man bobbing with a flash of red atop his head. "I think ye might be right, lass. That does look like a red bonnet."

Sophie exchanged a look with Rafe.

"Surely that's merely coincidence," she said. "Red bonnets are common among Scotsmen, even burly, bruiser ones, right?"

Rafe continued to stare at the men, eyes narrowing as if to bring them into better focus.

"Aye," he said after a moment. "It's not so uncommon as to *not* be coincidence. But this weather is frightful." He pulled his own cloak tighter. "And we've had more than our share of coincidences as of late." He turned his horse and met her gaze. "If the rain turns to snow in earnest, we may need to seek shelter."

Shelter? Where? Sophie shivered, scanning the empty moor. There was nothing over three feet tall for miles.

They continued onward for another hour or so, crossing a high plateau and passing an ancient cairn before descending to a wooded forest. The fir trees provided some relief from the endless wind, but the rain had turned entirely to snow. Big fluffy flakes dusted the tree branches.

"We need to find shelter," Rafe said, looking back at her. "This snow is too much."

Sophie nodded, her teeth chattering.

"There," Rafe pointed.

Through the snow, Sophie spotted a structure tucked against the hillside. A small stream and rudimentary bridge sat in front of it.

Reaching the bridge, they clattered over it and instantly aimed for what appeared to be a small ruined cottage beyond, the roof removed in an attempt to keep its former occupants from returning.

"Hah!" Rafe pointed to a small stable beside the cottage, this one with an intact roof. "Seems they left the stable to serve as a bothie." He noted Sophie's raised eyebrows and then added, "A shelter for travelers."

He reached the old stable first, dismounted, and pulled open the door. Smelling hay and, eager to get out of the cold and sleet, the horses crowded in behind him, pushing into the structure.

Sophie dismounted and followed. The interior was basic—four stone walls and a timber roof with slate tiles. But without windows, there was scarcely any light. She pulled the door nearly closed behind her, allowing only a small strip of daylight in so they could see.

Together, they worked to situate the horses, drying the beasts as best they could and finding scraps of hay for them to eat.

Finally, Rafe nodded his head and, pulling a rickety bench from the debris of the stable, angled it for her to sit upon. He positioned himself closer to the door, snagging his rifle and resting it against the door jamb, within quick reach should they need it. He laid his brace of pistols on the bench beside him.

"Will we be stuck here for long, do you think?" she asked, tugging off her gloves and blowing on her cold hands.

Rafe shrugged. "'Tis hard to gauge. The snow comes and goes this time of year. It's unlikely tae last for the rest of the day. For now, we'll wait a wee while and see if it doesn't clear out a bit."

"Should we be concerned about the travelers we saw behind us? They will need shelter, too, won't they?"

"Perhaps. But they are likely friendly. And if not, we are prepared." He patted the pistols beside his thigh. "They will not catch us unawares."

Sophie shivered, pulling her earasaid closer. Without the heat of movement, the damp seeped in. Rafe noticed her chattering chin with a frown.

"Come closer." He pulled her nearer to him, extending his greatcoat to cover her, as well. "The horses should help keep us warm, but we should all stay huddled together."

Shamelessly, Sophie tucked into Rafe's side, seeking his warmth. He obviously needed no further encouragement, as he instantly wrapped an arm around her, pulling her into him until they were touching from thigh to shoulder. He was deliciously warm.

"Better?" he asked.

She nodded, taking in a deep breath of the scent of pine and sandalwood that was so essentially *him*.

How her opinion of him had changed in such a small amount of time. From wastrel rake to seeing this gentle, kindhearted man. One who sacrificed his every happiness for his mother.

She sighed, relaxing further into him, resting her head on his shoulder. Memories of that fateful night at the ball years ago surfaced. It all seemed like a lifetime ago, and yet, being back in the circle of Rafe's arms, Sophie recalled it all in vivid detail. The supporting strength of his arms around her. The hitch in his breath as their lips first met. The soft press of his mouth. The way his hands had trembled as he kissed her.

How was she to survive this trip without giving her whole heart to this man?

And at this point, did she even wish to fight it anymore?

21

Rafe pulled Sophie even closer, desperate to hold her, to keep her safe.

The snow fell harder, obliterating even the road from view.

She relaxed against his side, half-turning into him, her soft curves melting into his chest, her head coming to rest on his shoulder. The horses snuffled as they munched on their hay, the combined body heat of four great beasts gradually warming the space.

Despite the gnawing worry over his mother and the quest to find Dr. Ross, Rafe felt a thrum of profound contentment.

This.

This is what he longed for his life to be.

Quiet stillness with a woman he loved.

He was quite sure this moment—a crofter's bothie, snow, and Sophie in his arms—might go down as the pinnacle of his existence.

And then . . .

. . . Sophie nuzzled.

There was no other word for it.

She buried her cold nose into the space between his jawline and shoulder and . . . nuzzled.

Heaven help him.

"Are ye . . . are ye nuzzling me, lass?" he asked.

She froze.

"Possibly," her voice muffled.

And then . . . she moved her nose again, drawing that much closer to him.

He chuckled, a low rumble.

"I would never have taken ye for the nuzzling sort."

That got her attention. "Whyever not?"

"You practically crackle with competence. I simply cannae imagine ye needing another tae the level of nuzzling."

"I need others. Think of me like a cat—"

"The barn cats again?"

"Hah." She poked him in the ribs.

He squirmed.

"Are you ticklish?" she asked, raising her head, looking at him with those lovely eyes.

"Perhaps."

She poked him again. He squirmed more emphatically.

"Mmmm, this might prove interesting," she grinned.

"Barn cats?" he prompted.

Her eyes narrowed. "Right. No matter how independently they behave, cats adore being petted."

"I'll keep that in mind." Rafe laughed, pulling her in for tight nuzzle.

Though, truth be told, he wanted significantly more than a mere nuzzle. His head spun at her nearness. The memory of their kiss all those years ago rose in vivid detail. As if he could ever forget. The way she had flowed into his arms, melting into him. He had cupped her cheeks and felt her entire body inhale and rise up. His hands had *trembled*, for heaven's sake.

Were memories all that he would be allowed of her? A talisman to cherish? If so, he would not waste this moment either.

He concentrated on the feel of her, the way the curves of her body melded into his, the light rose scent of her soap, the warmth of her breath on his neck.

Would her lips still taste the same? Would his hands shake again, were he to kiss her?

Why, of all women, was she forbidden him? He swallowed back the anger, the rage that flooded him. Was there no way to be free of his father?

"I cannot believe your father will force you to marry Miss Sykes," she whispered.

Her words may have seemed like another of her *non sequiturs*, but Rafe easily followed her logic. Their minds were too attuned, it seemed.

"He can and he will," Rafe replied, noting the bitterness in his tone. "Not all fathers are truly caring of their offspring."

She stirred at that, pulling back to look at him.

"The man is a fool," she whispered, eyes imploring. "How could he not adore you?"

The outrage in her voice caused him to snort, a soft breath of sound.

"The. Nerve," he said.

Sophie smiled, though it was edged with pain.

"Kendall is a monster," he continued. "There is no other way to describe him." A pause. He looked past her to the snow still falling through the cracked door, the world a perfect sheet of white. "I *hate* him, in fact. Thoroughly and utterly."

There.

He had said it.

And as if a dam burst, he could no longer stem the flood of words. "I detest everything my father stands for. His innate cruelty, his obsessive need to command every person within his sphere. It's an illness of the mind just as surely as that of my mother." He shook his head. "The worst part? I *hate* that I hate him." He laughed, so caustic. "I hate that I allow my emotions to control my behavior. That I *react* to him, instead of remaining indifferent and uncaring."

The horses snuffled again, one bumping him in the shoulder in the small space. He reached up to rub its nose with his free hand, his other arm still firmly around Sophie.

She leaned forward and stroked a hand down his cheek, her chilled fingers leaving a trail of fire in their wake.

"Hate can be crippling," she murmured. "I would know."

"You? I struggle tae imagine ye hating anyone."

She laughed, the same bitter sound he had just made. "Do not flatter me, my lord. I am hardly a saint."

"Truly? I dinnae believe it, lass." He caught her hand, unable to stop himself from pressing a kiss into her palm. She shivered and Rafe was quite sure it wasn't only from the cold, as she did not pull her hand out of his grasp. If anything, she leaned closer to him.

"You didn't see me during my marriage to Jack," she whispered.

That had Rafe lifting his head.

"Captain Fulstate? Was he unkind to ye?" If so, Rafe might have to exhume the man's body and send him to his Maker a second time.

"Unkind?" She paused. "Not with his fists, if that's what you mean. But yes, in other ways."

Her voice drifted off before she brought her gaze back to his. Rafe hated the pain he saw reflected there.

Yes, Jack Fulstate was fortunate to already be dead.

"Words can be as hurtful as fists. Behavior, too," she continued, answering his unasked questions. "He gambled to excess. He was chronically unfaithful to me. Worse, whenever I would confront him over his behavior, he was baffled that I found anything amiss with him visiting bawdy houses or slaking his lust with the occasional willing lady. It's what a gentleman does, after all . . ."

"Ah, Sophie—"

"I know." She gave that same mirthless laugh. "I *know*. How could I have been so *stupidly* naive? But . . . we had discussed it *before* marrying. Jack *knew* how I felt about my parent's marriage, about their infidelities, particularly those of my mother. I refused to be in a marriage such as that. I refused to have my children grow up in a house of lies and betrayal. In the end, I realized that Jack had simply heard that *I* would be faithful to *him*—something he crowed over, like I was a possession to be hoarded from others—but he clearly did not believe that same obligation of fidelity should extend to himself."

Rafe's anger stoked higher, fury quicksilvering his veins. This woman. How had he not known? How had he not fully discerned that this was how her marriage had been? She had alluded to it before, but it had not fully sunk in.

She had been in a marriage like that of his mother's . . . tied to a man who treated her abominably.

Worse, a thread of guilt wound through him. Rafe could not deny that his behavior had been a catalyst of a sort, practically forcing her into Jack's arms. If Rafe had been able to follow through with his word, would she have chosen him instead?

As for now . . . what could he say? "You are deserving of fidelity and honor. *Those* are the hallmarks of a true gentleman."

"Yes, I knew that then, and I know that now. But when in the middle of my marriage, it seemed impossible to remember." A brief pause as she brought her gaze to his. "I hated him for it."

"Jack?"

"Yes. I detested him. Every tender emotion I had felt prior to our marriage was burned and stamped out within a few months. And then I let the hate grow. I fed it. I nurtured it. Every word, every glance added fuel to the flames until our marriage became a conflagration. We fought . . . bitterly at times."

She stopped, eyes wide with pain and an almost horrified wonder.

"And . . ." he prompted. Because he had heard the word in her tone that the story did not end there.

"And then . . . he died," her words a mere breath of sound, swallowed up in the hush of the falling snow. "He caught a putrid sore throat and was gone within two weeks. Just . . . gone."

"Did your anger not die with him?"

"No!" A huff of nearly baffled laughter. "It did not. It was as if he held on to me from beyond the grave. To be clear, I felt relief that he was finally gone, but my anger toward him still seethed within me. My hate for him ruled me until I thought the anger and betrayal would consume my soul."

"I know that emotion well." Rafe clenched his jaw. "It is my oldest friend, my constant companion—"

"Yes, I can imagine. But, you see, I came to realize several important things." She trailed her fingers down his cheek again. He caught her hand in his before she could pull away.

"Aye?"

"My hate, all that bitterness and anger . . . it was only hurting *me*. All that energy, all that animosity, had nowhere to go, and so it was eating me alive from the inside out." Again, a bitter burst of laughter. "Jack was gone. My anger couldn't hurt *him*. It certainly couldn't right his wrongs or force him to apologize and change. It could not give me the loving husband I had thought to marry. My hate could do *nothing* but destroy me."

"All true. Anger toward a dead man does no good." He shifted his legs and looked down at her. "But my father is, tae my deep regret, very much alive. My anger and hatred can bear some fruit. Moreover, simply knowing something is poisoning you isn't enough tae squelch it. I don't *want* tae hate my father, and yet the emotion never ceases."

"I believe you. I wanted the hate gone, too. But scenes and words would tumble through my mind with alarming frequency. Months after Jack's death, I still felt captive to it, despondent even. I wasn't eating. I spent days in my bed chamber, only emerging to take long walks through the countryside. Until one day . . . it all came crashing down. I had just had *enough*. I was so tired of my hate. That man had taken so *much* from me, and I refused to give him any more of my soul."

Rafe huffed a laugh of his own. Easy words, but nearly impossible to follow. Just the thought of it left him choking. "How did you manage it?"

"I won't pretend it was simple or easy. But I realized something important . . . hate is a shield. A dam holding back a tidal wave of other, more painful emotions."

"A *shield?*" Rafe nearly snorted the word. "That seems . . . unlikely."

She raised an eyebrow. "Perhaps, but that is the way I think of it. I firmly believe that hate, as an emotion, rears up to protect us from other emotions that we would prefer not to feel. As I said, I had all this energy focused on trying to make Jack pay for his cruelty to me. But why? To what purpose? The man was *dead*. And no matter how hard you try to avoid it, the pain lying underneath hatred and anger will eventually catch up with you."

"You believe so?"

"I do, Rafe. I sincerely do. About three months after Jack's death, I sat in my bed chamber one evening—after having spent hours earlier having a good cathartic weep—examining the roil of emotion in my chest, mentally poking and prodding it, desperately wanting it gone but not knowing how to manage it. Eventually, some bit of it broke free . . . and the truth hit me all at once—my hatred was simply a dam holding back my pain."

"Your pain?"

Sophie nodded, eyes bright. "Pain that my marriage was such a failure. Pain that I had chosen so poorly. Pain that I was unwanted and unloved by the person who had pledged before God to do those very things. All that hatred I aimed at Jack was partly my own self-loathing and self-pity. But it is far easier to hate a wastrel husband than to feel all the horror of one's poor choices, the pain of one's insecurities. And so I *loved* my hate. I fed it and stoked it because it shielded me from a mountain of personal pain. But once I had removed the shield—or, as I said, a dam, if that metaphor works better for you—emotions flooded me, hurt and pain and such *bitter* regret."

Rafe instinctively pushed away Sophie's words. There was no underlying emotion going on. His father was a manipulative, controlling brute. Full stop. *That* was the beginning and end of Rafe's hatred. It was not a covering protecting him from something else. It was not a dam holding back an ocean of pain or regret.

And yet . . . his heart reverberated, as if Sophie's words had rung a bell deep within his soul and his chest clambered and resonated from the tumult of it.

Sophie continued, "But despite the horrific pain, I also realized something equally important—hate and anger are fuel. Hate is a species of violent anger aimed at another person. When left unchecked, it can be incredibly destructive. But that hate—that anger—can be channeled. And so I decided to put that fuel to better use, to turn it into determination to move past Jack and his cruelties, to heal the pain in my soul. I refused to give him more of myself than he had already taken. And so I took that hate and molded it from anger into tenacity and strength and, most importantly, into forgiveness—forgiveness toward myself for being so incredibly foolish.

"And in doing that, I finally saw Jack for what he was . . . a weak, pitiful man who needed to buoy himself up by making me feel small. He ceased to have any hold over me." She took in a deep breath. "But, to be truly honest, I am still working on forgiving myself. It is difficult to face one's own shortcomings. The process isn't easy. I still feel unwanted and unloved. But I feel hope that, if I continue forward, I *can* have a full and happy life in the future."

Rafe nodded, his throat abruptly tight and painful.

I still feel unwanted and unloved.

He blinked and looked out the door to the still falling snow, eyes stinging.

She wasn't quite done. "I am concerned for your own soul, Rafe. I sense so much rage in you. I'm not saying you need to like Kendall or trust him or even release your anger over his cruelty. But the hate? The rage you feel toward your father specifically? It *will* destroy you. Perhaps you could ask yourself: 'Is there some pain or fear that my hate is protecting me from?'"

"There is only my father's brutal cruelty!" He gave a harsh bark of laughter.

"Perhaps. But at the very least, consider harnessing all your rage and molding the energy into determination for good. Otherwise, I fear the power of it will destroy your soul. You will burn on the pyre of your hatred."

His breath caught. Why did her words pound through him?

Could he move beyond anger and hate? Could he move on—

No!

He instinctively rejected it. His father was a repugnant human being. Kendall *needed* to be abhorred, reviled. He deserved it. It was the only way to deal with a man such as him—

Something cold brushed his cheek. He looked down into her eyes, shimmering pools of forest green, her palm pressed to his jaw.

"Your father isn't worth your hate," she said. "Your hate is a reaction to his behavior. Another way in which he owns you, another way he controls you. Do not give him the satisfaction of such emotion."

The very thought felt impossible. His rage was a vast chasm, dug over too many years of hurts and cuts and cruelty. He couldn't imagine a day when he would *not* despise his sire, no matter how damaging to himself.

But yet . . .

Her words rang in his ears.

I loved my hate. I fed it and stoked it because it kept me from a mountain of personal pain.

Your hate is a reaction to his behavior. Another way in which he owns you.

"If hate and anger are fuel," he began, voice low, "I have enough of it tae energize an army."

"Then motivate that army. Pour that rage into hope, into determination to fight free of him. Take back your future. Do not give him any more of yourself. Your soul is too precious to squander on *that* man."

Her words increased the thundering in his chest, the rackety pinging resonating deep.

Take back your future.

Was that even possible at this point?

Your soul is too precious . . .

Did she really mean the implications of that? That his very soul was something she prized?

He was unsure, and his emotions were too dazed to create a coherent thought.

He scoffed at the idea that his hate covered more painful feelings. Worse, how could he let go of his hate?

His father was a monster of a man; he deserved every ounce of Rafe's spite.

Case in point—

Kendall had forced Rafe to give Sophie up, and the duke's actions had not only affected Rafe. What had Sophie said earlier?

I still feel unwanted and unloved.

Rafe's heart cracked at the thought.

How could Sophie not know how desperately he loved and *wanted* her.

Oh! The want of her!

It ate at him, consumed him until, at times, he felt unequal to breathing because of it.

A cascade of images tumbled through his brain. Sophie in his arms, laughing, his head dipping to kiss her. Sophie cuddled with him before a roaring fire, discussing an essay on Mexican fruit bats, pausing to let him kiss her over and over.

Such heaven. To simply *kiss* her again. Four years ago, at that ball, he had been bold, sweeping her underneath that staircase and into his arms.

But after that evening, he had lost hope of ever kissing Lady Sophie again.

And now . . .

To find themselves like this . . .

It seemed almost madness to *not* kiss her. To not dispel the lie that she was unwanted and unloved.

Using his teeth, he tugged off the leather glove of the hand not currently wrapped around her.

She leaned back slightly in his arms, eyes a question mark at his movements.

"I cannot promise to give up my hate for Kendall," he said.

"You cannot?"

"No." Dropping the glove into his lap, he lifted a single finger to her cheek, drawing it down the soft, downy curve.

Heavens but she was so soft.

Her eyes dropped to his mouth.

"I cannot forgive him," Rafe whispered, "because he denies me you."

"Me?!"

"Aye." He pressed his forehead to hers. "How can you think yourself unwanted? Undesired? I desired you then." He pressed a kiss to her cheek. "I desire you now. That has *never* changed."

"Oh!" Her sharp inhalation was more breath than sound.

He could no more stop gravity than cease the descent of his mouth to hers.

The first press was a testing, teasing sort of glide. A question.

Is this all right? Will you allow more?

The gentlest taste, her lips pillowy under his.

Sophie sighed and lifted upward in reply.

Yes. More, please.

Rafe needed no further encouragement. Cupping her head in his hand, he pressed his lips to hers in earnest.

He devoured. He feasted.

Sophie met him as an equal, no hesitation or shyness.

This woman.

She sang through his blood, the sheer *rightness* of her settling into his very bones.

And just as they had four years ago, his hands trembled at the thought.

22

After another hour, the snow finally eased, turning back to rain. Though Sophie hardly noticed, as she and Rafe spent the better part of that hour shamelessly kissing.

Sophie supposed she should be shocked by such wanton behavior, but kissing Rafe was so delicious and her own heart so battered, she struggled to care.

Regardless, she knew they needed to continue onward. They had to make Aboyne before nightfall.

And so she followed Rafe out of the bothie and swung back onto her horse, continuing up the narrow road. But she feared she had left her ridiculous brain back in the bothie, because all she could think upon was Rafe's thrumming, life-altering *kisses*.

In short, her body buzzed like a rung bell.

I desired you then. I desire you now.

How glorious to be wanted!

The magic of it hummed through her blood and addled her thinking and made her ache for a different future than the one she had been pursuing. A future where along with her barn cats and research, she raced across the Scottish moors with Rafe, the wind tugging her hair loose, their laughter floating around them as he caught her in his arms, pulling her against him while his head dipped down—

Enough.

You shall drive yourself mad with such thoughts.

She needed to focus on Rafe's revelations about his own inner turmoil, about the hate festering in his soul.

Or, more immediately, the danger of the weather around them.

The rain was chill and the wind cut through her clothing, a rude shock after the warmth of Rafe's arms. They pushed past the small forest which had surrounded the bothie and climbed up another rise, the road steep and muddy. The hill descended into more trees, meandering its way down the mountain.

The trees parted and, as if a mirage, a bridge appeared up the track, shimmering in the rain. Not a simple, perfunctory bridge, but an elegant curve of stone, spanning what appeared to be an imposing gorge.

Moreover, the bridge was enormous, wide enough for a haywain to cross or horsemen four abreast. The structure was a startling sight in the harsh landscape, like a fairy castle in a desert.

Two small towers flanked each side and a deserted house sat to one end of the bridge, testament to the structure's history as a toll bridge.

But the buildings stood empty now. They rode over the bridge, past the towers with broken window panes and a battered door. Water rushed through the gorge far below, the wind battering their cloaks.

Once past the bridge, they ascended yet another ridge, climbing out of the trees again. They crested the hill, the ever-present wind whipping at Sophie's earasaid. From the top of the ridge, she could see clouds gathering again over the mountains in the distance. Rafe guided his horse around a large puddle and began descending—

CRACK!

A loud retort echoed through the canyon.

A bullet whizzed past Sophie's shoulder, disappearing into the heather and gorse beside her.

Her horse shied.

Sophie screamed.

Pandemonium erupted.

Crack! Crack!

Another bullet. And then another.

Rafe's horse reared, nearly unseating him. The two spare horses pulled at their leads, causing Sophie's horse to stumble. Only her skill as a horsewoman kept her in the saddle.

"Bloody hell! The shots are coming from the valley ahead!" Rafe wrested his mount under control and turned around, pointing behind her. "Run!"

Sophie turned her own mount around and kicked her horse into a gallop, the sturdy gelding needing little encouragement to race back up trail from whence they had come. Rafe followed, galloping alongside her.

"Damn brigands," he swore, voice carrying over the wind. "It's the men that were behind us before. They must have decided against seeking shelter, as we did, but skirted around us and then lay in wait ahead!"

Risking a glance behind, Sophie could see the men in the valley below, kicking their horses forward, rifles pointed toward Sophie and Rafe, that red bonnet clearly visible now.

Bruiser.

It had to be.

Bloody hell, indeed.

Sophie neared the summit of the hill, rushing over the curve and down the other side. A vicious blast of wind greeted her. Pelting rain soon followed. Fortunately, the path was more rock than mud, but the weather was rapidly deteriorating again.

She and Rafe raced onward, hearing no more bullets. Would putting space between them and Bruiser be enough? Or was it merely the landscape and weather providing them with some protection? How long would the men follow them?

And why, why, why had Bruiser done this? Followed them, circled around, and now *fired* upon them from the front?! What plans had the men been hatching while she and Rafe were blissfully unaware, kissing in the bothie?

"Make haste," Rafe shouted, pointing ahead. The enormous bridge they had crossed earlier came back into view. "We can take a stand against them once we're across."

Excellent idea.

Sophie urged her horse onward, teeth chattering.

She raced back over the enormous bridge, Rafe right behind. He led them into the shelter of the trees beyond.

Swiveling in his saddle, he pointed back toward the road. "If we wait here, we can see the bridge. It's likely they will give chase—I doubt they have come this far to leave us be—but they won't be able to cross the gorge without using the bridge, not down in this weather."

Sophie nodded, teeth still chattering. They dismounted, drawing their horses deeper under the cover of the enormous firs.

Rafe grabbed his rifle. "Fortunately, they don't know yet that we are armed. So we will have the element of surprise if they continue pursuit." He pushed the rifle into Sophie's hands. "I assume your sport-mad father taught you to shoot?"

"Of course."

"Do you mind keeping watch while I tether the horses?"

Despite the looming danger, warmth blossomed in her chest. After their discussion earlier, something had eased within her. Lingering pain from Jack she hadn't even been aware of carrying.

She appreciated that Rafe handed her the gun and had faith that she could keep them safe. *She* knew she was competent, but most men would not assume so. Jack certainly would never have trusted her in this situation.

But Rafe was not like most men. He treated her as a partner, a friend in every sense of the word.

She and Rafe . . . they were equals. Working together.

She hid her body behind the trunk of a large fir tree, its enormous branches providing shelter. Once more, the weather was fickle. The clouds Sophie had seen at a distance had arrived, turning the drizzle into snow again, raindrops mixed with soft, white fluff.

"Blast it," Rafe muttered coming to stand beside her.

Sophie nodded. "This weather is too changeable."

"Aye. I hope they are still coming toward us. I would prefer a head-on confrontation. We cannot proceed forward with them between us and Aboyne."

"Rafe—" She put out a hand, stopping him. "Why haven't you asked the obvious? I am certain one of those men is Bruiser. I saw him quite clearly—"

"Sophie—"

"Are you *sure* your father isn't behind this attack? That he isn't willing to stoop to bodily harm to thwart us?" It was a dreadful question, but she felt compelled to ask it.

"I truthfully cannot say." He clenched his jaw, looking at the ground, hands on his hips, before shaking his head. "I dinnae ken what to make of it, lass. Until we know for sure it is Bruiser who fired upon us, it's a moot point."

Silence for a moment.

Side-by-side, they watched the bridge and road beyond. No sound reached them. No jangle of horse tackle or clop of hooves. Just the soft rustle of water through the gorge underneath the bridge.

Sophie continued to mull over their predicament. "I am still puzzled. The men are obviously targeting us, specifically. They circled around us in order to stop our forward progress. You have been ambushed twice now on this trip, both times in broad daylight."

"Aye."

More silence.

"It seems impossible to believe both attacks are simply coincidence."

"That it does."

"Does someone wish you dead?"

"Wish me dead?" He laughed at that, a breathy, bitter sound. "Aye, there are a few."

That got Sophie's attention. She twisted to face him more fully. "Who wishes you ill?"

A slight hesitation, and then, "There is something of a list, though I doubt the people to be in this corner of Scotland, so it's a bit puzzling."

"Are you always so blasé about death threats?"

"I've heard it adds to my overall panache." He smoothed a hand down his chest.

She found she greatly disliked him making light of his own mortality. She shivered and pulled her wet cloak and earasaid tighter around her shoulders.

"Could this be linked to the letters you all received?" she asked.

"Aye, it is possible. I am ruling out nothing." He stilled, looking beyond her to the road. "I hate simply sitting here, waiting to be fired upon."

Sophie followed his gaze, looking out over the bridge. The snow continued to melt on the road but was now sticking to the grass and trees. It would begin sticking to the bridge soon. The towers flanking the bridge were already sporting traces of snow.

Like Rafe, she did not like waiting here, passively accepting whatever might occur. Were the men following them?

She paused, studying the towers again. Her eyes darted to the coiled length of rope dangling from her saddle bag.

What if they . . .

She touched Rafe's arm. "I believe I have an idea."

23

Ten minutes later, Sophie was tucked once more against the trunk of the fir tree, rifle in hand.

Rafe had taken their two pistols and was crouched behind the stone ramparts of one of the towers that flanked the bridge.

Snow continued to fall, fluffy flakes swirling down.

Sophie forced herself to breathe calmly as they waited.

They did not have to wait long.

Horse hooves announced the arrival of the men. Sophie saw them as they cleared the small rise and descended quickly toward the bridge.

Ah. She had been right. Bruiser's red hat and bulky body were unmistakable.

The men scanned the trees as they rode, rifles held loosely across their saddles, but they seemed unconcerned about any real danger from Sophie or Rafe, likely thinking them to be a pair of pampered aristocrats.

Sophie met Rafe's eyes where he crouched, hidden.

She nodded. He winked in return.

Bruiser and his friend hit the bridge, side-by-side, their horses at a canter.

Please let this work, Sophie plead.

Bruiser was slightly in front.

He hit the rope first. The cord had been strung across the road, between the two towers, right at chest height, the snowy weather hiding it from view.

Momentum swept Bruiser off his horse; he hit the stone bridge with a loud thud.

His companion immediately followed.

Both their horses continued onward, unharmed.

The men moaned on the stone bridge, the tumble having badly jolted them.

Rafe leapt over the bridge railing and was on the men in an instant. He rounded on Bruiser, making quick work of tying up the man's hands as he lay on the ground, gasping for breath.

The other man rolled to his stomach, trying to get his feet underneath him.

Sophie pushed out from her hiding place, pointing the rifle at the man.

"Don't move!" she ordered.

The man froze, his back to her.

Rafe finished tying Bruiser's hands, propping the man up against the side of the bridge. He then grabbed the second man, trussing him up as well.

Sophie walked a few feet closer, keeping her rifle trained on Bruiser. The Scot glared at her, blood trickling down his cheek from a cut above his ear.

Rafe finished with the second man, dragging him to sit beside Bruiser. He retrieved his pistols and then surveyed both men.

"Well, I'm right glad we could have both of ye here for a wee blether." Rafe gave the men a cheeky grin, brogue broad.

Sophie kept her rifle trained on them.

"As ye can see," Rafe continued, pointing at Sophie, "I have my trusted assistant with me. She may look like a proper Sassenach lady, but she is dead aim with a gun, so dinnae think that ye will catch her out."

Bruiser scowled at Sophie.

"Now," Rafe said, "I have several questions I would like ye to answer. Ye will answer the questions eventually, so ye may just want tae volunteer the information easily."

Bruiser shifted his gaze to Rafe. "Why should I talk to ye?"

"Why? Because I'm holding a pistol, you lot are tied up, and this snow looks tae get worse afore it gets any better. We'll start easy. What is your name?"

Bruiser paused, shifting his gaze to Rafe's pistol, perhaps gauging how serious Rafe was.

"I am dead earnest, I assure ye." Rafe's grin vanished in an instant, replaced by a grim intensity.

Bruiser shifted, as if what he saw in Rafe's eyes gave him pause.

"Michael Grant," the man said.

"Thank ye, Mr. Grant." Rafe nodded. "Do ye know who I am?"

"Lord Rafe Gilbert, son of the Duke of Kendall."

"Excellent. Are ye in the employ of my father, the Duke of Kendall?"

Grant paused.

"Come now," Rafe continued. "I dinnae understand why ye would protect Kendall. The man's a right bastard. He will show no loyalty tae you. He'll cast ye off for this mishap regardless. You're better off tae talk to me. I, at least, will treat ye both fairly."

Sophie shifted the rifle, reminding the men that she was there, too. Grant's eyes darted to her and then moved back to Rafe.

"Aye. I am employed by the Duke of Kendall," he admitted.

"Why are you firing upon us?" Sophie asked. She had to know. Why was Rafe's father trying to kill them?

Grant glowered at her. "Ye are both fools tae be up here on Cairn O'Mount in this weather, chasing after Dr. Ross like proper eejits. I was merely trying tae warn ye off."

Sophie froze, mind churning. "You fired on us as a *warning*? That seems ... the opposite of warning. A warning is more along the lines of a timely note or a shouted word."

"Aye," Rafe agreed.

Grant shrugged. "'Tis the truth. Ye werenae exactly friendly in Edinburgh, were ye?"

"Pot meet kettle," Sophie muttered.

Grant continued, not having heard her. "I was merely encouraging ye to turn back. Ye are daft tae be out here in this." He tossed his head, indicating the falling snow. "Kendall is concerned about ye, as any father would be."

"*Concerned?* Kendall has never once expressed concern for my well-being." The scorn in Rafe's tone was palpable. "Besides, Beadle sent you, not my father. Kendall doesnae know I'm here—"

"Beadle is a good man who intuitively understands his employer's wishes," Grant all but growled.

"Beadle has an odd way of showing *concern*." Rafe laced the word with heavy sarcasm.

Grant's eyes narrowed. "Your father would not want ye here. You've taken it into your head tae go chasing after Ross, but the doctor is likely dead. He was ill last year, and his sister begged tae take him home to Drathes Castle to die. The man is long passed on."

Sophie's heart sank.

Was this all true? Was Grant to be trusted?

But they had come so far. How could their quest end without any hope at all?

"That's a likely story," Rafe said, his tone reflecting Sophie's own skepticism. "Why would Kendall know or care about what happened to Dr. Ross?"

"They were friends," Grant shrugged.

Rafe laughed, a bitter sound. "My father doesnae have friends. He has lackeys and sycophants. Beadle's a sycophant. Which are you?"

Grant's expression became stonier. "I cannae rightly say about Ross. Alls I know is this—Ross spent some years as Kendall's personal physician, and Kendall awarded the man a house in Edinburgh in his later years as token of his esteem. Sounds like friendship to me."

Sophie darted a look at Rafe. He absorbed Grant's words with a stoic calm.

Unfortunately, it all made sense. If Dr. Ross had been a servant of Kendall's, perhaps one who had his father's confidence at one time, it made sense that his father had provided the man with a house in Edinburgh. Then, when Ross' health had deteriorated further, the man retired to Drathes Castle and the care of his sister.

Rafe shook his head. "I dinnae believe your Bambury tale, Grant. If Ross were dead, if there were nothing to be had for us at Drathes Castle, ye woudnae be here—"

"Ye should return to London, my lord," Grant interrupted. "Your father wants ye there, I'm sure. Not here in the wilds of Scotland, chasing after a dead man, where anything could happen to ye."

Rafe gave another harsh laugh. "Touching," his voice so sardonic. "How truly moving for dear old papa to care so about me." He turned from the men. "I think we've gotten all the information we need here."

A FEW MINUTES LATER, Rafe and Sophie were back in the saddle, following the road through a thick forest. Rafe had placed the men, still trussed up like pigs, and their horses into the shelter of the forest, out of the elements as much as possible.

"They'll get free eventually," Rafe said. "Until then, they won't freeze to death. The horses will keep them warm."

The attack had terrified him. Rafe's hands still shook as he gripped the reins. If anything had happened to Sophie—

He swallowed back the terror of that thought, rage at Beadle and Kendall flooding him.

How could those men have threatened Sophie's life like this? How dare they?!

Harness the anger. Use it for good.

Hah!

That was proving easier said than done.

The snow had tapered at the moment, though a dark bank of clouds roiled on the horizon, promising more before evening. He urged their horses onward, Sophie behind him. They had to make Aboyne and the drovers inn before nightfall.

Sophie guided her horse around a muddy puddle, nudging her horse forward to ride beside him. "Do you think Grant will continue after us?"

"'Tis possible, I suppose." Rafe tugged his cloak closer. Thankfully, the surrounding trees cut the wind.

Sophie sniffed. "I certainly doubt the truth of what Grant said, that he only wished to warn us. However, the true reason he fired upon us is a mystery."

"Precisely. Perhaps Bruiser is simply an opportunist. This pass is the fastest route to Aboyne and Drathes Castle. He could have simply come this way, knowing me to be the son of a wealthy duke and thinking to rob us."

"Also possible, but unlikely. I think Grant and Beadle are acting based on something Kendall expects of them. But what? Your death?"

"I have no idea." He breathed through the anger in his chest. "My father may threaten, but I do not think he wishes me dead. He prefers manipulation over brute force. Besides, even dukes are not outside the law when it comes to killing others—"

"But Grant was sent to deter us from continuing onward, and he did shoot at us," Sophie pointed out. "Is there a reason your father would wish to kill you?"

"Besides my own intransigence?" he snorted, shaking his head. "There is nothing. My death would be a disaster for him, to be honest. My elder brother has yet to produce an heir. I am Kendall's best hope of continuing the ducal line.

"Besides, the bastard takes great pleasure in having me at his beck and call to do his bidding. My death would remove his favorite toy." His tone so bitter. "The bigger question is this—" Rafe looked at the looming clouds. "Do we continue onward to Drathes Castle?"

Sophie answered him readily. "Of course, we do. There is a chance that Grant was telling the truth, that Dr. Ross is dead. But it all seems havy-cavy to me. It is just as likely that there is some secret here that Kendall wishes to protect. And uncovering such a secret could be the first step to freeing yourself."

"What possible secret could there be, though?"

Sophie shrugged. "Is it not odd that Dr. Ross knows your father? That Kendall knows the man who is most likely to have the knowledge to help your mother?"

"Have ye always been this clever?"

"Oh, aye, laddie."

Rafe chuckled, but it quickly faded. "I have thought that, yes. My father knows Ross well enough to give the man use of a townhouse in Edinburgh. Surely he knew that Dr. Ross might be able to assist his duchess. And yet . . . I had never heard a whisper of the man until Alex mentioned him."

"If you ask me, it's all the more reason to continue on to Drathes Castle."

"Agreed."

They rode in silence for a while, side-by-side, Rafe trying to curb his wayward thoughts, to stem the habitual anger and helplessness he felt whenever pondering his father.

But so many questions loomed.

What was truly going on between Kendall and Ross?

Was there possibly a link between his father and the mysterious letters sent to the Brotherhood? It seemed almost farcical to think that, and yet, it was impossible to dismiss.

Though Rafe believed what he said. Kendall would not kill him. To injure Rafe would be to lose his favorite pastime—tormenting his second son.

But by sending Grant after them, his father had taken the gloves off between them.

Harness the rage. Use it for good.

Perhaps it was time to rebel more earnestly.

How desperate was his father to have a grandson? Desperate enough that Rafe could hold it over the man's head? And if Rafe could prove that Kendall had hired Grant to fire upon him . . . even dukes were not immune to prosecution for attempted murder . . .

And if Dr. Ross were able to improve his mother's health even partially . . .

Mmmmm.

"You're smiling," she observed. "I take it you have found some hope?"

He bent in the saddle and kissed her lush mouth, unable to stop himself.

"Aye, lass," he vowed.

Somehow, he would make this come aright.

24

Drathes Castle emerged from the sleet and fog in jagged bits. A tower first, then a crumbled bounding wall, the side of a fractured turret.

A broken fairytale.

Ahead of Sophie, Rafe guided their horses along the rutted path barely visible through the snow.

After leaving Beadle's men at the bridge, they had reached Aboyne without further incident and stayed the night in the drovers inn there, a spartan but clean place.

But when they had asked the innkeep in Aboyne about Drathes Castle, he had crossed himself before saying he did not meddle in the affairs of his betters and then refused to say another word on the matter.

That was ominous.

Fortunately, an ostler had given directions to Drathes. And so at first light, they had traveled the last three miles to the castle, eyes peeled for ambush, turning down smaller and smaller tracks until following a battered sign across an old stone bridge to the castle itself.

Drathes Castle came more fully into view, emerging from the mist. The building rose as a single rectangular structure from the base, branching to cantilevered turrets supported by impressive corbels on the upper floors.

Nudging her horse forward, she pulled alongside Rafe. He shot her a glance, face wet from the weather.

"So this is Drathes Castle, is it?" Sophie pulled her earasaid and cloak tighter around her.

"Aye."

"It doesn't appear very . . . castle-like." She had to say it. Though it had several fanciful turrets, it looked more like a single keep than a typical walled castle, as if someone had begun a castle and then petered out after only constructing the central tower.

Rafe surveyed the building, squinting as if to see better through the sleeting rain, before shrugging. "Eh, it's a Scottish castle. Unlike castles in England, the Norman motte-and-bailey construction never reached this far north. And we Scots are a practical lot. We don't waste time on embellishments that do not contribute to survival. Only an eejit spends money on bonnie bits and bobs instead of gunpowder, lead shot, and more manpower. Scots built their castles to allow a handful of men to withstand marauders with only a single door reinforced by a yett. Most are more multi-storied tower house than castle in any real sense."

Sophie nodded at his explanation. They rode into the large clearing before the castle, bringing the entire structure fully into view.

"Is it . . . Am I . . ." She started, stopped, and then turned to him. "Is Drathes Castle . . . pink?"

He nodded.

It was, indeed, pink. A mottled, splotchy pink.

The color stood in stark contrast to the barren hills behind it.

"Why . . . pink?" Her tone was utterly baffled.

Rafe smiled. "Pink castles are not as uncommon as ye may think."

She turned and fixed him with a *look*. "Surely you jest. Scots are supposed to be fearsome warriors, inspiring terror. A pink castle is more merry than intimidating."

"Nae, ye have it all wrong, lass. We're practical, remember? Most Scottish buildings are covered in harling—"

"Harling?"

"Uh . . ." He mentally searched for the English word. ". . . roughcast, the lime plaster that keeps the damp out of the stones. Many of the hills in this part of Scotland have red-tinted soils. So when the harling is mixed, it creates a pink color. 'Tis nothing more than that."

Sophie absorbed his explanation with a raised eyebrow. "The pink is practical, then? How disappointing. I wanted to find it amusing."

"Amusing?"

She shot him her primmest look. "I have bravely refrained from making a scathing remark about men who wear skirts and live in pink castles. You should appreciate my forbearance."

Rafe laughed.

Of course, the closer they came, the more dilapidated the harling appeared, crumbling in places, revealing rough, gray stone underneath. A single trail of smoke drifted up from only one of the many chimneys.

No one was about as they circled to find the door. No groom or stable boy came to snatch their reins.

The place felt abandoned. In fact, if the chimney smoke didn't indicate someone was in residence, Sophie would have thought the structure derelict.

None of it boded well. Perhaps Grant had spoken truth, after all. Dr. Ross was dead, and the castle was barely inhabited at the moment.

They stopped before the entrance, a solitary step leading to an imposing-looking door, an iron grate before it ajar—the yett, she supposed.

Frowning, Rafe dismounted and then helped Sophie down. The misty sleet was rapidly turning to snow. If this entire journey had been for naught, they faced a cold ride back to the inn in Aboyne.

Rafe knocked loudly with the affixed rapper, the sound echoing beyond the door.

Nothing.

Sophie looked to him, arching an eyebrow.

He rapped again, more vigorously.

Nothing.

"Truly?" he muttered. "We have come so far."

Just as Sophie considered actually *trying* the door handle, they heard the sound of shuffling feet, then metal grinding as the lock was thrown.

The door creaked open.

A wizened elderly manservant peaked out, a shock of white hair sticking from underneath a blue bonnet. He wore old-fashioned knee breeches and a frock coat, but a length of green-and-brown tartan circled his chest almost like a blanket.

The old man was a wee bit worse for wear. He looked at them, eyes blinking against the light, and then shook his head.

"I dinnae know yous." The man waved a gnarled hand. "On yer way."

He turned and slammed the door shut.

The lock engaged with a loud *sha-shunk*.

The sound reverberated up the entire structure.

Sophie was quite sure it knocked the air out of her lungs as well.

Of all the—

After everything—

She shot Rafe a glance. Was her expression as outraged as his?

RAFE STUDIED THE door before him, struggling to rein in his temper.

They had come so far, been shot at (twice!), suffered cold, wretched food, and snowy mountains. Not to mention the snow that had commenced falling, yet again.

Someone would damn well answer this door!

Rafe would learn if Dr. Ross lived. He would have some reasonable explanation as to why his father wished to warn him away from this place.

He rapped again, louder and longer than before.

The same shuffling sound, the same lock being thrown.

The door opened again to the same elderly manservant.

"We are here to see Dr. Ross," Rafe said before the man could say anything.

"Who?" the man blinked. "Who did ye say?"

"Dr. John Ross. We would like to speak with the good doctor."

"The doctor?"

"Aye, Dr. Ross. We've come all the way from London, in this weather—" He waved a hand to indicate the falling snow. "—with an urgent matter for him."

"Who?" the old man scanned Rafe from head-to-toe, brows puzzled.

"*Dr. John Ross*," Rafe repeated, enunciating each word clearly.

I . . . I . . ." The man froze, that frown still in place. "I dinnae ken anyone by that name."

Sophie gasped at Rafe's side. Or perhaps it was only his own sense of surprise.

"Is this not Drathes Castle, sir?" Sophie leaned in. "We were told that Dr. Ross lives in Drathes Castle."

"Drathes?"

"Yes." She gave the man a dazzling smile.

The poor old chap didn't know what hit him. He blinked and stared at her, instantly enraptured.

Rafe could hardly blame him. Sophie's smiles did have a tendency to dazzle the senses.

"Is there anyone else we could talk to?" Rafe asked.

The elderly man jolted, looking away from Sophie, eyes confused. He shuffled sideways and glanced at their horses, standing before the door. But like a compass finding north, his eyes swung back to Sophie again, staring at her intently.

"Horses shouldnae be left in the snow, Cat," he said to her.

Before Rafe could reply to that bewildering statement, the man turned and yelled, "Boy!"

A scuttling noise and then a lanky young man popped his head out from a side door.

"Horses!" The old man snapped his finger.

The lad took in Rafe, and then gave a start when his eyes landed on Sophie, jaw dropping slightly—again, Rafe couldn't blame the lad, Lady

Sophie was rather alarmingly pretty—before touching a forelock and racing into the snow to take their horses toward the dilapidated stables.

Rafe turned back to find the old man still staring at Sophie.

"Come," the man said, turning away.

Rafe waved Sophie inside before closing the door behind them. They stood in a small vestibule that sported a pair of doors on two sides and a staircase on the third. The old man was slowly climbing the steep stairs, obviously expecting them to follow.

Hanging their dripping cloaks on a pair of convenient hooks and setting gloves and hats on a side table, Rafe and Sophie followed the old man deeper into the castle, quickly catching him as he reached the top of the steep staircase.

Turning to his left, the man walked through an arched doorway, leading them into what had to be the great hall, a standard feature of all Scottish castles.

In medieval times, the great hall had served as a dining room for the clan, a gathering place in times of war, and a municipal hall when the local laird had to mete out justice. Nowadays, it was demoted to a grand sort of drawing room.

This particular great hall appeared to have been untouched over the centuries. A large table dominated the center of the room, flanked by windows on one side and an enormous fireplace on the other. A low fire smoldered in the hearth.

Snowy sleet continued to lash the windows, rendering the room dim and gloomy despite it being only midday. But bits of the room came into shadowed focus. White-washed walls soared two-stories up to a decorative plasterwork ceiling, the walls dotted by paintings and the odd piece of medieval weaponry. Chests and chairs lined the perimeter, giving the space a hodge-podge, lived-in feel.

Rafe's eyes followed the old manservant. The man muttered to himself, slowly shuffling into the room, Rafe and Sophie forgotten.

Now what were they to do? Was Dr. Ross even among the living?

"Sir?" Rafe said. "We need tae speak with Dr. Ross. Do ye know where we might find him?"

The man turned around, eyes slow to focus on them. "Eh, what did you say? Dr. Ross?"

This again?

"Aye," Rafe answered.

The old man blinked. "Why do ye wish to speak with Dr. Ross?"

Ah. Perhaps there was hope here after all.

"We seek his medical advice on a matter of some urgency. Is he at home?"

The old man laughed in reply, turning toward the fireplace, probing it with a convenient poker.

Rafe grimaced, exchanging a glance with Sophie.

"Perhaps there is someone else we can speak with," he muttered. Surely there were more people about than just this old man and the lad who took their horses to the stables?

The old man shook his head, reaching for a brick of peat from a basket beside the hearth. He tossed it on the fire where it hissed and popped.

"Will the boy return from the stables soon, do you think?" Sophie murmured at Rafe's side. "This poor old man is clearly doddering."

"Aye, that he is. Would it be too much tae hope that Dr. Ross still lives and takes on men like this as charity cases? Diseases of the mind are his area of specialty, after all." Even to Rafe's ears, this idea seemed far-fetched.

"Or perhaps this man was a loyal retainer at one point, and the doctor hasn't the heart to turn him off?" She shot Rafe a wan smile, as if to buoy his own flagging optimism.

They both looked back at the old man as he tossed another two bricks of peat onto the fire, sending sparks cascading up the chimney.

A gust of wind battered the windows opposite the fire, sleet hammering the glass.

The man stood, wiping his hands on the tartan wrapped around his chest. Reaching for a taper, he lit it in the fire, carrying it over to a candelabra atop the large table. The old man attempted to light candles, but his trembling hand made the task nearly impossible. Rafe took several steps forward and gently took the taper from him, lighting the candles himself before blowing out the taper and setting it on the table.

The fire crackled merrily, and the candelabra sent much-needed light into the dim space. The flickering light illuminated the furniture, glimmering across the claymores and shields and family portraits on the walls.

Abruptly, Sophie gasped beside him.

"*Oh!* Good gracious me!" she whispered.

Rafe whirled around.

Her jaw was slack in shock, her eyes wide and fixed on a point to the left above Rafe's head. Turning, he followed her gaze, looking up.

His eyes snagged on the enormous portrait above the fireplace, finally illuminated by the cheery candlelight.

"Bloody hell," Rafe gasped.

The portrait featured a woman in the satin and silks of the previous century—small corseted waist, voluminous skirts, hair pulled across one shoulder in a cascade of dark curls. Rafe was quite sure there was a similar portrait of his mother and her sisters somewhere, painted by Gainsborough or Reynolds or the like.

But this particular painting spoke of more exotic climes, of a skilled artist from Paris or Rome. The lady stared at the viewer with a bemused expression, eyebrow slightly raised, as if challenging the artist to fully capture her personality in mere paint.

More to the point . . .

"Th-that's not m-me," Sophie stammered, still staring at the painting. "I know it looks like me, but I haven't sat for a portrait in nearly a decade—"

"She is your very image," Rafe breathed.

It was true. The woman in the painting could be Sophie's twin. The same wide green eyes, high cheek bones, and pointed chin. The same courageous spirit in her eyes.

"Well, I am utterly unnerved now," Sophie shook her head.

"Aye. Quite the coincidence." He gestured toward the painting.

"Coincidence?" Sophie snorted. "Or, more likely, we will find more answers than we had anticipated here. I wonder who she is."

They both stared at the unknown woman for a moment, Rafe scrambling to make connections from all the pieces of this puzzle.

"Ye are sure Lady Mainfeld is your mother? Because this woman . . ."

He didn't need to say anything further. He was quite sure Sophie understood the implication of his words.

The woman in the portrait could easily be her mother or sister.

"Yes, Lady Mainfeld is truly my mother." Sophie nodded her head, eyes never leaving the portrait. "I am as sure as anyone could be about that fact. I do resemble her in many ways. Despite my odd parentage, I have never doubted that she is my *Mater veras*."

"Yes, but—"

"Why are ye still standing there blethering with that rakeshame?" the old man growled from across the room.

Rafe and Sophie turned toward him.

The man was glaring at Sophie. "I told ye tae stay away from the likes of him." He jabbed a finger at Rafe. "Only bring ye heartache, a man like that."

"Pardon?" Sophie breathed.

"Ye must be more mindful of yerself, Catharine. I willnae see ye hurt again," the man said, beckoning her forward. "Come."

25

Sophie froze, staring at the old man.

"Catharine?" she repeated. She shot a glance at Rafe before cautiously crossing the worn carpet to where the man stood beside the now-roaring fire. "Who is Catharine?"

"Eh?" the man cocked his head. "Catharine?"

"Yes, you called me Catharine just a moment ago. Is the lady in the portrait Catharine?" Sophie motioned toward the portrait looming overhead. It abruptly seemed imperative that she know the identity of the woman in the painting.

Having spent her entire life as an outcast—her origins unknown—to discover an image of a woman who could be her twin . . .

Well, it felt impossibly momentous.

If only someone here could help her understand.

The elderly man studied her and then took a step out to better examine the portrait. He paused, looking back and forth between Sophie and the painting. He frowned, confusion clouding his eyes.

"Is that Catharine?" Sophie repeated.

The old man stilled before licking his lips, turning back to the fire.

"I cannae rightly say." His voice had a wondering, wispy quality to it. "I cannae remember."

Oh.

"I don't ken that he's lucid enough tae answer," Rafe said at her elbow, startling her.

Sophie swallowed the disappointment in her throat. "You are likely right." She shivered, pulling her earasaid tighter around her shoulders, grateful for the warm wool. She regarded the elderly man, now fussing with fire poker. "His memory appears gone, poor dear. Hopefully the boy returns from the stables soon—"

"Och, brother, what scrape have ye gotten yerself into this time?" A woman's voice sounded from behind them, nearly startling Sophie out of her skin. "Ian said ye had guests, a fine gentleman and his lady."

Sophie turned to see an older woman rounding the large central table, crossing the room. Dressed in a blue morning dress and a white mobcap, she pulled a Paisley shawl tighter around her shoulders, warding off the chill. Something about the woman tugged at Sophie's memory, as if she knew her somehow. Had they met previously?

Sophie stepped toward the table, the light from the candelabra washing her face.

The woman raised her head at that moment, locking eyes with Sophie and coming to an abrupt halt, skirt swinging forward with her momentum. The woman blanched white, her knuckles clutching at her shawl.

The woman's gaze darted to Rafe at Sophie's side, expression sagging further, if possible. She gasped, a hand covering her mouth, before swaying, almost as if she would faint.

Rafe darted forward, possibly thinking to catch her should the woman actually crumple.

But the woman caught herself with one hand on the back of a dining chair, the other palm outstretched facing toward Rafe—*stay where you are.*

Still wild-eyed, the woman pulled the chair out and sat down, hands shaking, chest heaving. The poor lady seemed equal parts horrified and stunned, her gaze swinging back and forth between Sophie and Rafe, up to the painting behind them on the wall, before coming back to Sophie.

Was it simply the resemblance between Sophie and the lady in the painting that caused this reaction? Or was more going on here?

And why did the woman appear familiar?

"Uhmm, we mean no harm." Sophie took a slow step forward. "The kind gentleman here let us in and showed us upstairs."

"Yes." Rafe smiled his charming smile. The one that deepened his dimples and took his handsomeness from simply dashing to utterly devastating.

But instead of softening, the woman's expression became more withdrawn and severe, her lips drawing into a straight line. Deep creases lined her face, wrinkles that spoke to a life of stress and strain.

Rafe, bless him, would not be deterred.

"We wish to speak with Dr. John Ross," he said. "We have journeyed from London with questions for the good doctor and were told he resides here."

The woman took in his words, her face closing off. She gave the impression of one not given much to emotion, that the shock she had experienced was a great one to cause her composure to slip so thoroughly. This aloof expression seemed to be her more accustomed mien.

But her hands betrayed her. They still shook, clutching her shawl like a talisman.

The elderly man hummed behind them. A quick glance showed that he had sat in a chair before the fire. Who were these people? They appeared to be near one another in age. Was it too much to hope they might be a husband and wife who cared for the good doctor in his illness?

"Who might ye both be?" the woman asked.

Sophie swung her head back around, meeting Rafe's raised eyebrow. She nodded at Rafe to make introductions.

"I am Lord Rafe Gilbert, at your service madam." He bowed, the courtly gesture at utter odds with his dress and the room in general. "And my companion here is Lady Sophronia Sorrow Fulstate."

He winced slightly as he said her full name, shooting Sophie an apologetic glance. Her full name truly was ridiculous.

"I imagine ye are," the woman replied, her tone unclear as to whether she was referring to Sophie's identity or the comical absurdity of her name. Perhaps both?

"Mainfeld's lass?" the old woman asked, shrewd eyes on Sophie.

The question set Sophie's heart to pounding. The woman recognized her last name. Not everyone would, particularly in this remote corner of Scotland.

"Yes." Sophie bobbed a small curtsy, as it seemed appropriate.

The woman turned to Rafe, eyes withdrawn and cool. "And ye are Kendall's son?"

"Yes."

"The heir?"

"No, that would be my elder brother."

She sniffed in reply.

So this woman knew of their respective fathers. Enough to tie a last name to a title. The woman must be a lady in truth.

The mystery surrounding this castle and its inhabitants only deepened.

Why had Kendall not wanted them to come here?

Silence hung for a moment, the old man still humming from behind. The woman studied them, eyebrows drawn down.

Sophie understood the feeling.

"I find your presence here most odd," the woman said, a hard wariness crossing her face. Sophie guessed this was a woman who trusted very few people. Now that she had absorbed the shock of their arrival, the lady retreated behind an impassive facade. "Ye say ye wish tae consult with Dr. Ross, but that seems almost . . . absurd. What questions would be so urgent as tae compel ye to travel so far and in weather such as this?" She waved a hand to indicate the sleet spattering the window. "Forgive me for not trusting ye, but your explanations are, in a word, *improbable*."

Sophie barely repressed a grimace. The woman was wise to be suspicious. Their pilgrimage did appear foolhardy.

It was just . . .

Desperation drove one to extremes.

She shot a look at Rafe. He returned a tight smile before speaking.

"You appear to have the advantage of us, madam," he said, laying his words with exquisite politeness. "You know of our respective families. May we have the pleasure of your name?"

Ever the gentleman, Lord Rafe. Sophie did not think a situation existed that the man could not navigate with charisma and a carefully laid smile.

The woman shook her head, eyes lost for a moment.

"Ye truly came tae see our John?" she asked instead.

Sophie swallowed back a triumphant crow of delight. At *last* confirmation that perhaps they were in the correct place.

"Yes," Rafe said.

"We have questions, you see," Sophie added. "I know it appears absurd at the outset, but our questions truly have warranted a journey such as ours."

The woman drummed her fingers on the table top, looking back and forth between them, as if trying to determine the truthfulness of their words.

Finally, she sighed, shoulders slumping. She tugged on her shawl.

"I fear ye have journeyed in vain," she said, voice soft. "John cannae help ye."

Sophie's heart sank. "Is the good doctor no longer with us, then?"

"After a fashion." The woman rose and motioned toward the fireplace behind them.

Sophie and Rafe turned.

The old man lifted his head, gaze unfocused.

"May I present my brother, Dr. John Ross," the woman continued.

Sophie gasped, her hand pressing to her throat, her eyes fixed on the dottering old man attempting to pull a blanket over his knees.

Oh!

Oh, gracious no.

This?

This helpless, elderly man, struggling with dementia, unable to hold a thought from one moment to the next?

Dr. John Ross *was* alive.

And yet . . . not.

"I would introduce ye, but he will not recollect ye in two minutes' time," the woman said.

So many pieces of the puzzle slotted into place. Kendall's actions came into sharper focus. Once Dr. Ross's dementia had become pronounced, having him as a tenant in Edinburgh would have been a burden. So Kendall had sent the doctor to live with his sister. Much better to cast him aside.

Sophie closed her eyes, disappointment stinging.

Perhaps Grant had spoken truth, after all. Perhaps the brute's actions had simply been as he said—a wish to keep them safe.

There likely was nothing here that would help Rafe.

They all watched Dr. Ross . . . John . . . as he tried one more time to pull the blanket upon his lap, his hands shaking and clumsy.

Rafe stepped forward and assisted him, lifting the wool and gently tucking the blanket securely to John's side.

No trace of monumental disappointment showed on Rafe's face. How did he do it? How could he hide his dismay?

Sophie bit her quivering lip, breathing in measured time . . . anything to stem the tears that threatened.

How could Rafe's hopes have come to this? What was he to do now to help his mother?

And as for herself . . .

Sophie turned back to the sister.

"I am Miss Catharine Ross." The woman pulled her shawl, her knuckles white where they grasped the fabric.

"Catharine?" Rafe asked, head snapping upright.

Sophie stared at the woman. As in, *truly* stared, taking in every feature. The pepper gray hair peeking out from underneath her mobcap, the point of her chin, the mossy green of her wide-set eyes.

Ah.

No wonder she had seemed familiar.

At least Sophie herself would likely find answers here. She swallowed before darting a glance at the portrait over the fireplace.

"That Catharine?" she asked.

Miss Ross nodded, a slow, almost mournful movement. "The very same."

RAFE HAD JUST finished pinning his great kilt when a knock sounded at the door.

Sophie stood on the other side.

"I can scarcely think at the moment," she said, walking straight into his room.

Miss Ross had said little after her announcement earlier, only a promise to discuss more over dinner.

A harried maid had shown them up a narrow spiral staircase—another ubiquitous feature of Scottish castles apparently—to a pair of guest rooms on the third floor. Small and rather spartan with only a double bed and washstand, the rooms were at least clean and relatively cosy once the fires were lit. Ian, the lad who had stabled their horses earlier, delivered saddlebags to their rooms.

Sophie crossed to the fireplace, warming her hands.

The earlier snow had melted back into rain, an incessant drizzle against the window panes.

"What are we to do, Rafe?" She turned to him, gaze imploring.

"I haven't the slightest idea," he responded truthfully.

She had changed out of her riding habit and into a simple dress of green wool, the color capturing her lovely eyes. She had wrapped Jamie's tartan around her upper body, forming a sash.

Even dressed so simply, she was almost breathtakingly beautiful.

"I feel ill." Sophie bit her lip, gaze going glassy before she reined back her emotions. "We had hoped to find answers for your mother."

"Aye," Rafe bit out.

He turned to look in the mirror, adjusting the pleats of his great kilt, smoothing the fabric.

His heart was a leaden weight in his chest.

Grant had likely spoken truth. There was nothing here for him.

Dr. Ross was alive. But no longer . . . Dr. Ross.

Rage and helplessness flooded Rafe in equal measure. All that learning and wisdom just . . . gone. Erased by old age and dementia.

Why had the man not published his knowledge in papers? Shared what he knew with others?

He caught Sophie's eye in the mirror. She, at least, should find answers here. Surely the resemblance between herself and Catharine was more than just chance. Sophie had to have some biological connection to the Ross family.

As for himself . . .

He had not realized how much hope he had until it was dashed—a delicate Venetian goblet that Fate had crushed into a thousand jagged shards.

At the outset, his quest had seemed so clear cut, so simple:

Find the doctor. Explain the situation. Discuss treatment options.

But now, faced with the reality of having traveled nearly the entire length of Great Britain to no avail, he had reached the end. There were no more solutions to chase.

He wanted to fight his father, but a fight required ammunition, a weapon of some sort.

At the moment, Rafe had only his anger. Nothing more.

He turned around, taking in the steadiness of Sophie's green eyes, the determined jut of her chin.

Longing swamped him, a sharp ache behind his ribs.

Why could this lovely creature not be his?

His father would never agree to a marriage between Sophie and himself, even if Sophie were amenable to the idea. Sophie knew nothing of the history there, Rafe's love of her, his father's vehement hatred of her specifically.

Moreover, how would Mainfeld feel about a union between them?

Even if Rafe's mother were hale and hearty, it would still be fraught. But without something to improve his mother's health, a future between himself and Sophie was impossible. He could not leave his mother to bear the brunt of his father's cruelty.

He pushed back the weight of it, the sinking sense of inevitability.

Something of his emotions must have shown on his face.

"I refuse to give up." She drew up her shoulders. "There are answers to be had here—"

"Sophie—"

"No, Rafe. Let me restate—I will not permit *you* to give up hope."

This woman. She would fight for him.

He reached for her, the movement almost unconsciously done. It was as if his arms were helpless to do anything else *but* reach for Lady Sophie.

She came with gratifying eagerness, wrapping her arms around his waist. Rafe tilted her chin upward, capturing her mouth in a punishing kiss—short but ferocious—before gathering her close, savoring the sheer pleasure of holding her. He pressed a kiss to the top of her head.

"We haven't come this far to give up yet." Her words were muffled against his chest.

"But, lass—"

"No!" She shook him, her hands tightening. "You are not permitted to despair. Not until we have answers. If nothing else, your father still needs a grandchild. There are options, even if the one here at Drathes Castle has proven a dead end."

He swallowed the despair he felt clawing in his chest. It tasted of ash.

Sophie spoke truth, but there would be hell to pay once his father learned of this trip—

A gong sounded somewhere below, summoning them to dinner.

26

"I assume you have many questions," Miss Ross said as Rafe sliced into his braised beef.

Questions? That was a mild way of putting it. Sophie had buoyed him up. Rafe was ready to grasp at anything to help his mother, anything to use as leverage with his father.

Anything to keep alive the dream that he and Sophie might salvage this yet.

Perhaps Miss Ross had answers that her brother could not give.

Dinner was a modest affair with Miss Ross at one end of the table and Rafe and Sophie to each side. The same harried maid had placed dishes on the table before bobbing a curtsy and hastily exiting the room. The fire crackled at Sophie's back across from him, casting long shadows up the walls of the great hall.

Dr. Ross had not joined them, as Miss Ross insisted her brother preferred to have a dinner tray in his room. Rafe wasn't quite sure he believed her. Miss Ross kept many secrets, that much was obvious.

The larger question? How willing would the lady be to share them?

For example, seeing Miss Ross and Sophie side-by-side only highlighted the similarities between them. They could easily be mother and daughter.

Sophie cleared her throat, slanting a glance at their hostess. "Miss Ross, perhaps I should—"

"Please, call me Catharine. I feel we will be on a first-name basis afore the night is through, so why not begin how we intend to carry on?"

Sophie smiled, tentative. Only a slight tremor in her fingers betrayed her nervousness. Rafe wished he sat closer so that he could hold her hand, lend her his strength.

"Very well, Catharine." Sophie set down her fork. "Let me tell you why I have sought out Dr. Ross, and then perhaps you would be willing to offer your opinions as to why you and I so greatly resemble one another."

Catharine nodded her head.

Sophie laid out her story. Her mother's well-known indiscretions, her own desire to know her true father.

"I simply wish to know my own biology, you see. My aunt insists that my father was present for my birth, and Dr. Ross was reported to be attending my mother," she finished. "I only vaguely resemble my mother. The portrait on the wall here leads me to believe that perhaps Dr. Ross was involved in my birth for more personal reasons."

Catharine took a slow sip of her wine, dabbing her mouth before answering.

"Ye are correct, my lady. Your mother and my brother—"

"Dr. Ross?"

Catharine inclined her head. "John attended your birth because he assumed himself to *be* your father, Lady Sophie. The fact that he was also a physician was ancillary to everything else."

Rafe studied Sophie, trying to gauge how she was taking this news. She swallowed, biting her lip.

"Dr. Ross is my father," Sophie repeated, as if burning the knowledge into her own soul. "My *true* father."

"Yes." Catharine paused, compassion in her tone. "I am sorry that he is not as he once was. He was a remarkable man before the dementia set in. Clever. Witty. Handsome in his youth."

Sophie met the woman's gaze, eyes too bright. "He would have to be for my mother to pursue him so. Did he never marry?"

"Nae. John was always too busy tae marry, he said. Medicine was his bride. Though, I think he would have found ye fascinating. You have many of his mannerisms, and I have heard report of the scientific bent of your mind. It is interesting how biology expresses itself." Catharine leaned toward her. "Our family traits run true in ye, Lady Sophie. John would have liked that."

Sophie nodded, her smile watery and tremulous. She turned and dabbed at the corner of her right eye with her napkin.

"And the painting?" Rafe asked, wanting to give Sophie a moment to compose herself.

Catharine glanced up at it. "It was done while I was in Naples on a Grand Tour. I remember the occasion well, as John received the painting the day before Mount Vesuvius erupted—"

"In '79?" Rafe interrupted.

Catharine paused, looking long at Rafe before answering, "Aye."

Rafe frowned, his heart beating faster. His mind raced to make connections. "My father was in Naples in '79 when Vesuvius erupted. I remember him recounting the experience over dinner once—"

"Your father?" Sophie asked, wiping her eyes one final time. "My mother was in Naples at the same time. She told us stories as children about watching the lava flow down the mountain, the amber glow in the evening. She even gifted me a watch and chatelaine with painted glass beads showing the stages of the eruption."

"Oh, that is lovely tae hear," Catharine breathed.

"It is?" Sophie's head whipped toward her, clearly finding the older woman's response as odd as Rafe did.

Rafe took in a deep breath, his mind racing to make connections.

His father was in Naples at the same time as Catharine and Dr. Ross? Grant had mentioned that Dr. Ross had been Kendall's personal physician for a while. Had that extended to a Grand Tour?

And Sophie's mother, Lady Mainfeld was there, too? Though she wouldn't have been Lady Mainfeld then, would she? She would have been a mere aristocratic debutante, Miss Anne Montague, if memory served him right.

Surely they had all known one another. The number of English aristocrats at that time in Naples would have been small.

Rafe met Sophie's gaze across the table, the downturn of her brows testifying to the similarity of their thoughts. They both turned their attention back to Catharine. The elderly woman had set down her cutlery, choosing instead to nurse her glass of wine.

"Aye. I wondered if you two would connect this bit of the story," she murmured.

Silence hung for a moment. The fire popped, sparks showering up the chimney.

The quiet only heightened Rafe's agitation. What wasn't Catharine telling them?

"And what bit is that?" he asked, struggling to keep a bite out of his tone. This woman did not deserve insolence, even if every instinct screamed that she was keeping secrets.

Catharine set down her glass.

"Your mother"—she looked at Sophie—"first met John in Naples, two years before her marriage to Lord Mainfeld. My brother fell madly in love with her. We all did, I think, as she and I became friends, too. Your mother was a remarkably beautiful, spirited woman—"

"She still is."

"Aye? I dinnae doubt it. John tumbled headfirst into love with her, and for her part, I think Anne—your mother—loved him in her way. The watch and chatelaine you mentioned were a gift to her—"

"From Dr. Ross?"

"Aye. I remember well the day he purchased it. I thought him fair mad, but then he *was* mad for Anne. Enough that when they met again years later in Bath, they began a torrid love affair."

"Why did they not marry initially, then?" Rafe asked.

Catharine took up her wine glass again, swirling it in the candlelight.

"Anne was the daughter of a wealthy English baron. And such a woman did not marry the lowly-born physician of a duke."

Catharine met his gaze.

Ah. That was his answer then.

"A *duke*," Rafe repeated. "My father." It was not a question.

Catharine nodded just the same. "The very same."

"Dr. Ross was my father's servant—his attendant physician—traveling with him tae Naples," Rafe said, again, not a question.

It was not unusual for a nobleman to take along his own physician when traveling abroad. As a gentleman, the physician provided companionship, as well as medical care.

"Aye," Catharine said. "John encouraged Kendall tae hire me as a companion to his aunt, Lady Sarah Gilbert, who also accompanied them."

Rafe sat back in his chair. He remembered his Aunt Sarah. A perfect harridan of a lady who had chided him endlessly on his bookish ways when he was a child. She had passed away nearly a decade ago.

Did Miss Catharine Ross still maintain contact with his father then? If so, would she report Rafe's intentions to Kendall? And at this point, did it even matter anymore?

"You have the look of him," Catharine was saying.

"Pardon?" Rafe lifted his own wine glass, regretting that the liquid wasn't something even stronger.

"Your father. You have the look of him. Not necessarily in your coloring, but in the size and shape of your body, in the way you carry yourself."

Rafe nearly flinched at the words.

I am nothing *like that wretched man*, hovered on his lips.

He only barely held the words back, choosing instead to pause and take a healthy sip of wine.

"I thought you him when first I saw you, standing before the fire," Catharine continued, indicating the blazing hearth. "It nearly stopped my heart until I realized that you are much too young to be *him*."

The way Catharine spat the word *him* indicated that she understood the kind of man his father was.

Rafe relaxed a wee bit.

"And who is my father tae you, Miss Ross?" Rafe had to know.

Catharine flinched, as if the words were ice water flicked upon her face.

"No one," her words vehement. "Kendall is *no one* to me. The duke has no reach here."

Clearly the lady had close experience with Kendall's heavy-handed ways.

Catharine pushed back her plate. "So now we know why Lady Sophie wished tae speak with Dr. Ross. Why do you seek Dr. Ross, Lord Rafe?"

He set aside his own plate. "I seek help for my mother—"

"The duchess?"

"Aye. She experienced the loss of an infant shortly after birth. Melancholy has taken her, and she has been unable tae recover. I had hoped that Dr. Ross . . . well . . ."

His voice trailed off, indicating the futility of his request now.

"Ah."

Sophie stirred across the table. "Did you assist your brother, Miss Ross? Might you have some knowledge that would ease the duchess's melancholy?"

Catharine sighed and shook her head, eyes going sightless, as if pondering the ramifications of it all.

"It says much of your devotion to your mother that you would travel so far in search of help." Catharine met Rafe's gaze. The pity he saw there left a sinking hole in his chest. "My brother worked seeming miracles in patients with a depression of spirits. But I know nothing of his practices."

In one look, Catharine communicated everything Rafe had already surmised.

Kendall had been acquainted with Ross for nearly forty years. The duke had known that the doctor might be of help.

And his father had done . . . *nothing*.

Rafe's hands nearly shook with the effort to rein in his anger.

He caught Sophie's eye. The portrait of the young Catharine rose above Sophie's head, underscoring the similarity between them.

He abruptly saw the entire situation through Kendall's monstrous eyes.

His sire knew of Catharine Ross. He knew of Dr. Ross's former devotion to Lady Mainfeld. It would be a simple matter to connect that Lady Sophie was their illicit child.

No son of Kendall's would so taint his blood with the illegitimate daughter of a former servant-physician.

Moreover, Dr. Ross would be prevented from treating Kendall's duchess. After all, what use was the woman whole? Kendall needed her broken to force Rafe's compliance.

Rafe let out a stuttering breath.

Fury choked him. He had heard of men's vision going red with rage, but he had never truly experienced it so literally.

How could that bastard of a man be so heartless?

If Rafe married Sophie, his father would truly consider it an act of warfare. There would be no quarter, no compromise. His father would throw every last ounce of his enormous power into destroying their happiness.

Huh.

Rafe blinked.

So this is what it felt like . . . absolute despair.

No hope.

"I am truly sorry," Catharine continued, gaze earnest. "You must understand how much I wish I could help the duchess, truly I do. Sometimes, Fate takes things from us—"

"No, you needn't apologize." Rafe drained his wine glass. "My father's cruelty is none of your affair."

Catharine shot him a tight smile that did not quite chase away the shadows lingering in her eyes.

Rafe set down his glass, staring at Sophie across the table, a feeling of agonizing finality settling over him.

They had tried.

They had lost.

What price would now be paid?

27

Two hours later, the fire in the great hall had burned low.

Sophie pulled Jamie's tartan tighter around her shoulders, huddling into its warmth, sinking back into the chair.

Rafe sat opposite her, eyes gazing into the glowing coals.

Catharine—her *aunt!*—had retired, saying her bones were too old to stay awake any longer.

A great hush settled over the castle, the darkness a velvety thing, hoarding sound and light.

Rafe lifted a single brick of peat, setting the turf on the coals. The fire licked to life. The scent of sweet grass and earth wafted out.

Sophie swallowed, pushing against a sense of impending doom.

The emotion banding her chest must surely be a biological reaction to the dark room and steel weapons on the walls, glinting in the firelight. The castle nearly echoed with the centuries of warfare that created it.

"I must leave at first light." Rafe's voice hung between them. He did not raise his head to meet her eyes.

Telling, that.

She shifted, swallowing again, attempting to force that same emotion down, down, down. It tasted of despair.

"I am for Aberdeen," he continued. "An acquaintance, Captain White, runs an express packet boat out of the harbor there. He leaves for London tomorrow afternoon. I intend to be on his boat, as it's the quickest way to Town from here. My father will surely have been apprised of this entire venture by now." He waved a hand to include the room. "I have already tarried too long. Any further delay puts my mother at greater risk."

Sophie did not disagree with him.

He left the unspoken question hanging between them.

Would Sophie go with him?

She had been contemplating that very thing and had reached a decision.

"I know you need to go, and I wish you well on your journey," she said. "As for myself, I have searched for so long for my father, to leave after having only seen him for an hour . . ."

She hadn't even had a chance to truly speak with the man, to look in his eyes, to study their similarities up close. And all was not lost, as there was Catharine herself to know. Sophie had acquired an aunt, and that was nothing to scorn.

"I understand." Rafe stared into the fire.

Sophie nodded, her throat so very tight. It was best for them to part now.

Her reputation, such as it was, might survive this sojourn to Scotland—as few knew of it—but arriving at the London docks arm-in-arm with Lord Rafe would be tantamount to waving a red flag at the bull of London gossips. A widow was allowed more freedom than a mere miss, but that did not mean ignoring *all* propriety.

She would find herself utterly ostracized.

And there were her servants and the carriage in Edinburgh to consider.

So no, she would not be leaving with Rafe.

"I am sure Catharine can assist me in making arrangements once I am ready to leave," she said. "I have ample funds for my needs. What will you do once you arrive in London?"

He scrubbed his hands through his hair before sitting back with a frustrated *thwump*. "I will turn my life over tae my father in exchange for a modicum of freedom for my mother."

Sophie's heart froze. The desolation in his voice wrenched her.

"But . . . *why*? We discussed other options while on Cairn O'Mount. If your father wishes a grandson, perhaps it could be used as a bargaining chip?"

"Yes, it is,"—tone bleak—"and I will use my willingness tae marry as a carrot to secure some safety for my mother . . ."

His voice drifted off.

"But?" she whispered.

"But . . . my father will never allow my bride to be you."

Sophie hissed in a breath. He spoke the words with a horrid finality, as if they were carved in stone—an unchangeable fact.

Moreover, the words *my bride* stuttered and tumbled around in her brain—*my bride, my bride, my bride*.

Did Rafe truly wish her to be his *bride*?

Sophie's heart pounded and skipped at the thought, giving its opinion on the matter. Logically, she understood that finding a way to carve a future together had been part of their quest.

But it was something else to hear the words from Rafe's mouth.

"But how can you be sure?" She had to ask it. "Why do you automatically assume . . ."

That we cannot marry.

Her unspoken words hung between them. She could not quite bring herself to voice them, to put the idea forth so baldly.

If he noticed or cared, Rafe did not show it. His expression seemed to assume that their marriage had been a foregone conclusion. Which, in and of itself, was a bit earth-shattering.

His hands rested atop his kilt, fisting and relaxing, over and over, as if helpless to stem the emotions in his chest.

"Kendall despises Mainfeld," he finally replied. "Remember what I told ye? He found out I had danced with ye that night at the ball and then forbade me—"

"I grant you that, but this isn't some honor blood feud. We do not live in the Middle Ages. At some point, our fathers have to move past that wretched duel so many years ago. But *my* father—well, Lord Mainfeld, I guess I should say—would grant his blessing, if he knew it was what I truly wanted."

"Bah! Kendall doesnae care what I want. I'm convinced that even without the bad blood between our fathers, he would still deny me simply tae be cruel. Ye dinnae know him—"

"You're correct, I do not. But if he is as desperate for an heir as you say, then why would he so vehemently oppose me? Despite my actual parentage, I *am* the acknowledged daughter of an earl."

He fixed her with a dark look. "Surely Kendall knows who your father is. You are the image of your natural aunt. Catharine traveled with Kendall and Dr. Ross as a young woman. My father, at the very least, knows her in passing. He cannot be blind tae the similarities between you—"

"Why are you assuming this?" she pressed onward. This was their *future* he was casting aside. The possibility of her being his *bride*. "Why are you assuming that he will say *no* to a union between us? Particularly, if you make it clear that it is the only way he will have grandchildren? Do you *wish* to marry Lord Syke's daughter?"

"Of course not."

She bit her lip, thinking to perhaps stem the words, but they tumbled free regardless, angry and frustrated.

"Then why will you not fight for *us*?!" She leaned toward him. "Do you not care?"

Something snapped within him, some tether holding back an avalanche of words.

"Fight for us? Care?!" He surged to his feet, one hand on a hip, the other in his hair. "Are ye daft, lass?!"

"*Daft?!*" She rose, as well, hands waving. "Remember that moment in the bothie?! The one where you said you wanted me?! Was that all a lie?!"

"Of course not! I adore you!"

"Forgive me if I'm struggling to believe it! How does your current line of thinking show that you want me? That you *adore* me?" She gestured wildly. "You're giving in and assuming that your father won't permit . . . that he will not allow us to. . ."

She drifted off, her nerve failing her.

"Marry?" He finished the sentence for her.

The word hung between them, nearly pulsing with life—*marry, marry, marry*.

She nodded, pulling the tartan closer, wrapping it tight around her, as if the wool would protect her from his words.

He laughed—a bitter, caustic sound.

Sophie winced, turning her head to the side, tears falling in earnest.

She moved to pass him, intent on retiring to her quarters.

He stopped her with the wall of his chest.

"No. Not tears." His arms wrapped around her, his tone instantly softening. "I think ye are misunderstanding this situation, lass. Ye don't understand what I'm saying."

She held utterly still in his arms, her own hands trapped between them, her knuckles pressed against his sternum. She kept her eyes on his Adam's apple, fearful that if he looked into her eyes, he would see the heartache in her soul.

Sophie swallowed back the tears choking her, sucking in a stuttering breath.

"Then what *are* you saying?" she whispered.

"Sophie?"

Silence.

"Sophie, lass, *please* look at me."

It was the plaintive note in his *please* that convinced her.

She lifted her eyes, expecting to see sadness or determination or wariness. Anything but the warmth and adoration that shone there.

He studied her, his expression one of wonder . . . almost awe. He traced the side of her face with two fingers, gently tucking a stray strand of hair behind her ear.

"Do ye remember our first meeting? Behind the curtain at that ball all those years ago?"

She nodded, not trusting herself to speak.

He continued, "Ye were the most beautiful thing I had ever seen. And not just your face—which is stunning, mind ye—but I noticed so much more than that. I admired the original turn of your mind, the clever way ye looked at the world. And I knew, in that moment . . ."

He drifted off.

"Knew what?" she whispered.

He drew that same finger down her cheek, his eyes tracing the path. "That my heart would always belong to you."

Sophie froze, her own heart literally giving a stuttering hiccup before racing away. "Pardon?"

He brought his eyes to hers, intense and weighty. "If ye believe nothing else from me, then hear this: Lady Sophronia Sorrow Fulstate . . . I *want* you. I worship you." He paused, releasing a deep breath. "I *love* you."

She sucked in a gasped breath.

"I love you," he continued. "It seems at times that I have always loved you."

He loved her?

He had *always* loved her?!

'But Rafe—"

"Lennon, lass."

Oh, for the love of—

"Lennon? Truly?! At a moment like this?!"

He laughed, this time a soft breath of sound.

"Lennon," he repeated, giving the word a slightly different intonation, though it still sounded like *lennon* to her ears. "L-E-A-N-N-A-N . . . *leannan*." He spelled it out for her.

"Leannan?" she repeated.

"*Mo leannan.*" He leaned forward, pressing his forehead to hers. "My beloved."

She gasped, those dratted tears spilling over. "*Leannan?* Beloved?"

"Aye."

And then he kissed her, right then, her mouth agape in surprised shock, tears on her cheeks.

The contact jolted her, scrambling her senses further.

It only took a fraction of a second for her to return his embrace, her mouth hungrily responding to his. Her hands were still trapped between them, but she freed one, wrapping it around his neck.

This man.

She was his beloved? His *leannan*?!

And he had deliberately goaded her into calling him *beloved* every time she said his pseudonym?

But, of course, he had. It was such a . . . *Rafe* thing to do.

She almost laughed at the sheer absurdity of it. To have the heart of one like Lord Rafe Gilbert . . .

The mind nearly boggled at the thought.

And yet, here she was . . . kissing him senseless in the great hall of her natural father's castle in the Scottish Highlands.

The kiss went on and on, Rafe's hands splayed across her back, lifting her to her toes, bringing her that much closer.

"*Mo leannan,*" he murmured. "*Mo chridhe.* My heart."

She threaded her hand into his hair, not allowing him to pull away from her. She would keep him here by sheer force, if necessary.

"How can you call me your beloved and then not fight for us?" she whispered against his lips, tasting the salt of her own tears. "How can you not want us to be together—"

He kissed her again, swallowing her words, his actions becoming more and more desperate.

"I want it more than anything," he replied, pulling back just enough to speak. "I would give just about anything tae keep ye, Sophie, love, ye must believe that. But, my father . . ." He paused, kissing her one more time.

She was quite sure her knees had gone utterly boneless. "Your father?"

He leaned his forehead against hers once more. "My father knows."

Sophie blinked. "Pardon?"

"My father knows how I feel about you. He knows that I love you."

"H-h-how? How could he know that?"

"He knows me. He deduced the reasons behind my behavior."

"I don't . . . I don't understand."

Rafe let loose a gust of air and stepped back, his hands leaving her body, as if greatly reluctant to let her go.

Cold swept over her at his loss.

"Ye know the ball where I kissed you?" he asked. "I have never enjoyed an evening more than that one. Truthfully. As I said before, I had every intention of courting ye in earnest after that night. But my father learned of my behavior and loudly voiced his disapproval of ye."

"Yes." Her heart plummeted. "You have mentioned this."

"Aye. But I have not told ye all." Rafe slowly nodded his head. "The day after the ball, Kendall tried everything to make me give ye up. I held fast. I refused. I was going tae take my mother out of the country. I hoped to convince ye to elope with me."

"Truly?" Sophie's voice cracked. "What a crazy, wonderful idea."

"It was." His eyes so very sad. "We would have taken off with Andrew on his adventure to the South Pacific."

"Oh!"

"It would have been incredible. But . . ."

"But?"

"My father was livid at my intransigence, at my refusal tae bow to his demands and give ye up. And so, Kendall took matters into his own hands. He forced me tae accompany Andrew—"

"Forced you?" Sophie's hand clutched her stomach.

"Aye. He ordered two burly grooms tae 'escort' me to *The Minerva* in Leith. He compelled me to go on the voyage, knowing that ye would be married when I returned. *That* is how much Kendall hates Mainfeld. That is how opposed he is tae a union between us."

She practically watched the fight drain from him.

Sophie didn't want to join him in his hate for his father, but it rose in her nonetheless. How could that callous duke take such a kind, generous son and deliberately crush him, grind him to dust like so much chaff?

Silence.

"So you see, Kendall will never allow our marriage. He practically took me up in chains the last time I mentioned it. If we were tae marry, we would do it without his blessing. And he would exact revenge upon my mother for it. Kendall would cast her into the worst asylum he could find."

"I agree with you. I would never do anything that would harm your mother so. Can she not be spirited away then? You had mentioned that before—"

"*That* option has passed. 'Twould be just as cruel to her, as she dotes upon her grandchildren so. I think she would prefer the asylum—"

"No!"

"Aye. 'Tis the truth. Regardless, I cannot purchase my happiness at the cost of condemning my mother to a life of captivity and misery. I cannot. Such a thing would poison my soul . . . and so I cannot think of a way . . ." He paused. Cleared his throat. And then continued. "Despite it being the absolute profoundest wish of my heart, I cannot see how there can be an . . . *us*."

Even though Sophie knew the words were coming, even though she knew he would—and *should*—choose his mother over her, hurt still lanced through her chest.

She licked a tear off her upper lip.

Rafe observed it in silence, dark eyes tracking the drops on her cheeks. He brushed them away with his thumbs, but more followed. Shaking his head, he let out a curse and bent down. He began kissing the tears away, murmuring his love over and over.

"I would give anything tae be the one to always kiss away your grief," he whispered, a hitch in his breath.

Sophie could not bring herself to answer. Instead, she pulled his mouth back to hers, communicating her anguish through a punishing kiss.

Finally, Rafe pulled back, pressing his forehead to hers, hands trembling, chest heaving.

"I hate him," he hissed. "It's unchristian and unholy and likely going to destroy me, but I don't care. I hate him!"

Despite having never met the man, Sophie could not bring herself to respond.

She felt like hating the Duke of Kendall, too.

But she had already fought so hard to rid her heart of such rage. It was an acid to her soul.

Hatred had nearly destroyed her once. She would not allow it purchase again.

But it was difficult. It was *so* difficult to not hate as Rafe continued to rage, as she had to stand as witness to the result of his father's cruelty.

She tried not to hate as she lay in her bed later that night, imagining more and more desperate ways that she and Rafe could be together.

And she viciously smothered the emotion as she watched Rafe ride out the following morning at first light.

Not knowing when, or if, she would see him again.

28

Rafe rode out of Drathes Castle at first light.

He did not look back.

One slight glance from Sophie would be enough to destroy his resolve, to claim her as his own and abandon his mother to her fate.

And he could not do that.

He *would* not claim his future on the back of his mother's misery.

Anger burned a hole in his chest. The more Rafe thought of Kendall, secure in his position, king of his fiefdom, basking in power and wealth . . .

Rage tasted acrid in his throat.

How could this be the end? After everything, Rafe would be forced into a marriage he did not want, dancing to his father's tune like a trained monkey, spending his days bending to *that man's* will. Just imagining such a life wrapped a vise around his chest, snatching his breath and constricting his lungs.

What was he to do?

Unbidden, images crawled through his mind . . .

Rafe arriving in London and luring his father away somewhere for a hunting trip. How simple it would be to contrive a convenient accident.

Or perhaps a vintage French brandy laced with sufficient nightshade to ensure death.

There were numerous ways to send the Duke of Kendall to an untimely end.

And with his death, Rafe's mother would be free. Free of his father's threats and abuses. Free to live as she chose.

Even if the deed were pinned on Rafe, he could flee the country. Sophie was adventurous; surely she would join him. They could be together.

Rafe only had to enact a plan . . .

Sophie's words from those hours in the bothie on Cairn O'Mount rattled through him.

Hate and anger can be molded into determination and strength.

He knew that murder was not what Sophie had meant. Would she forgive him for killing his father?

And was he actually contemplating patricide as the only viable solution to this?

Didn't he try to kill you first on Cairn O'Mount? an insidious voice whispered. *Grant said he was only to warn you, but how do you know?*

If Grant had been successful, no one would have ever tied Rafe's death—in a ravine on a moor in the Scottish Highlands, a brigand's bullet through his skull—to his father.

Was death truly what his father had intended for him? And if so, didn't Rafe have a right—even an *obligation*—to protect himself?

Only the dissolution of her marriage bonds would release his mother. Divorce was impossible. Therefore, his father's death was the only viable solution.

Rafe tried to push the dark thoughts away—they had no proof that Kendall had ordered Grant to kill him, the likelihood of it seemed slim and illogical—but the idea of being free took on its own life.

Images and ideas flooded him. So many options; so many ways he might go about ending his sire.

The violent thoughts acted like tinder to the flame of his rage, stoking it higher and higher, until it felt as if he *had* to kill Kendall. That it was the only logical place for his hatred to go.

Rafe cantered into Aberdeen in the early afternoon, heading straight for the harbor. It was a simple task to locate Captain White and book passage on the packet boat leaving for London in two hours.

Captain White, a good friend of Kieran's and hence an acquaintance of Rafe's, was a looming, no-nonsense fellow.

"'Tis a pleasure to see ye again, my lord. I trust Kieran is well?"

"Aye." Rafe fished coins out of his sporran. "He was hale when I last saw him in Edinburgh. He was for New York then."

"Eh, New York always agrees with a man." White took Rafe's payment and then consulted his pocket watch. "We leave with the outgoing tide in precisely ninety-five minutes. Be punctual. Dinnae make me search for your sorry arse."

Rafe nodded. He had no intention of being late. He had to reach Kendall as quickly as possible, anything to stem the tide of damage.

Rafe made his way to a nearby livery stable and arranged for his horses to be returned to a stable in Edinburgh. He then bolted down a quick luncheon of haggis and neeps at a crowded dockside tavern across from the packet boat. As he finished eating, he could see Captain White and one of the crew directing passengers into several skiffs to be rowed out to the packet boat bobbing in the harbor. The ship would leave promptly at the hour; Rafe didn't have much time.

He paid his account and crossed the wharf, pushing through the lines of sailors unloading cargo and the crowds of passengers milling about, intent on Captain White and the skiff. The captain turned and motioned to him to hurry. Rafe picked up his pace.

But as Rafe stepped aside to allow a group of drunk sailors to pass, a familiar voice reached him through the din.

". . . I cannae say precisely how long we'll be gone, but the voyage should take at least two weeks, mayhap three."

Rafe froze between one step and the next, feet locked in place, heart in his throat.

No!

It cannot be.

Surely, he was hearing things. That voice did not belong to whom he thought.

And yet . . .

The voice continued, moving away from him, "I can look at the charts and give ye a better estimate, if ye'd care to call upon me tomorrow."

Rafe whirled around in the crowd, desperate to track the speaker. He circled a group of sailors fresh into port.

Surely he was simply hearing things.

Surely it was merely the anger over his father bleeding into other aspects of his life.

The sailors parted, almost magically revealing a path that ended in the form of the last man Rafe expected to see—

Martin Cuthie.

Captain of *The Minerva.*

A man reportedly lost at sea nearly four years ago.

Rafe's limbs were encased in ice, breaths labored in and out as he struggled to process what he was seeing.

He stared at Cuthie, checking over and over again that this was, indeed, who he thought it was.

The same salt-and-pepper hair.

The same craggy face.

The same voice that haunted Rafe's dreams.

This man . . .

The cause of so much hurt . . .

A thousand images flashed through his head. The most vivid being Cuthie's order to his men, lip curling—

Hold him steady, lads.

And then the searing heat of Cuthie's knife slashing across his upper cheekbone.

To see Cuthie here. Now.

Cuthie had survived. Somehow, someway . . . the bastard had lived.

No need to wonder who had been sending them threatening letters and posting those notices into the *Advertiser*. It is exactly the sort of cowardly thing Cuthie would do.

Did the captain plan to blackmail them? Did he really think that Rafe and the others were so easily taken down?

Fury was a lit fuse inside him, anger a battle pulse in his ears.

Jamie had died, and despite every damn thing this man had done, *Cuthie* had lived.

Just like Kendall, Cuthie was a rat. A pestilence. A scrabbling parasite of a man, intent on sucking the life's blood of everything and everyone around him.

There was no justice in this.

Why?

Why did those who killed and maimed and hurt prosper?

While those who tried to live a virtuous life—like Jamie, like himself—were doomed to be their punching bags? Taking the hits and never having a chance of truly getting free?

Rafe was moving toward Cuthie before consciously thinking about it.

Something in the air must have shifted, alerting the older man to Rafe's presence.

Cuthie's head swiveled.

He did not mistake the murderous look in Rafe's eyes, the recognition there.

If Cuthie had even looked confused for a second, Rafe might have believed him to be someone else, that this man's survival would have been impossible—

But Cuthie knew him instantly, understanding flashing across his expression.

The man stood taller, gaze wary.

"Lord Rafe," he began, startling looks from those around him, heads whipping to look at Rafe. After all, lords did not generally stalk along Aberdeen's wharf. "What a surprise to see ye here."

Rafe kept coming, closer and closer.

The men around the captain stood back, correctly reading the murderous bent in Rafe's eye, smart enough to not involve themselves in Cuthie's business.

Cuthie finally understood that Rafe would not be stopping until he had his hands around the captain's throat. The captain glanced around, quickly ascertaining that none of his supposed companions would be helping him. There were no crewmen nearby to protect him. No ruffians to do his bidding.

And so, like the inherent coward that he was, Cuthie turned tail and ran.

Rafe was more than ready for it, sprinting after him.

Dimly, Rafe heard someone shout his name, but the blood roaring in his ears drowned out all sound.

Cuthie dashed across the wharf, pushing his way through the crowd, Rafe close at his heels.

The older man didn't stand a chance. Rafe had six inches, twenty years, and a lifetime of pent-up rage on Cuthie.

He caught Cuthie just as the older man darted into a narrow close beside an inn.

Snatching the captain's jacket, Rafe whirled him around, slamming his back into the harling lining the stone building, the motion generating a satisfying *thwap*. The noise was so gratifying that Rafe did it again and again, punching Cuthie in the face and stomach with each *thwump*.

He initially intended to knock Cuthie's head about and then demand some answers. Soften the man up so he would talk.

What had happened to *The Minerva*? What had happened to Jamie? Who else had survived?

But Cuthie struggled away and pulled a wicked-looking knife from his boot.

All questions flew out of Rafe's brain. Blind rage filled the vacuum.

Cuthie came at him, knife raised. Rafe didn't doubt that the man knew his way around a fight.

But Rafe wasn't Scottish for nothing. He side-stepped Cuthie's swipe and pivoted sharply, hacking an arm across the man's forearm, sending the knife skittering along the cobblestones behind them.

And then Rafe truly let his fists fly. He danced on his feet, weaving in and out of Cuthie's punches. Every thrown fist, every grunt was tinder for his anger, feeding the fury that raged within him.

Cuthie had held him prisoner, had hurt those he loved, had hurt Jamie . . .

Just like his father. Just as Kendall cut with his words and manipulative behavior.

And just like Kendall, Cuthie deserved to die for his crimes.

The captain was no match for Rafe's fury.

Finally, Rafe slammed Cuthie face-first into the wall, pinning him with his body, wrenching one of his arms up between his shoulder blades. Cuthie squirmed and bucked, but Rafe was twice the man's size and infinitely stronger.

"Did ye think to frighten us, old man?" Rafe shouted. "Did ye think a few letters and a posted advert in the *Advertiser* would scare us?"

"An advert?"

"Aye, ye eejit."

"I dinnae know anything about any notice in the papers—"

"Shut it." Rafe didn't believe Cuthie, that the man knew nothing of the notice in the *Edinburgh Advertiser*. It was simply more of his lies.

"'Tis truth. I sent the letters—"

"Did ye? Why? Hoping tae scare us? Ye should've known we dinnae scare so easily. Ye were better off with us thinking ye dead."

"I'll see ye pay—"

"For what?! For trying to save our own lives? For saving the lives of those villagers?"

"Ye deserve it—"

"Like hell, we do. Andrew's a wealthy earl. I'm the son of a powerful duke. Despite your legal technicalities, slave trade is a nasty, foul business. Do ye think ye can touch us now? We have the law and public opinion on our side."

"I wouldnae be so sure as to what ye know, lad."

"Where is Jamie Fyffe, old man?" Rafe hissed in Cuthie's ear.

"J-Jamie?" Cuthie grunted. "I'll n-never tell ye."

"Ye will!" Rafe pulled harder on the old man's arm.

Cuthie yelped in pain.

"D-dead," the man spat. "Jamie is dead."

"You lie!"

Cuthie grunted again but remained mum.

Rafe dug his elbow into the man's spine, causing him to cry out. "Perhaps another round will loosen your tongue."

Rafe shoved Cuthie's face into the stone, punching him in the kidneys. The man twisted away, but Rafe was on him in an instant, taking them both to the ground. Rafe straddled the captain, pounding fists into the man's face.

After a moment or two, some sense of rational thought broke through his blinding anger.

Cuthie was no longer fighting back. The man was whimpering, hands up to protect his head.

Rafe was pummeling an older, weaker man. It was anything but a fair fight.

When did Cuthie ever fight fair with you? When he chained you in the hold of The Minerva? When he had his men hold you down so he could slash your face?

Cuthie deserved this . . . his past behavior, his cruelty needed to be avenged. Rafe may not be able to attack his father directly, but he could mete out punishment to Cuthie.

It was Rafe's *right*.

Jamie was dead.

But . . . Sophie's words floated through him.

Harness your rage and mold the energy into determination for good. Otherwise, I fear the power of it will destroy your soul. You will burn on the pyre of your hatred.

Abruptly, he saw the scene through her eyes—

Rafe beating an older man within an inch of his life, anger and hatred in his fists.

This wasn't the man he wanted to be.

This wasn't the man he wanted Sophie to love.

Rafe pulled away from Cuthie, standing up. The captain lay still. Unconscious.

What had Rafe done? The man still breathed, so Rafe hadn't killed him, but what—

A whistle sounded from the harbor.

Dammit!

The packet boat!

But he couldn't leave now, not with Cuthie here. They needed answers—

A hand wrapped around his elbow, pulling him backwards. Rafe went to shrug it off and looked into the eyes of Captain White.

"Ye bloody eejit, picking a fight at a moment like this. And with *Cuthie*, no less. His men will be here any moment," the captain growled, turning away, half-dragging Rafe with him.

Rafe pulled on his arm, but White was determined, his grip a vise.

"I should let them beat ye senseless. That might cool yer anger, but Kieran would have ma hide," White continued. "You will board my ship *now* if ye value yer own life!"

Some sense trickled through to Rafe. He knew first-hand how vicious Cuthie's men could be.

Rafe finally noticed the crowd of people watching the scene from the mouth of the close, grim-eyed and wary. He saw the scene through their eyes . . . him bloodying an older man, being hauled off like a madman.

Nausea clawed up his throat.

He could run from Sophie. He could run from his father, from his past with Cuthie, from his responsibilities to his mother.

But . . . he could never outrun himself.

If he allowed Kendall and Cuthie to turn him into a monster, how was Rafe any different from them, in the end?

He allowed Captain White to lead him, the need to get away nearly suffocating.

Sophie's words from days before cut into him.

Hate is a shield. A dam holding back a tidal wave of other, more painful emotions.

He had rejected those words.

But now . . .

Now . . . he *felt* them, viscerally, a raw twisting in his gut.

Emotion pounded through him . . . scouring, cutting, caustic.

Later Rafe would wonder how he managed to hold himself together as Captain White led him across the dock, as he was rowed out to the ship, as he was led to his private berth, the door slamming behind the captain.

Once there, Rafe lowered himself onto the small box bed, his shoulders crumpling, his body curling around itself. His fists ached, bruised and scraped. There was a twinge in his ribs where Cuthie had landed a lucky punch.

But with a heaving sob, he looked further inward.

And . . .

. . . there it was, behind his rage, behind his hate . . .

The promised tidal wave of pain and grief.

A veritable ocean of hurt, so deep and fathomless, its existence threatened to drown him.

Sophie had been so very *right*.

Just the thought sent a torrent of emotions flooding him.

How could his own *father* treat him with such cruelty? How could Kendall—the one person who should love and protect him above all else—treat Rafe with such brutal callousness?

The dam burst.

For hours, Rafe sobbed his grief.

Crying for the little boy who had been desperate for any scrap of attention from his father, who had sought the duke's approval despite Kendall's harsh words and biting disregard.

Crying for his mother and her pain and Rafe's helplessness to stem it, the years of inaction and simply allowing Kendall to control them all.

Crying for every cruel and cutting remark, for every gleeful order.

Sophie *was* right.

Kendall might have been the catalyst, but it was Rafe's own rage and hatred that were destroying him. He might be limited as to how he could respond to Kendall physically, but he could stop allowing his father to control his thoughts. Rafe *could* stem the hatred eating away at him.

Sophie cared about the welfare of his soul. Maybe he could harness his love for her and allow it to save him, to carve new paths into his thinking, turning his rage into a power to save himself from the drowning ocean of his hatred.

Finally—*finally!*—Rafe saw the Duke of Kendall for what he truly was:

A petty, small-minded man who had to prey upon others in order to feel some self-worth. A man who was incapable of love.

And in that realization—in the cleansing wake of his pain, in his soul-deep understanding of how to harness his hatred for change—Rafe knew his life would never be the same.

29

Sophie moved through the next several days as if in a fog.

Rafe had left. Part of her longed to race after him, to force him to battle for a solution.

To *fight* for them.

But no matter how many hours she spent thinking through possibilities, there simply wasn't a solution for his mother without Kendall relenting in some way.

And, heaven knew, there was nothing she, Lady Sophronia, could do to force the Duke of Kendall to relent.

And so, instead, she did what she had set out to do when she left London—

She returned to her origin, her natural father.

John.

The man spent his days lost in his dementia, curled into a chair before the fire in the great hall, tartan wrapped around his shoulders and chest for extra warmth.

Sophie sat at his side.

Why had her mother never told her about John? Why the secrecy? Surely it wasn't just his station in life. Sophie's other siblings had similarly non-aristocratic fathers, and her mother spoke of them on occasion when Lord Mainfeld was not about.

But even an oblique reference to Sophie's natural father would send her mother into panicked hysterics. Why was Dr. Ross a banned topic of conversation? Had their love affair ended badly?

But even that theory didn't seem quite right. Lady Mainfeld clearly felt something for John, as she had gifted Sophie the chatelaine and watch he had given her in Naples. Her mother had kept the memento all these years, so it followed that she didn't *hate* John.

Sophie could make no sense of it.

Instead, she spent time each day mentally cataloging the numerous ways she and John resembled one another. Their hands were eerily identical, the same long fingers and narrow fingernails, the same protruding bony wrists. She shared his ears and hair, the general structure of his face, but her eye shape and overall body structure belonged to her mother.

How she longed to learn more than surface, physical things about him.

Sophie would have liked to know her aunt, Catharine, better, too. But after their dinner together that first night, her aunt had retreated.

Oh, Catharine was polite and kind when Sophie *did* speak with her, but the woman gave every appearance of stringently avoiding Sophie's company.

When John decided to nap, Sophie wandered the castle, just her and the whispered ghosts of the past.

What had her father been like twenty-five years ago? Who was the man that her mother fell for?

Catharine merely smiled sadly when Sophie asked her about it during the rare minutes that her aunt appeared.

"John was obsessed with the mind, with all the ways it can betray you," Catharine said, watching John awkwardly dangle a bit of yarn to entice a kitten who had sneaked up from the kitchen. "It was as if he saw his own future and spent a lifetime kicking against it. All to no avail." She waved a hand toward the back of the great hall. "There is a small study across the landing that houses all of John's books, if you are interested."

Sophie was very much interested. Perhaps there was something in John's books that could help Rafe's mother?

She spent an entire day closeted in the study, poring over the books that were important to him. John had liked to write comments in the margins, arguing with the authors. His intellect sparkled and shot off the page.

She went to bed that night unsure if reading her father's comments had helped her to know him better or only deepened her sorrow over his current mental state.

Moreover, there had been nothing in John's writings that outlined ways to treat melancholy.

John himself was no help, either. He was in an advanced stage of dementia. He remembered little from minute to minute. He would ask who she was a hundred times a day and each time Sophie would tell him—"I'm Sophie. I'm here to call upon you."

Sometimes he would respond. Often he would forget, only to ask her yet again.

Every now and again he called her Catharine, thinking her to be his sister.

Occasionally, he would become agitated until Sophie placed her chair beside his and wrapped his hand between hers. The simple human touch calmed him, grounded him.

Sophie didn't mind the silence.

It gave her time to think, to realize that this was all she would ever have of her natural father.

There would be no joyous reunion, no homecoming.

The pilgrimage to piece herself together seemed to have gone all topsy-turvy.

She was supposed to go back to the beginning, to find herself there . . .

But like John, she feared she had gotten lost along the way. She had been sent down unexpected paths, losing her heart to a man she could not have.

And now, her search ended here, in a lonely castle buried in the Scottish Highlands, watching John struggle to remember people, to gather the scattered shards of himself . . .

Ironically, it all felt too much like herself.

Lonely. Lost. Unsure of where she had been.

Her current destination unknown.

FOUR DAYS AFTER leaving Aberdeen, Rafe stood in the hallway staring at the door to Kendall's study, steeling his resolve to face his father.

Thanks to Captain White's iron will, the packet boat had made excellent time on the journey southward.

Rafe had spent most of the trip in his private berth, sorting through the emotions his altercation with Cuthie had raised, the pain and hurt of Kendall's behavior.

Rafe's fists and side were still bruised, a solid reminder of what had happened on that wharf in Aberdeen.

He reeled from the implications of those minutes in that alleyway.

The blinding hatred taken too far. The soul-rattling understanding of himself. The knowledge that Captain Cuthie had survived the wreck.

If not for his smarting hands, he might have convinced himself that he had imagined the whole thing.

But no, Cuthie had been there. Someone had survived the sinking of *The Minerva*. Who else had lived?

Cuthie said Jamie had died . . . but was that to be believed?

If Jamie had survived—and that was a truly enormous *if*—the youth would have contacted one of them by now, particularly Kieran. Knowing Jamie's sense of loyalty as Rafe did, Jamie would never allow the Brotherhood to assume the worst. Their lost friend would have found a way to get a message to at least one of them.

Nearly four years of silence was proof enough of Jamie's death.

Regardless, they would hunt for answers. Cuthie would not remain at large for long. The Brotherhood had time, money, and power on their side. They were no longer helpless passengers on the far side of the world. Cuthie had been wise to keep his existence a secret from them.

Rafe would write the Brotherhood as soon as he finished speaking with his father, apprising them of what had transpired.

As for his father...

Rafe had no idea what he would say. His stomach knotted at the thought of facing the man, but Rafe had to do it, if nothing else than to check on his mother's welfare.

Fortunately, he was well-heeled at the moment. He had stopped by his rooms for a quick bath and change of clothing, allowing his valet to give him a careful shave and thoroughly brush his clothing.

But when he reached Gilbert House, the butler informed him that his mother was no longer in residence in London. His Grace had decided that the duchess needed some country air.

The man refused to tell Rafe where his mother had gone.

Rafe was no fool. His father wished Rafe to have no contact with her, to heighten the perceived threat to her person.

And now, staring at the door before him, Rafe paid the price for his journey north.

Straightening his shoulders, he rapped on the door.

"Come," Kendall's voice called.

The duke looked up from his desk as Rafe walked in.

As usual, the duke oozed power and arrogance. Kendall's pale-ice eyes glittered in the gloomy light. The ducal seal flashed on his finger as he drummed the desktop.

"Ah, the prodigal returns." His father raked his gaze over him from head to toe, posture rigid. "You have been quite busy, I understand. Beadle and Grant have sent me reports of your activities."

Rafe said nothing.

He *had* been busy, desperate to salvage something of his future.

All for naught.

Sophie's green eyes flashed through his head, the warmth of her laughter.

After accepting the pain behind his hate—knowing that he needed to change the way he thought about his father—Rafe had spent every minute of the past four days thinking through how he would behave once faced with his sire. He expected to feel that same visceral anger, the same clenching bite in his chest.

And those sensations certainly were there, but mingled within it was a sense of Sophie's trust, of her strength and determination for him.

Harness your hate and anger for something good.

He liked the sound of that. He wanted to do it.

But it was the *how* of it all that got him. How could he fight his father when the man held all the cards? When his mother's very sanity hung in the balance?

Kendall sat back in his chair. "I must say, tying up Grant was hardly sporting of you, boy. Not particularly gentlemanly."

That, Rafe could not let pass.

"Well, given that Grant was firing upon me at the time, it seemed a prudent course of action," Rafe replied, holding his sire's gaze.

If Kendall was surprised by this, he didn't show it. Instead, the duke studied Rafe intently, as if searching for something. Perhaps some sign of remorse?

Rafe refused to give the man anything. He was done allowing Kendall the ability to control his emotions; it was one area that Kendall could not affect—Rafe's attitude.

"Did you reach Drathes Castle then?" Kendall asked.

There was no point in denying it. "Aye."

The duke pinched his lips. "And did you find what you sought there?"

Rafe paused. It was an odd question for Kendall. How to answer?

"I found . . . enough," Rafe replied.

"But not all?"

Rafe did not reply. His silence was answer enough.

The tense quiet between them stretched and stretched, a band about to burst. Kendall continued to search Rafe's gaze, eyes narrowed and shrewd.

Finally, the duke gave a small smile and relaxed slightly into his chair. "You know how I hate it when you force me to be cruel to you, boy." The nearly gleeful look in his father's eye said he was more delighted than disappointed. "Shall I jump right to the point? Your mother is gravely ill."

The duke's smile widened. It was not a pleasant expression.

But instead of flooding anger, Rafe only felt pity as he stared at his father. How would it be to live one's life so devoid of love? Of basic human compassion?

"It distresses me greatly to see her so indisposed," Kendall continued. "I have spoken with her physician, and we both agree that a strict regimen of restraints, ice baths, and bloodletting are the best course. She is en route to a sanatorium even as we speak. The treatments will begin in three weeks' time. Unless, that is, you have something else to offer me in exchange for altering the course of her . . . treatment . . ."

Rafe said nothing for a moment. His father knew Rafe's wishes. The old man likely wanted to hear Rafe beg.

Instead, Rafe shifted on his feet and said the thing that truly haunted him:

"Who hurt you?" The baffled wonder in Rafe's voice astonished even him, the genuine sincerity of his tone. "Who formed you into such a hate-filled, spiteful man? What horrid events occurred in your past to have this outcome?"

Kendall's nostrils flared. Something flashed across his granite-like face. Had Rafe struck true?

Silence.

Kendall firmed his jaw. "Lord Sykes' house party begins Thursday next." His father leaned forward. "Let us discuss how you are going to repent of your behavior over the past few weeks, shall we?"

AFTER A WEEK at Drathes Castle, Sophie knew it was time to return to London.

Catharine had continued to avoid her. Sophie didn't know what to make of it. Looking at Catharine was to see thirty-odd years into her own future. Sophie longed to know the woman better. Was Catharine disinclined to others' society? Or did she simply find Sophie's company distasteful?

Regardless, any real friendship or touching familial reunion with the woman appeared unlikely. How odd, to have an aunt who was nearly one's twin, and yet be unable to forge a connection of any sort.

Would Sophie end her days like Catharine? Keeping house for a dotty older brother, all her personal dreams dried up?

She hoped not.

She *would* not.

Sophie had survived a disastrous marriage to Jack. She would survive losing Lord Rafe Gilbert, too. She would continue breathing. She would move forward.

Tenacity, after all, would prevail.

She made arrangements with Ian to return to Edinburgh, hiring several people from Aboyne to accompany her to Alex's residence. Once there, she could return home with Martha and her father's men. Sophie would surely have to reassure Martha that she had not been sold into a harem, nor captured by highwaymen (though there had been a close call or two which she would definitely *not* mention).

The afternoon before her departure, Sophie sat with John one last time. The dreary skies of the past week had evaporated, sending cheery sun streaming through the windows of the great hall, illuminating the space.

The sunlight improved John's mood, it seemed. He smiled more and kept calling her Catharine, watching Sophie pet the kitchen kitten, who had clearly decided that she needed to be a great-hall kitten and insisted on a place in Sophie's lap whenever she sat before the fire.

Sophie watched the creature stretch and yawn, curling its orange tail upward.

"Ye're not Catharine," John abruptly said at her elbow.

She turned her head to him. "Pardon?"

She noticed instantly that something was different. John was alert, the unfocused, haziness in his eyes gone. Instead, she met the gaze of an intelligent, focused man.

"Ye have her look, but ye are not her. Ye're not Catharine," he repeated.

She swallowed. "No, sir. I am not Catharine. I am Sophie."

"Sophie?" John frowned. "Sophie who?"

"Lady Sophronia Sorrow."

She expected that her name would mean nothing to him. That he would nod and reach for some yarn to tease the kitten.

But instead he froze, eyes going so very wide.

"Sophronia?" he whispered, voice wondering and astonished. "*My wee Sophronia? Anne's child?*"

Sophie gasped, the world going blurry in an instant.

He looked her up and down, gaze so very wide-eyed. "Ye grew up, lass. Last I held ye, ye were a tiny, wee bairn in my arms."

He reached out and caught a tear from her cheek.

"You r-r-remember," she hiccupped.

"Aye." He swallowed. "For the now." His eyes skimmed her face, as if greedy to memorize every last inch. "I made it a point, over the years, tae keep track of ye. I saw ye once, from a distance, riding in Hyde Park. Ye've a fine seat in the saddle, lass. And I hear tell that ye have an affection for the natural sciences, aye?"

Sophie was crying in earnest now. Not soft sniffles or polite tears, but embarrassing gusts and sobbing snuffles. She couldn't speak, only nod her head in agreement. She wrapped an arm around his shoulders and pressed her face into his chest.

"There, there, lass. 'Tis no need to weep over me, greetin' away." He patted her shoulder, the motion at once so tender and so fatherly-awkward, Sophie couldn't stem another bout of tears. "Most ladies find me quite handsome and charming, ye know."

She choked out a laugh, made more painful because she would never know this version of John. Her father as he had been.

Sophie was not foolish enough to think that John's lucidity would last long. She had minutes, at most.

Sucking in a stuttering breath, she lifted her head, smiling through tears. She pressed a kiss to his grizzled cheek.

"It is l-lovely to meet you." She swiped at her wet cheeks. "I have longed to know you for so many years."

"Aye, lass. It was my deep regret that yer birth happened as it did. I would have liked tae have known ye over the years."

Ah, heavens. How was she to stem the flood of tears?

He waited patiently as she retrieved a handkerchief and dabbed and wiped until she felt equal to the task of speaking again.

"Th-thank you," she finally said. "I should like to have known you better myself."

"Has Mainfeld been a good father to ye? He promised me he would be."

"Pardon? Lord Mainfeld promised you?"

"Aye. After ye were born, I didnae want tae let ye go. I wanted ye for my own, tae raise you myself. Yer were my wee girl. I couldnae part with ye."

What—?!

John had wanted her? As his own?

Yer were my wee girl.

Sophie hiccupped a sob.

His eyes went soft. "I loved yer mother . . . from the first moment I set eyes on her all those years ago in Naples. She was such a beautiful, vivacious thing . . . so full of life." He brushed a tear from Sophie's cheek. "Ye had the look of my family from birth, what with all yer dark hair. I knew instantly that no one would ever think ye tae be Mainfeld's. I wanted tae raise ye as my own daughter. But Mainfeld . . ." John paused, shaking his head before clearing his throat.

Sophie pressed her handkerchief to her face, futilely trying to mop up her tears.

"M-Mainfeld?" she prompted. What had Lord Mainfeld to do with this?

John smiled. "Mainfeld is a good man. He loves your mother and, because of that, he loves her children. Never met a man quite like him. He pointed out that if I were tae raise ye, ye would never escape the stigma of being illegitimate. But with his name, he could protect ye, give ye a true family, raise ye as a fine lady. He said he wanted ye tae be with him. It was the life ye deserved."

She crumpled into a sobbing mess, her mind stuttering to take in the onslaught of information.

Lord Mainfeld had *fought* to raise her as his own?! He had deliberately *chosen* to be her father?

She had been loved.

She had been wanted.

Not by one father . . . but by *two*.

The knowledge swelled within her, a balloon of joy.

Finally, she managed to raise her head.

"There, there, child." John surveyed her. "I can see it all turned out a'right."

Affection and love surged through her heart for this man, John, who had sired her.

But also love for Lord Mainfeld, the man who raised her, who never once made her feel like anything other than his own child.

She had been so fixated on finding her natural father, she had lost sight of that fact.

"Lord Mainfeld *has* been a good father to me. The best of fathers." She felt the truth of it spread through her chest, a glimmering blossom of light. "But I have so longed to know *you*—" Her voice cracked at the end.

"Well," he huffed a laugh, "I am here for the moment, it seems. What would ye know?"

A thousand questions ran through Sophie's mind, all the things that she wanted to know about him, about her.

What had he felt at her birth?

When had his love of medicine begun?

What did he adore most about being a scientist? What was his greatest struggle?

But instead, the words that tumbled out were, in the end, not about her.

"What would you recommend as a treatment for melancholy brought on by childbirth?"

John sat back, clearly nonplussed by the sheer randomness of her question.

"It's for a friend," she clarified. "To help his mother."

Because if Dr. John Ross had a moment of lucidity, Sophie realized that she would use it to help Rafe. His happiness and his mother's happiness were directly related to Sophie's own. So the question was actually monumentally selfish and not nearly as altruistic as it appeared.

She loved Rafe. She wanted to be with him.

"Melancholy brought on by childbirth?" John repeated "Does the patient appear tae suffer from a surfeit of anxiety, as well?"

Sophie thought back to Rafe's descriptions of his mother. "I don't believe so."

He pondered that for a moment. "I'm not sure there is a cure, per se. But the symptoms can be eased. I know my methods have been considered unorthodox, but I have seen them work time and again—"

"One moment. Allow me to fetch pen and paper." Sophie scrambled for the small desk sitting on the opposite wall.

Returning with pen and paper in hand, she wrote down John's recommendations. They seemed so simple—remove worries and troublesome situations, create an environment where the patient feels safe and loved, administer a strong tincture of distilled St. John's wort and willow bark. He gave her meticulous instructions.

"The tincture is unusual in its preparation, but I find that the process creates a more robust medicine that eases the symptoms of depression of spirits."

Sophie blew on the paper when she was done, drying the ink, tucking it safely into her pocket, determined to see it delivered to Rafe as soon as she arrived in London.

John remained clear-minded. They moved off to speak of other things. Sophie told him about her research with barn cats, and he told stories about his travels and work in medicine.

An hour passed. And then two.

He forgot her name once.

And then he lost the thread of a story midway through telling it.

She watched the dementia claim him—one tiny piece at a time—until he was a stooped elderly man again, no recognition in his eyes.

It was agony to witness, to know the brilliance that John had once been.

But, despite the pain and tears, she wouldn't trade those hours of lucidity. The incredible gift of finally meeting her natural father.

Her mind stuttered to accommodate everything she had learned about herself over the afternoon.

John had loved her. He had wanted her as his daughter, to raise her.

But Mainfeld had stepped in. He had claimed her as his own.

Sophie let that settle deep into her soul.

All her life, thinking herself an outcast . . . unwanted by her natural father, foisted upon her legal father . . .

And now . . .

She felt a little like a ship righting itself after a lifetime of storms.

She didn't have a lack of fathers . . .

Selfish, foolish woman.

She had an *abundance*.

Memories flitted through. Lord Mainfeld—oh bother, her *father*, as she had always thought of him—trundling her out to the barns on an autumn morning, lifting her before him on his horse. Listening with a bemused expression that she now recognized as love, not just tolerant fondness, as she explained her theories about barn cats. Opening his arms to hold her when she arrived back home after her disastrous marriage to Jack. Traveling to Yorkshire to retrieve a feral tomcat because he thought it might help ease her melancholy.

He had always been there, always supported, accepted, and loved her in the only way he knew how. He had shared with her the things he adored—hunting and horses and dogs. And she, in her stupidity, had not seen those actions as love.

She had gone searching for similarity and like-mindedness and biology, thinking that love would be inherent in it, but she could not have been more wrong.

Love did not need similarity of thought or interest. Love required only attention and care, thoughtfulness and generosity of soul.

Things that Lord Mainfeld exhibited in abundance.

Tears pricked her eyes again.

She was a thousand ways a fool. She did not deserve such devotion. She did not *deserve* his love.

And yet, she knew she had it anyway.

Love, she realized, was not the sort of thing to neatly fit into parameters and boundaries.

No . . .

Love took many forms and needed to be accepted as it came. To do otherwise was to risk a life of eternal disappointment.

John picked up the kitten with fumbling hands, scratching its head as it nuzzled for affection.

Sophie watched, letting her heart grieve what might have been. John would have been an excellent father, as well.

But she did not regret his decision. Her life *had* been infinitely more secure growing up the acknowledged daughter of an earl, surrounded by brothers and sisters, looked after by their mother.

But she still mourned that she would never know John. She was not foolish enough to think that his lucidity this afternoon would ever be repeated.

It had been a miraculous gift.

Though her chin was yet wobbly, she managed a smile and sat beside John for another hour, petting the kitten with him.

He lifted his head. "Ah, there ye are, Catharine."

"Yes." Sophie smiled wide, even though the gesture nearly broke her heart. "Here I am."

"I'm glad yer here."

She swallowed back the lump in her throat. "I'm glad to be here, too."

"I never did like it, Catharine. I didnae like what ye did," he muttered.

Sophie angled her head. "What did I do?"

"Eh?" He lifted his head, meeting her haze.

"What did I do?" she repeated.

"How can ye ask that!" His voice so outraged. "I told ye not to, Catharine. That marrying that man would only bring us all heartache. He's no' a fit husband for any lass, much less my sister."

John's words jolted her. Marriage? *Husband?!*

"Pardon? My *husband?*" Sophie paused.

Catharine had never married. She had introduced herself as Miss Ross. Had she married after all? And if so, why the secrecy?

"Och, dinnae play that game with me, Cat." John snorted. "We both know ye married him, even though ye like tae pretend ye didnae. I was there, remember? Ye practically forced the man tae the altar, ye did."

"I did?" Unbidden, Sophie felt her heart speed up. "And what man is that?"

John frowned at her. "Why the Duke of Kendall, of course."

30

Rafe stood to the side of the crowded ballroom. It was the night of Mrs. Bartlett's annual winter ball, the inaugural event heralding the opening of the winter session of Parliament two days hence.

It had been nearly three weeks to the day since his arrival in London. Rafe had managed a brief meeting with Andrew—who had come into town to attend Parliament—to discuss how to find Cuthie and deal with this twist of fate.

But otherwise, Kendall had commandeered Rafe's waking hours. Rafe had attended Lord Sykes' house party. He had danced attendance on Kendall, playing the dutiful son at every turn. And in exchange, his mother had been returned to the family townhouse in London. Rafe would do what he must to ensure her continued health.

Tonight marked his last night of freedom.

Kendall had made it clear that Rafe would call on Miss Sykes tomorrow morning and propose marriage to her.

"The evening is well-attended," Miss Sykes said beside him, fanning herself slowly. "Mrs. Bartlett will be so pleased."

Rafe smiled his reply, tight. He had already danced the requisite two dances with Miss Sykes this evening. After returning from the house party in the country, he had also escorted Miss Sykes and Lady Sykes to the opera and to view the Elgin Marbles on display at the British Museum. He had sent Miss Sykes flowers courtesy of his father's hothouses and, despite the chilly November weather, had taken her driving twice in Hyde Park.

Basically, everything a gentleman should do to court a young lady.

Across the room, Kendall was conversing with Lord Sykes, their heads leaning toward one another. As if hearing his son's thoughts, his father raised his eyes, fixing Rafe with a dark warning.

You will do as you are told, boy, that look said.

Rafe broke away first, swallowing the acrid taste in his mouth.

Though hatred no longer scoured him, Rafe felt scrubbed raw from the iron chain of his father's heavy-handed demands.

He was quite sure that aristocrats headed for the guillotine had perhaps appeared cheerier than he. At least death would send him to a theoretically better place.

This . . . *this* was a living hell.

His Sophie would soon be lost to him for good.

She had returned from Scotland. He knew this because he had seen Lady Sophie riding Rotten Row the previous morning. His eyes had lingered on her—less polite and more like a dying man staring down a desert mirage—knowing that the pain of losing her would simply have to become a part of him.

Miss Sykes stirred at his side. "I fear I am a bit thirsty, my lord. Would you be so kind as to fetch me some ratafia?"

"Of course, Miss Sykes." He bowed and strode out of the ballroom proper. He could feel his father's eyes following him into the dining room and the buffet table there.

The man didn't want to let Rafe out of his sight. Did he think Rafe would bolt? Or did he simply enjoy watching Rafe thrash and squirm, forever that fish pinned to the earth and struggling for freedom?

Pain constricted his breathing.

How was he to do this? How could he go through with this marriage?

Rafe pushed through guests in their silks and tailcoats to the refreshment table. He accepted a glass of ratafia from an attending footman, downing the drink in one swallow, wishing desperately that the sickly-sweet wine were something infinitely stronger. He reached for a glass for Miss Sykes—

"Lord Rafe!" A familiar voice sounded near his elbow.

Rafe turned to see Lady Lilith's fine eyes smiling up at him.

"Lady Lilith." He nodded his head.

Out of the corner of his eye, he noticed his father enter the dining room, clearly trying to locate Rafe in the crowd.

Heaven forfend the man let Rafe out of his sight.

The emotions in his chest coalesced, tightening until Rafe feared he would explode with the agony of it.

His hands shook and a sort of panic seemed to overtake him.

His chest tightened, a vise around his lungs.

The noise in the room rose to an almost deafening clatter, guests laughing and crystal clanking.

His heart beat a frantic tattoo, hot and anguished.

He gasped for breath. Once. Twice.

Why could he no longer breathe?

He set down the glass meant for Miss Sykes—the wine sloshing from his trembling hand.

Kendall was pushing through the guests, drawing nearer.

Rafe whirled around, desperate for fresh air. In the process, he nearly ran over Lady Lilith, who was still at his elbow. She grasped his arm in a surprisingly firm grip, holding him steady.

He met her gaze and was startled by the compassion he saw there. Lady Lilith, despite her flirtatious behavior, could be quite perceptive.

"That bad, eh?" she murmured, taking a sip of her own drink.

He barely managed to shake his head. Why was it so blasted hot in here? Why were his lungs not functioning?

"Mmmm." Lady Lilith set down her own glass. "You need cooler air. Come."

The pain in Rafe's chest would not abate. His skin practically crawled with the heat of his father's gaze.

He *had* to get away. He couldn't stay another moment here, another moment in this life.

Later, he would blame his panic for distracting him, for allowing Lady Lilith to lead him through a side door and along a narrow hallway. The cooler air felt so good, loosening his lungs, that he made no protest as she continued up a short flight of stairs and into a darkened study.

He noted the dim room, a fire smoldering in the grate, a single candelabra burning on a table. A desk sat to the left of the door, the fireplace and some chairs to the right. Ahead, velvet curtains enclosed a pair of windows.

He came to his senses with the *snick* of the door closing and the *clack* of the lock being thrown. He whirled to look at Lady Lilith.

Despite everything, Miss Sykes did not deserve a betrothed who carried on with another woman the night before becoming officially affianced.

If only the panic in his chest would subside.

"Lady Lilith—" he began, lungs heaving, taking a step to the side, intent on leaving the room.

A knock sounded on the door.

Rafe froze.

Lady Lilith stilled.

The door handle jiggled.

"Rafe?" His father's voice sounded through the wood. "If you are in there, boy, you will open this door immediately."

No!

Not now.

Not this.

Caught, alone, in a room with Lady Lilith.

Could his situation become any worse?

He stared at the door, as if he could will his sire away, as if he could do something, *anything* to stop the current course of his life, to turn it into aught but a runaway carriage hurtling down a hill.

That same panicky feeling seized his chest. Where had all the air gone?

The handle jiggled again.

He darted a glance back to Lady Lilith.

He wasn't sure what he expected her expression to be, but amusement was *not* it.

She rolled her eyes and pressed a finger to her lips. Tugging on his arm, she dragged him across the room.

"Trust me," she whispered.

She shoved him behind one of the velvet curtains, pulling it around him.

Her footsteps retreated, and he heard the lock snick open, the sound muffled through the heavy curtains.

"Lady Lilith." His father's voice carried through the room. "I assume Lord Rafe is with you." The anger in his tone was nearly palpable.

"Heavens, Your Grace. What sort of lady do you take me for? Lord Rafe most certainly is *not* with me. I left him at the bottom of the stairs as I needed to tend to my hair, and the withdrawing room is an absolute crush at the moment. Fortunately, I remembered that this small study had a mirror over the fireplace. Lord Rafe must have returned to the ballroom."

A pause.

"Would you be so kind as to accompany me downstairs?" she asked, her tone syrupy-sweet.

His father grunted, a noise Rafe knew meant a grumbling *yes*.

A swish of skirts. The door closed. Rafe heard nothing more.

He let out a slow, painful breath.

Bless Lady Lilith for seeing, for understanding that he needed a moment to pull himself together, to somehow stem his involuntary panic.

How long before this pain would become easier to bear? Would Sophie's loss never cease to bring him to his knees?

As if hearing his thoughts, the curtain to his right stirred.

Rafe looked to the side and nearly yelped in a surprise.

Sophie's glorious eyes met his.

What—?!

Sophie.

His Sophie.

Was he dreaming? Hallucinating, even? Had his blind panic come to this?

He blinked and shook his head.

But . . . she was still there, beside him.

His beautiful, brave bird.

He reached out and traced a finger down her cheek. Solid. Real.

No . . . she was not a mirage.

Sensations assaulted him, jumbling his senses.

The hitch of her breathing at his touch.

The silvery sheen of her moss-green evening gown, the low-cut bodice exposing a glorious amount of alabaster skin.

The soft folds of Jamie's tartan wrapped as a sash across her chest.

The wafting scent of rose and Sophie.

The rough rasp of air in and out of his lungs.

Ah.

So *this* was what it was like to breathe again.

She peeked out of the curtains, surveying the room.

"They're gone." She left the heavy velvet ajar, light from the candelabra illuminating the space between them.

Rafe's brain struggled to piece together what had just happened.

Lady Lilith had . . .

And then . . .

Sophie was here.

His Sophie.

How had this—

"I bribed her," Sophie whispered, looking tellingly back at the closed door. "Well, my sister did. Lady Lilith owed her a favor, and so she lured you up here."

"Ah."

Sophie touched the curtains, her fingers drawing down the velvet. "Meeting behind curtains seems to be a theme with us."

An almost agonizing ache started behind his lower right rib, spreading slowly across his chest.

Seeing her lovely face, hearing her voice . . .

It was the most exquisite torture.

"Why?" he whispered, the word so anguished.

Why are you here? Why are you doing this to me?

"You needed saving." She met his gaze, eyes fearless. "And so I'm saving you."

He closed his eyes at that, horrified to feel them *pricking*, of all things.

Damn and blast.

This woman.

"Sophie—" His voice cracked. The room was rapidly blurring.

Whatever she proposed, whatever she thought . . .

He sucked in a fortifying breath.

"Sophie," he began again, tone hoarse, "*mo leannan*, you know this cannot be." He motioned between them. "As long as my mother lives, she will be under my father's thumb. Such is English law, and I cannot leave her to Kendall's cruelty. I simply *cannot.*"

The sheer anguish in his voice astonished him.

"I know," she nodded, her own eyes suspiciously bright. "I know, Rafe." A tear tumbled down her cheek, nearly unmanning him. "You are a good son. The *best* of sons."

She smiled, lips tremulous.

Heaven above how he longed to kiss her. To hold her close and lose himself in the sheer rightness of *her*.

He closed his eyes, holding his hands at his side with an almost fervent desperation, trying somehow to hold himself back.

This moment.

This moment had to be enough to carry him through a lifetime without her. Tomorrow, he would betroth himself to another . . .

She shifted, sending a waft of rose his way. Her hand cupped his cheek, a deliberate caress.

Unable to stop himself, he turned his head toward that hand, his lips planting a kiss in the center of her palm.

But tonight . . . he was not betrothed yet.

He reached for her before the thought even cleared his brain. She came with shocking willingness, no hesitation.

A law of nature had asserted itself, it appeared. A newly discovered law that insisted Lady Sophronia exist only in the arms of Lord Rafe. They were symbiotic pairs, better only by being together.

His mouth found hers, and he was a lost man.

Her lips were every bit as pillowy as he remembered. The feel of her curves in his arms.

His thoughts spooled out.

How had she—

Why was she—

What was he—

He was a stuttering mess.

He tasted salty tears, no longer caring if they were hers or his.

Her hands were in his hair, tilting his head, holding him exactly as she pleased.

"Rafe." Her lips breathed against his. "*Leannan.*" Her thumbs skimmed his cheeks, palms pressed to either side of his head.

She kissed away his tears, scooping them up with each press of her lips.

"Sophie—"

"Shhhhh." She stopped him with a kiss. "Let me tell you."

She waited until he met her gaze.

He blinked.

There was no pain in her eyes. No fear. No agonized worry.

Only joy.

Absolute, soul-rending *joy*. As if her heart would burst for . . . *happiness*.

His own heart stuttered.

How—

How did she have such . . . *hope?*

She continued, "I pray what I have to tell you will be good news. But regardless, you must know that nothing will be done with this information unless *you* will it."

A pause as he absorbed her words and then, "Tell me."

She smiled. "Several days after you left Drathes Castle, Dr. Ross had a spell of lucidity. He remembered *everything*." Her eyes went glassy again, wonder in her tone. "My mother. My birth. Me!"

"Ah, my darling. That is wonderful news, sweetling."

"I shall have to tell you all of it. But he also spelled out how to treat your mother for her melancholy."

Hope roared to life in his chest, a dragon bursting free from its chains.

"Truly?"

"Yes,"—she placed a staying hand on his chest—"but that isn't the most important bit."

"It's not?! It's glorious!"

"It is, but I've something even better. Well, at least I hope you think it will be better."

Rafe stared at her, his mind trying to think of anything that would be better than this.

"Unless you are to tell me that my father is not my father, I cannot think what would be better, Sophie," he laughed.

Sophie, notably, did not laugh with him.

Her silence spoke volumes.

He froze, mouth open.

"The thing is, Rafe," she said slowly, "Dr. Ross let slip an enormous secret, one that has far-reaching implications for you. For your mother. For your entire family."

He stared into her eyes.

"W-what is it?" His voice the barest thread of sound.

"Your father married, and is *still* married, to Catharine Ross. He married her two years *before* he wed your mother."

Rafe would relive those words—that moment—for years afterward. The sheer *shock*—

Your father is still married . . .

He dropped to his knees, his legs abruptly no longer up to the task of holding him upright. Sophie sank with him.

"W-w-what did you say?" he whispered.

"The Duke of Kendall is a bigamist. Your parents were never legally married."

He let that sink in, thoroughly drill into the depths of his soul.

The Duke of Kendall is a bigamist.

Your parents were never legally married

. . .

. . .

. . .

Hallelujah!!!

He closed his eyes, his chest expanding, the news blazing through his blood.

He opened his eyes to meet her brilliant green gaze.

"Allow me to explain," she continued. "The Duke of Kendall married Miss Catharine Ross in the parish church in Aboyne two years before he wed Lady Elspeth Gordon, third daughter of the Earl of Ayr. His first marriage is entered, neat and legal, in the parish records in Aboyne—George Gilbert married Catharine Ross on the 9th of November, 1781. The marriage was even registered with the local sheriff. No one could contest the legality of their marriage. Of course, being that his first wife still lived, your father's subsequent marriage to Lady Elspeth Gordon was never legal."

Rafe blinked and then blinked again.

His parents were never married.

But that meant—

"I'm a bastard!" He said the words in a tone of utter wonder . . . like one might exclaim, *I'm a father!* or *I've won a lottery!*

She laughed, a giddy, soft breath of sound. "You are."

He joined her laughter. He longed to whoop his joy, to crow it from the rooftops. He settled for standing and pulling her to him.

"I never thought I would be so happy to be declared a *filius nullius*. Are you certain?" He snatched her shoulders. "Can this truly be proved?"

"Yes, absolutely." She grinned widely, pressing her palms to his chest, bopping up on her tiptoes to place a kiss on his mouth. "I would have approached you sooner, but I wanted to make sure that everything was ready to be set in motion. Your father has gone to considerable effort to hide his first marriage—including dire threats to John and Catharine—so it took some effort to convince her to cooperate."

"But that poor woman . . . now *she* will be married to him—"

"Not for long, I do not think. Scottish law, unlike English law, allows a woman to file for divorce on the basis of abandonment. She will have a clear-cut case. At the very least, your father will have to grant her a legal separation."

He rocked back on his heels, shock and wonder fizzing in his blood.

Sophie grabbed the lapels of his evening coat. "Honestly, there is so much to tell. Once Catharine realized that her voice needed to be heard—that she would have support and friends to bring Kendall to justice—she poured out the entire sordid tale. How Kendall had pursued her throughout their Grand Tour—Catharine refusing to become his mistress, and Kendall refusing to marry her. Eventually, Kendall followed her back to Drathes Castle which had been left to John by an uncle. Kendall capitulated and agreed to the marriage, thinking to do a less-traditional hand-fasting that would be unlikely to stand up to scrutiny in an English court. Catharine, no slow-top, insisted on the marriage being done proper-like in the parish church in Aboyne, the bans read for three Sundays and the marriage registered with the local sheriff."

"I can scarcely believe he married like that—"

"I cannot agree more. But he was furious with Catharine's intransigence in becoming his mistress and wished her capitulation. He likely figured he could brazen his way through any consequences."

"Sounds like my father."

"Indeed, it does. Not surprising, the marriage collapsed rather quickly. There were, thank goodness, no children from the union. Your grandfather summoned your father back to London and insisted he marry your mother, Lady Elspeth. Your father, being a coward at heart, never mentioned his first marriage. He married Lady Elspeth and then sent Beadle to Catharine and John with a threatening letter, telling them both to stay silent *or else*. That was a message he reiterated over and over again—"

"Does Catharine still have all those threatening letters?"

"Of course! She is frightfully intelligent, once one excuses her poor lapse in judgment with regards to Kendall. Apparently, John wished for years to expose the duke's perfidy, but Catharine refused to allow him to say anything. She was terrified Kendall would have Ross killed in order to silence him."

Rafe paused. "She was wise to be so concerned."

"I agree. Regardless, John kept his silence. He worked in Bath for many years, well away from London and Kendall. But then my mother—no longer Miss Anne Montague, but Lady Mainfeld now—removed to Bath, and she and John reignited their love affair. Catharine says that Kendall became incensed, worried that his secret would slip out. That worry only increased with my birth—"

"No *wonder* my father hates you with such vitriol. Seeing you would be like looking at Catharine reincarnated. All it would take is one person remembering her and then digging into the odd resemblance between you to uncover nearly everything—"

"Precisely! Kendall repeatedly threatened my mother, too, sending her letters periodically. So much so, that even the mention of my natural father sent her into hysterics. She refused to tell me about Dr. Ross for fear of what Kendall would do. It is why she delayed my come-out for years, terrified of Kendall, as I so greatly resembled Catharine.

"As for John, he eventually moved to London, as his practice thrived more there. But Kendall didn't catch on for years that John was in London. Of course, by that time, John's health had deteriorated such that he needed to retire. Apparently, the doctor's slide into dementia happened slowly, and he was decidedly vocal about his sister's marriage. Kendall didn't want John to blurt out the information to someone, and so the duke insisted on placing John under house arrest in Edinburgh with Beadle as his guard. Of course, it was all for naught, in the end, as John told me about Catharine's marriage."

Rafe shook his head, so many puzzle pieces slotting into place. "No wonder Beadle appeared so shocked to see us together . . . me with you, the image of Catharine. And then us, together, asking after Dr. Ross. The man must have panicked."

"You have the right of it. Which explains why he sent Grant to deter us from arriving at Drathes Castle. I understand Grant regularly treks up to Drathes Castle and 'reminds' Catharine of Kendall's power to destroy her, basically ensuring her continued silence."

"Bloody eejit."

"Truthfully. So much effort to protect Kendall from the consequences of one monumental lie." Sophie paused. "I hope you are not upset, but I had to approach my father with this—"

"Lord Mainfeld?"

"Yes. I needed help, as I wasn't sure how to proceed from this point. It's one thing to know that a duke is a bigamist. It's something else to then take legal action. But my father knew what to do. He is already marshaling support in Parliament. A duke, of course, can only be accused and tried for a crime such a bigamy in the House of Lords—a jury of Peers. Therefore, the accusation could be brought against your father when Parliament opens on Monday. My father believes that the charge will stand up to any legal test."

She swallowed, running a hand down the lapel of his evening clawhammer coat, before giving him a small smile. "Of course, all this supposes that you would like to go forward with this. Obviously, your mother and sister should be consulted, too. If you do not wish to expose your father as a bigamist and a fraud—knowing the consequences, that you and your siblings will be declared illegitimate—then nothing will happen. At the very least, you should be able to use the information to blackmail Kendall into giving your mother her freedom."

Rafe absorbed her words, the hope of them finally sinking deep.

However, his logical mind picked through the salient points, cataloging the rippling effect of this knowledge.

His parent's marriage was invalid. And English law being what it was, *nothing* could make it retroactively valid at this point.

Absolutely nothing.

Rafe and his siblings would be declared illegitimate.

His brother would lose the title. The dukedom would likely pass to their insipid Cousin Frank. His father's entire legacy would be destroyed in an instant.

But... his mother would be free. It would be as if the marriage had never happened, Kendall forever banished from her life.

For Rafe's part, he would retain his properties and monies, as they were all tied to his maternal grandmother's will, not his father's estates. His mother's dowry would revert to her and provide her with sufficient income to live.

Kate and her children would suffer some loss of status, but Kate's husband was a good man. He would likely support whatever decision Rafe's sister made.

But what did *Rafe* wish to do?

Blackmail his father?

Or publicly, openly, *thoroughly* humiliate the man?

Rafe instinctively wanted to side with humiliation. The scorn of being exposed as a bigamist would torment his father.

Kendall deserved that and more.

But...

... the decision hinged on more than mere revenge, Rafe realized.

Kendall was, simply put, not to be trusted. Blackmailing the man might work for a time, but the duke was wily and cunning. Rafe wouldn't put it past him to kill Catharine or John in order to ensure their silence.

No, it would be better for all parties to have the truth out in the open.

So in answer to Sophie's question, Rafe had only one reply—

"I would see Kendall's crime's exposed to the light of day," he said. "Let the battle begin."

He would still need to consult with his mother and sister, but his own decision had already been made.

He threaded his fingers through Sophie's. Had anything ever felt so momentous? Holding the hand of a woman he *finally* had no intention of ever losing?

He pressed his forehead to hers, emotion welling in his chest.

"Thank you," he whispered.

"For what?"

"For never giving up." He leaned in and kissed her.

"You do realize that this is just the beginning of a long fight? Your father will contest this with everything he has."

"Aye, but he doesn't have right on his side. I intend to see justice meted out."

31

Two days later, Sophie sat in the gallery in the House of Lords, nestled between her mother on one side, and Lord Rafe on the other. Lady Hadley, Rafe's cousin of sorts, sat beside him.

Lord and Lady Hadley—or Andrew and Jane as Sophie now thought of them—had both mustered their own considerable support throughout the peerage for Rafe and his mother. Kendall had made many enemies over the years with his heavy-handed ways, so it was not difficult to rally members of Parliament to their cause.

Lord Hadley currently sat beside Lord Mainfeld on the floor of Lords, both sporting their official robes in honor of Parliament convening, their earl coronets of alternating laurels and pearls glinting in the sunlight washing from windows high above.

Rafe's weekend had passed in a blur. First, he had visited Kate and her husband, telling them the news. Kate had broken down, sobbing. Rafe had been concerned, until he realized, that like himself, hers were tears of relief. Kate vehemently wished their mother's freedom. Her husband stood at her side, asserting that any slight to their social standing and that of their children was a small price to pay.

After that emotional moment, Rafe and Andrew began planning their attack, while ignoring the increasingly incensed letters from Kendall, demanding Rafe propose immediately to Miss Sykes. His mother remained in residence at Gilbert House, but Rafe refused to set foot inside the place, not knowing what Kendall might do.

This morning, after his father had left for Parliament, Rafe and Andrew had arrived at Gilbert House with a contingent of footmen and removed the Duchess of Kendall from the residence. His father's butler had stood by, angrily fuming but otherwise helpless.

His mother had devolved into a weeping mess when told of her husband's perfidy. But to her credit, the duchess instantly supported the dissolution of her marriage. In fact, the very idea greatly rallied her spirits. They had left her in Kate's care, playing happily with her grandchildren.

Now as Sophie sat in the visitor's gallery, she studied the back of Kendall's head. He sat beside the Duke of Montacute with a haughty expression. Did Kendall suspect what was to come? If so, he gave no sign of it.

The man was supremely arrogant, used to heaven and earth bending to his will. Rafe had returned from Scotland, after all. So Kendall assumed that Rafe, if he had reached Drathes Castle, had found nothing.

Regardless, given the lengths Kendall had gone to in order to suppress the information about his first marriage, Sophie did not think he would succumb easily to the accusation of bigamy. They faced a long fight. The House of Lords, this morning, was simply the opening salvo. And in the end, the only punishment that could be meted out to Kendall was the dissolution of his second marriage. As a duke, he could not be sent to prison, nor could his lands and title be removed.

Sophie clenched her hands together, willing them to stop trembling. Rafe smiled at her and wrapped her fingers with his, easing her nerves.

The Prince Regent arrived, his portly body waddling the length of the hall, the creaking of his corset heard clearly even up in the gallery. Though resplendent in royal robes of red and ermine, His Highness was not in the best of health, his heaving chest and pallid skin apparent even from a distance.

He sat upon the throne at the far end of the hall, raising a hand in greeting before giving his traditional speech to open parliament.

Sophie tried not to let her attention wander as Prinny lamented that his father, King George III, was yet indisposed. Manufacturing concerns required their attention. The military needed to be strengthened, and so forth.

After His Highness finished, Earl Manvers rose to make some obsequious remarks, all but fawning over Prinny's speech. Lord Churchill agreed. Earl Grey then rose and spoke at such length—and in such a convoluted manner—that Sophie despaired of making heads or tails of it. Even Prinny nodded off. Finally Earl Grey sat down to harrumphs and sighs of relief.

Then . . . the Earl of Mainfeld stood.

"Your Highness." He nodded to the Prince Regent. "My peers in Lords, I have a grave matter to bring before you at this time."

"Indeed," Prinny intoned. "Continue."

The Duke of Kendall *finally* turned in his seat to look at Mainfeld standing several rows behind him.

Mainfeld met Kendall's gaze, steely determination in his eyes. Never had Sophie been so proud of her father as in that moment.

Kendall's expression morphed in an instant, rage darkening his features.

He *knew*.

He knew what was to come.

But Mainfeld was already talking, "It has come to my attention that one among our illustrious members has been shockingly dishonest, both with us, and with God—"

"YOU ARE A LIAR!!" Kendall lurched to his feet, whirling to face Mainfeld, expression mottled and ugly. He lunged forward, as if he would reach across the intervening row to grab Mainfeld's robe. Mainfeld shied back.

Pandemonium erupted.

"I say!" Someone called out.

"What is this?" asked another.

A woman screamed in the gallery.

The Duke of Marlborough hauled Kendall back into his seat.

The Lord Speaker pounded his gavel, calling for order.

"You will stay SILENT!!!" Kendall roared, shaking off Marlborough and lunging again across the row of earls to get at Mainfeld.

Hadley threw himself between Kendall and Mainfeld, while a group of lords pulled Kendall back.

"ENOUGH! SILENCE!" Prinny rapped his scepter on the marble floor. He waited in stony silence.

Kendall jerked himself free, chest heaving, shooting daggers at Mainfeld.

He pointed a shaking hand at Sophie's father, turning to Prinny. "Whatever this man says is a lie, Your Highness! You all know Mainfeld has hated me for—"

"I said *silence*, Kendall," Prinny said, eyes narrowing. "Clearly, you suspect that whatever Mainfeld will say pertains to you, but as of yet, Lord Mainfeld has made *no* accusations."

Kendall opened his mouth and took a small step forward, as if he would continue to speak. Prinny held up a staying palm.

"I find it rather odd, Kendall," the prince continued, "that you would jump to protest your innocence before your name has been mentioned, much less any accusation laid against you. You will be seated."

Kendall faced the Prince, chest still heaving.

Finally, with a shake of his head, Kendall turned back to his seat.

Though as he moved, the duke turned his head and met Sophie's gaze in the gallery above, as if feeling the weight of her eyes.

Sophie stared him down. The fury in Kendall's gaze sent a skittering sensation across her skin. The duke's eyes darted to Lady Mainfeld beside her and then to Rafe on her other side.

He retook his seat, but Sophie could see growing panic in the set of his shoulders.

Prinny waved his jeweled fingers at Mainfeld. "Please enlighten us, Mainfeld, as to the cause of Kendall's distress."

Her father straightened his shoulders, shot a glance at Kendall, and then addressed Prinny: "Your Highness, after reviewing evidence and hearing the testimony of witnesses, it is my belief that the Duke of Kendall should be charged with bigamy."

Lords erupted into pandemonium once again. The Duke of Kendall shot to his feet, shouting his innocence, denouncing Mainfeld. Others called and hollered, pointing fingers.

The Lord Speaker pounded his gavel, shouting, "Order!" over and over.

Finally, Prinny rose, rapping his scepter again, both hands outstretched, demanding silence.

Slowly, quiet descended.

"Mainfeld." Prinny fixed him with a shrewd eye. "This is a heavy accusation, indeed. I can appreciate why Kendall was quick to denounce it, if he suspected your words. Do you contest that this bigamous relationship occurred before or after Kendall's current marriage?"

"Before, Your Highness."

"Ah." Prinny sat back, nodding slowing. "That is, indeed, unfortunate. This crime, if true, would result in Kendall's current marriage being dissolved and his children, specifically his heir, being declared illegitimate. I assume you would not make such an accusation lightly. Have you adequate witnesses and testimony, as you say?"

"I do, Your Highness."

Prinny nodded. "So be it. I command the Lord Chancellor and Lord Speaker to give this matter their utmost care and attention." He fixed Kendall with a steely look. "Bigamy is not to be tolerated in this country. Given Kendall's rather violent proclamation of his innocence, I should like us to examine the evidence forthwith."

The rest of the day continued in organized chaos.

Mainfeld listed the bare facts before Lords. He described the evidence collected, the witnesses' testimony, the words of Catharine Ross herself, and Kendall's damning letters to her.

Mainfeld even named his wife as a witness.

"Lady Mainfeld," her father said, "knew of the clandestine marriage. She had formed a friendship with Catharine Ross while in Naples, and the ladies corresponded regularly. Kendall, upon learning that Lady Mainfeld knew of his first marriage, threatened her in order to ensure her silence on the matter. As you all surely know, I overheard the slight and challenged Kendall to a duel because of it. We all know the outcome of that duel. Lady Mainfeld never clarified for me *why* Kendall had threatened her in the first place."

The testimony went on.

Rafe leaned into Sophie. "Today has gone better than we could have hoped. Kendall is done for," he murmured in her ear. "You can see it on their faces. Kendall doesn't stand a chance. They will convict him and make an example of it. Lords will overlook many things, but they will *not* tolerate one of their own making a mockery of their laws of inheritance and primogeniture."

Sophie could see it herself. Her father had presented the proof of Kendall's crime as convincingly as any skilled barrister. Kendall attempted to rally support, but the evidence was too damning. The man's second marriage was all but annulled.

Lords adjourned not long after.

SOPHIE, RAFE, AND all their friends celebrated that night at Lord Hadley's townhouse.

After a lengthy dinner and even lengthier conversation in the drawing room, Sophie managed to pull Rafe aside, drawing him into an alcove, partially covered by what else? A heavy curtain.

"We always seem to meet behind these." He touched it with his fingers. "People will assume we are up to no good back here."

Sophie smiled, tugging on his waistcoat, bringing him closer. "We *are* up to no good, Rafe Gilbert."

She kissed him.

She adored kissing him. The feeling of his hands around her waist, the strength in his arms as he pulled her to tiptoes in order to reach her lips. The power in his shoulders under her hands. The rasp of his evening whiskers and the warmth of his mouth on hers.

They did not speak for a moment or two.

Rafe finally broke their kiss, leaning his forehead against hers.

"You are right," he said, voice breathless. "We are up to no good."

"Are you content then to live your life as Mr. Rafe Gilbert? No one will ever 'my lord' you again."

"I am *frighteningly* content to be mere Mr. Rafe Gilbert."

He smiled, those dimples she so loved popping in his cheeks.

"I love this smile." She kissed each dimple. "I love that the shadows in your eyes are gone."

"I cannot describe the relief—the elation—of no longer having that man in my life. It's such freedom . . . I did not realize the pain of its weight until it was removed."

"Do you still hate Kendall?" she asked, curious to know. He had told her about meeting Captain Cuthie, about the violence inherent in his rage, about the ocean of pain his hate had been covering.

A long pause. "No. As I've told you, I stopped truly hating him before I even arrived back in London. I had decided, then and there with Cuthie in that alley, that I would not be that man. That I would not allow hate to have such a hold on me."

"And now?"

"And now today, when I saw my father in Lords, I felt nothing more than vindication. A sense that a wrong and been righted. I haven't forgiven him. That will take much longer, perhaps forever. But I have moved on. Kendall no longer has a hold on my thoughts and actions."

Sophie wrapped her arms around him, burying her face in his shoulder, breathing in deep lungfuls of him.

"Still smelling me, I see." His voice rumbled in her ear.

Sophie responded by taking another deep breath—sandalwood and spice and Rafe.

Heaven.

Emotion welled in her chest, pricking her eyes.

How could she not have seen, all those years ago, that underneath the *Rakus lasciviosus* persona, was this loyal, sincere, bookish man—a true *Virum nobilis?*

Her *leannan*.

Her beloved.

She instinctively knew that a life with him would be nothing like it had been with Jack. Rafe would treasure her heart, just as she would protect his.

She pulled back and looked up at him.

"I love you," she whispered, popping up to kiss his lips. "I didn't mean to give you my heart, and yet here we are."

"Ah, *mo leannan*, you have owned mine for more years than I can quickly count. Are you sure you don't mind associating with an illegitimate man?" He waggled his eyebrows.

She laughed. "I have contemplated the absurdity of our situation. I am illegitimate in truth, but legally not. You, my darling heart, are the exact opposite: legitimate in truth, but legally not. Regardless, I adore you just as you are, Rafe Gilbert—"

"Have I told you that I intend to change my surname?"

"You do?"

"Aye. I have no wish to carry about the name of that man. I most certainly don't want my children to bear it. My mother's maiden name is Gordon, and I quite like the idea of living my life in Scotland as Rafe Gordon. Besides, I shudder at the thought of referring to my wife as Mrs. Gilbert."

"Wife, eh? Do you have someone in mind?"

He grinned. "I just might at that." He kissed her nose. "You'll find out soon enough."

TWO DAYS LATER, Sophie paused in the doorway of the breakfast room. Her family were already eating, a cacophony of sound and laughter.

Thomas and Robert were discussing a recent hunting trip and feeding snippets of bacon to the dogs, sending them into a typical frenzy.

Lord Mainfeld, with wee Henry on his knee, asked eager questions about the prospect of a fishing trip to Aberdeen the next summer.

Mary, Harriet, and Lady Mainfeld were discussing a possible visit to the haberdasher.

Sophie pondered the difference a couple months could make. How had she not seen this joyous ruckus as love? How had she not felt the energy and affection within her own family? How necessary they were to one another? They were not perfect, but they were dedicated and loyal. Case in point, her entire family had insisted she recount every last detail of her adventurous journey to Scotland, gasping and ahhing at all the right places.

She walked into the room, running a hand across her father's shoulders. He turned and smiled up at her.

Bending down, she kissed his cheek.

"Thank you so much for all you have done, Papa," she whispered. "You mean the world to me. I love you."

"'Twas nothing." He winked at her. "And I love you, too, poppet."

After giving her father another kiss, Sophie filled a plate from the sideboard and took a seat across from her brothers. She was halfway through her eggs and toast when Thomas snagged her attention.

"So it was the doctor in the end, eh?" Thomas leaned across the table, fixing her with a bemused look.

"Pardon?" Sophie smiled at her brother.

"Your natural father," Thomas clarified. "It was the doctor."

Robert reached for more sugar for his tea. "I had my money on Kendall, actually."

"*Pardon?!*" Sophie repeated, nearly screeching. "Kendall?! What are you both on about?"

"I thought the Duke of Kendall was your natural father," Robert said, face entirely too benign for such a ghastly statement.

Something that tasted like horror stuck in the back of Sophie's throat. She darted a quick glance at their mother—who, thankfully, was fully engrossed in a conversation with Mary—and then looked back at her brothers with their innocent expressions.

"You wagered on who my natural father would be?" she asked.

"Aye," Robert nodded, matter-of-factly. "Lost me a full canary, it did."

"None of us had money on the doctor," Thomas added, mournfully.

Far too many thoughts crowded Sophie's brain.

First, *ewww*. Thank *heaven*, Kendall was not her father.

Second, there was a record somewhere—likely the betting book at White's—where men had wagered as to the identity of her natural father?

And third—

"But if Kendall had been my father, that would have made Rafe and myself—"

"Brother and sister?" Robert snickered.

Thomas kicked him. "Well, thank goodness it *was* the doctor, in the end. Otherwise, poor Sophie would have been faced with a rather unsavory decision—"

Now it was Robert's turn to kick Thomas into silence.

Before Sophie could reply, a footman entered the room, silver platter held high, skillfully dodging the rowdy dogs. He paused before Sophie, presenting a solitary letter to her.

Thoughts of her brothers abandoned, she lifted the letter with a nod of thanks and broke the seal.

It was a proposal, written in the style of those submitted to the *Transactions of the Linnean Society of London*.

> *Proposed*: A change to the genus and species of one specific *Rakus lasciviosus*.
>
> *Reasons for proposed changes*: The behavior of this particular *Rakus lasciviosus* does not match that of others of the species. Specifically, the *Rakus* in question does not, nor ever had, displayed truly lascivious behavior. Previous reassignment to *Rakus falsus* is also inaccurate.

Reassigned genus: It is put forth that this particular member of *Rakus* be reassigned to genus *Matrimonius*, species, *sophronia*. He will be the only species in the genus, but we feel that this is the preferred state of this particular specimen.

Sophie's hands were shaking by the end.

Oh, the glorious man!

Trust Rafe to make her feel everything . . .

. . . as in, *all* the things.

And the wretch wasn't even here to receive her reply—

A sudden drop in noise caught her attention.

Sophie lifted her head from the note.

Rafe was on a knee before her, in front of her entire family.

Lady Mainfeld wiped a tear from her cheek. Her sisters watched, wide-eyed. Her father smiled with his good-natured bonhomie. Her brothers grinned, elbowing one another. Even the dogs were behaving.

Rafe met her gaze, those beloved dimples popping. "Lady Sophronia, will you do me the honor of becoming my wife?"

What else was she to say?

Sophie gasped out a "Yes!"

With that, cacophony returned.

Her brothers whooped, making some ribald comment about "definitely not brother and sister." The dogs barked and ran in circles, startling wee Henry. Her sisters instantly began giving advice on wedding clothes and the venue.

Sophie, of course, hardly noticed.

She was too busy kissing her rake.

EPILOGUE

After spending so many years apart, Rafe had no intention of waiting through a lingering betrothal with Lady Sophie.

Three weeks to the day after his proposal, Rafe and Sophie were wed in St. George's Church in Hanover Square, just four days before Christmas.

The church was packed to the rafters with friends and relatives. Sophie's large family—Lord and Lady Mainfeld's Sorrowful Miscellany—were all present. Their grinning faces and bumping elbows attesting to their affection. Lady Mainfeld sat in the midst of them. Rafe was quite sure he would never understand Sophie's parents' odd marriage, but it appeared to work for them.

As for Rafe's family, his mother had been most prominently seated on the first row, a radiant smile on her face. Just a week prior, her marriage to the Duke of Kendall had been officially invalidated by the Archbishop of Canterbury. Cousin Frank had been named his father's heir presumptive. Rafe was quite sure his father was apoplectic at the thought of Frank inheriting the dukedom. But laws of primogeniture being what they were, there was nothing Kendall could do aside from marrying legally and siring another son.

To that end, Kendall had already begun the process of divorcing Catharine officially, as Scotland's marriage laws were more accommodating than those in England. In his more fanciful moments, Rafe imagined his father sitting alone in the ash of his own life, scrambling ineffectually to reconstruct it.

As for his mother . . .

The former Duchess of Kendall had followed Dr. Ross's suggestions, and though Rafe knew his mother still had much healing to do, her dark days were already less dark. An enormous weight had clearly been lifted from her.

He had long suspected that the horror of her marriage had contributed to his mother's melancholy, but its dissolution confirmed it in spades. She laughed more frequently and no longer got lost for hours staring into the fire. Bit by bit, the woman he knew as a child emerged. He had hope that, with time, his mother would continue to blossom.

In addition to his mother, the entire Brotherhood of the Black Tartan were in attendance. Rafe stood in front of the altar, Andrew as best man at his side. Alex and Ewan sat with Jane beside Rafe's mother. Kieran had rushed from the London docks to attend, sneaking into the back row of the church just before the ceremony began.

But everyone had faded into the background once Sophie appeared at the end of the nave. Rafe saw only his bride as she walked down the aisle, her hand loosely resting on Lord Mainfeld's arm. Sophie had kissed her father's cheek, both their eyes overly bright, before turning her radiant gaze to Rafe.

He remembered little of the ceremony afterward. Just that he had pledged to adore this woman for the rest of his life—a promise he couldn't wait to keep.

Several hours later, after a raucous wedding breakfast at Andrew's London townhouse, the Brotherhood and their wives gathered in the library. The wedding guests had all departed, racing to reach home before the weather turned truly foul.

Snow fell lightly outside, but the fire roaring in the hearth sent a cheery warmth through the room. A bottle of aged Scottish whisky and a tea tray laden with biscuits and sandwiches helped as well.

"I haven't found a trace of Cuthie," Andrew said, sipping from his tumbler. "The man has surely gone to ground, now that we know he lives."

"*Eejit*," Kieran spat, gaze hooded. "We'll find him. I'll make it ma life's purpose to bring that monster tae justice."

"There may be others who lived, too," Rafe said. "Cuthie said that he sent the letters but knew nothing about the notice in the *Advertiser*. So it could be that others survived. We simply don't know at this point."

"Aye," Andrew agreed. "Did ye ever track down who was responsible for the highwaymen who fired upon ye in Yorkshire?"

Rafe shook his head. "As far as I can tell, they were simply highwaymen, unrelated to all this. But we would have to investigate further to be sure."

"Winter isnae helping our efforts, either," Alex agreed, accepting a cup of tea from Jane. "Getting north right now is a true challenge. We will need tae wait for fairer weather."

Ewan shifted his large body, adding several sliced-beef sandwiches to his plate. "Aye. I am away for Aberdeen in February. I can make inquiries while I am there and have a report for ye when we meet on the anniversary of Jamie's death on the nineteenth of March."

"That would be excellent, Ewan," Rafe said. "Sophie and I intend to go tae my estate outside Perth as soon as we're able. We can remain in contact and help, if ye need."

"Aye," Andrew nodded. "I'd also like to hire a Runner or two from Bow Street. See what they can uncover about the demise of *The Minerva*. I know we have been hesitant to open up old wounds—" he paused, shooting a look at Kieran, "—but Jamie would want us tae know what happened."

"I agree," Rafe said. "We shouldn't shy away from the truth."

Kieran sipped his whisky, eyes staring sightlessly into the fire.

"What if Jamie *lived*—" Kieran's voice broke on a pained gasp. He blinked his eyes too quickly. "What if we've been remembering that day of death and going onward with our lives and yet—" Kieran drifted off. He swallowed, chest heaving. "I couldnae forgive myself for giving up hope, for leaving Jamie alone tae—" He bit his lip and looked away.

Sophie leaned over from her seat beside Rafe, placing a comforting hand on Kieran's shoulder.

"Kieran, I am so sorry," Alex's tone carried the weight of his regret. "But ye know that Jamie didnae survive. Cuthie himself said so. If anything, as we've been saying, Jamie's *silence* is proof enough of this. Dinnae allow yerself to hope, my friend. Dinnae do it. Jamie is *gone*."

Kieran nodded, wiping at his eyes.

Neither of them stated the obvious.

Jamie's loss had nearly killed Kieran the first time. To raise his hopes and have them dashed again . . .

"All we can do is search for answers," Ewan said.

"Aye," Andrew agreed. "And we will. But—" He fixed a smile on Rafe and Sophie. "—this evening is one of celebration. Let us raise a glass to our good fortune. To our friendship. But, most of all, let us salute Rafe and his lovely bride." He raised his glass. "*Slàinte mhath.*"

To your health.

To a person, each raised the glass in their hand, giving the traditional response.

"*Slàinte!*"

AUTHOR'S NOTE

I know this book has been a long time coming. So first of all, I wish to thank everyone who sent encouragement and helped me finally (finally!) finish it.

As usual, a book is a mix of fact and faction, particularly a historical romance. Allow me to suss out some of the specifics for you, though be warned there are minor spoilers ahead.

First of all, Sophie's family situation was modeled after the real-life Earl of Oxford. The first Earl of Oxford and Earl Mortimer, Robert Harley, was a man of letters. Upon his death in 1724, Samuel Johnson himself wrote *The Harleian Miscellany,* a series of volumes cataloging the late earl's library.

Fast forward fifty years, and we arrive at Edward Harley, the 5th Earl of Oxford and Earl Mortimer (1773-1848). This particular earl was not quite as illustrious. Most significantly, his countess, Jane Scott, was notorious for her philandering ways, including a rather public affair with Lord Byron. Because of this, it was assumed that many of Lord Oxford's eight children were not his own. This fact led many in Polite Society to refer to the earl's children as the Harleian Miscellany.

Traveling in 1819, particularly into the Highlands of Scotland, was a fraught endeavor. Roads north of Edinburgh and Glasgow, in particular, were not well-maintained. In fact, Cairn O'Mount is still a fairly dicey road today, though a lovely drive in the late summer when the heather is in full purple bloom.

Highwaymen were definitely on the wane in 1819, but it would be another fifteen years before they would be eradicated entirely.

The plot for *Romancing the Rake* revolves around ideas of emotional abuse and mental illness. Obviously, neither thing was clearly identified or discussed in 1819. Melancholy or depression was thought to be something a person could simply snap out of. Much of the treatment for it, therefore, was similar to shock therapy—ice water baths and physical restraints. Worse, a man who had charge of a woman (a husband, father, or brother) could have the woman confined to an asylum for almost any behavior that he deemed unsuitable, such as voicing an opinion with which he disagreed or refusing to obey him. (Because, obviously, a woman who was not submissive to the men in her life must be mentally ill in some way.) Cases such as this eventually resulted in public outrage that finally led to legislative change.

Allow me to also comment on Scottish language and pronunciation. It's always a struggle to know how to write an accent, particularly in a historical novel. Scotland today recognizes three distinct languages: Scottish Gaelic, Scots, and English. Historically, Scottish Gaelic has been spoken in the Highlands. Most Lowland Scots in the early 1800s (i.e. those from Glasgow and Edinburgh) would have spoken a mix of Scots and English. (Sidenote: If you want to read some Scots, Wikipedia actually has an entire dictionary written in Scots—sco.wikipedia.org.)

Of course, I realized fairly quickly that a modern, primarily American, audience would struggle to understand Scots.

So, what to do?

After much consideration, I decided to go with a slightly more modern Scottish accent and syntax, simply to aid readability. I write novels, after all, not history texts. I've used modern spellings of Scottish pronunciations and, even then, restricted myself to a few key words to give a Scottish flavor to the text. So at times, the accent as written is not perfectly consistent; this was done to help readability. That said, I have continued to use more common Scots words wherever possible—e.g. *ken/kens/kent* (think, know), *eejit* (idiot), *glaikit* (foolish), *fou* (drunk), etc.

I have created an extensive pinboard on Pinterest with images of things I talk about in the book. So if you want a visual of anything—including Jamie's tartan or Cairn O'Mount, etc.—pop over there and explore. Just search for NicholeVan.

As with all books, this one couldn't have been written without the help and support from those around me. I know I am going to leave someone out with all these thanks. So to that person, know that I totally love you and am so deeply grateful for your help!

To my beta readers—you know who you are—thank you for your editing suggestions, helpful ideas, and support. And, again, an extra-large thank you to Annette Evans and Norma Melzer for their fantastic editing skills.

Again, I cannot thank Rebecca Spencer and Erin Rodabough enough for their insights. And a shout-out to Julie Frederick for her keen observations, particularly in helping me to layer in more fully Rafe and Sophie dealing with the anger and hatred from their respective abusive relationships. Thank you to Joan Runs-Through for honing in a couple key problems and helping me to address them.

Finally, thank you to Andrew, Austenne, Kian, and Dave for your endless patience and support.

And to all my readers who waited so long for this book, thank you for continuing to read and support my work!

Reading Group Questions

Yes, there are reading group questions. I suggest discussing them over lots of excellent chocolate (solid, liquid, frozen, cake . . . I'm not picky about the precise state of matter of said chocolate. Chocolate in any form is good chocolate.)

Also—fair warning—there are faint spoilers inherent in these questions if you have not finished reading the book as of yet.

1. The book has a rather lengthy intro section that details Rafe and Sophie's initial romance, before moving on to the main plot. Why do you think the author included the scenes? Did you like seeing the beginning of their romance? Why or why not?

2. How did you feel about the Duke of Kendall's threats to send his wife to a lunatic asylum? Do you feel that Rafe acted appropriately in response to his father's constant threats?

3. Do you agree with the author's viewpoint, that hate and anger are a shield for other emotions that we would prefer to avoid? Why or why not?

4. What does it mean to forgive someone? Do you feel Rafe should, or will eventually, forgive his father? Why or why not?

5. Did you see the final twist coming, the Duke of Kendall's big secret? If not, what did you think would happen? Did you like the resolution the book came to? Why or why not?

6. Clearly, this book contains a lot of information about Scotland and Scottish culture. Did you learn something new or unexpected? If so, what was it?

7. Did you agree with how the love story progressed? Did you truly feel like Rafe and Sophie had come to genuinely love each other? Why or why not?

Other Books by Nichole Van

BROTHERHOOD OF THE BLACK TARTAN
Suffering the Scot
Romancing the Rake
Loving a Lady (Ewan's story, coming Autumn 2020)

OTHER REGENCY ROMANCES
Seeing Miss Heartstone
Vingt-et-Un | Twenty-one (a novella included in *Falling for a Duke*.)
A Ring of Gold (a novella included in *A Note of Change*.)

BROTHERS *MALEDETTI* SERIES
Lovers and Madmen
Gladly Beyond
Love's Shadow
Lightning Struck
A Madness Most Discreet

THE HOUSE OF OAK SERIES

Intertwine
Divine
Clandestine
Refine
Outshine

If you haven't yet read *Seeing Miss Heartstone*,
please turn the page for a preview of this
Whitney Award Winner for Best Historical Romance 2018.

Seeing Miss Heartstone

> ... My lord, news of your current financial pressures has reached many ears. I know of an interested party who would be honored to discuss a proposed joint venture. They have asked to meet you along the Long Water in Hyde Park tomorrow morning, where they shall endeavor to lay out the particulars of their proposal ...
>
> —*excerpt from an unsigned letter posted to Lord Blake*

In retrospect, Miss Arabella Heartstone had three regrets about 'The Incident.'

She should not have worn her green, wool cloak with the fox fur collar, as Hyde Park was warmer than expected that morning.

She should not have instructed her chaperone, Miss Anne Rutger, to remain politely out of earshot.

And she probably should *not* have proposed marriage to the Marquess of Blake.

"P-pardon?" Lord Blake lifted a quizzical eyebrow, standing straight and tall, rimmed in the morning sunlight bouncing off the Long Water behind him. A gentle breeze wound through the surrounding trees, rustling newly-grown, green leaves. "Would . . . would you mind repeating that last phrase? I fear I did not hear you correctly."

Belle straightened her shoulders, clasped her trembling hands together, and sternly ordered her thumping heart to *Cease this racket.*

Swallowing, she restated her request. "After much consideration, my lord, I feel a marriage between you and myself would be prudent."

Lord Blake stared at her, blinking over and over. Belle was unsure if his reaction denoted surprise or was simply the result of the dazzling sunlight off the water behind her.

Silence.

Birds twittered. Branches creaked. Leaves rustled.

Eternities passed. Millennia ended and were reborn.

Belle gritted her teeth, desperate to bolster her flagging confidence. *You are strong and courageous. You can do this.*

In the past, her passivity over the Marriage Matter had nearly ended in disaster. So, Belle had set her sights on a more forthright course—propose marriage herself. Yes, she struggled to talk with people and preferred anonymity to attention, but her current situation was critical.

She needed a husband. Decidedly. Desperately. Immediately. As in . . . yesterday would not have been soon enough.

At the moment, however, her mental encouragement barely managed to convince the swarming butterflies in her stomach to not free her breakfast along with themselves. Casting up her accounts all over his lordship's dusty Hessian boots would hardly nurture his romantic interest.

At last, Lord Blake stirred, pulling a folded letter from his overcoat. He stared at it, eyebrows drawing down, a sharp "V" appearing above his nose.

"You sent me this message, asking to meet me here?" He flapped the letter in her direction.

"Yes." Belle bit down on her lip and darted a glance behind at her companion. Miss Rutger stood a solid thirty yards off, studiously facing the Long Water. "Well . . . uhm . . . in all truthfulness, Miss Rutger wrote the letter."

Lord Blake raised his eyebrows, clearly uncaring of the minutiae involved. "So you are *not* a gentleman interested in my business venture in the East Indies?" He unfolded the letter, reading from it. "'*I know of an interested party who would be honored to discuss a proposed joint venture. They have asked to meet you along the Long Water,*' et cetera. This 'interested party' is yourself?" He returned the letter to his pocket.

"Yes, my lord." Belle commanded her feet to hold still and not bounce up and down—the bouncing being yet another effect of those dratted nervous butterflies.

Lord Blake's brows rose further. "And you are offering . . . marriage?"

"Yes, my lord," Belle repeated, but she had to clarify the point. Apparently, she had no issue with being thought forward and brazen, but heaven forbid Lord Blake imagine her a liar, too. "Though . . . I *am* proposing a joint endeavor."

"Indeed," he paused. "Marriage usually implies as much."

Lord Blake shuffled a Hessian-booted foot and clasped his hands behind his back. A corner of his mouth twitched.

Was the man . . . amused? If so, was that good? Or bad?

And at this point, did it matter?

Belle soldiered on. "There would be significant advantages to both of us with such a match."

More silence. An errant draft of wind tugged at his coat.

"You have me at a disadvantage, Miss . . ." His voice trailed off.

"Heartstone. Miss Arabella Heartstone."

"I see." He removed his hat and slapped it against his thigh. "And why have we not met in more . . . uh . . . typical circumstances? A ball, perhaps? A dinner party where we could be properly introduced and engage in conversation about the weather and the latest bonnet fashions before leaping straight to marriage?"

"Oh." It was Belle's turn to blink, absorbing his words. *Oh dear.* "We *have* met, my lord. We were introduced at Lord Pemberley's musicale last month. We did discuss the weather, but not bonnets or . . . uhm . . . marriage."

She hadn't expected him to recall everything, but to not even *recognize* her? To not remember their brief conversation—

"How do you do, Miss Heartstone? It's a pleasure to make your acquaintance." Lord Blake bowed.

"The pleasure is all mine, my lord." Belle curtsied. "Lovely weather we're having."

"Indeed, we are."

It did not bode well.

The butterflies rushed upward, eager for escape.

"Right." Blake let out a gusting breath and shook his head, sending his hair tumbling across his forehead. The morning sun turned it into molten shades of deep amber, curling softly over his ears.

Lean and several inches taller than her own average height, Lord Blake was not classically handsome, she supposed. His straight nose, square jaw, and high forehead were all too exaggerated for classical handsomeness.

And yet, something about him tugged at her. Perhaps it was the breadth of his shoulders filling out his coat. Or maybe it was the ease of his stance, as if he would face the jaws of Hell itself with a sardonic smile and casual *sang-froid*. Or maybe it was the way he ran a gloved hand through his hair, taking it from fashionably tousled to deliciously rumpled.

Mmmmm.

Belle was going to side with the hair. Though sardonic smiles were a close second.

Regardless, her decision to offer marriage to him had not been based on his physical appearance. She was many things, but *flighty* and *shallow* were two words that had never been attached to her.

Replacing his hat, Lord Blake studied her, blue eyes twinkling.

Yes. Definitely amused.

That was . . . encouraging? Having never proposed marriage to a man before, Belle was unsure.

"Enlighten me, if you would be so kind, as to the particular reasons why you think this . . . joint endeavor . . . would be profitable." He gestured toward her.

Oh! Excellent.

That she had come prepared to do.

With a curt nod, she pulled a paper from her reticule.

"A list?" His lips twitched again.

"I am nothing if not thorough in my planning, my lord." She opened the paper with shaking fingers, her hands clammy inside her gloves.

"Of course. I should have expected as much. You arranged this meeting, after all." He tapped the letter in his pocket.

Belle chose to ignore the wry humor in his tone and merely nodded her head in agreement. "Allow me to proceed with my list. Though please forgive me if my reasons appear forward."

"You have just proposed marriage to a peer of the realm, madam. I cannot imagine anything you say from this point onward will trump that."

"True."

A beat.

Lord Blake pinned her with his gaze—calm and guileless. The forthright look of a man who knew himself and would never be less-than-true to his own values.

His gaze upset her breathing, causing something to catch in her throat.

Belle broke eye-contact, swallowing too loudly.

"Allow me to begin." She snapped the paper in her hand. The words swam in her vision, but she knew them by heart. The paper was more for show than anything else. She had done her calculations most carefully.

Taking a fortifying breath, Belle began, "Firstly, you have newly inherited the Marquisate of Blake from a cousin. Your cousin was somewhat imprudent in his spending habits—"

"I would declare the man to be an utter scapegrace and wastrel, but continue."

"Regardless of the cause, your lands and estates are in dire need of resuscitation." Belle glanced at him over the top of her paper. "You are basically without funds, my lord."

"As my solicitor repeatedly reminds me." He shot her an arch look. "It is why I am trying to fund a business venture in connection with the East India Company, as you are also undoubtedly aware."

"Yes, my lord. That is why I am proposing an enterprise of a slightly different sort. Allow me to continue." Belle cleared her throat, looking down to her paper. "My own family is genteel with connections to the upper aristocracy—my great-great grandfather was the Earl of Stratton—though we have no proper title of our own, leaving my father to make his own way in the world. I, as you might already know, am a considerable heiress. My father was a prominent banker and left the entirety of his estate to me upon his death three years past."

Belle clenched her jaw against the familiar sting in her throat.

Blink, blink, blink.

Now was *not* the time to dwell upon her father.

"Are you indeed?" he asked. "Though I do not wish to sound crass, I feel we left polite discussion in the dust several minutes ago, so I must enquire: How much of an heiress are you, precisely?"

Did she hear keen interest in his tone? Or was Lord Blake simply exceedingly polite?

"I believe the current amount stands somewhere in the region of eighty thousand pounds, my lord," she replied.

Lord Blake froze at that staggering number, just as Belle had predicted he would.

"Eighty thousand pounds, you say? That is a dowry of marquess-saving proportions."

"My thoughts precisely, my lord."

Her father had originally left her a healthy sixty thousand pounds, but she was nothing if not her father's daughter. Numbers and statistics flowed through her brain, a constant rushing river. She had used these skills to grow her fortune.

It was what her father would have wanted. Refusing to see her gender as a barrier, her father had taught his only child everything he knew—financial systems, probabilities, market shares—even soliciting her opinions during that last year before his death.

By the age of sixteen, Belle understood more about supply-and-demand and the mathematics of economics than most noblemen. Knowing this, the conditions in her father's will allowed her to continue to oversee her own interests with the help of his solicitor, Mr. Sloan. At only nineteen years of age, she currently managed a thriving financial empire.

She could hear her father's gruff voice, his hand gently lifting her chin. *I would give you choices, my Little Heart Full. A lady should always have options. I would see you happy.*

Belle swallowed back the painful tightness in her throat.

Now, if she could only land a husband and free herself from the guardianship of her uncle and mother.

Family, it turned out, were not quite as simple to manage as corn shares.

Her mother, hungry for a title for her daughter, was becoming increasingly bold in her attempts to get Belle married. She had all but forced Belle to betroth herself to a cold, aloof viscount the previous Season. Fortunately, the viscount—Lord Linwood—had asked to be released from their betrothal.

But the entire situation had left Belle feeling helpless.

She *detested* feeling helpless, she realized. And so she used that unwelcome sensation to suppress her inherent shyness and overcome her retiring personality.

Belle would solve the husband problem herself. She simply needed to reduce the entire situation to a statistical probability and face it as she would any other business transaction.

"Eighty-thousand pounds," Lord Blake repeated. "Are husbands—particularly the marquess variety—generally so costly?" He clasped his hands behind his back, studying her. "I had not thought to price them before this."

"I cannot say. This is my first venture into, uhmm . . ."

"Purchasing a husband?" he supplied, eyes wide.

Heavens. Was that a hint of displeasure creeping into his voice?

"I am not entirely sure I agree with the word *purchase*, my lord—"

"True. It does smack of trade and all polite society knows we cannot have *that*."

A pause.

"Shall we use the word *negotiate* instead?" she asked.

He cocked his head, considering. "I daresay that would be better. So I receive a sultan's ransom and your lovely self, and you receive . . ." His words drifted off.

"A husband. And in the process, I become Lady Blake, a peeress of the realm."

"Are you truly so hungry to be a marchioness? Surely eighty thousand pounds could purchase—forgive me, *negotiate*—the title of duchess." His words so very, very dry.

"I am sure my mother would agree with you, my lord, but I am more interested in finding a balance between title and the proper gentleman." She cleared her throat. "You come highly recommended."

"Do I?" Again, his tone darkly sardonic.

Oh, dear.

But as she was already in for more than a penny, why not aim for the whole pound?

"I did not arrive at the decision to propose marriage lightly. I had my solicitor hire a Runner to investigate you. I have armed myself with information, my lord."

Belle wisely did not add that, after crunching all the statistical probabilities, Lord Blake had been by far and away her preferred candidate. She was quite sure that, like most people, he would not appreciate being reduced to a number.

"Information? About me?" he asked.

"Yes. For example, I know you recently cashed out of the army, selling the officer's commission you inherited from your father. All those who served with you report you to be an honest and worthy commander—"

"As well they should."

"Additionally, you are a kind son to your mother. You send her and your stepfather funds when you are able. You visit regularly. Your four older sisters dote upon you, and you are godfather to at least one of each of their children. You are a tremendous favorite with all of your nieces and nephews. All of this speaks highly to the kind of husband and father you would be."

After her disastrous betrothal to Lord Linwood last year, Belle was determined to not make the same error twice. She learned from her mistakes. Her mother and uncle would not browbeat her into accepting one of their suitors again.

If nothing else, eighty thousand pounds should purchase—*negotiate*—her a *kindhearted* husband of her own choice.

Lord Blake shuffled his feet. "I-I really am at a loss for words, Miss Heartstone. I am trying to decide if I should be flattered or utterly appalled."

Belle sucked in a deep breath, her mouth as dry as the Sahara.

Stay strong. Argue your case.

She pasted a strained smile on her face. "Might I suggest siding with flattery, my lord?"

Visit www.NicholeVan.com to buy your copy of
Seeing Miss Heartstone today and continue the story.

ABOUT THE AUTHOR

THE SHORT VERSION:

NICHOLE VAN IS a writer, photographer, designer and generally disorganized crazy person. Though originally from Utah, she currently lives on the coast of Scotland with three similarly crazy children and one sane, very patient husband who puts up with all of them. In her free time, she enjoys long walks along the Scottish lochs and braes. She does not, however, enjoy haggis.

THE LONG OVERACHIEVER VERSION:

AN INTERNATIONAL BESTSELLING author, Nichole Van is an artist who feels life is too short to only have one obsession. In former lives, she has been a contemporary dancer, pianist, art historian, choreographer, culinary artist and English professor.

Most notably, however, Nichole is an acclaimed photographer, winning over thirty international accolades for her work, including Portrait of the Year from WPPI in 2007. (Think Oscars for wedding and portrait photographers.) Her unique photography style has been featured in many magazines, including Rangefinder and Professional Photographer. She is also the creative mind behind the popular website Flourish Emporium which provides resources for photographers.

All that said, Nichole has always been a writer at heart. With an MA in English, she taught technical writing at Brigham Young University for ten years and has written more technical manuals than she can quickly count. She decided in late 2013 to start writing fiction and has since become an Amazon #1 bestselling author. Additionally, she has won a RONE award, as well as been a Whitney Award Finalist several years running. Her late 2018 release, *Seeing Miss Heartstone*, won the Whitney Award Winner for Best Historical Romance.

In February 2017, Nichole, her husband and three crazy children moved from the Rocky Mountains in the USA to Scotland. They currently live near the coast of eastern Scotland in an eighteenth century country house. Nichole loves her pastoral country views while writing and enjoys long walks through fields and along beaches. She does not, however, have a fondness for haggis.

She is known as NicholeVan all over the web: Facebook, Instagram, Pinterest, etc. Visit http://www.NicholeVan.com to sign up for her author newsletter and be notified of new book releases. Additionally, you can see her photographic work at http://photography.nicholeV.com and http://www.nicholeV.com

If you enjoyed this book, please leave a short review on Amazon.com. Wonderful reviews are the elixir of life for authors. Even better than dark chocolate.

Made in the USA
Monee, IL
13 February 2024

52879231R00208